David Butler was born in Scotland. Son of a headmaster he was educated at Larkhall Academy and St. Andrews University. After studying at the Royal Academy of Dramatic Art, he became popular as an actor on television, starting with the long-running series *Emergency – Ward 10*. During *Ward 10* he began to write for the stage and television. Amongst his many successes are *The Strauss Family*, *Helen*, *A Woman of Today*, *Within These Walls*, *The Adventures of Black Beauty* and *Edward VII*.

David Butler is married and lives in Hampstead with his wife, Mary.

Also by David Butler

EDWARD VII: PRINCE OF HEARTS
EDWARD VII: THE PEACEMAKER
DISRAELI: THE ADVENTURER
DISRAELI: THE GREAT GAME

David Butler

# Lillie

Futura Publications Limited
A Futura Book

A Futura Book

First published in Great Britain by
Futura Publications Limited in 1978

Series format and television play scripts
Copyright © London Weekend Television 1978

This novelization Copyright © David Butler 1978

To Mary

ISBN 0 7088 1407 7

Printed by
William Collins Sons & Co Ltd
Glasgow

Futura Publications Limited
110 Warner Road, Camberwell
London SE5

# CHAPTER ONE

The sunlight glinting on the rocks was almost blinding for a moment and he pulled the visor of his cap down sharply to shade his eyes. His horse snorted and trembled, tossing its head in protest, and he gripped tightly with his knees, steadying it. It snorted again as he urged it forward, its hooves slithering and sliding on the rounded, polished stones, but then they were out of the glare and on to firm sand.

Lieutenant Charles Longley, newly appointed Assistant Paymaster to the garrison at Fort Regent in Jersey, the largest of the Channel Islands, was a strikingly handsome young man. As he sat, tall and ramrod-backed on his powerful, dark chestnut gelding, it was easy to see why he already had something of a reputation for horsemanship among his fellow officers. He had risen early that morning, dressing by candlelight and breakfasting on a pint of scalding hot tea from the urn in the guardhouse, to give himself a good three hours of riding exercise before first parade. He had ridden down into the small town of St. Helier from the massive fortress that overlooked it and round by the Weighbridge built across the entrance to the two main quays of its harbour and was well along the sweep of the bay beyond before the first, faint breaks of dawn came up behind him.

Once clear of the town and the spread of new houses along the sea front, he had cut up behind the fisherman's cottages at Millbrook and struck out across country. With the late summer sun beginning to warm his back, he had paused only once, to take off his black undress uniform jacket and tuck it under the lip of his saddle, before giving the gelding its head. Strong-legged and deep-chested, it had taken off like a signal rocket, scarcely seeming to draw breath. Across fields of green pasture where the sun sucked spirals of mist from the lush, ankle-deep grass, past groups of startled, gentle-eyed Jersey cattle, over hedges and ditches, down and climbing again through wooded valleys, they galloped on, stopping for nothing, in as direct a line as possible with the rising sun at their backs.

An hour after leaving St. Helier, they were picking a path along the grass and bracken of a stony headland on the south-west of the island. The sun was now above the horizon, sailing free in a blue, cloudless sky. Straight to the south, only fifteen or so miles away, was the coast of France and Charles was almost sure he could see its dark line at the extreme limit of sight. At this height, there was a light breeze and he opened his shirt to let it cool the skin of his chest and sides.

Here on the headland there was no opportunity for fast riding. Rabbit runs and pitted slabs of granite just protruding from the thin carpet of turf, the spaces between them filled with tangled roots of heather, made the going difficult. They paced for a time, enjoying the breeze, then headed back inland to skirt the next headland and the next, until they found a path winding down. In a few moments, they had passed from sunlight to deep shade as the path twisted and turned down the steep, shadowed side of the cliff, like the dried-up bed of a stream. It was bordered by dense ramparts of blackberry and hedgerose and branches of trees stretched overhead, some so low that Charles had to lean forward almost to the gelding's mane. The branches had all been swept in one direction by the prevailing, Atlantic wind, like gnarled fingers clutching towards the hillside, bent into fantastic shapes and completely masking the view. The lower the path descended, the darker and more chill the air had become and so, when they finally turned the last corner and came out on the beach, the heat and light reflected from the polished, ruby granite of the rocks had been all the more unexpected.

Charles found himself near one end of a superb bay, the finest of several separated by towering headlands. To his left, the cliffs dropped sheer to the sea. To his right was a long, empty stretch of beach, ending at the natural barrier of a tumbled mass of the same red granite rocks. He rode slowly forward, crossing another line of pebbles and drying seaweed, to reach the lower broad expanse of sand. He reined in almost at the water's edge. The tide was just on the turn and the gelding raised his forelegs in nervous steps as the water made little rushes towards its hooves.

Ahead of them was a small island, topped by an ancient, broken tower. The sea was just closing round it. Earlier, at low tide, one should be able to ride right up to it. The perfect setting for a Gothic romance, Charles thought, and smiled at his own fancy. It was really warm now and the sun glistened on the rippling surface of the water. He had quite resented being posted to Jersey, instead of one of the more exotic territories of the Empire. He dreamt of India or the Cape. With his family connections and his own capabilities, he knew it would be comparatively easy to arrange a transfer to almost any regiment he chose, even to crack outfits like the Hussars or the Blues. But, as his father said, there was time enough for that. And already, in a few weeks, he had come to love this tiny island, British, self-governing, with its own parliament or assembly presided over by a Bailiff. Quaint that. Apparently, the Channel Islands had already belonged to Duke William before the Norman Conquest of England and had accepted him as their Lord, when he became King William the First. Ever since, the islands' loyalty had been given directly to the Crown and not to the Parliament at Westminster. The Queen, Victoria, in this year of grace 1868, was represented in Jersey by a Lieutenant Governor and the presence of the garrison.

Although intensely loyal, everyone spoke French and, most of the country people at least, a Norman patois from the olden days that was damned difficult, wellnigh impossible, to understand. English was spoken by the educated classes, of course, and coming into more general use through the growing numbers of well-to-do people who wintered in the islands. Charles liked a sense of history in his surroundings, and here it was all round him.

As he breathed deeply, gazing at the sea and the eggshell blue sky, he heard the clatter of hooves on the stones at the top of the beach and looked round. Another rider had emerged from the path down which he, himself, had come and had paused at the sudden glare before moving forward off the slippery rocks on to the higher stretch of sand. It was a slim youth in loose, woollen trousers and a Breton fisherman's blouse, a wide-brimmed hat. His mount was a beauty, a grey pony with a silver mane and tail, fine-boned but strong, with a racer's legs. It was obviously a farmer's son, or perhaps a stable boy, out like Charles for an early morning exercise run.

It was the first living soul Charles had seen since he left the harbour area at St. Helier where the night mailpacket had been unloading. He had noticed smoke rising from the chimneys of some of the low, grey granite farmhouses and dogs had barked as he passed but, apart from that, he might have had the island to himself. 'Good morning!' he called. 'Beautiful day!' The boy hesitated, then raised one hand slightly in greeting.

Charles waved back. He enjoyed meeting the locals, trying to make out the patois. 'Feel like some company?' he shouted. The boy rode on without replying. Charles took the movement for assent and turned his horse's head, riding up on a diagonal path to join him. The grey pony seemed mettlesome and the boy, young man or whatever he was, certainly wasn't a child to manage it as he did. 'Hold on!' Charles called. 'Tell you what – I'll race you to the rocks at the end there!'

Almost before he finished, the pony took off, at scarcely a flick of its rider's heels, surging ahead with such speed it caught Charles completely by surprise. He whooped and spurred the gelding, racing after him.

The going was perfect on the level sand and Charles had little doubt he would catch up before the halfway mark his steeplechaser's eye had chosen the second they set off, a length of shattered spar thrusting diagonally from the band of pebbles. But as he thundered up to the spar and passed it, the pony's silver tail still streamed ahead of him, its rider rising clear of the saddle but bent low over the pony's neck to give the least resistance to the wind. Even at full gallop, because of the surprise start, the gelding had no chance of catching them at that distance. In a longer race, it would have been a different matter, but the pony reached the barrier of tumbled rocks first and its rider slowed down, circling.

After a moment, Charles raced up and reined in, laughing. 'Whoa, boy! Whoa, there . . . Where'd you learn to ride like that?' he asked, admiringly. 'You're a regular flyer!' He swung his foot out of the stirrup and jumped down, crouching to run his hand down the gelding's right front fetlock. It had seemed to give him trouble lately, but all was well. Charles straightened. 'It was no race, though,' he said. 'You didn't give me a chance to . . .' His voice trailed away. He was looking directly at the other rider for the first time and saw to his astonishment that it was a girl.

She was looking down at him with a faint smile at his surprise. As she smiled, the breeze tugged at the wide brim of her hat and she pulled it off. Rich, golden brown hair tumbled to her shoulders and down her back. She was breathtakingly beautiful, with a perfect, natural complexion heightened by a slight tan and clear, wide, violet-blue eyes. The leather belt buckled round the rough trousers emphasised the smallness of her waist and the smooth swell of the blouse above was unmistakenly feminine.

'You're a gi – !' Charles breathed. 'Forgive me, I'd no idea – I say . . .' As he gazed at her, the girl was disconcerted by his obvious admiration. She smiled again, with a touch of embarrassment, then turned her pony and headed away through the high rocks. 'No, wait!' Charles called. 'I'm sorry. I didn't mean to – Oh, dash it!'

The girl had gone. Charles remounted quickly to follow her, but his breeding stopped him. He looked back along the beach across which they had raced, and again at the rocks through which she had disappeared, like a vision. It was no use. He had to find out where she had gone and headed for the apparently solid wall of rocks. Turning as she had done, he found a narrow passage between two high boulders leading to a vaulted space. An even narrower passage led off at right-angles from that, much easier for the

9

pony than the heavier gelding. But once he had scraped his way through, Charles came out on to a shorter continuation of the beach, enclosed by the cliffs of the next headland. Higher up was a shelf of turf and another, steeper path winding up. Charles thought he saw a momentary flash of grey between the branches, but then it was gone. He shook his head. It was time for him to get back to barracks. 'I say . . .' he muttered.

On the following morning, and the next, he returned to the headland, the path with its gnarled trees and the empty beach with its island and ruined tower. Each day he came earlier and stayed later, but there was no further sign of the girl. He had not told anyone at the garrison about the meeting for fear they would laugh or, worse, follow him. He would have began to believe she really was a vision conjured up by his imagination, if it had not been for that path on the other side of the rock barrier.

On the third morning, he returned to the beach for the last time. He had realised it was pointless and, in any case, the girl could not possibly be as lovely as he remembered her. She would be some farmer's daughter, pink and pretty, and he would be lucky if he could follow two words she said. But no, at least she had understood English. He had shaved and dressed very carefully, wearing his black, frogged tunic buttoned high at the neck, dark blue breeches, black riding boots and military cap. Very correct and handsome, he rode again out of the darkness of the path on to the beach. And his heart seemed to turn over.

The girl was riding slowly away along the edge of the water. This time, it was she who stopped and looked round. When she saw Charles riding towards her from the cleft in the hillside, she looked away again quickly, but made no attempt to ride on. He came up to her, moving round to see her more clearly.

It had not been imagination. She was even lovelier than he had remembered. She was not wearing her hat and the sun brought out a sheen of auburn in the gold of her hair. Her eyebrows were well-marked and swept up over those wide eyes. The line of her forehead and nose was straight, almost Grecian, her upper lip slightly short, her mouth full and curving. Her face was saved from classic prettiness by the strong line of her chin with its faint cleft. Even the clumsy, male clothes, the heavy blouse tucked into rough, shapeless trousers, could not disguise the perfection of her figure, more revealed than it would have been in a softer blouse and full skirts.

Charles was excited, and felt clumsy and tonguetied. He saluted and smiled. 'Hello again! What a charming surprise.' The girl looked at him and, as her violet-blue eyes turned to him he was thrown by the utter candour of her look, the hint of a smile. '. . . Well, no, I'll confess,' he stammered. 'I'm not here by chance. I've ridden this way every morning, waiting – hoping . . . I'd almost given up.' She looked away. 'You must think me an awful ass.'

The girl looked at him again and, this time, she smiled more openly, though shyly.

'You don't mind?' Charles blurted eagerly. He remembered his manners and straightened. 'Oh, forgive me. I am Lieutenant Longley. Newly posted to the Jersey garrison – and very much at your service.'

He smiled again, greatly relieved that she was allowing him to speak to her and the thought that she might even have looked forward to seeing him, too. But she lowered her eyes. When she raised them again, she was no longer smiling and again he was thrown by her direct gaze. He felt as if she were assessing him, ready to take flight. He could not bear it, if she left so soon through his clumsiness. 'I realise it is a frightful impertinence,' he said, 'but – may I at least know your name?'

She paused as if reluctant to give away even that much of herself, then said very quietly, 'Emilie.'

She had pronounced it in the French manner. Charles savoured it. 'Emilie . . . How delightful!' She looked away with a slight frown. He was nonplussed. Apart from the strangeness of their meeting, she was the most unsettling girl he had ever met, and yet the one he wanted to impress more than any other. She was disconcerting and ravishing and, quite definitely, not the daughter of a farmer. More likely the daughter of one of the local Seigneurs, poor as churchmice, but of old feudal stock.

Her pony was restive at a light wind that blew along the beach into its eyes and it pawed the sand to be off. 'This is a dreadful intrusion, I know,' he said quickly. 'But may I accompany you?'

After the slightest pause, without answering, she began to ride slowly on along the beach. Charles turned his horse and followed her, catching her up.

For a minute or two, they paced slowly, in silence. Charles could not resist glancing at her, fascinated by her attraction and that mysterious reserve. 'I must ask – are you French?' She shook her head. 'English?' She shook her head again and Charles was puzzled for a moment, before he understood. He laughed. 'I have it! You were born on Jersey. You are Norman.'

She smiled. 'Yes.'

'A daughter of the island,' he said. 'You know, before I was sent here, I thought of the Channel Islands as the back of beyond.' Her head turned towards him and he smiled. 'I admit now it was sheer ignorance. I never expected to find anything so lovely.'

She looked ahead to the golden sand, the green slopes of the cliffs under the cloudless sky, the headland in front of them where the wind drove the waves in long rollers to smash and spume high into the air over the sentinel rocks at its foot. One thing he could tell about her. She loved her island. 'It is very beautiful,' she murmured.

'. . . I wasn't referring to the island,' he said quietly.

She glanced away from him and rode on. He caught her up, cursing himself for risking everything too soon. 'I'm sorry,' he apologised. 'I'm too forward. I had no wish to embarrass you.'

She neither reacted to his apology nor put him at his ease. But he was relieved that she let him still accompany her, content merely to watch her, which he managed to do more openly by allowing her to draw a little ahead.

Over the next two weeks, he met her again several times. It was never arranged. He went to the beach every morning without fail. If she turned up, he was there and they rode together. Each time, she seemed more pleased to see him, but she always let him leave first, since he had to return for parade. He felt more and more drawn to her. Sometimes they walked on the sand or sat on the high rocks and talked about life on the island or his family and career. She would not talk about herself. It was some while before he realised that they never left the beach together. Then she asked him, and he promised, not to try to follow her. He was afraid to press her for answers, in spite of the hundreds of things he wanted more and more to ask, in case she simply stopped coming. It should be easy to identify her on an island this size, only forty-five square miles, but so far discreet enquiries among his few civilian acquaintances had produced nothing. Speculations about her and the reasons for her secrecy tormented him, although some of them he realised were fanciful.

His fascination for her was not merely that she was beautiful. He found her interesting to talk to, again unlike any other young lady he had known. He had been to Oxford, yet her reading in the classics of literature was at least as extensive as his. And what she had read, she had thought about. Her mind was quick and lively and conversation with her was often stimulating, yet he was aware of barriers, a private inner world into which he could not see. And just when he thought he knew her, she could completely confound him by a silence or that questioning look that was so direct and unsophisticated. He wanted her desperately, but there was a sense of innocence about her and a total trust in him that made it impossible for him to take her in his arms as he longed to. He had never even held or touched her hand.

One day, when the tide was late, they had ridden to the little island and climbed on foot to the ruined tower. Once the home of a hermit, she told him, or some said, the tomb of an exiled poet. They walked round it and sat on the rocks, waiting until the last moment when the tide was about to turn it into an islet again. The setting was idyllic and Charles had never felt so close to her. He began,

haltingly, to tell her that he had discovered a new contentment and a new peace since knowing her, when she turned
away and slipped down the slope of the rock to the beach.

'Please . . .' he began. He rose and followed her, jumping
down to the sand. She was kneeling, crouched over, with
her back to him. 'Please, forgive me. I had no intention
of . . .' He moved round and stopped, seeing that she was
bent over a little, bedraggled seabird that lay dead against a
stone. She looked up at him, distressed. 'It's only a little
gull,' he said.

'Its wings are broken.'

He crouched beside her. 'Perhaps it was dashed against
the rocks.'

'Yesterday it was skimming the waves,' she whispered.
'And today the waves will carry it away – and no one cares.'

'We could bury it above the waterline,' he said.

He smiled as he said it, half joking, but she looked up at
him seriously. 'Could we?' She picked the dead bird up
gently.

Above the high water mark of seaweed and pebbles,
Charles scooped a small grave in the sand and shingle. She
laid the bird in it, smoothing its feathers, and he patted
down the covering over it, piling a little cairn of stones on
top. She was kneeling opposite him. She lowered her head,
closed her eyes and joined her hands in prayer.

Charles went slowly down on both knees, his hands by
his sides, watching her. The whole incident had touched
him and he gazed at her, intrigued and grateful to have
shared this moment with her. He knew without doubt that
he was very much in love.

That afternoon, walking down King Street in St. Helier,
he met an acquaintance who had been invited to a dining-in
night at the Mess, Edward Langtry. He was a goodlooking,
plumpish, indolent young man of twenty-five or twenty-
six, reputedly fairly well off, with a string of yachts and a
rich father, who was something in shipping. He was a keen
angler and Charles and he had been drawn together by that
common interest. He was on a return visit to Jersey, where
he had met and was about to marry the eldest daughter of

one of the most respected families on the island. He was slightly priggish, but much more a man of the world than any of the local younger set and it occurred to Charles that Langtry might be just the chap who could help him. There was no one else he could think of confiding in and he accepted with pleasure the offer of a drink at the Yacht Club, explaining his problem as they walked down towards the harbour.

The lounge of the Yacht Club was spacious, with wide, low windows looking out to sea. Decorated in white, with white tables and chairs and a broad white staircase leading down into it from the entrance landing, it had the air of a fairly opulent stateroom. In his stylish yachting cap, reefer jacket and white trousers, Edward Langtry fitted into it perfectly. He was well liked and several people beckoned to them. Out of deference to Charles's confidences, however, he would not join any of the groups and headed for an empty table by the windows, pausing only to order two tankards of hock and seltzer from one of the stewards.

They settled at the table. Charles's story had just become really interesting and Edward wanted to hear more. 'Dressed as a boy, you said?'

Charles nodded. 'For ease of riding, I presume. I was quite startled when I realised.'

'I can imagine,' Edward smiled.

'But she is feminine perfection. Her figure . . . She is exquisite!'

'Sounds a paragon. If a trifle fast.'

'Oh, just the opposite!' Charles protested. 'I've never seen such a – such a spiritual expression. She is not only perfectly beautiful – but perfectly pure.'

'Naturally,' Edward commented. He was amused by his new friend's earnest enthusiasm.

Charles was rapt. 'Her skin is like ivory. Her hair like warm honey and her eyes . . .'

'Limpid pools?' Edward suggested, drily.

Charles glanced at him and flushed. 'You're laughing at me.'

'Perish the thought,' Edward murmured.

For a moment, Charles was resentful, then he smiled and shrugged. 'Well, I can't blame you. I've completely lost my senses over her.'

Edward smiled. 'As bad a case as ever I've seen.' The steward brought their two silver tankards and they toasted each other. 'You say she's a Jersey girl?'

'Yes.'

'That explains it.' Edward took another pull at his tankard and set it down. 'The islands are filled with stunners. Natural coquettes.'

'Not Emilie,' Charles said quickly.

Edward chuckled. 'Aha! So that's her name. Emilie who?' Charles was silent. He had tried to tell the story, giving as little away as possible and he kicked himself, mentally. 'Oh, come.on,' Edward urged him. 'I'm getting married next month. I'm not liable to steal her away from you.' He was incredulous when Charles confessed that he did not know her second name, that she would not tell him. 'Are you sure she's of good family, Charles?'

'Oh, she must be.'

'But she goes riding unchaperoned in the morning? Well . . . does she live in St. Helier?' Charles shrugged. Edward stared at him. 'Hasn't she told you that, either? Well, haven't you followed her home?'

'She made me promise not to,' Charles said quietly.

Edward laughed. 'Oh, my sainted aunt . . . ! All's fair in love and war. You're a soldier – haven't you learnt that?'

Charles smiled, with some embarrassment. He saw Edward wave to someone and glanced round. A tall, fair-haired young man in his mid twenties was coming down the stairs. He wore a light brown civilian suit, but carried himself like a soldier. 'Here's someone who can solve your problem,' Edward said.

'How d'you mean?'

'He and his brothers know every girl on the island. Just describe her to him – '

'No, please!' Charles protested quickly. 'I'd rather you didn't mention it. I feel enough of a fool already, having told you.'

16

Edward sat back, slightly huffed. 'Suit yourself, old boy. Only trying to help.' The newcomer reached them and nodded. 'Hello, there. Lieutenant Longley, may I present William Le Breton, a fellow officer.'

Charles rose. William and he shook hands and they made room for him at the table.

'Hock and seltzer all right?' Edward suggested. He signalled to the steward.

'You're not stationed here?' Charles asked.

'No, I'm home for a spot of leave,' William told him. 'Just been posted to India – Royal Artillery.'

'Lucky devil,' Charles said enviously and William smiled, liking him.

Edward finished his drink and wiped his thumb over his upper lip. 'It's thanks to William that I met Jane, my fiancée.'

'Blasted cheek,' William snorted. 'He sails into the harbour on his yacht and, because he's becalmed for a few days, I introduce him to some amusing company. And he ends up by carrying off the prettiest girl on the island.'

As they laughed, Edward looked across at Charles. 'Bar one,' he said pointedly. Charles shook his head in embarrassment. William noticed and was intrigued, but the moment was broken when the steward came up to them. Edward pointed to the two tankards on the table, then held up three fingers. The steward bowed and left.

Charles was impressed by Edward's style and saw that William was, too. 'Le Breton?' he said. 'You must know Dean Le Breton.'

'I should do,' William smiled. 'He's my father.'

'Ah.' Charles nodded.

'Something wrong?' Edward asked.

'A breach of good manners, I'm afraid,' Charles admitted. 'I promised my father I would call on the Dean as soon as I was settled. But . . .'

'Charlie's had other preoccupations,' Edward finished for him.

'I shouldn't worry,' William said easily. 'We don't stand much on ceremony here. Are our fathers acquainted?'

'They used to be. It is a purely courtesy call.'

'I should have warned you,' Edward told William. 'We all have to mind our Ps and Qs in front of Charlie. His papa is the Archbishop of Canterbury.'

William was on his way home and, when they had finished their drinks, he invited Charles to come back with him for tea. Edward agreed to accompany them as far as the Deanery. They walked back through the town and up the long, steep curve of the hill beyond. Edward was shorter than the other two and, with his extra weight, perspiring by the time they neared the top. 'Ooh!' he panted. 'Should have hired a carriage, or something.'

'Do you good,' William said. 'You spend too much of the year at sea. You need to get some walking in, when you're ashore.'

The hilly lane curved around to the left and there, behind rough stone walls, was a large, mediaeval church with twin, pointed gables over the nave and a high, square tower. Its walls of weathered, granite blocks glowed a rich amber in the sun. 'That's my father's church,' William said. 'St. Saviour's.'

'You're sure he won't object to my just turning up like this?' Charles asked.

'Not at all. It's always open house at the Deanery.'

They took a shortcut through the large graveyard that surrounded St. Saviour's. Many of the stones were ancient and almost indecipherable, leaning at odd angles. Among the newer were headstones to local men who had been killed in India and the Crimea. To join the services was almost the only means of getting away from the island, William explained. Of his five brothers, three were already commissioned in the Army like him, and a fourth soon to join them.

They carried on down a narrower lane beyond the church and soon came to the drive leading to the Deanery, known as the Old Rectory until William's father had come to live here as head of the Anglican Church in Jersey. Turning from the drive, they came into a wide, open courtyard. In front of them was an old, two-storeyed house, built of grey granite, taking up three sides of a square. The two main sides were living quarters, the third a row of outbuildings. With a flowering thorn set in the centre of the courtyard and its walls nearly covered by white, red and blush climbing roses, ancient cherry and pear trees and, framing the lower and upper windows on the right, a huge white jessamine, it was remarkably picturesque. There were two entrances, one in the main body of the house for the Dean and his official visitors, the other in the corner between the living sections for his wife and family. That door was enclosed by a glass portico, making a small conservatory, filled with flowering plants. William led the way to it, opened the outer door and showed the others in.

Edward crossed first towards the inner door. As he moved forward, his cap was snagged and knocked backwards off his head. 'What the devil? . . .' he spluttered, catching at it.

Following him, Charles ducked and looked up. A wire was stretched across the entrance at hat level between two nails. William laughed and unhooked it at one end. 'It's the children,' he explained. 'There's no end to their tricks. They must have set it up for me.'

Charles smiled, but Edward was not amused and smoothed his ruffled hair.

Inside, the rooms of the house were surprisingly small, built originally for strength and snugness. In fact, the Dean, in keeping with his position, was just building a more spacious diningroom and upper drawingroom at the rear. They met William's mother, Mrs Le Breton, in the hall, a small, very pretty woman. Considered exceptionally beautiful at the time of her wedding, now at fifty, poor health and the cares of a family and marriage had aged her, but she was gentle and charming.

'Visitors, Mother,' William announced, as she came down the steep stairs.

She was pleased to see Edward. 'Why, Mr Langtry, how nice of you to call!'

'I must confess, I only looked in in passing, Mrs Le Breton,' he said, and bowed. 'I'm on my way to the Prices.'

She smiled. 'Dear Jane will be looking forward to the wedding.'

'Not half as much as I,' he assured her. He introduced Charles, who explained that he had come to pay his respects. The Dean, Mrs Le Breton told them, was in his study.

Dean William Corbet Le Breton was a fine looking man, somewhat over six feet, well built, handsome and fresh complexioned. His fair hair had turned white quite early and now, although receding on top, it was white and full at the sides, adding to the dignity of his appearance. He was in his mid fifties. From one of the oldest of the island's families, he had been educated on the mainland at Winchester and Oxford, where he had taken his BA at Pembroke and become one of the youngest ever Fellows of Exeter College. Shortly afterwards, he took holy orders and was appointed curate in the London parish of St. Olave's, Southwark. At only twenty-nine, he had been offered the appointment as Dean of Jersey, a position held by previous Le Bretons, but he agreed with his father that he was too young for the responsibility and elected to stay in his working class parish in Southwark, where he felt more needed. By that time, too, he was married, with a growing family of boys. Part of the reason for his decision, although he did not announce it, was the disapproval of his family at his marriage to a mainland girl from the broad middle class. Five years later, however, when the position was offered to him again, he had reconsidered. He had now been Dean for twenty years, popular, intelligent, understanding, a vigorous, even inspiring preacher. He spoke at the Assembly and dined with the Lieutenant Governor, yet he had the common touch. He visited his poorest parishioners in their cottages as happily as he called on the local seigneurs and would often wait in his carriage at the foot of St. Saviour's Hill to give the market women a lift to the top with their heavy baskets.

Charles had heard part of this story from his father, with whom the Dean had been friendly in earlier years. He was interested to meet him and found himself genuinely impressed by the older man's personality.

Wearing a black frockcoat, black waistcoat, breeches and gaiters, a costume that might have been designed to show his physique, Dean Le Breton stood with his back to a large, open, stone fireplace in the study. He strode forward and clasped Charle's hand in both his. 'Welcome to Jersey, Mr. Longley' he said, smiling, 'and to St. Saviour's. I thank your esteemed father for his good wishes.'

'I apologise for not having come to present them before now, sir.'

'Nonsense. You've had your duties, I'm sure. We were about to take tea on the terrace. You will join us, won't you?' Charles hesitated politely. 'I insist. And you, Mr Langtry.'

'Unfortunately, I have to run along,' Edward told him.

'What a pity,' the Dean said, sincerely. 'Still, you know you can come any time. You're always welcome.'

'You wouldn't have thought so a minute ago,' William chuckled. 'He was nearly decapitated on the way in.' His father looked a question. 'A trip wire at the front door – set to knock off visitors' hats. I've taken it down.'

'Oh, no,' the Dean sighed. 'These children are incorrigible.'

'There was no harm done,' Edward said magnanimously. 'Pray do not punish them on my account, Mr. Dean.'

Dean Le Breton looked at him. He had no intention of punishing them. 'Good of you to say so,' he nodded. 'I'll speak strongly to them, of course. One day they may go too far.'

The Dean brought Charles out on to the wide, gravel terrace at the rear of the house, leading on to a broad lawn that sloped down to trees, partially concealing the distant view of St. Helier that lay at the foot of the hill. 'Yes, there have been Le Bretons on the island since before the Conquest,' he said.

'You, yourself, served for a time in London, though, didn't you, sir?'

The Dean nodded. 'I had a small, very poor parish in Southwark for some years. I was frowned on in some quarters for, there, I saw it as my duty to attend as much to the physical wellbeing of my parishioners as to the state of their souls. You cannot preach abstinence to a man who is starving.'

'No,' Charles agreed, more and more impressed.

'Eventually, I had to choose between the poverty and grime of my tenement parish and the light and air of the island. But it was not an easy choice. Yet I had to think of my young family and many years of tradition.'

'Of course.'

'So I decided to return here, and I have never regretted it,' the Dean smiled, then added briskly, 'Well, I see my daughter waiting for us. And there are the boys. If you'll excuse me, I'll give them a call.' He moved forward. 'Clem! Reggie! Teatime – come along!'

At the far end of the lawn, Clement, a fairhaired boy of seventeen, was playing French cricket with his youngest brother, Reginald, thirteen. Reggie had his legs pressed tightly together, holding a bat in front of them, while Clement circled him with a ball, ready to bowl it to hit Reggie on the legs.

Charles turned. There was a table already set with things for tea near him. Beyond it, a girl in a lacy, light blue dress was sitting on the low balustrade of the terrace, reading, turned away from him. The sheen of her hair and the straight line of her back was unmistakable. He moved forward, almost disbelieving, and stopped.

The girl lowered her book and looked around. She was as startled as he had been, but quickly covered it. It was the first time he had seen her not in trousers and that ugly, fisherman's blouse. In the simple blue dress, moulding the full curves of her figure, she was entrancing.

Dean Le Breton came to them, smiling. 'Tell your mother we're ready for tea, will you, my dear?'

She rose. Clement and Reggie came running to the terrace and Charles had to turn to be introduced. He heard their names and shook hands, almost in a daze. He looked round. She was just reaching the corner of the house and glanced back with the suggestion of a smile, before she moved out of sight.

Charles had no opportunity to speak to her during tea. She helped her mother hand round cups and passed plates of cake and buttered scones, staying in the background, while her father and brothers plied Charles with questions about the garrison and William and he exchanged comments on the service. He promised to forward messages from the Dean to his father. It was pleasant and informal and friendly, but he did not know how he stopped the trembling of his hands.

After tea, the Dean excused himself to prepare for Evensong. Mrs Le Breton cleared the table with Reggie. Clement took William to show him the new extension to the vegetable garden, and Charles excused himself from going with them. They showed no concern at leaving him alone with their sister. He was over the shock of seeing her, but that was another surprise. No mainland family would leave the daughter of the house alone with a complete stranger. It showed the strong element of trust there was between them all.

Charles was anxious that, at any moment, one of the others might return. For a few minutes, they made inconsequential conversation. When she suggested showing him round the house, he jumped at it. Anything, rather than to talk polite nothings. He could tell that she had been under the same strain. He rose swiftly and held her chair. The momentary pressure of her shoulder was like a burn on his hand. In a dress, she seemed taller and he was more than ever aware of the firm curve of her breasts.

At least, now they could talk like old friends. She showed him the stable and the coachhouse, then the outbuildings which once had been used for making cider, the stone vats and troughs and the massive wheel for crushing the apples. She led him through the Dean's door into the narrow, panelled hall of the oldest part of the house, first built about 1100. The door to the left was to the old sittingroom, now used as her father's study, which he had entered from the other side. A short flight of stairs faced them, turning to the left to the bedrooms of herself and Reggie.

She opened the door on the right of the hall and showed

23

him into a cramped, square room, with windowseats under its recessed double windows filled with small panes. There were maps and drawings of plants and animals on the walls. Down the centre was a wooden table with a bench on either side. Facing it, at one end, was a blackboard and easel. He hardly needed to be told that this was the schoolroom where she had been taught with her brothers. The Dean's sons went to the splendid, new Victoria College for boys, but wanting to give them every advantage, he had also arranged for private lessons at home.

In the schoolroom, Charles felt very close to her, as if he shared a part of her life. 'And this is where you had your lessons,' he said.

She paused. 'I still do. When my brothers' tutors come.'

Charles smiled. 'And what do you study?'

'The Classics. French and German. Drawing. Mathematics.'

'Mathematics . . .' he repeated, surprised. 'But why?' It was an unheard of study for someone in her position.

'Father says it teaches you to think clearly,' she told him. 'He cannot see why a young lady should grow up, knowing less than any schoolboy.'

'So he believes in the education of women?' Charles said. She took it more as a matter of astonishment than a question, and did not answer. He watched her as she moved to the windowseat and sat, half turned from him. Seeing her silence as a reproof, his mind raced and he suddenly realised that his attitude had been insulting to someone of her intelligence, woman or not. He caught himself up again. One spoke glibly of woman being the partner of one's life. With education, they could truly become so. 'Well, why not?' he agreed. 'If you are the proof. A remarkable man, your father. You should be very proud of him.'

'I am,' she said quietly.

'To add knowledge and wisdom to beauty.' He smiled. So much was becoming clearer. 'That's why you ride so well! You learnt with your brothers.' Her smile in reply told him he was right. 'And what else did they teach you?'

'Everything they do,' she shrugged. 'Running, climbing,

24

swimming.'

He moved closer, surprised. 'But surely – forgive me – surely as a girl you could not join them in everything?'

'I wanted to be like them,' she said simply. 'I soon realised they'd leave me at home, if I could not keep up – if I was afraid, or if I cried.'

'You are amazing, dear Miss Le Breton!' he marvelled. 'How formal that sounds . . . You must admit, I did not give it away – that we had met before.'

'Yes.'

He moved closer. 'Shall we still meet? I could not believe it, when I saw you here! My heart leapt – I beg your pardon. I shall not embarrass you again. But I think you understand what I would say.' She was silent and he was again afraid that he had offended her modesty. He lowered his voice. 'Social convention puts formality between us. At least – when we are alone – may I call you Emilie?'

She looked away and, after a second, she shook her head.

He stiffened and stepped back. 'As you wish,' he said, hurt. 'I know I am too precipitate.' It was true. Before he left England, he would never have dared to presume on an acquaintance of only a few meetings, and without receiving her parents' consent.

'. . . My full name is Emilie Charlotte,' she said quietly. 'I hate them both.' She made a slight grimace of distaste. 'My brothers – my family calls me Lillie.'

It was several heartbeats before he understood what she had said. 'And – and may I?' She glanced at him and away. No wonder she thinks I'm a fool, he thought. It was a major step in their relationship, to be allowed to use her private name . . . 'Lillie . . .' he breathed. 'How perfect!'

She looked at him and smiled. It hit him like a battery of lanterns. He laughed aloud with relief. 'Lillie . . . One thing puzzles me. Your father said he was going to speak sharply to the children. Where are they?'

'It is what he calls us all,' she told him.

'How galling for you,' he laughed.

The door opened and Reggie came in. 'Here you are.' He was a bright, fairhaired boy, with the same blue eyes as

Lillie and the Dean. He looked angelic, but Charles suspected a hidden deviltry. 'We've been looking everywhere,' he went on. 'Mother thought you'd got lost.'

Charles saw that he had led Lillie into a fairly compromising situation. It was, perhaps, fortunate that it was her youngest brother who had found them. 'Miss Le Breton was showing me over the Deanery,' he said stiffly.

'I can't think why she brought you to this Chamber of Horrors,' Reggie smiled. 'I've to remind you that it's nearly time for Evensong.'

Charles nodded. 'Yes, of course.' He offered his hand to Lillie to help her up. 'Miss Le Breton –' She hesitated, then laid her hand in his, rising.

Reggie grinned, watching them.

St. Saviour's Church was fairly full, with an enthusiastic congregation. A good sign, Charles thought, a real tribute to the popularity of the preacher. Wearing his surplice, Dean Le Breton stood above them in his pulpit, leading the singing in the closing verses of the chosen hymn. Charles stood in the family pew. Along from him, Lillie was with her mother, William, Clement and Reggie. As he sang, he could not keep his eyes from her profile, nor on the words of the hymn. As it ended and the congregation sat, he still watched her. As the congregation settled, the Dean's voice sounded suddenly, full and dramatic, electrifying his listeners. Charles's attention was wrenched back to the pulpit.

'I say to you – be bold for God!' The Dean called. 'Fight the good fight in His name! He sees the struggling of your soul against the torrent of iniquity – and His great arm will reach down to support those whose strength is weak, but whose heart is strong!'

The Dean's expression was lit by a pure conviction and certainty that was spell-binding, a holy fire of goodness and strength that made Charles acknowledge the guilt of his thoughts, and yet the same fire was comforting. He looked again at Lillie, understanding more about that purity and stillness in her, seeing how she gazed at her father, responding to his presence and the power of his words.

The next day, she did not come to the beach. Nor the next. As the days passed, Charles felt unable to survive without at least a glimpse of her and called again at the Rectory. He saw her through the window of the new drawingroom, seated at the garden table, playing what looked like chess with Reggie. But William had been his excuse for calling and he found himself making conversation about the prospects of promotion in the Indian Army and agreeing to walk over to the Prices to look up Edward Langtry.

On Sunday, he excused himself from attending the Garrison Chapel and went instead to morning service at St. Saviour's. Lillie smiled warmly when she saw him and Mrs Le Breton invited him to share their pew again. This time, he stood next to Lillie, sharing her prayerbook and hymnbook. Holding them for her, he could not help glancing at her and her shy smile in return dried his throat and brought back that betraying tremble to his hands. By the end of the first lesson, he had already developed an uncharitable longing to kick her little brother, who kept grinning knowingly along the pew at him.

After the service, he waited outside with the family, while Dean Le Breton shook hands with his parishoners as they came out. He managed a few words with Lillie, who explained that her pony had been lamed by Reggie riding it fulltilt at a five-bar gate, a jump it could never have taken. As a rider, Reggie was more fearless than skilled, another mark Charles chalked up against the little brute. He was heartened, however, when Lillie told him her pony had nearly recovered and she hoped to begin her morning rides again quite soon.

The following week was torment for Charles. William Le Breton had gone to visit a friend on Guernsey, so he no longer had an overt reason for calling at the Deanery. He still rode to the beach every morning, although the memory of the first idyllic days there seemed to mock his loneliness. He tried to think if he had said or done anything to offend her, but honestly could not. There was no one else courting her, he was sure of that now. She was far too honest not to have told him. He cursed his timidity at not having made

27

his intentions more clear to her, for he knew now that he could not live without her. And he cursed the way he had discovered who she really was. He could not speak to her parents without confessing the secret meetings, and it was more than likely that the Dean would consider his visits to William as an underhand means of winning the family's trust. He could not throw doubt on the perfect confidence that existed between Lillie and her father. Perhaps he was being too scrupulous, but that was his nature.

It worried and obsessed him to such an extent that his brother officers began to notice, and finally, one afternoon when Charles sat on the ramparts of Fort Regent, staring moodily down at the small boats tacking with the wind in St. Aubin's Bay, his colonel tackled him about it.

Colonel Wallace was a practical, experienced but considerate man, concerned in case Charles was losing his taste for soldiering, which would have been a loss to the regiment. He questioned Charles closely, but got nothing out of him and, at last, warned him to pay more attention to his military obligations.

'I owe you an apology, sir,' Charles admitted. 'I have been . . . distracted. But I have not let it interfere with my duties.'

'Let what interfere?' Wallace asked.

Charles hesitated. 'There is a certain, young lady . . .' he began.

Wallace nearly laughed. Now, damme, why didn't I think of that?, he wondered, then frowned. 'Not in any kind of trouble, are you?'

'Oh, no, sir,' Charles protested. 'Certainly not.'

'All right. No, not with your background, I suppose. So what is it? Has she turned you down?'

'. . . I have no reason to think she would,' Charles said.

Wallace grunted. 'You mean you don't know? Is she playing hard to get?'

'She's not at all like that, sir,' Charles told him. 'She's quite unlike any – any young lady I have ever met.'

'Of course,' Wallace smiled. 'Who is this charmer? Would I know her?'

Charles decided to confide in him fully. 'The daughter of the Dean, sir. Miss Le Breton.'

Wallace was puzzled. '*Miss* Le Breton? . . . I don't believe I've met her. Though, come to think of it – I've heard him mention a daughter.' The Dean was a guest at occasional official dinners in the Mess and always attended the Garrison Ball at the end of the season. He shook his head. 'I don't remember her at any of our dances. Keeps her pretty close to home, does he?'

'She is devoted to her family, sir.'

Wallace nodded. 'Well, if you don't think she'd turn you down, I don't see what's wrong.'

Charles hesitated again. 'I can't seem to raise the subject with her, sir. I'm fairly sure she enjoys my company, but – she doesn't ever seem to hear, when I try to tell her how I feel.'

'So you haven't actually – uh – stormed the fortress?' Wallace asked delicately.

'Oh, good Heavens, no, sir!'

No. No, Longley was not a rake like some of the other younger officers who laid bets on how many of the local girls and visitors they could get aboard each summer. 'Quite strictly brought up, of course, these island girls,' Wallace observed. 'If you're not a recognised suitor, she may be trained not to respond. What's the attitude of the parents?'

'I've hardly seen them,' Charles said. 'I – I've usually met Miss Le Breton alone.'

Wallace considered him. 'I take it your intentions are honourable. If so, there is only one course open to you. The Dean is, I would imagine, approachable.'

It was something Charles had been reluctant to face. '. . . Yes, sir.'

'Very well. You're excused duties for the rest of the today, Lieutenant,' Wallace said briskly. 'Can't have my junior officers mooning about. Attack boldly, it's the best way in any campaign.'

Charles had come to attention. 'Yes, sir.'

'Cut along, then,' Wallace nodded. 'And good luck.'

Charles was glad he had decided to speak to him and

smiled. 'Thank you, sir.' He saluted smartly and went quickly down the ramp to the lower courtyard.

Colonel Wallace had returned the salute and let himself smile openly, when Charles had turned away. Yet he had to admit he felt a little envious. He had reached the age when a long, slow campaign was the only one possible.

Dean Le Breton showed Charles into his study. He was pleased to see him, but was pressed for time. 'You just caught me,' he said. 'Some ladies have been making needle-work designs for the new altar cloth. Another few minutes and – ' He broke off, seeing that Charles was tense and nervous. 'Do forgive me. You wanted to talk to me.' When Charles still did not speak, the Dean decided to let the altar cloth wait. The boy was clearly troubled. 'Is something the matter, Mr. Longley?'

'I had to see you, sir,' Charles told him.

'Yes?'

'Before writing to my father.'

This time, it was the Dean who paused. He smoothed his hands over his waistcoat and nodded. 'On what subject?' he asked, carefully.

Charles coughed. 'My family is known to you, sir. I am, I trust, not unworthy of it. I am, as yet, only a Lieutenant, but I have a private income and, with my connections, believe I have every possibility of succeeding in my career.'

What he said fitted none of the probable reasons for the meeting which had occurred to the Dean. He nodded again, non-commitally. 'So I would imagine.'

Charles felt slightly encouraged. 'I realise that your acquaintance with me is short, but you may judge the depth of my sincerity when I tell you that I have decided to speak to you first.'

'About what?' the Dean pressed.

'To ask permission to propose to your daughter.'

The sudden silence in the room once he had spoken was so profound that he could hear the tick of the miniature carriage clock on the mantelpiece. It seemed to stretch on without end.

'. . . You wish to marry Lillie?' the Dean asked at last.

'As fervently as I hope for Heaven,' Charles assured him. 'I beg you not to doubt my sincerity.'

'I do not, Mr Longley. Have you . . . had converse with her?'

'I have spoken to her several times,' Charles said, cautiously. 'Without your knowledge, I admit – yet in all innocence. Nothing has passed between us that I would blush to confess.'

The Dean brushed the thought aside. 'Of course.'

'I have never known a young lady so above the normal arts of her sex. So tender and reticent, yet so direct. So spiritually refined that her modesty will not allow her to accept the slightest compliment.'

'Yes . . .'

Charles saw that the Dean was watching him closely, with the beginnings of a frown, and hastened to add, 'May I say? My admiration extends to yourself and your household – to which I would consider it a privilege to belong.'

The Dean looked away, towards the window. 'You honour me, Mr Longley,' he said mildly. 'What you say about Lillie is, to some extent, true. She has a touch of her mother's beauty. And yes, she is shy and reticent – which is only natural . . .' He turned back to Charles. 'You see, she may have the developed physique, the apparent maturity of a grown woman, but, surely you have realised? – she is not yet fifteen.'

Charles stared at him, shocked. He wanted to protest, but now he could tell that what he had taken for the Dean's frowning disapproval was really concern and, what was even more shaming, pity.

'She is nearly of an age with Reggie,' the Dean went on. 'She is shy and tender as a young girl is. Emotionally, quite untouched and undeveloped.'

Charles was shaken and bewildered. Listening to her father, he realised all too well the reason for her modesty, the teasing, enigmatic silences. He wanted to protest that he would wait, that he would return, but already he could hear the sniggers and the raucous teasing in the Mess. She had not trapped him. She had not deceived him. He had done it to himself!

'Her only companions have been her brothers,' the Dean was saying gently. 'If she does not respond to compliments, it is because she does not recognise them for what they are, to what they might lead. Her purity is the untested, un-suspecting purity of a child.'

Lillie was sitting crosslegged on a pile of cushions under the windowseat, in her small, low-ceilinged bedroom, the end room on the upper floor of the Deanery, directly above the schoolroom, its windows framed by the white jessamine and clusters of dark red, damask roses. Leaning down, she pushed the hair back from her face as she pasted coloured, cut-out figures of red-coated guardsmen into her scrap-book. Reggie came in and smiled, highly amused. 'Poor Lieutenant Longley . . .' he said and she looked up. 'He's applied for immediate transfer and left the island.' He laughed. 'Did he really want to marry you?'

She looked back at her scrapbook, concentrating.

Reggie moved closer, still laughing. 'What fun! . . . What a rotten time he'd have had.'

Lillie scooped up one of the cushions and shied it at him, scrambling up. He shouted and dashed back out through the door, with her after him.

Mrs Le Breton had picked some fresh beans in the vegetable garden and was returning to the house. As she crossed the terrace, Reggie came flying out, nearly knock-ing her over. Lillie raced out after him and chased him down the lawn, tripping him up and sending him sprawling. 'Do be careful, children!' Mrs Le Breton called. She shook her head and smiled, going inside.

On the lawn, Lillie and Reggie were rolling over and over, laughing. She got him on his back and stradlled him, sitting on his chest. He tried to fight her off, but he was weak from laughing, and she caught his head, banging it on the grass.

# CHAPTER TWO

St. Saviour's churchyard lay dark and silent as midnight approached. The sky was cloudy after rain and the wind had dropped, so that the trees made only the faintest rustle. The cry of a hunting owl sounded eerily in the valley.

A middle-aged couple, out late after visiting, had taken a shortcut past government House and were coming up the lane towards the church. The churchyard had a reputation for being haunted and the man smiled at the way his wife held tightly on to his arm. He headed directly for the path through the churchyard, to cut out the large bend in the road.

The moon had shone only fitfully as they climbed the hill. Now, for the moment, it was unveiled apart from tattered wisps of cloud, but it was light enough to make out the path between the tall, carved tombstones and the woman was grateful. All at once, she saw a movement off to the right and caught her breath. Her husband had seen it, too. A shapeless, ghostly figure draped in white seemed to glide between the tombstones nearer the church wall, disappearing into the pitch-dark shadows. They advanced more slowly, wide-eyed, trying to dismiss it as a trick of the light.

Where the path began to curve, the bank was quite high, topped by the tallest of the tombstones. Just as they reached it, another spectral figure rose from behind it. They gasped and stood frozen to the spot, staring, as the white figure reared to enormous height, the black eyes in its featureless face staring down at them, raising its white arms and groaning. Crying out, the couple turned on their heels and raced back down the hill.

As the sound of their yelling voices and running footsteps faded, the tall spectre split into two and Reggie, who had been sitting on Clement's shoulders, jumped to the ground, tripping over the white sheet that was wrapped round him. Over his head, he wore a white flour bag with black, painted eyes. Laughing, Clement hauled him to his feet and pulled him back to sit on the bank. The third ghost ran to join them. It was Lillie. She pushed her head out of a slit in the sheet that covered her, just like the ones draped round the other two, and collapsed on the bank beside them. Faint shouts could still be heard from further down the hill and they were nearly helpless with laughter at the success of their haunting.

Two days later, they stood in line in the schoolroom, thoroughly subdued, while Dean Le Breton walked slowly along, looking at each of them in turn. He was carrying a folded newspaper and held it up as he surveyed them.

'I make no accusations,' he said seriously, 'for I cannot believe that children of mine would stoop to anything so puerile and irresponsible. However – let me read you a letter from this morning's paper.' He opened it and read, 'Sir, with reference to the spectral figures which have been frightening travellers of late on the lane by St. Saviour's graveyard, I beg to state that I have frequent occasion to use that road by night and that I shall be carrying a loaded shotgun. If the aforesaid "ghosts of St. Saviour's" appear again, they shall be exorcised with two barrels of buckshot. Yours, etc. J. Wilkins.'

When the Dean stopped reading, Clement, Lillie and Reggie glanced at one another. Their father's solemnness and their own feelings of guilt made it difficult for them not to laugh, but they managed to control themselves. He sighed and crossed to the door. 'I hope the point has been taken,' he said, and went out.

As they looked at one another again, the laughter they had been stifling broke out. 'We're famous!' Reggie giggled. 'We're in the papers . . .' They had to muffle their laughter with their hands, in case their father heard and was upset.

Dean Le Breton shook his head as he joined his wife in the drawingroom. 'What are we to do with them?' she asked, concerned.

'Oh, they're just high spirited,' he said mildly.

'I never know what they'll get up to next!' she exclaimed. 'I've lost count of the number of people who have come here to ask for their doorknockers back.'

He smiled. 'Yes, they seem to have a positive mania for doorknockers.' The game of stealing doorknockers had been dreamt up by Clement, the more ornate and the more difficult to remove, the better. He had soon tired of it, but Lillie and reggie had developed a genuine collector's passion. No distance was too far for them to walk to pick up a really prize specimen and, eventually, their collection was too large to conceal. They had to dig a pit in a corner of a field and bury it, wrapped in sailcloth. Soon, the pleasure of mere acquisition was not enough and special projects were born. An early favourite was to exchange the knocker of every door in a street with the one next door. That caused satisfying confusion. It was increased when the door-knockers on one side of a street would be found exchanged with those of the houses opposite. It required iron nerve and perfect timing, and the highest reward was to join the crowd of puzzled and irate householders in the road the next morning, listening to the chorus of guesses and accusations. The demure Lillie and angelic Reggie were never even faintly suspected. Then alarm increased, when door-knockers were mysteriously translated from one end of St Helier to the other. Clement was the only one in on the secret and he helped to spread the rumours of poltergeists and visitations. A certain quixotic element began to appear in the raids. Knockers from the most imposing of the town mansions, massive, richly carved, brass lions' heads and dolphins, would appear on the doors of rickety, thatched cottages. These were not always returned. Yet still no one connected the phenomenon with Lillie and Reggie's habit of walking in the dark after supper, until one night a group of self-appointed vigilantes spotted Reggie and gave chase. He escaped, but had been recognised.

Next day, an angry householder arrived at the Deanery to demand the return of his doorknocker. A search of Reggie's room revealed not one, but dozens. More were found in Lillie's room, and a huge hoard under sacks in the old vats in the outbuildings. Soon there was a procession of carriages and people on foot beating a path to the door of the Deanery, where Mrs Le Breton directed them to the outbuildings to identify their knockers from the rows laid out. The Dean made Lillie and Reggie replace personally those that were claimed. Many were lost forever. It was generally agreed that the mischief was too extensive to have been carried out by only the two of them and that others must be involved. Lillie and Reggie regained some credit for steadfastly refusing to inform on their non-existent accomplices.

'It's not funny, William,' Mrs Le Breton objected. 'Little wonder folk look at me so pityingly.' It worried her that, whenever anything extraordinary happened anywhere on the island, it was automatically attributed to her children. What can you expect, people whispered, from a household like that? It was nearly too much for her. She was still in mourning for her third son, Trevor, a lieutenant in the Royal Marines, who had died suddenly at Toronto at the early age of twenty-three.

Her husband patted her shoulder, comfortingly. 'It will end soon enough. Clement will be off to join the Army, like his elder brothers. And Reggie will have to prepare for college.'

'It's not them I'm worried about,' she told him. 'It's Lillie – growing up like a boy. Just as wilful and boisterous as her brothers.'

The Dean smiled. 'She'll settled down.'

'How? She takes no interest in female accomplishments. She needs the companionship of girls of her own age.' She hesitated. 'Of course, it's my fault that we have little social life.'

'Nonsense, my dear.'

His wife would not be comforted. 'Oh, you know as well as I do,' she said, 'that the parishioners have never forgiven you for choosing someone from the mainland. And your family has always thought you married beneath you. That is why we are seldom invited anywhere.' She had tried very hard to be accepted, carrying out all her many obligations as his wife scrupulously and cheerfully. She worked tirelessly for the poor of the parish and they adored her. Yet apart from the Prices and a very few others, most of the more prosperous parishioners seemed to avoid her. It was hurtful. As was the way she was excluded from most official functions. Even when he was invited to dine at Government House, the invitation was pointedly only for him.

'It is their loss,' he said gently. 'And we are sufficient unto ourselves.'

'*We* are,' she agreed. 'We have had to be. But it is not fair to Lillie, when all she meets are occasional visitors to the island.'

It was the visitors on whom Mrs Le Breton decided to concentrate. With their wider outlook and more polished social graces, wealthy visitors to Jersey could serve as models to Lillie. Many of them payed courtesy calls on the Deanery as a matter of course, unaffected by local prejudices. The worldly-wise Dean, his wife and the attractive, younger members of their family, in fact, became favourites and were often invited to picnics and At Homes. The invitations they sent in return were usually accepted. It was in that manner that the family became acquainted with Lord Ranelagh.

Ranelagh had been a notorious swell and rakehell, a dashing soldier and a lover of the fabled Lola Montez, among others. Now nearly sixty, he wa not as rich as he had been, having spent a fortune in the pursuit of pleasure, but he was still comfortably wealthy. He built a pretty, little stone house at Portelet, a remote, unfrequented bay on the south-west of the island, where Lillie and Reggie often went to swim. The house was divided by a track from a small farm. He installed a housekeeper in Portelet House with a young son, Arthur Jones, who was only slightly older than Reggie. Since Jones was Ranelagh's family name and he came to stay with his two daughters at the house as often as possible after the end of the social season in London, it was widely and rightly believed that Arthur was his son. Lillie like Lord Ranelagh's daughters very much, especially the younger, Alice, while Arthur and Reggie became fast friends.

Even more welcome, from Mrs Le Breton's point of view, were the charming Lord and Lady Suffield. Rich and impeccably respectable, high even in Court circles – Lord Suffield, it was said, served frequently as Gentleman-in-Attendance to the young Prince of Wales – the Suffields had been taking a house in Jersey for a month or two each spring, for several years. They also had two daughters and it was natural that, as Lillie grew up, they should gravitate together. The Suffield girls were a little older than she was, poised, perfectly mannered, and quite happy to accept her as an occasional, holiday companion. She was aware of something faintly condescending in their attitude to her, but their handsome, elegant father made up for it. A worldly man in his forties, he was struck by Lillie's developing beauty, natural grace and clear mind, and made much of her when the families were together. He often joked about the co-incidence of his younger daughter also being called Lily, although spelt the more conventional way. Lillie always pretended to be amused, although she did not find it exceptionally funny. To her mother's distress, she much preferred to romp with Reggie and Arthur, than to sit in the garden under a parasol with either set of girls. The secret was that, with Reggie now at Victoria College, the Dean could no longer afford to keep a pony for her use. But Arthur had one, which he let her ride.

One afternoon, in the summer of Lillie's sixteenth year, Mrs Le Breton came to her husband's study. He was at his desk, checking through the parish accounts, and did not pay much attention when she began to speak again about her concern for their daughter's future. She tapped him on the shoulder. 'I said, for her own sake, she must learn what will be expected of her as a young lady.'

He could tell that she had reached some decision. 'You have something in mind?' he asked.

'. . . Do you remember the picnic at Easter, when we were with Lord Suffield?'

He nodded. 'A most agreeable gentleman.'

'Very,' she emphasised. 'I have never forgotten what he said to Lillie. "Do you know, Miss Le Breton, that you are very, very beautiful? You ought to have a season in London.'"

She paused expectantly. He saw at once what was in her mind and hated to dampen her enthusiasm. 'My dear . . . like you, I want the very best for our children. But there are limits. A stay of several months in London is far beyond our means.'

'I wasn't suggesting a whole season,' she explained. 'Only a short visit, a week, say. Just Lillie and myself.'

That was, at least, feasible. 'But what use would that be?'

'It would broaden her outlook – make her aware of the world outside.'

Dean Le Breton had vivid memories of London, the contrasts of plenty and misery, extravagance and squalor. In his privileged position as a clergyman, he had seen something of society. As newly appointed Dean of Jersey, he had even been presented to the Queen at Windsor. He knew the world he had glimpsed was immensely powerful and fiercely exclusive. Many, even of the richest, were not permitted to be members of it. Lillie might see just enough to resent the limitations of her station in life. 'With no entry to fashionable society, it might only make her envious.'

Mrs Le Breton smiled. 'But we have an entry! I'm sure if I write to Lady Suffield to tell her of our visit, she and her daughters will invite us to call. We may even be asked to dinner – or a party!'

She was becoming quite excited, but the Dean was still doubtful. 'That will mean new dresses and – '

'Our Sunday dresses will do for day wear,' his wife broke in. 'And Madame Nicolle will run up an evening gown for Lillie, in the latest fashion. Very reasonably. You'll see.'

He did not have the heart to disappoint her. 'Very well, my dear,' he said, yielding. 'Write to the Suffields that you are thinking of coming. If they do invite you, then I'll just have to find the money for it all, won't I?'

She clapped her hands and kissed him.

Lillie was naturally excited to be visiting London. She had never in her life been away from the island. She had heard enough about 'the season' from Alice and from Elizabeth and Lily Suffield to know that its balls and parties were grander than anything she had ever imagined. They had still not had an answer from Lady Suffield, but her mother would not put off the trip.

Somehow, the thought of the visit made Lillie feel more grown-up. She had learnt that one of the main objects of the season was for the young ladies to find husbands. Was that what her mother had in mind? Was she going to London to look for a husband? The idea was funny. There had been no man in her life, since Charles, and even him she only vaguely remembered. She had liked him, although some of the things he had said to her made her feel uncomfortable and unsettled. Was that what it meant, to be in love? It had never happened to her again.

She found men odd. Her father was the finest and noblest man who ever lived. She knew that, and that there was no one else like him. Her brothers, and a few others like Arthur, were fun. And she envied them their freedom and strength. There was so much they could do without even having to ask permission, without anyone thinking it strange. All the money available to the family was for their education, their careers, to buy them commissions in the Army. Any of them who chose could even take holy orders like Father and learn to be a guide and inspiration to others like him. Yet even with all their advantages, men were odd. When she talked to them, they laughed at nothing and said silly things. Or showed off to impress her, when there was no need. At the Grand Review on the Queen's birthday and at the promenade concerts, young men followed her or sat and gazed at her, but when she smiled to them, they became bashful and stupid. At the Garrison Balls to which she was now invited, the young officers crowded round her, jostling one another to be her partners in the quadrilles and old-fashioned Sir Roger de Coverleys that were the only dances considered permissible by the prim social leaders of the island. She had discovered that the tiniest smile and a glance from her violet eyes were enough to bring any man to her from the other side of the room. Remembering how beastly they had been to Charles, it amused her to become silent and distant for no reason and see the eager looks and swaggering laughter all round her turn to bewilderment. Once there had even been a fight to decide who would escort her to her father's carriage at the end of the ball. Men were definitely odd.

The best thing about the trip to London was the gown being made for her by Madame Nicolle. St. Helier's most fashionable dressmaker, a plump and voluble Frenchwoman, she had welcomed the esteemed wife of *Monseigneur le Doyen* and her daughter to her establishment in Halket Place, almost overwhelmed by the honour of being asked to create a gown for Mademoiselle's coming-out in society. Hardly that, Mrs Le Breton explained. Lillie was not yet of an age. Madame Nicolle could not believe it. Still less, when Lillie stripped in the fittingroom to be measured.

Standing only in her sleeveless vest and long cotton drawers, she plucked nervously at the tapes at her waist, looking at herself in the full-length cheval mirror. She had never been embarrassed by her body before, but now she was made to feel so, with her mother and the sharp-eyed Madame examining her.

'No corset?' Madame Nicolle whispered.

'She has never needed one.'

'No, of course, not. With a figure like that . . . *Elle est ravissante!*'

It was bad enough being a girl, Lillie thought, without having to wear instruments of torture like corsets and stays – even if they could have flattened her breasts. She wished they were not so obvious. Breasts were awkward things that made running and climbing more difficult. They even hurt sometimes when she galloped. And they seemed to swell once a month, when she was reminded most forcibly of her sex.

Madame Nicolle approached her from behind, measuring her height from the nape of her neck to her heels, then from her shoulder to elbow and elbow to wrist, reading off the measurements on her tape for her assistant to take down, a bright, black-haired, Italian girl, named Dominique. She lifted the heavy mass of Lillie's hair. 'It

41

cannot be worn loose, Madame,' she said to Mrs Le Breton, 'not if we are to show *les épaules*. It must be swept up, with ringlets. *Voilà* . . .' She separated the hair with her hands and held it up in two bunches, one on either side of her head.

It looked so comical that Lillie nearly giggled but, seeing the seriousness with which her mother, Madame Nicolle and the girl, Dominique, were considering her, she composed herself.

'Ye – es,' Mrs Le Breton agreed. 'Ringlets. But the dress mustn't be cut too low.'

'Oh, no! No, no, no,' Madame Nicolle assured her. She touched herself below the collarbone. 'Just so. Enough – no more.' She finished the measurements, exclaiming over the slenderness of Lillie's waist, licking her teeth in surprise when she read off the measurements of bust and hips. 'It is the height. It disguises.'

'There is only one snag,' Mrs Le Breton told her. 'We are leaving exactly a week from today.'

Madame Nicolle spread her hands and smiled. 'That is no problem. For a dress such as this, we shall work day and night, *n' est-ce pas*, Dominique?'

Dominique bobbed and nodded in agreement, then smiled when she saw Lillie stick out her tongue at her reflection in the mirror.

Six days later, Reggie sat on the window seat in Lillie's bedroom, disgruntled, watching her pack a travelling case. A small cabin trunk, already filled, stood near the door. 'Why d'you have to go to London?' he muttered.

'Mama wants me to see it.'

'Why can't I come, too?' he demanded, and scowled when Lillie shrugged. 'You won't have any fun, just with Mother. You should've asked them to let me come with you.'

'I did,' she told him. 'But Papa said he couldn't afford to send all of us.' Going alone with her mother made it seem all the more special. The more she had thought about it, the more exciting it seemed. The men of the family were all given their chance. This was hers.

Mrs Le Breton bustled in. 'Nearly ready? Good. The trunks have to go down to the packetboat this afternoon. Reggie, run down and see if the carter's here yet.' He did not move. 'Don't sit there sulking. Run along! She folded a nightdress for Lillie and put it in the travelling case.

Reggie moved reluctantly to the door. 'Do you think you'll see the Queen?'

'Nobody has for years, not since Prince Albert died,' she said. 'So it's not very likely. Run along!'

On the chest of drawers by the door, Reggie noticed a little flowered bonnet with pink bows. He picked it up, laughing. 'Is Lillie going to wear this?'

'Put that down, Reggie!' his mother ordered. 'Now, be off with you.'

'I wouldn't want to come, anyway,' he said, dropping the bonnet back on the chest of drawers. He marched out, then stuck his head back in. 'You'll probably die of seasickness on the crossing!'

They heard his footsteps thumping disconsolately down the stairs and Mrs Le Breton sighed. 'That boy . . .' She saw Lillie smiling and laughed, herself. 'Thank Heavens, he's not coming with us. As soon as we've finished, we'll pop down and collect your evening gown from Madame Nicolle. It's going to be so pretty!'

It was. It really was. It was the prettiest dress Lillie had ever worn, in pastel blue, with a fairly high neck trimmed with lace. It had small puff sleeves, also trimmed with lace, and darker blue bows on the hoop skirt and on the wide tangerine sash which slanted across her waist.

'As Mademoiselle does not wear a corset, the sash is to de-emphasize the fullness, you see?'

Mrs Le Breton was delighted. 'Oh, it's beautiful, Madame Nicolle! Really perfect, isn't it, Lillie?'

Lillie was silent, looking at herself in the sewing mirror which Madame's assistant, Dominique, angled for her. The dress was so perfect, she almost did not recognise herself. It was like looking at a tinted fashion plate, yet it was her face. She realised what Madame had meant. To show the slope of her shoulders and the line of her neck, her hair would have

to be raised. How strange to be thinking of such things . . .
She was beginning to feel like a different person.

'*Vous êtes troublée, Mademoiselle*?' Madame Nicolle
asked.

Lillie shook her head slightly. '*Non, Madame. Pas du
tout.*'

'She is to wear it at a ball in London – Upper Grosvenor
Street,' Mrs Le Breton said with pride.

'Then I am glad I made it in the very latest style,'
Madame Nicolle smiled. 'Mademoiselle will be, as they say,
"the belle of the ball."'

In spite of her feeling of awkwardness, Lillie was reassured. She swung her body gently from side to side,
seeing how the skirt of the gown like a narrow bell swayed
with her. The gown was so pretty, her first real ballgown,
and it would not be wasted on the officers at the garrison.
She would wear it for the first time in the magical city that
everyone said was the centre of the world. They had heard
that very morning from the Suffields who had invited them
to a ball at their home two days before the end of their stay.

The crossing to Southampton was fairly rough, but Lillie
loved it. For her, the rougher the sea, the more she enjoyed
it, and she had never been on a paddle steamer before. Her
mother, however, had to spend most of the time lying
down. Lillie laughed at the way she struggled out of the
cabin, worried in case she had fallen overboard or had got
smuts of soot on her second-best dress which she had worn
for travelling.

Compared to the four or five miles of railway at home, the
train journey from Southampton to London was another
great excitement. They covered so many miles at such
speed and passed through so many towns. It was almost
frightening to think of the millions of people there were
here. Even Southampton had over twice as many as in the
whole of Jersey.

It was evening on the day after they set off that they
reached London. From the first suburbs to the train's final
stop in the terminal station, the city had seemed to stretch
on for ever, the buildings becoming larger and more densely

packed the closer they came to the centre. Lillie had had less than two hours sleep on the boat, but the noise and bustle, the amazing number and variety of carriages in the streets, from hired cabs to horse-drawn omnibuses, jolted her awake. She wanted to rush out, to see everything at once, but her mother insisted on her going to bed that first night. It was not until she lay down that she discovered how tired she was. Even the constant rumble of traffic on the cobbled streets outside the small, family hotel could not keep her awake.

It was the noise of the traffic that woke her again in the morning. She had never heard anything like it. In the streets, it was quite deafening, the sound of the hooves of the horses, the creaking, clanking and rattling of all the different vehicles, the shouting and ringing of bells. It took her a full three days to become used to it. And to all the people, all of them seeming in such a hurry, pushing past her when she stopped in front of the windows of one of the countless shops. Crossing the road was a nightmare and she marvelled at the ease with which the Londoners winked in and out of the traffic. When she had to cross, herself, she clung to her mother's arm as if she was a little girl again.

Here, in the city, she saw that her mother was a changed person, livelier and more confident, and Lillie and she became more like real friends, sharing each other's excitement. They went to see the house in King's Parade, Chelsea, where she had lived with her own widowed mother and where she had been courted by the young curate, William Le Breton. She told Lillie how she had also been courted by Charles Kingsley, the author, then a theological student and by his brother, but she had chosen the Jerseyman for his blue eyes and humour and gentle manners. It drew Lillie even closer to her. She could imagine her father, young and strong and handsome, winning love and his position in life by his own merit.

Every day they set out on a dizzying round of sightseeing, from the Tower of London to Kew Gardens, from the British Museum to Greenwich Observatory. They watched the elite of society riding in Hyde Park in the early morning

45

and, in the late afternoon, the great ladies taking the air in their carriages. Every evening, they returned to their room exhausted. Lillie would have liked to go to a theatre. From the newspapers, she knew everything that was on and the names and histories of most of the leading actors, but she had never been inside a theatre nor seen a play. Regretfully, her mother explained that it was not possible for two unaccompanied ladies to go out at night. The evenings were the most disappointing part. But each day they were both so tired by suppertime that it did not matter.

On their second last day, they got back early to rest and change for the Suffields' Ball.

All week they had looked forward to it more and more. Lillie was glad it was being given by people she knew. She was nervous at the thought of stepping into the company of the fashionable ladies and gentlemen she had watched in the Park, who lived unimaginable lives in palatial homes like the ones spaced out along the north side of Piccadilly. It was comforting that Lord Suffield and his daughters would be there to look after her and introduce her.

Mrs Le Breton was in a flutter of excitement. She did not really know what to expect, but this was the climax of the week and the event that could change Lillie's life. Stranger things had happened. Her daughter was undeniably lovely and perfectly turned-out. If she caught the eye of some eligible bachelor – Mrs Le Breton would not let herself speculate too far. Other invitations were bound to follow the success of the evening. She had already made up her mind to accept them and to send a telegraph message to the Dean that circumstances had detained Lillie and herself a little longer in London. She booked a cab to take them to Upper Grosvenor Street.

The Suffields' mansion was ablaze with lights. Huge gas globes burned outside the doors, where footmen in livery waited to escort guests from their carriages. A knot of spectators had gathered by the railings on either side, to cheer the nobs and call greetings to the celebrities. Lillie flushed at being given a small cheer and whistles of appreciation as she was handed down from the cab.

Inside, the house was a revelation. An immense hall with a long, sweeping staircase, chandeliers, marble columns, portraits on the walls. The staircase was lined with more bewigged and liveried footmen. At the top a majordomo took their names and conducted them to the open door of the ballroom, where the Suffields waited with their fair-haired, younger daughter, Lily, to greet their guests.

Lillie was wearing her new gown. Her cheeks were still flushed and her eyes sparkled. Her hair was freshly dressed, parted in front and drawn back in thick, twin loops to end in bunches of ringlets over her ears. She had begun to feel dwarfed by the opulence of the house, but the music of a quadrille from inside the ballroom and the sight of the Suffields lifted her spirits. Her mother was wearing a simpler, dark green version of the gown, which she had kept as a surprise. Like Lillie, she was smiling and animated.

Lord Suffield, bearded and, as always, supremely elegant, stepped forward when he saw them. 'Mrs Le Breton,' he exclaimed, 'how delightful to see you!'

She curtsied slightly. 'It was most kind of you to invite us, Lord Suffield.'

'Not a bit of it. Not a bit!' he chuckled. He was gazing at Lillie, who also gave a slight curtsey.

Mrs Le Breton moved on to Lady Suffield, who smiled charmingly. 'How nice you could come. But what a pity the Dean could not be with you.'

Suffield had taken Lillie's hand. 'And the lovely Lillie . . . so we've enticed you to London, at last?' She smiled shyly. 'What have you been doing so far?'

'Sightseeing.'

'And what have you seen?'

'Everything.'

He laughed. 'Yes, you've probably seen more in a few days than I have in nearly fifty years.' He turned to his wife. 'It's so annoying that we were booked up earlier in the week.'

'Yes, most annoying,' she agreed. More guests were arriving and she beckoned to her daughter. 'Lily, will you

47

keep Mrs Le Breton and Lillie company?'

'Introduce your near namesake, Lily,' Suffield chuckled.

'Yes, Papa.'

'See you later, then,' he said to them. 'We'll have a chat.'

Lillie smiled and turned with her mother and Lily to pass through the ornate entrance. She had taken only a few steps, when she paused, gazing at the ballroom. It was the most spectacular room in the mansion, lit by thousands of candles in a line of giant, crystal chandeliers. Other candles burned in sconces set in the marble half-pillars dividing the walls, which were hung with wine-coloured damask. A Viennese orchestra played in the raised rostrum at the far end. Round the walls, elderly chaperones sat and watched, while groups of younger guests chattered and laughed. The dancers had reached the last section of a rather stately quadrille, the gentlemen in immaculate eveningdress or uniform.

It was the ladies at whom Lillie was gazing. Meeting Lord and Lady Suffield, she had been too conscious of herself to notice what anyone else was wearing. Now she realised that all the ladies' dresses were full skirted. More than that. They spread out from the waist in enormous, ruffled hoops. It was the height of the crinoline fashion. Their necklines were low, leaving the shoulders and upper arms bare, with long, white gloves reaching to the elbow. A few wore their hair in a single, fat coil over one shoulder. The rest wore it swept up into elaborate, high coiffures.

Across the floor, Suffield's older daughter, Elizabeth, attractive and waspish, sat with a row of other young ladies. Her rather superior financé, George Bentham, leant on the back of her chair. 'What on earth is that with your sister, Elizabeth?' he drawled.

'Don't be naughty, George,' she warned.

His eyes opened wide. 'Well, I didn't know it was a fancy dress ball.'

She giggled and rapped him on the wrist with her fan. 'She's a sweet girl, a dear friend of mine. The daughter of the Dean of Jersey, in the Channel Islands.'

'Ah, that explains it. She has come as a milkmaid – and

left her cow outside.'

Elizabeth almost laughed aloud, but made herself look prim. 'You're being very wicked,' she said, reprovingly. 'For that, you must dance with her.'

'Oh, Lord . . .' he sighed. 'Must I?'

Lillie's smile had faded. She glanced down at her gown, which suddenly looked tasteless and countrified. The fashion drawings which Madame Nicolle had used as her models must have been years out of date. And now she understood why the hairdresser that afternoon had smiled, when her mother described the style they wanted, and said, 'Yes, I remember it,' She looked again at the elegant ladies with their upswept hair, their billowing gowns and glittering jewellery.

Mrs Le Breton had also reacted with some surprise, but comforted herself that Lillie would stand out more by contrast. Lily Suffield, at a loss for what to do with them, was heading round towards her sister. 'Come along, my dear,' Mrs. Le Breton said confidently.

The dancers finished the last set of the quadrille and bowed and curtsied to one another. The gentlemen escorted the ladies back to their seats.

Elizabeth had risen to greet Lillie and Mrs Le Breton, introducing them to George. As they made conversation, so unlike the unforced chatter of their holiday meetings, Lillie was aware of other women, seated beyond, making amused, whispered comments about her appearance. 'It's such a pity we didn't have another day free,' Elizabeth was saying. 'I'd so have adored to spend some time with you, talking about your lovely island.'

'Do you think you may come again, Miss Suffield?' Mrs Le Breton asked.

'Papa is always talking about it, isn't he, Lily?'

'Always,' her sister agreed quickly.

Elizabeth smiled. 'Now, dearest Lillie, I must tell you that George has been dying to meet you. I vow I'm quite jealous! He insists on dancing with you.'

'Oh . . . rather. Can't wait,' George assured her. Lillie smiled to him. He bowed. 'May I have your card?' She handed him her dance programme, in which partners who wished to book dances with her would write their names. It was obviously empty, but he opened it with a flourish. 'Now let me see . . . I do believe I have first choice. So – may I claim the next dance, Miss Le Breton?' He bowed to her mother. 'With your permission, Madam.'

'Please, Mr Bentham, please,' she said warmly.

He smiled to Elizabeth and signed his name with the little pencil hanging from Lillie's card, and handed it back.

Lillie was grateful to Elizabeth and to him. She knew that Elizabeth's formal manner did not mean she was not welcome, and her fiancé was charming. It meant a great deal to have the first name in her programme. She looked at it and, for a second, her teeth caught her lower lip. '. . . It's a waltz.'

'Yes,' George beamed. She was a pretty girl, with a fine, healthy figure, in spite of her outlandish get-up.

'I – I don't know how,' Lillie said, hesitantly.

Elizabeth was surprised. 'To dance a waltz?'

'They are never played at our dances,' Mrs Le Breton explained. 'It is considered . . .' She could not think of the right word.

George was smiling. 'Oh, we in the metropolis have been exposed to the waltz for a number of years now – and have suffered no serious moral effects.'

Elizabeth and Lily laughed with him. Lillie was embarrassed. It was hateful to feel so provincial. She tried to smile, but the music was starting.

George leant towards her. 'Have no fear, Miss Le Breton,' he said reassuringly. 'You'll soon pick it up. If you'll excuse us, ladies.'

He held out his arm for Lillie. She laid her hand nervously on his forearm and he led her out on to the floor. Other dancers were beginning to waltz round them and she watched them, trying to catch the rhythm. 'Come on, partner,' George said. He took her in his arms, holding her left hand. She copied him, resting her right hand on his waist. He corrected her, lifting it to his upper arm, and began to waltz. She stumbled and hopped, trying to follow him.

Elizabeth indicated the empty chairs and Mrs Le Breton sat with her and the fairhaired Lily. She was anxious, watching her daughter among the other dancers, seeing her bite her lip, unable to catch the step. If only it were not so fast . . .

As they danced, George chuckled, 'No, no, it's three steps, basically. ONE, two, three, ONE two three. That's it . . . Look out!'

Lillie stumbled and he caught her. She was conscious of the other dancers watching them as they swirled past. 'I'm sorry,' she apologised. 'I can't – '

'Nonsense,' he encouraged. 'Try again. Just follow me. ONE two three, ONE two three.' He hoped she would pick it up soon. After all, it was not too difficult and many of the other guests were now watching them. 'No, don't look at your feet,' he told her. 'Follow me. ONE two three. ONE two three. That's it. Splendid! ONE two three.'

Lillie was beginning to get it. She loved dancing and, as her feet started to move naturally to the rhythm, fast and lilting, she was exhilarated. George tried a spin and she followed him perfectly, to her relief. So he said, it was not too difficult. She was dancing the waltz! She looked up at him gracefully. He was still repeating 'ONE two three' loudly. With shock, she saw that he was smiling broadly to the other dancers, who were amused as they passed them by his attempt to teach an obvious carthorse to dance. In her embarrassment, she lost the beat and tripped over the hem of her dress, sprawling and nearly falling.

George just managed to catch her. 'Steady on!' he chuckled. The people round them were laughing.

Watching from the side, Mrs Le Breton tensed. Lily giggled, but stopped when Elizabeth glanced sharply at her.

George and Lillie were isolated on the floor, in a space which the other dancers left clear. 'If at first you don't succeed – ' he chuckled. 'Come on.'

She was selfconscious and upset and avoided him, when he reached for her. 'No. No, please. I'd rather sit down,' she said. 'I'm sorry.' She turned away and headed back through the dancers towards her mother. He shrugged and followed her, rather disappointed. He had been enjoying himself.

Elizabeth rose, as Lillie came to them. 'Are you all right?' she asked.

Lillie was holding herself tightly under control. 'Yes, thank you. I'm sorry, I – '

'Came a trifle unstuck, I'm afraid,' George cut in. 'Never mind, we'll try again later, eh?'

She knew that with a more considerate partner she might have managed, but not with him. It had amused him to make her seem more awkward than she was. 'Thank you, Mr Bentham – but I don't think so,' she said calmly. She turned to Elizabeth. 'If you don't mind, I'll sit down. Please, don't let me keep you from your fiancé.'

Elizabeth frowned. 'Well . . . if you're sure?'

Lillie smiled fleetingly and sat beside her mother. George bowed to her, then led Elizabeth out to dance. As they left, Lillie heard them laughing, discreetly.

Beside her, Mrs Le Breton was rigid, upset for her. 'My poor darling – ' she whispered.

'Please, Mother,' Lillie said quietly. She looked straight ahead at the swirling couples on the floor.

They sat in silence for a minute, watching, then Lily remarked, 'Don't you dance at all?'

'Oh, yes, Miss Suffield, Lillie dances very well,' Mrs Le Breton explained. 'Only – not the waltz.'

If that was true, Lily Suffield thought, it was a pity the evening had begun so badly for her. She looked quite out of place, perhaps it had been a mistake to invite her. Well, she would have a chance to redeem herself later on.

But Lillie was not given the chance. To avoid embarrassing her still further, none of the gentlemen Elizabeth introduced offered to partner her. As the tempo of the ball increased, more and more people were dancing, in a succession of waltzes, progresses, Scottisches and Polkas. Throughout, she sat alone with her mother. As the sets formed and the music began for the final quadrille before supper, she looked to either side and saw that, apart from them, only the oldest of the chaperones were still seated. Of all the young ladies, she was the only one not dancing. She found that, unconsciously, she had crushed her dance card in her hand and she tried to smooth it out without anyone noticing, smiling, determined not to show how hurt she really was.

She looked forward to the supper interval as an escape from the hideous embarrassment and disappointment, but it turned out to be another ordeal. The ranks of knives, forks and spoons laid out round her place mat confused her, and all the differently shaped glasses. In all, there were sixteen courses. She had not expected so many and ate too much at the beginning. There were courses which were served by the footmen. Others to which ladies were expected to serve themselves. Still others at which, by unwritten law, a lady was served by one of the gentlemen one either side of her. And, she discovered too late, there were certain courses which, following the same unwritten laws of etiquette, all the other ladies declined. It made her more and more confused. She was conscious of the suppresed amusement of Bentham and his friends, although they pretended not to watch her. She knew she looked as clumsy and inexperienced as she felt. And all the time, she kept thinking of the second half of the ball that was to follow and wondering how soon she and her mother could decently leave.

Returning to the hotel in their cab, Mrs Le Breton wept and asked Lillie to forgive her. It was her fault, she said. She had insisted on their coming all this way, only to be humiliated. How could people be so cruel? Lillie would not let her blame herself. She was taut, but dry-eyed. She would have felt even more humiliated, if she had let herself cry. All she wanted was to forget the evening as soon as possible. Before going to sleep, she wrote a short note of thanks to Lady Suffield, asking her to pass on her regards to her daughters and to Elizabeth's charming fiancé, whose name, she was afraid, she could not remember.

She had never imagined such happiness as when the

53

homecoming packetboat docked at St. Helier and she saw her father and Reggie waiting. A few private words passed between the Dean and his wife and afterwards, by unspoken agreement, although Lillie and he talked about such things as the marbles in the British Museum and the wonders of the National Gallery and Westminster Abbey, the ball at Upper Grosvenor Street was never mentioned.

That late summer, shortly before her seventeenth birthday, Lillie fell in love.

After their return from London, the new closeness to her mother did not continue. It was not because of coldness on either's part, but simply because Mrs Le Breton became ill with a kind of nervous trouble. She moved to a separate bedroom from the Dean and was often confined to it. For some months, the family saw little of her and Lillie took over as many of her duties as she could, shopping in the covered market and bargaining for the best of the day's catch with the fisherwomen like any young Jersey housewife, as well as visiting the poor of the parish and teaching in Sunday School. She was grateful she was so busy, because she was often alone. Her father was frequently out for most of the afternoon or evening on business. Clement had gone to do his military training at Aldershot. Reggie began by helping her, but soon became bored and took off to visit Arthur or help on the fishing boats.

As he was growing up, he became more wilful and moody. Because of his intelligence, the Dean expected him to do well at school, but he was so filled with nervous energy that he could never sit and study for as much as half an hour. On the evenings when his father and Lillie read aloud, the poems of Walter Scott or a Shakespeare play, he yawned and fidgeted, until he was sent out of the room. He reacted violently to any attempts at discipline, so a career like his brothers in the Army or Civil Service seemed out of the question. Only Lillie could manage him and he resented anything that kept them apart, even his mother's illness. When Mrs Le Breton seemed to be recovering in early September and took over the running of the household again, although she rarely went out and had few visitors,

Reggie's only thought was that Lillie would now have more free time to spend with him.

She had been subdued since her return from London and absorbed in the responsibilities forced on her, but after a few weeks the memory of the ball was less sharp. The long days of summer seemed to stretch on for ever and her energy, which more than matched Reggie's, made her chafe at being indoors. There were so many things she had missed and she could not think which she wanted to do first, although she felt a twinge of guilt at leaving her mother alone. 'I should stay and help her,' she told Reggie.

'Oh, she's fine!' he protested. 'Come on – let's go to the beach. We'll find Michel.'

'Who's he?' she asked.

'Michel Corbet,' Reggie told her. 'A new friend. Come on.'

They begged a lift from a carter who was setting off down the hill, perching on top of the assortment of crates of farm produce and coils of rope in the back of his wagon. He made one short stop in St. Helier and took them on as far as the slipway at La Greve d'Azette. From there, they walked round the next bay to La Rocque. Michel was a fisherboy whom Reggie had met, shrimping. He was a year and a bit older than Reggie, about the same age as Lillie, and lived with his mother and two aunts in a cottage out towards Gorey. The main attraction about him was that he had the use of a small boat.

On the south-east of the island, the coast was much lower and the beaches more stony. The tide was on the ebb when they reached La Rocque Point, leaving long, jagged spines of rock stretching far out towards higher fangs that made this part of the coast so dangerous. There was no gentleness here. As far as they could see, the view was savage and primitive. They hurried along the narrow strip of sand. Below a squat tower built for defence at the time of Napoleon, they came to a little, wooden hut, where Reggie hoped to find Michel. It had only one window covered with sacking and Lillie wrinkled her nose at the mingled smell of tar and fish. It was empty apart from a pile of nets and some old creels. 'He'll be down on the rocks,' Reggie said.

Slipping and sliding on wet stones covered with slime and seaweed, they began to search the foreshore, until Reggie spotted him working farther out. 'Hola, Michel!' he shouted.

When they reached him, Lillie saw that he was a fresh-faced boy about seventeen, really handsome, with golden brown hair and eyes nearly the same shade of blue as her own. He was quite tall, wearing an open shirt and rough trousers rolled up to his knees, leaving his legs and feet bare. He was on one of the higher rocks and rose as they came to him, smiling down to Reggie, then glancing uncertainly at Lillie.

'This is my sister,' Reggie said.

She saw a wicker basket by his feet and asked, 'What are you doing?'

'Gathering whelks, and mussels.' He spoke slowly, his accent soft and guttural.

'To eat?' she asked in patois.

He was surprised that she could speak it and answered warily, 'Some. The rest we use for bait.'

'We'll help you,' Reggie offered.

Michel hesitated, looking at Lillie's shirt-blouse and skirt and soft ankle boots. 'Not her,' he said. 'It's too slippy on the rocks.' He crouched and began to work again, loosening the molluscs from their hold with firm, sideways blows with a stone.

Lillie pushed the front of her skirt between her legs, then caught the back and pulled it up, tucking it into her belt, so that it looked as though she was wearing a pair of baggy breeches. She was barelegged. When she pulled off her boots, Reggie laughed. They both chose a stone to hammer with and clambered up on to the rock.

In the weeks that followed, they saw Michel nearly every day. He was a strange boy, Lillie thought, so quiet and impassive. He hardly ever showed what he was thinking and, sometimes, scarcely spoke more than a word or two in an hour. He had never known his father and, helping to support his mother and aunts, his whole life was spent working. At first, he was very unsure of Lillie, but gradually he came to accept her, even to seem pleased to see her. That was after he had learnt there was no need to make allowances for her. She was as strong and as quick as Reggie. The three of them became inseparable.

At first, it was annoying that he had so little free time, but they soon discovered that, if they helped him, working really hard for three or four hours, gathering bait for the night's fishing or mending nets in the hut, between them they could complete his day's work. Then they could relax and enjoy themselves. In return, he showed them where to find the best crabs, how to cast for bass in a rising tide and to catch the big conger eels in sandy patches between the rocks. Sometimes, they went out in his small lobster boat to fish with lines. The boat was fairly flatbottomed, with just enough room for the three of them. If the wind was right, he would fix up the patchwork sail and they shouted with exhilaration as the surprisingly buoyant, little craft danced over the waves.

One morning, they left the Deanery taking their breakfast with them. They were going climbing on the sea cliffs with Michel, to collect gulls' eggs, and Lillie wore a shirt and a pair of Reggie's trousers, with her hair pushed up under a peaked cap. Michel laughed, when he saw her dressed like that. It was the first time she had really heard him laugh and she liked it strangely. Somehow, with her dressed like this, he was more at his ease and it was one of the best days.

The climbing was hard, even dangerous, but he kept an eye on her and Reggie and showed them how to test foot and hand holds before trusting their weight to them and how to keep their attention on the next move up or across, not on the drop below. Lillie was glad she had worn trousers, for some of the cliffs were fairly sheer. The wind plucked at them and, sometimes, angry gulls flew at them, pecking and beating at them with their wings. She was more afraid for Reggie than for herself, since he kept trying to match Michel and to race him up rockfaces that needed to be approached with caution. The eggs they collected went into canvas satchels slung round their necks and, as they became heavier, made the risk of overbalancing greater. When Michel called down at last that they had enough, she was tired and sweating. Her arms and leg muscles ached with climbing and the satchel hung like a dead weight, making every step an effort. They had worked right round the cliffs of one of the more northerly headlands, slanting up higher and higher from the shore. Momentarily, she glanced down and her head spun as she realised how far away it was. She clung to the surface of the cliff, with her eyes tightly shut, until her breathing slowed again and she could make herself look up.

Michel had already reached the top and sat on a projecting slab of stone, smiling down to her. Reggie was inching up on his right and she held her breath as one of his feet dislodged a large pebble that had been wedged in a narrow crevice and slipped, but he climbed on. The pebble skittered down the sloping top of the cliff and fell past her into silence, until she heard it smack on the rocks below. She knew if she waited any longer, she would never be able to move. She reached up and pulled herself over the lip of the topmost slope, inching up as Reggie had done, searching with her toes for firm ledges and cracks as Michel had taught them. The slope was only fifteen or sixteen feet and she covered it in three minutes, but it felt like hours until Michel's hand closed round her wrist and he pulled her up beside him.

Reggie had also been reaching down for Lillie and, for a second, he was hurt that she had not even seemed aware of him. Then he grinned as she rolled over on her back, laughing and panting with relief.

The rest of the day they spent exploring the further bays, which none of them really knew. The last was quite small with nearly pure white sand that whistled when they scuffed their feet on it. Lillie and Reggie had left a note to tell their mother they would be late. The Dean had been so busy out and about in the parish recently that he would not notice their absence, so they stayed on, while the shadows vanished at sunset, then reappeared as the moon rose.

The sea was still. It was a cloudless night, almost as clear as day in the moonlight. They lay on their backs on the warm sand, watching the shimmer of the water, 'Sainte Marie . . .' Michel breathed. 'It's so hot . . .'

'Let's go for a swim,' Reggie said. 'Lillie won't mind.'

Michel glanced at her. During the day, dressed as she was, he had stopped thinking of her as a girl. Reggie had jumped up and headed down towards the water, pulling off his shirt. Michel hesitated before following him. He was conscious of Lillie behind them, as Reggie and he stripped. Then Reggie looked round and laughed.

Lillie had slipped off her shirt and trousers and was coming towards them, wearing only short culottes, trimmed with scalloped lace, completely unselfconscious. Michel gazed at her. Her hair floated free, darker in the moonlight, which silvered her pale skin, gleaming on her arms and the high, firm gourds of her breasts. He had never dreamt that a woman's body could be so perfect.

Her nakedness had no effect on Reggie. 'Come on!' he shouted, impatiently.

The three of them ran, laughing and splashing into the water.

There was a change in their relationship after that night. Before, when Reggie had decided to visit Arthur, instead of going to look for Michel, Lillie had either gone with him to Portelet or stayed at home. Now, she went alone to the hut by the Martello Tower and, although neither she nor Michel spoke of it, both of them enjoyed the times when there was just the two of them more than when Reggie was also with them. He was only half aware of it, but slowly began to resent the feeling of being excluded by both his sister and his friend. One afternoon when they were hunting the rocks for peeler crabs to use as bait, he became separated from them. Climbing higher to look for them, he saw them crouching on opposite sides of a little rockpool, intent, fascinated by the miniature world it contained. After a moment, Lillie reached down and stirred the surface of the water with one hand. Michel copied her. As they drew their hands out, he touched his dripping fingertips to hers and smiled. She smiled back, very slightly, withdrew her hand and gazed again down at the little pool, while Michel sat and watched her. It was only a moment, but for that moment Reggie felt such a wrenching spasm of jealousy that he was ashamed.

The next day, they were to meet Michel again, but Mrs Le Breton was not feeling well and sent Reggie to fetch a joint of beef she had ordered. When he got home, Lillie had already gone without him. He had told her he would hurry and she had said there was no need. Obviously, they did not want him. He was hurt and angry.

As he stood disconsolately in the hall outside the empty schoolroom, he heard a noise upstairs. He hurried up the stairs and stopped in surprise, seeing a tall, young man in the uniform of a Lieutenant in the Royal Fusiliers closing the door of her room. The young man turned and he shouted, realising it was his brother, Clement. Clem came to meet him and they hugged each other, slapping each other on the back, laughing. 'You've grown,' Clem said.

'So have you,' Reggie answered, grinning. 'It's marvellous! When did you get here?'

'Ten minutes ago. Where is everyone?'

'Mother's lying down. She's . . . you know.'

Clement nodded, serious. 'And Father and Lillie?'

'They're both out,' Reggie told him, and smiled. 'So what's it like at Aldershot? Are they going to make you a General?'

They laughed.

In the fisher hut, it was warm and quiet. The door was open to give more light. Michel knelt, mending and knotting the broken meshes of a net. Lillie was kneeling quite near him, working on the wicker cage of a lobster pot. She wove the new strands through the old, pushing them in tight. She finished and laid the pot down. When she turned, she became motionless, seeing Michel on his knees beside her, the net in his lap, watching her.

Slowly, as he leaned towards her, she leaned to meet him, until their lips were very close. Her eyes were huge. Their arms were by their sides, neither daring to touch or hold the other. When their lips met, Lillie's eyes closed.

Dean Le Breton had arrived home to find Clement in the drawingroom with Reggie. He clasped Clement's hand, delighted. 'Splendid, splendid. How good to see you, my boy! I daresay you'd like a glass of sherry, eh?' As he crossed to the sideboard, he smiled wryly to Reggie. 'And I suppose you'd better have one, too.' He was in good humour as he took out three glasses and unstoppered the decanter. 'A family cherishes the moments it can be together.'

Clement smiled. 'Yes, sir. It's good to be home.'

The Dean nodded and began to pour. 'I'm sorry your mother – well, she'll be down this evening. Where's Lillie?'

'Out, Reggie says.'

'Oh, where to?'

Reggie felt faintly excluded again, by the warmth of his father's welcome to Clem. 'She's with Michel,' he told him. And immediately wished he had not, but it was too late.

'Michel?'

'Michel Corbet,' Reggie said. He saw his father's back stiffen and Clem turning towards him in surprise. 'She's always with him,' he added, tense.

Clement looked hard at him, warning him to stop.

The Dean set down the decanter and turned, holding two glasses. 'No doubt she'll be back soon,' he said, evenly. He handed one glass to Clement, then the other to Reggie, who could not look at him.

Michel walked part of the way home with Lillie. She was as animated and carefree as he was silent. They had kissed only once, but he knew it was a commitment. It had been unexpected and had roused pleasurable, disturbing feelings in both of them. Only their inexperience stopped it from going further. For the moment, she had no thought of what would come next, yet he knew it was only a matter of time before they made love. The impulse to hold her and feel her against him was almost overpowering.

They were cutting across country and came out of trees on to the green slope of a hill. 'Oh, I don't want to go home!' she said, 'I just want to walk and walk. Don't you, Michel?'

He was silent, watching her as she paused, looking at the view. 'This must be the most wonderful island in the whole world . . .'

'You'll leave it one day,' he said.

'Never!' she protested. 'Why do you say that?'

He shrugged.

'I couldn't leave Father, and Reggie and – and you.' She put her hand on his arm. He smiled and covered it with his, but she was troubled. 'You wouldn't leave, would you?'

'I couldn't,' he told her. 'All I know is fishing. I'm not educated like you.'

'Do you think that matters?' she said softly. She looked up at him, waiting for him to kiss her again. But he hesitated a fraction too long. As he leant towards her, she broke from him, smiling, and ran on down the slope. He smiled and ran after her.

There was a stile at the end of the field. He caught up with her in time to help her over, her hand warm in his. She was standing on the step on the other side, her face level with his. 'Are you going out fishing tonight?' she asked.

'On the ten o'clock tide.'

'I'll come with you,' she said. 'I can get out again, after they've all gone to sleep.'

His throat went dry. 'We'd be alone,' he said slowly. 'I wouldn't get much fishing done.'

She was indignant. 'I can help you just as much as Reggie!'

'That's not what I meant,' he told her. She flushed and stood very still suddenly, her eyes fixed on his. He made himself smile, as if he had been joking. 'I'd better be heading back. I'll see you tomorrow.'

'I'll see you tonight,' she said and kissed his cheek. When he reached for her, she jumped off the stile and ran towards the corner of the lane. Reaching it, she turned and waved to him before running on. He waved back, but she did not see. He watched her out of sight.

Lillie came into the hall of the Deanery. She paused, looking at herself in the mirror and flicking her hair back over her shoulders. As she headed for the stairs, her father opened the study door and she smiled to him.

'Would you come in here, please?' he said curtly.

She was surprised by his tone. She followed him and closed the study door, watching him as he moved to the centre of the room.

'You were not at home to greet your brother.'

She knew that Clement was due on leave and laughed. 'Is Clem here already? Where is he?'

Her father turned to her, his voice cold. 'Where have you been?'

'Out walking.'

'Where?'

'By the cliffs.'

'Alone?'

She hesitated. 'With a friend.'

'Who? he asked, repeating it when she did not answer. 'Who is this friend?'

Her surprise increased. He had never questioned her like this before. '. . . His name is Michel – Michel Corbet. A fisherboy.'

The Dean sucked in his breath. His brow lowered. 'How long have you known him?'

'A few weeks.'

'What do you know about him?'

'Nothing,' Lillie said. 'I like him.'

The Dean's mouth twisted. 'Like him? . . . Have you met frequently?' She was silent. She was so fair, he thought, so seemingly innocent. Yet, was her silence really evasion? There were serpents hidden here, but he had to go on. 'Have you?'

'Yes.'

'Have you been seen together?' he demanded.

She could not understand his growing anger and displeasure. 'Perhaps,' she faltered. 'I don't know.'

'You don't know? . . . Yet you sneak out of the house by day and by night to meet him!' When she made to speak, he swung away from her. 'Don't try to deny it! I have been told.' He moved swiftly to the window and stood with his back to her.

Obviously, someone had been carrying tales, she thought, making everything seem secret and deceitful. Who could have told him? It must have been Reggie. For what reason? Her father's hands were clasped behind his back. One was clenched like a fist. She saw it beat into the other's open palm. He was turning.

'Why?' he asked, tautly. 'What is there between you?' She hesitated. 'Yes?'

'I love him,' she said quietly.

He stared at her, disbelievingly. '*Love* him?'

Until that moment, she had not known what she really felt for Michel. He had forced her to put it into words. 'I am happy with him – just to be with him.'

'You don't know what you're saying,' the Dean muttered.

It was important for her father to understand, more important than anything in the world, and he would, when she explained. She smiled. 'I think about him all the time,' she said shyly. 'He's so gentle and – '

'That is enough!' he shouted. 'Have you so little care for your reputation? No thought for whose daughter you are?' She was shocked by the fury of his anger. She had never ever seen him like this. He stepped forward. 'How far has it gone?' What has taken place between you?'

'Nothing,' she whispered.

'You expect me to believe that?' he rapped. 'You meet him alone – at night!'

'He has never touched me.'

'Never?' As he stared at her, he saw her hurt and bewilderment. It was not feigned and some of his alarm subsided. She was still innocent. That he must believe. He mastered himself. 'No . . . no, of course not,' he said thickly. 'Well, that is – that is something. Now, listen to me – you are not to see him again.'

'But Papa – !' she began.

'Do you hear me?' he insisted. 'Not ever again.'

It was too cruel. He had not even given her a chance to explain. 'I – cannot – '

He drew himself up sternly. 'I mean to be obeyed. I will

be obeyed in this! I – I apologise for doubting you, but it is unthinkable that you should go on meeting him.' She wanted to protest, but he was so righteous and authoritative that she could not find the words. 'I'll have no arguments, Lillie!' he said firmly. 'You must be ruled by me. You will go to your room until you accept what I have said. This boy is *not* for you! And I forbid you, strictly forbid you, ever to see him again.'

She did not know how she reached her room. Her eyes were unseeing, her mind whirling. It was unjust! The island was ruled by convention and prudish morality. Her father was against Michel, merely because she had been alone with him and people might gossip! It was so unlike him. He had always been so understanding and wise – not like those mealymouthed – one thing she knew. Nothing would make her give up meeting Michel as often as she chose! Even if she had to defy them all, even if they had to hide. And she would never forgive Reggie, if it was him who had betrayed her.

She heard the door open behind her and turned quickly, expecting her father, ready to be defiant.

It was Clem. He closed the door softly behind him, watching her, very serious. 'I heard some of it,' he told her.

'How could he?' Lillie protested. 'It's so unfair!'

'Yes . . .' Clem said. 'But you must do as Father says.'

She stiffened. 'Never! If he sent you –'

'He did not.'

His quiet voice was at once calming and irritating. She was sorry she had misjudged him, but she could not pretend to be reasonable. 'He has never spoken to me like that before. He has no right to stop me seeing Michel!'

'He has every right, Lillie.'

'You're all against him!' she flared. 'Just because he's poor, because he's not grand enough!' Clement shook his head and moved nearer. She stepped away from him. He had always been her closest ally, next to Reggie. Now they were all turning on her. Too much was happening. She sat on the side of her bed. 'I thought you'd be on our side, Clem,' she said. 'I – I love him.'

L.—C

'You have every reason to,' he told her.

Something in his voice puzzled her. She looked up at him and saw that he was troubled.

He sat beside her. There was something he wanted to say, yet found difficult. 'Why?' he asked at last. 'Why do you love him?'

'Because he's kind. He's fun to be with.' At least, she could explain to Clem. She smiled. 'I feel as if I'd known him all my life. He's just like one of us!'

'Just like Father, you mean,' Clem said quietly. 'And that's why you must have nothing more to do with him.'

She heard what he said. It meant nothing. 'But – '

'Lillie, don't you understand? Michel is your brother,' She gazed at him, unable to take it in. 'He is Father's son . . . by another woman. There are . . . others. That is why Mother has been unwell. She did not know, until a few months ago. Everyone else did. Everyone pities her. Don't you see? . . . Michel is our half-brother.'

Lillie was shaken and horrified. She thought of Michel's golden, fair hair and blue eyes, so like she had imagined her father as a young man. His strength, and the smile that had made her love him. She tried to deny it, but could not, and trembled. All at once, she realised why her father was out of the house so often, and the business that detained him.

Clement put his arms around her and held her, feeling her whole body shake. 'Cry if you want to, my dear,' he said. 'It will be better.'

She clung to him, needing the assurance of his arms around her. Too much else in her world had fallen to pieces. After a moment, she pushed herself away and sat straight. Her eyes were clear. He had never seen her so bleak and withdrawn.

'I shan't cry,' she said. 'I shan't ever cry.'

She went with her mother to church on Sunday. Neither Clement nor Reggie would come with them and they sat alone in the long, family pew. She knew now how shamed and conspicuous her mother felt. She heard her father's voice, deep and eloquent, which used to thrill her with its conviction, and made herself look up at him in the pulpit.

'Fight – resist!' the Dean called. 'Sin is the Enemy! When he comes stealing towards you, be on your guard – do not let him find the chink in your armour. Hold up the shield of Faith before you and be bold, bold for God!'

She glanced at her mother, who sat motionless, looking fixedly ahead. She took hold of her nearest hand and her mother grasped it tightly.

# CHAPTER THREE

By the time she was nineteen, Lillie's reputation as the most beautiful girl on the island was almost unquestioned. Other local girls came briefly into fashion, but none of them could compare with her in grace and poise. The others were soon married. She remained unattached and unavailable.

She thinks no one in the island good enough for her, the older women sniffed, and whispered the shocking rumour of how she rolled naked in the morning dew in the field by the Deanery to make her skin supple, and lay for hours every evening with her face covered by strips of raw liver to keep her complexion. Lillie laughed when she heard the stories. It was fun to be courted and to be talked about, but she had her own private dream which she confided in no one.

She enjoyed the companionship of men, much more than of women, but had to take extreme care of her reputation. Because of her father's compulsive misconduct, she was watched very narrowly by the respectable ladies of the community. As more children began to appear with a striking resemblance to the Dean, he was known mockingly as the Father of St. Saviour's. Mrs Le Breton continued to lead an almost separate life from his, although she ran his house and joined in on family occasions. She depended more and more on Lillie's help with her parish duties. Reggie, as he grew up, was her main problem. He was quite unmanageable. Wild and reckless, he showed no interest in choosing a career. The Dean had nearly given up trying to discipline him and he led an erratic, almost solitary life, more and more obsessed by Lillie.

She had forgiven him long ago.

Wealthy visitors to Jersey still called at the Deanery and were struck by the beauty and charm of the Dean's daughter. Lillie accepted their invitations to picnics and lunches, but had learnt not to take their condescension as an offer of friendship. She was guarded and they thought her touchingly shy, aware of her place. She, in turn, observed them and their manners, style and conversation, absorbing what she learnt. When subjects and personalities were discussed of which she knew nothing, she developed a trick of listening, poised and slightly detached, which made the people with her exert themselves to try to keep her interest. Reggie called it her Duchess look.

Most of the time, she much preferred being with him. Although she had learnt control, she could be just as reckless and determined as he was. She liked best to ride fast with Arthur Jones and him, the three of them sighting on a distant landmark and making breakneck for it, whatever the obstacles. When Lord Ranelagh and his two daughters were there, Reggie and she sometimes stayed at Portelet House with them and Arthur. Ranelagh was a sprightly, old rake who enjoyed being surrounded by young people and, for them, it was a welcome change from the uneasy atmosphere of the Deanery.

Lord Ranelagh was furious once, though, when Clement was on leave and came with them. Clem was much taken with the younger daughter, Alice, and when Ranelagh heard that he had begun to court her, he ordered Reggie and him out of the house, until they possessed better manners. The ban did not apply to Lillie.

He had no need to worry about Reggie, either, if he had known. His energy and nervous good looks made him attractive to girls and he often carried on affairs with several at once. But they were only substitutes and none of them lasted more than a week or so. None of them could take the place of Lillie, for whom all his devotion was reserved.

Shortly before her twentieth birthday, he noticed a change in her. She spent long hours reading, or working in the Deanery garden. She had a passion for flowers. Even when they were at Portelet, she often would not come out with Arthur and him and stayed behind to tend the section of the terrace garden that everyone called hers. Her touch was amazing. Plants and flowers flourished for her, when they would for no one else.

When the summer came, she spent fewer and fewer days with Reggie. He resented the work she did in her garden and often thought of uprooting it to teach her a lesson. Mrs Le Breton was again unwell and Lillie took over her charity work. Reggie resented that, also, finding her in the evenings discussing projects with neat, earnest, young wives and the ladies bountiful of the island. She became very friendly with one of them, her brother William's fiancée, Elizabeth. She was a Price, a sister of the young woman whom the yachtsman, Edward Langtry, had married and who had died tragically of tuberculosis not long after the marriage.

Reggie came on them in the schoolroom one day. The table, benches, chairs and windowseats were covered with linen and knitting clothes for babies and infants. Elizabeth, a delicate, dark-haired girl of twenty, was helping Lillie to sort them out.

'Bit premature, isn't it?' Reggie laughed. 'You're not getting married for three months yet.'

Elizabeth blushed and Lillie glanced at him in annoyance.

'Sorry,' he pretended to apologise. 'Just my coarse tongue.' He leant back against the door, watching them, amused. 'Who's it all going to, anyway?'

'The poor children of the parish,' Lillie told him.

'Did Elizabeth and you collect it all?'

'Most of it,' Elizabeth said. 'It was Lillie's idea.'

'Quite the little angel of mercy . . .' Reggie murmured. 'Don't you ever get tired of standing in for Mother?'

Lillie laid aside some vests to be washed. 'There are so few things a woman can do to be useful.'

'Oh, come on,' he laughed. 'Let's go for a walk.'

'Not today.'

He grimaced in annoyance and pushed himself off the door, about to retort. He saw Elizabeth looking at him curiously and stopped. 'Suit yourself,' he muttered, turning away.

He was gone for the rest of the afternoon, riding his horse

savagely as far as St. John before he had worked off his annoyance. In the evening, when Lillie sat reading in the drawingroom, he strolled in and stood looking at her. She glanced up and went on reading, while he poured himself a glass of sherry from the decanter. 'You're always reading nowadays,' he complained. He leant over her and tipped the cover towards him. 'The Book of Beauty,' he read, and laughed. 'That explains all this nonsense about not going out in the sun – ointments for your arms, primping your hair. What's got into you?'

Lillie laid the book on her knee. She wore her hair tied back now, gathered with a bow. She had begun to take a more deliberate care of what she wore and how she looked. 'I must do as the others do,' she said quietly.

'You were fine as you were! Why must you?'

She paused. 'No man likes his wife to be to different.'

He was shaken. 'Wife? You're planning to be married?'

'One day – if I'm ever to leave this island.'

He did not know what she meant. The island was enough for him. 'To go where?' he asked, puzzled.

'London,' she told him. 'It's all I think of.'

'But you hated it there!' he protested. 'It was awful.'

'Only because I didn't know anyone,' And because of my inexperience, she admitted to herself. She was ashamed now at how awkwardly she had behaved at that ball, and longed for another chance. She had grown out of her childhood and the island, which had then seemed magical, was like a prison. Everything she heard and read about the world outside made her more conscious of the frustrations and limitations of her life. She remembered vividly all the details of her short trip to London. And there was so much more. 'Everything's there – everything I ever wanted. If I were married . . .'

'You don't mean it,' he laughed. 'You can't want to be *married*? . . . I mean, I don't ever intend to. I thought – we'd go on, the two of us. Just as we are.' He looked younger and more vulnerable, when he was perplexed. Lillie smiled to him and closed the book.

The autumn storms were bad that year. For days on end,

the paddle steamers could not leave the harbour and many of the little fishingboats were wrecked, even at their moorings. The late harvest looked like being ruined. It would be a hungry winter for many of the islanders with food and work scarce.

One night, Lillie was in bed, sleeping fitfully because of the storm outside. A violent clap of thunder brought her awake and, as she lay watching how her whole room flickered into brightness with the flashes of lighting, she thought she heard the sound of her father's carriage on the gravel of the courtyard. A minute later, she heard the door open downstairs and his voice shouting, 'Reggie – Lillie! Someone!'

In the hall, Dean Le Breton struggled to close the front door against the wind. He was supporting a much younger man, wearing yachting clothes, so tired he could barely stand. It was Edward Langtry.

As the Dean managed to get the door shut, Lillie came hurrying down the stairs in her nightgown, pulling on her wrap. An oil lamp stood on the hall table, burning with a low flame. She turned it up.

'Is the fire lit in the study?' her father asked, urgently.

'Yes.'

'Good.' He took the lamp from her. 'Get some blankets. It's Mr Langtry. His yacht nearly foundered.' She ran back to the stairs.

When she returned to the study with the blanket, she found her father poking the fire into a blaze. Edward sat huddled in a chair, shaking with cold, his hands stretched out to the fire. His jacket was soaking and lay on the floor beside him. He had been fighting the storm in his large yacht for nearly five hours. 'There were times I didn't think Red Gauntlet was going to make it,' he muttered.

'Yet you brought her into harbour. A fine bit of seamanship, Mr Langtry.' The Dean with others had watched the last stage of the yacht's battle from the quayside. They had cheered when she finally beat round and made anchor in the shelter of the harbour, some of her sails in tatters and her crew exultant, but exhausted. Various people had taken them off to their homes to rest and recover. The Dean took the blankets from Lillie, laid one over Edward's knees and the other over his shoulders. 'How did you come to be caught out?'

'I was on my way from . . . Southampton to Harfleur,' Edward said. 'When the storm struck, the wind drove us in this direction. A blessing, really. At least, I know the waters round Jersey.'

Lillie had picked up his jacket and watched him, fascinatedly, as she folded it. His dark hair was tangled. He looked pale and quite handsome, although a full moustache he now wore made his face seem heavier.

He was shivering again and tried to rise. 'If you'll forgive me – I must find lodgings.'

Dean Le Breton pressed him back down. 'You'll do no such thing,' he declared. 'You'll stay here.'

'I couldn't presume – '

'No presumption, sir,' the Dean smiled. 'You are a friend of my son, and we have more rooms than we know what to do with. You may stay as long as you choose.' Lillie had poured a glass of brandy. 'Ah, good. Thank you, Lillie.' He passed the glass to Edward.

'Thank you,' Edward panted. He gulped at the brandy, coughing as it burned down his throat. Then he realised what the Dean had said and glanced up in surprise. 'Little Lillie? . . . I must apologise. I hadn't recognised you.'

He slept for most of the next day and she heard more about his feat of bringing his yacht, *Red Gauntlet*, in safely through the rocks and shoals in the teeth of the storm. Everyone was talking about it and it was exciting to have the hero of the hour in their house. She would have loved to see it. Even more, to have been on *Red Gauntlet* with him. She was annoyed with Reggie who said, he did not see why they were all praising Langtry, when he had a captain and a crew of five to do all the real work.

The following day, Edward had fully recovered. His captain, Merritt, came to report on damage and that the storm showed no sign of lessening. It might not blow itself out for several days yet. At least, Edward consoled himself, the race he had planned to enter at Harfleur would have been cancelled. He fretted at being inactive and studied the wind every morning and evening.

The main consolation he discovered was Lillie. She had definitely become most attractive. And was such a quiet and sensible, young woman. The first he had taken notice of, since his wife died. She would make some lucky man very happy.

He was watching the driving rain and fierce waving of the treetops from the drawingroom window, when she came in. 'Still between Force Six and Seven. I'd say,' he commented.

'Are you impatient to leave?' she asked.

It occurred to him that he might appear ungrateful for her parents' hospitality. 'Only to be at sea again,' he assured her. Her smile was delightful. And her carriage, the way she held herself. There was breeding there, although the family were all a bit hail-fellow-well-met. Of course, he had known them for years. He realised she was waiting for him to speak. He had very little smalltalk and was not at his ease. He coughed. 'You mustn't let me keep you, eh, Lillie. After all, it doesn't do for us to be together – unchaperoned.'

She thought he was being amusing and smiled. 'The door's open.'

'Ah – yes,' he nodded. 'So it is.'

She sat by the fire. He hesitated, then sat also, on a chair by the window. They were well apart. No one could possibly take exception. Certainly, in her artlessness, she saw nothing wrong in their being together like this. He thought it charming and smiled.

'There can be no scandal,' she said. 'We are practically related.'

'Oh?' He did not follow her.

'Your late wife's sister, Elizabeth, is to marry my brother William quite soon.'

'Why yes, that is so,' he agreed. He lowered his head.

'Forgive me, if I have raised a painful subject,' she said quickly.

'No, no, no.'

'I did not really know the late Mrs Langtry very well,

74

but I am a great friend of her sister's.'

'Dear Elizabeth,' he sighed. 'A charming girl. But she does not have my Jane's refinement. My wife was so lovely – so delicate.'

'Yes.'

'Consumption is a cruel disease. It heightens and purifies the beauty of its victims, while it eats away their strength,' He was genuinely saddened and, at the same moment, surprised. He never talked about Jane.

Lillie was touched. It was a romantic and poignant story. 'I hear you were always at her side.'

'When my interests did not drag me away,' he nodded.

'Your interests?'

'Sailing. Fishing,' he told her.

Lillie had never actually met a man who lived only for his hobbies. 'Is that all you do?' she asked.

'When one has no need – ' He shrugged. 'And now I am alone, I spend most of my time with my yachts.'

'You have more than one?' she wondered.

'Three others – yachts and cutters. The Red Gauntlet is my pride, though. She's an eighty footer.'

'Do you live on board her?'

'Not all the time,' he smiled. 'I have a house on Southampton Water.'

Lillie was more and more impressed. He must be even richer than she had imagined. She had already been surprised to learn that there was only seven years difference between them. With his poise and reserve, she had always thought of him as much older. She rose and, as she laid some more coal on the fire, asked casually, 'Did your wife always sail with you?'

He shook his head. 'Hardly ever.'

'I cannot imagine why,' she said.

'She was no sailor,' he explained. 'The slightest wave made her unwell.'

How sad, Lillie thought. If she had the chance – Edward was looking at his hands again. 'I would love to see the Red Gauntlet.'

He looked up. 'Really?'

'And to go for a sail in her,' she suggested, adding quickly, 'If that were possible.'

Edward was delighted. He liked nothing more than showing off his yacht. And Lillie would make an enchanting passenger. He could not remember when he had found it so easy to talk to someone of her sex. 'You mean it?' he smiled. 'Well, why not? If one of your parents would agree to come along. Are you serious?'

'It sounds wonderful,' she told him, controlling her excitement. She did not want him to think her forward. 'Provided it was not too rough.'

'Naturally.' He rose and glanced at the window. 'Well, then – as soon as the wind has dropped, and the sea is calm.'

By the end of the week, it was difficult to believe it was the same month. The weather had cleared into a perfect, Indian summer, as happened so often on the islands. Dean Le Breton needed little persuasion to accompany Lillie on a short cruise.

The *Red Gauntlet* was the most beautiful thing she had ever seen. The crew had used the time to clean and repair. The yacht was almost breathtaking, long and thrusting and white, the cabins below deck so luxurious that Lillie knew she would dream of them. The crew was smartly uniformed and she liked the captain very much, George Merritt, a capable, friendly man.

Because of the seamen's superstitions, the Dean was not wearing his white dogcollar. He sat with Lillie on canvas chairs on the deck, under the stern awning. They were both well wrapped in rugs and she wore her best outdoor dress and a straw sunhat. They were making a circuit of the island and the Dean saw her look from Edward, who stood with Merritt and the helmsman at the brassbound wheel, to the crewmen working the sails and rigging. Her eyes were alight as the yacht spanked along, slicing the waves.

'I'm surprised you're not helping the crew,' he murmured.

She sighed. 'Edward wouldn't think it suitable for a young lady.'

Her father chuckled. 'But you've been sailing fishing

boats in all weathers, since you were a child. He must know that.'

'I haven't told him,' she said. 'And I hope no one else will.'

Just then, Edward turned and waved to them. As she waved back, a gust of wind tugged at her hat. She made a tiny gasp of surprise and caught the brim. It looked so spontaneous, and yet was so calculatedly feminine, that the Dean nearly snorted.

Edward laughed indulgently and came to them. 'Everything all right?'

The Dean nodded. 'Most enjoyable, thank you, Mr Langtry.'

Edward looked at Lillie. 'Not too choppy for you?'

'No,' she smiled. 'It's very exciting.'

'Good. Just say the word when you've had enough.'

'Oh, I don't have to be back till this afternoon,' she said quickly. 'We have to decide on the bridesmaids' dresses.'

He was pleased that she enjoyed it so much. He had to admit to himself that he wanted to impress her. She made him feel quite boyish.

In the next two weeks, he took her sailing several more times, either with the Dean or Mrs Le Breton. Once, they went as far as the coast of France and he even let her take the helm for a minute or so. The impression of holding all the thrust and power of Red Gauntlet in her hands was intoxicating, Lillie found. There was no other sensation to compare with it. If she had been Edward, she would have done all the steering herself, until her arms ached. Merritt had been prepared for the worst, but she caught the knack of it so quickly, he joined the crew in applauding her.

There was now no reason for Edward to remain in Jersey, but he could not bring himself to say goodbye. He decided to stay for William's wedding to Elizabeth. It was welcomed by both families, except for Reggie, who disliked the way he was always looking at Lillie, walking with her in the garden and showing off about his rich family. And she encouraged it, blushing and simpering like one of the townie girls. She was completely dazzled by the damned yacht. The sooner he sailed off in it, the better.

William was a Captain now, tall and bronzed. He brought them all messages and presents from another brother, Maurice Le Breton, who was also in India. He had begun a notably successful career in the Indian Civil Service and they were proud of him.

It was like the old days to have William at home. Then Clement came on leave, too, for the wedding and they had a family party to celebrate. Elizabeth was there with her parents, and Edward.

William and Elizabeth were especially grateful to Edward. 'It was so good of you to stay on,' she said.

'Nothing could tear me away,' he told them.

Reggie tensed when he saw him glance towards Lillie, who looked down demurely.

'I confess I'm beginning to feel nervous already,' William laughed. 'I'd no idea it was going to be such a grand affair.'

The Prices had invited nearly two hundred guests. Lillie was to be principal bridesmaid and Reggie one of the groomsmen. The Dean was to conduct the wedding himself, assisted by the Vicar, with a full choir. The bridesmaids were to be in military style.

'The hats and dresses are so pretty!' Elizabeth said. 'Madame Nicolle is making them specially.'

'I've had experience of her,' Lillie smiled. 'Madame Boielle is making mine.'

Elizabeth had been unsure about that, but agreed, provided it was in the same colours and material. Madame Boielle was the most expensive of St. Helier's dressmakers and, as chief bridesmaid, it was Lillie's right to go to her, if she chose.

Listening, Edward had a brilliant idea. With three brothers at home and the family excitement over the wedding, not all Lillie's attention was fixed on him, as it had been. He had enjoyed being a celebrity and having her look up to him. It had become important to him, he realised. 'Look here – Mr Dean, Mr and Mrs Price, Elizabeth, William – ' he announced loudly. 'I'd like to contribute to this occasion. As my present, let me give a wedding ball for you at the Yacht Club.'

It was worth it to hear the exclamations of surprise and to see Lillie so excited, looking at him so admiringly.

'Ned, you couldn't possibly – ' William began.

'No, no, please!' Edward insisted. 'Please. After all, your marriage will be the main social event for many years. Let me make it unforgettable!'

For the convenience of the guests, the wedding was held in the early evening. Two hours before, the churchyard round St. Savoiur's was filled with spectators. The unreserved seats inside the church had been taken already. No one could remember such anticipation. It had been growing for weeks. More and more people came crowding in from the countryside and up the long hill from St. Helier, eager to see the guests in their finery and the splendours of the bridal group. Before long, the churchyard was crammed, with people standing on the tombstones and climbing up to sit on the walls. More were outside, clamouring to get in and jamming the road. The carriages of the guests had to be diverted along the narrow track at the side of the church and, soon, stretched back to nearly halfway down the hill.

Pushing and jostling, the spectators parted only reluctantly to let the guests through and the police on duty called for volunteers in case of violence. But the crowd was goodnatured, cheering William and Clement in their dress uniforms, when they arrived with Edward Langtry. Then there was a special cheer for the Dean, escorting Mrs Le Breton in his full vestments, beaming and waving to the shouts of congratulation.

Inside the church, Edward stood with Elizabeth's mother and family. Her brothers were serving as the other ushers with Reggie. The excitement and the hubbub of the crowd infected them all. He nodded encouragingly when William looked round nervously from where he stood with Clement, then they heard a commotion from the mob outside and he knew that the carriages bringing the bridesmaids and Elizabeth and her father had arrived, led by Captain Merritt and the sailors from Red Gauntlet carrying red and green, port and starboard, lanterns. The ushers went out to help the police clear a path for them and, after a full five minutes, while the crowd yelled and whistled and cheered, the organ played the wedding march and all the guests rose as Elizabeth in her bridal gown came down the aisle on her father's arm.

She was tremulously beautiful, but most of the gasps of admiration were for the four bridesmaids who followed her, in their scarlet, black-frogged military tunics over white silk dresses, with red tricorne hats, decorated with pearls and white ostrich feathers. Edward only saw Lillie. Her tunic was undeniably better cut than the others, moulding the incredible slenderness of her waist and the perfect line of her bust and shoulders. She was smiling as she advanced, aware of Edward gazing at her.

For the wedding ball, the main room of the Yacht Club was hung with flags, pennons and bunting. The stairs and hall were lined with sailors in white uniforms. The stewards circulated with champagne and the music was played by a small French orchestra which Edward had brought over from St. Malo. Everyone was agog at the extravagance of it, and still excited by the near riot after the wedding, when the bridal party emerged from the church. the ushers, police and Red Gauntlet's sailors had literally had to fight a passage through the crowds for them. Several lady guests had their dresses torn and one gentleman had even lost his boots.

As the first quadrille ended and the dancers applauded, Mrs Le Breton could not think what had happened to Lillie. She could see the other bridesmaids in their red tunics, but no sign of her daughter. Mr Langtry, she knew, was quite agitated, in case she had become unwell. She saw Lillie's and Reggie's young friend, Arthur Jones, passing and stopped him. He was a very likeable young man. Fairly tall and goodlooking, he had become, always natural and goodhumoured. 'Arthur, have you see Lillie anywhere? Where's she got to?'

'I think she said something about changing,' he told her.

'Oh – well, thank you.' She stopped him again. 'Do help me, will you, Arthur? Try to make sure Reggie doesn't drink too much champagne.'

He grinned. 'I'll *try*, Mrs Le Breton.'

They heard murmurs of surprise and interest round them. People were turning to look at the stairs.

Lillie was coming down, between the lines of sailors. Unlike the other bridesmaids, she had taken off the scarlet tunic to let her dress be seen properly. It was of white silk like the others, but with a much fuller skirt. And the skirt was not plain, but sewn with dozens of tiny, blush roses. The neckline of the dress was deep, leaving her shoulders and upper bust bare, and she wore white elbow-length gloves. Her hair was tied back in a white bow, then rolled into one gleaming coil which rested on her left shoulder. Using all the lessons she had learnt since that evening at the Suffields', she came down slowly, with a faint, teasing smile. She was stunning.

Some of the gentlemen began to move forward and clustered at the foot of the stairs to escort her to her table.

Edward hurried forward and reached the stairs just as she took Arthur's arm. 'I don't believe I've had the pleasure,' he said stiffly.

Lillie was surprised. 'Don't you know Artie?'

'How do you do, Mr Langtry?' Arthur said, holding out his hand. 'I was at school with Reggie.'

Edward relaxed. 'Ah – a friend of the family.' He smiled and shook hands. 'Well, I'm sorry.' He looked at the others. 'Sorry, gentlemen. But as host, I claim the privilege.'

The gentlemen laughed and stepped back as she took his arm and he led her proudly across the floor to the family group.

During the next Lancers Quadrille, the two families chattered and gossiped. They were all lively and animated, except for Reggie. He could not bear Edward and stayed aloof, drinking solidly. Arthur passed on his mother's warning. They laughed and settled down to consume as much Langtry champagne as possible.

Lillie stood with Elizabeth and William. At least as many people complimented her on her appearance as congratulated them, until she felt quite embarrassed. 'You'll be

81

next,' Elizabeth whispered, and kissed her cheek.

Most of the gentlemen were eager to dance with her, but felt warned off by Edward. They wished he would claim his first dance and get it over to give them a chance. He was waiting impatiently. The whole reason for this ruinously expensive evening had been to impress her, and he had a shrewd idea she had done herself up so ravishingly for his benefit. If so, it was certainly worth it. He would have to move in fast, though. Most of the other fellows couldn't keep their eyes off her. As the music finished again, he lifted two glasses from a passing tray and presented one to Mrs Le Breton.

'Oh, I couldn't, Mr Langtry!' she protested.

He bowed. 'It's a special occasion, Mrs Le Breton.'

She gave in and accepted it. He offered the second glass to the Dean.

'I mustn't,' the Dean said, and took it.

They laughed and Edward had the group's attention again. 'With your permission?' He bowed and, turning, took Lillie's hand. 'Lillie – '

She smiled. 'What? What is it?'

He led her across the empty floor towards the bandstand. She was flushed, knowing that everyone was watching. Her certainty that he had really given this ball for her made it all the more exciting.

They reached the bandstand, where the conductor bowed to them. Edward smiled. 'Now, it's your choice.'

She did not understand. 'Choice?'

'What they play next,' he explained. 'Whatever you please.'

She caught her breath and looked at the conductor, who nodded, waiting. 'Will they play a waltz?' she asked Edward, tautly.

'Why not?' Edward smiled. 'Let's have a waltz.'

The conductor knew the customs of the island better and hesitated, but it was a request from the host. He bowed and turned to the musicians, whispering quickly, and they began to play the Morning Papers Waltz by Strauss.

There was a gasp of astonishment in the room. Some of

the younger people did the waltz at private parties and others had danced it on the mainland or in France, but it was never played or danced in public here. No one took the floor.

Lillie was looking at Edward. He bowed to her. She laid her right hand on his right wrist, her left on his upper right arm, and they began to dance. As they waltzed to the centre of the empty floor, there was a ripple of applause at her daring. The lilting music was having its effect and people began to sway to it. After a moment, William and Elizabeth began to dance, to more applause. Only three other couples joined them. The rest stood swaying, watching Lillie who turned and spun gracefully with Edward.

'You look – you look radiant!' he told her. 'Where did you learn to waltz?'

She smiled. '. . . in London.'

'I'm glad you're not there now,' he said.

'Why?'

'You'd be surrounded by young blades – swept off your feet.'

Her eyes were shining. 'You think so?'

'You'd take the Town by storm!' he swore, seriously.

She glanced to the sides as they spun. Men were darting past them, stooping. Some of the little roses were falling from her dress and the men were laughing, scrambling to pick them up as trophies. She laughed, too, with pleasure and happiness, spinning and spinning in Edward's arms.

Two days later, she sat alone in the schoolroom in the Deanery. She was curled up on the lefthand windowseat, thinking about Edward. He was easily the most wonderful and generous man she had ever met. As well as his yachts, he owned a house and a coach and horses. He had been to Oxford and studied law, but had no need to take it up as a profession. His family's shipping line from Belfast to Liverpool and London was famous and, after his father's death, he had been given a yearly allowance, fitting his position as a gentleman and sportsman. She thought of his first marriage and how tragically it had ended for him. Only last night, he had told her how he had never thought he could fall in love again – until now. She hugged herself, remembering how he had held her, telling her he could not live without her. Anything, everything she wished in the world was hers, that was in his power to give. She had felt him tremble as he held her, and it excited her. If he had taken her then, in the dark shadows of the garden, she would not have been able to resist. The sudden passion that had filled her, the longing, with the strength of his body against her, had shaken her. She had hardly been able to stand – and he had mistaken it for fear, apologising and turning away.

She knew now that she truly was her father's daughter. She had flirted with men, sometimes leading them on, but the shock of learning about her father, and the way she had heard about him – and Michel – the heartache and revulsion of it had closed her heart. No man's touch could affect her, nor mean anything to her – until now. Just like Edward. He had brought her to life and her own excited reactions were a revelation. She realised now that she had been denying herself. And yet she was glad she had denied herself, for his sake.

She looked at her left hand. On the fourth finger she was wearing a diamond ring he had given her, to wear in secret. The stone was large and its facets glittered and sparkled as if a hundred tiny fireflies were imprisoned in it. Edward – Ned – was experienced and capable and rich, and he loved her desperately. Why had she hesitated before taking it? She smiled. On impulse, she turned and scrawled her name with the ring on the bottom righthand pane, Lillie Le Breton. Soon, she would write something else.

As she began to go over her name again, etching it deeper into the glass, the door was thrust open and Reggie came in. 'It is true?' he demanded. 'Langtry? . . . You're going to marry Edward Langtry?!'

He was taut and deathly pale. She hesitated for a second, before holding up her hand and showing him the ring.

'How could you?' he protested. 'It's against all reason! Are you marrying him or his yacht?'

It was deliberately insulting, but he was obviously distressed and she did not want to fall out with her dearest brother. 'Reggie – ' she began gently.

'He can't even sail it!' he went on. 'He has a captain to do that. He's nothing!'

'That's enough,' she said.

'More than enough! Do you know what you're doing?'

'I'm marrying the man I love,' she told him.

'Love? . . .' he sneered. 'There must be more honourable ways to get off the island. There are women who sell themselves. Do you know what they're called?'

She rose slowly. All at once, without warning, she slapped him hard across the face.

Her mother begged her to take longer before deciding. Her father gave her the same advice. He saw the advantages in her marrying Edward Langtry, but there were other considerations. She knew what he meant. Ned and she had little in common, but with marriage they were bound to develop similar interests. For one thing, she was passionately fond of sailing. And they would have a wonderful life together in London, when he took her there as he had promised.

Nothing they could say would change her mind nor make her wait. She insisted on being married at once, as Ned wanted, or she would go off with him. Too late, her father realised that opposition had only made her more determined. If she was to be legally married, he would have to give his consent. She was only twenty and he wished she had waited another few years. But at least, Langtry would be able to support her properly. The wedding was arranged for six weeks later, in March, 1874.

It took place in the early morning so that *Red Gauntlet* would not miss the tide.

Mrs Le Breton fussed round Lillie's room, checking that everything she needed had been packed and taken down to the yacht. After today, she would have only Reggie left at home, and he had become more moody and unpredictable than ever. She knew she was going to miss Lillie dreadfully and could have wept, but she did not wish to spoil the wedding. Though there was precious little to spoil – no guests, no proper ceremony. 'What will people think?' she muttered.

Lillie was fastening the long row of buttons up the front of her blue woollen dress. 'I don't care what they think,' she said..

'You haven't really taken time to know him. Your Father wonders if – '

'It's my choice, not anyone else's.'

Mrs Le Breton blew her nose. 'When I think of William's wedding – And now you're to be married in your travelling gown.'

'I don't want Edward to waste his money, Mother. He's spent enough already on William and Elizabeth.' She took up a little straw hat, trimmed with blue flowers. 'Where's Reggie?'

She had spoken casually, but her mother knew she was hurt that Reggie had been avoiding her. It was dreadful to see them falling out, when they used to be so fond of each other. 'He went out riding, very early,' she told her.

Lillie frowned. 'But he'll be at the church?'

'I'm not sure, dear,' Mrs Le Breton said, upset.

Lillie had a sudden memory of Reggie's face jolting as she slapped it and the awful, scornful way he had looked at her. He had deserved it, but she was still sorry. And would have said so, if he had apologised. Instead, he had withdrawn from her. When they met, he was silent and distant. In the last few days before today, she had not seen him at all.

There was a knock at the door and she tensed, hoping. That would be the best present she could be given. But it was Clement, who had come home again for her wedding. She smiled to him, grateful that he was here, at any rate.

Like the others, he was not completely happy at her choice, but he thought the rest of the family was being unfair. She had the right to decide the kind of life she wanted. 'Well . . .' he said brightly. 'It's time.'

The church was almost empty. There were no brides-maids. Lillie wore her travelling dress and hat. Clement stood behind Edward as best man.

In the front, there were only Mrs Le Breton and Elizabeth's mother and father. Behind them were Mrs Le

Breton's cook and maid and one or two poorer people from the parish who had known Lillie since she was born.

As Edward laid the ring on the bible which the Dean was holding and the Dean presented the open book for him to take back the ring, Lillie glanced round anxiously, hoping that Reggie had come. She had heard someone arrive. It was Arthur Jones, who sat alone at the back.

She started, when Edward touched her left hand, and looked at him, as he repeated after her father, 'With this ring I thee wed, with my body I thee worship, and with all my wordly goods I thee endow – in the Name of the Father, and of the Son, and of the Holy Ghost. Amen.' Now they were man and wife.

He kissed her chastely on the cheek.

They had rather a silent breakfast at the Yacht Club Hotel and her mother cried, when they left.

After all her determination and defiance, there had been a nagging feeling of disappointment, but everything suddenly came all right as soon as they were on *Red Gauntlet*. The leading seaman piped her aboard and the sailors cheered her. There was a fast tide running and a fresh wind and the big yacht slipped easily away from her moorings and out past the grey mass of Elizabeth Castle into open water. Full sails were set and they snapped in the wind.

Lillie had wanted to steer *Red Gauntlet* out of port, but Edward would not hear of it. He, too, had seemed subdued that morning. With a deck beneath him and a blue sea creaming back at the bows of the yacht, he had come alive. He settled her in one of the seats under the stern awning, with a rug over her knees, then sniffed the wind and smiled, going off to confer with Captain Merritt and check the compass.

She swivelled round and watched the long wake curving away. It was a moment she knew she would never forget. As the island dwindled and sank out of sight behind them, she felt only the briefest pang before excitement took over. How could any of them have understood? She wanted to shout, to sing. She was free!

When Edward returned, he smiled to see her so keyed-up and she laughed to him, out of sheer enjoyment. He sat on the seat next to hers and put his arm round her shoulders. With a swift glance towards the crew, who were all carefully not looking at them, he kissed her. She laid her head back against his arm. She felt protected and pampered. 'Which direction is England?' she murmured.

Edward pointed vaguely back. 'Over there to port, I should think.'

'Can we go there soon? Just the two of us.'

'Where?'

'To London.' Her voice was longing. 'Even for a few days.'

'I can't abide the place,' he chuckled. He took his arm from around her and eased it.

'But you promised,' she reminded him, sitting up. 'And I want to, Edward. I really want to.'

He laughed indulgently. 'Yes, but I don't. Don't care if I never go there again,' he said. 'You're my wife now, my dear, and we do as I say. Just you sit here and look pretty.' He rose. 'I'll be back presently.' He pinched her cheek and strolled off towards the helm.

Lillie was left puzzled and confused. Her excitement had been cut off too abruptly. She wanted to call him back, to protest, but already he was walking towards the bows with Captain Merritt. Surely he did not mean they would never go to London? He had as good as promised. Perhaps she had mentioned it too soon, she thought. That was it. They were just married. All he could think of was having her here on their yacht – on their honeymoon. She smiled and relaxed.

Throughout the morning, Edward came back and sat with her several times. He was rather preoccupied, concerned at the way *Red Gauntlet* was handling. She had to be at the peak of condition, it he was to enter her for the first class races. He was reassured by lunchtime, however, when he and Captain Merritt toasted Lillie in champagne. Their course was set for Southampton, he explained, but they would use this to carry out some trails and would not actually dock until the afternoon of the following day.

After lunch, he let Lillie take the wheel again and once more she had that incredible sensation of controlled power, responding to the lightest touch of her hands. The sensation was almost purely physical, a tingling excitement that made her catch her breath. The helmsman was standing by her to make sure she did not deviate too much from their course and she hoped he did not notice. When the feeling passed, she smiled to him and asked how the wheel behaved in rougher weather. He had only begun to reply, when Edward cut him off and made her hand over, leading her back to the stern. He did not want her to tire herself, he said, nor to distract the crew from their duties.

He was so odd, she thought, and overprotective. She promised herself that she would soon show him how capable she could be. He must not think of her merely as an ornament. There was so much they could share.

The afternoon passed pleasantly enough, although Edward was busier than he had been in the morning. Sails were set, then struck and refurled. Stayropes and spars tested and adjustments made. She longed to join in, at least to ask the reason for the adjustments, but Edward spent most of the time midships or nearer the bows. Still, it was wonderful to be at sea on her husband's yacht, her own yacht, to feel the deck move beneath her and hear the wind in the cordage and the hiss and purling slap of the waves as they cut through then. All afternoon, she saw only one small steam freighter on the horizon and the sense of solitude, of space stretching away without limit all round them, was almost mystical. In a spell when the wind dropped and *Red Gauntlet* floated motionless apart from a slight roll, the steward brought her tea.

When the breeze picked up again and they began to move forward, she noticed to her surprise that the sun was quite low and would soon set. She looked for Edward. He was talking to two of the crew and pointing to something in the fore-topmast. Captain Merritt joined them. As Edward turned towards her, she smiled, but his look passed over her and up to the clouds beyond the stern. He breathed deeply, patting his chest with one hand. She remembered her tumult of feelings on the times he had held her, her longing for him to loose the self-control with which he kept his own passion in check for her sake. It was not needed any more . . . She thought of the master cabin below, warm and comfortable, a private world of mahogany and brass and shaded lights. She saw him speak to the captain, who touched his cap and moved back to the helm. The two sailors went to the foremast and one started to climb. He was standing alone.

In spite of his thick jacket and muffler, the air was chilly and Edward rubbed his hands smartly together. He noticed that Lillie had risen. As she came towards him, he moved to meet her. 'There you are, my dear,' he smiled. 'Enjoying the breeze?'

'Yes, Edward,' she said, and added softly. 'It is growing late.'

'It's been a long day,' he nodded.

'Mother woke me at half-past four, to finish packing and get ready.'

He looked contrite. 'My poor dear, you must be tired out.' She smiled and shook her head slightly, expecting him to understand. He took her arm, leading her towards the door to the steep companionway down to the cabins. 'Thoughtless of me. You must get some sleep.'

'You, too, Edward.'

'Oh, no,' he smiled. 'I'm quite used to long hauls. I only catnap, when I'm under sail.'

She stopped and hesitated shyly. ' . . . It's our wedding day.'

He was conscious that they could be seen by the captain, helmsman and most of the crew, even though they were out of earshot. 'Yes, my dear, but . . . we are not the only ones aware of that.' He could tell she was puzzled, and lowered his voice. 'Don't you see, Lillie? You are the only young lady on board. If I came down to the cabin with you, it would be obvious that I – that we . . .'

'Are we not man and wife?' she asked him.

'Of course.'

'Then, don't you want . . . to be with me?' He was carrying his scrupulousness and care for her to an extreme. 'Don't you love me?'

'I adore you. You know I do. But try to understand – some things are not possible on board.' He squeezed her hand and smiled. 'Tomorrow evening when we reach Southampton, when we are at Cliffe Lodge, in our own home, our life together can begin – more fittingly.'

She looked at him for a long moment. She did not care what those sailors thought. Why should he? It was the first night of their honeymoon and nothing could be more romantic, more *fitting*, than to – to give themselves to each other here, as she had dreamed of it. But she could not argue with him.

'You turn in now, if you wish, my dear. I'll call you in the morning,' he told her. He seemed almost embarrassed to be standing talking to her. 'Good night.' He kissed her cheek. It was as light and impersonal as the kiss he had given her in church.

'Good night,' she said very quietly, and went down the companionway alone.

Standing near the wheel, Captain Merritt shrugged to the helmsman and scratched his chin, as they saw Edward step briskly down the deck, his hands in his pockets, studying the set of the sail between the fore-topmast-head and the jib-boom.

Lillie looked up in surprise as she stepped out of the carriage at the front door of Cliffe Lodge, Edward's house on Southampton Water. Set in its own gardens, a seventeen roomed, Victorian mock-Tudor villa, it was even more imposing than she had imagined. The coachman was lifting their bags down from the carriage. The dark evening added to the sombreness of the house and she was glad when the door opened and Edward led her into the brightly lit hall.

Edward pulled off his plaid ulster and handed it to his butler, Evans, a superior man in his late forties, whom he introduced. Lillie smiled to him and looked round at the broad, dark-panelled hall with its stand and barometer and the main staircase, turning right under arched, Gothic windows. Edward held her arm and showed her into the drawingroom.

Although lit by gaslamps above the fireplace, the drawingroom gave an impression of shadows. With its heavy, overstuffed furniture and dark drapes at the windows, it was full of odd angles. Edward crossed to the carved, stone fireplace and turned, warming his back. Lillie still wore her cape and travelling gown, with a flowered hat. The impassive butler and the size and solidity of the house had made her feel nervous and she wondered if she should have left the cape in the hall. It was not the kind of question she could ask Edward. He was so masterful, so used to all this that he would merely laugh. She took off her hat and was trying to think where to put it down, when Evans, the butler, brought the rest of the staff in to be presented.

They stood with him in a row by the door, an elderly cook, a middleaged maid called Norah, and the coachmangardener who had driven them up from the harbour. 'From now on, you will be given your instructions by Mrs Langtry,' Edward told them. 'If any problems arise, you will, naturally, refer them to her. Is there anything you wish to add, my dear?'

'. . . No,' she said, hesitating. She was not entirely unused to servants. Her mother had a woman who came in to cook and another to clean and act as maid, but it was a different thing to have them living in. It must be strange for them, too, she thought. Edward had been away so much and now they suddenly had to adjust to an unknown woman. They were watching her and she smiled to the maid and cook. 'I expect we'll get on famously.'

They did not respond and there was an awkward pause.

'Will you be requiring supper, Madam?' Evans asked.

Lillie was unsure and looked at Edward.

'Not tonight,' he said. 'We shall probably retire shortly. If you'd see that Mrs Langtry's things are unpacked.'

Evans bowed and spoke quietly to the others. 'That will be all.' He followed them to the door. 'May I say again, welcome home, sir? Madam – ' He inclined his head and went out.

Lillie was disappointed. 'I don't think they like me,' she said.

'Rubbish!' Edward laughed. 'How could they fail to?'

She was pleased by the compliment. Part of her discomfort had been caused by his distant manner. As a man of the world, he had schooled himself to show very little in public, certainly no emotion nor enthusiasm. But now they were alone at last, in their own home. She moved to him impulsively, to be kissed. His lips touched hers briefly and lightly. She wanted him to take her in his arms, to feel herself pressed against him, to be reassured by his need for her. But he moved away. 'There is one thing, my dear,' he observed.

'Yes?'

'We are not in the Channel Islands now. On the mainland, things are a touch more formal. One must learn not to treat servants with familiarity. They do not like it.' He raised his eyebrows, asking if she had understood. 'Firmness, with a slight distance, is the correct attitude.'

'Yes, I see, I'm sorry,' she apologised. She still had so much to learn. She took off her cape and smiled. 'This is a beautiful house, Edward.'

'You like it? Good.' he was gratified. 'I chose it for Jane.'

He smile faltered. 'This was her house?'

'She never lived to see it. Still –' He shrugged and sighed. He saw Lillie holding her hat and cape, watching him. 'Perhaps you had better go up now.'

'You'll come, too, Edward?' she asked quickly.

'After a moment. I shall give you time to . . .' He paused, making his point.

Lillie wished he was not always so tactful. Just to go up to the bedroom and prepare herself seemed so coldblooded. Then she realised he was right. The maid, Norah, would be there and they would need time to unpack. It could be embarrassing, if all three of them were there. 'Yes, of course,' she said, gratefully. 'Thank you.'

The bedroom was cold and Lillie shivered as she brushed her hair. Wearing a white, highnecked nightgown and a white wrap with ruffles at the shoulder, she sat at a table by the curtained windows. On the table were a stand mirror and an oil lamp. Another lamp glowed on the bedside table. In spite of them, the room seemed gloomy because of its maroon flock wallaper and mahogany furniture. There was a door in the corner to a small dressingroom, in which a single candle was burning. This house is so dark, she thought. She saw that the maid had put the last of her underthings in the chest of drawers and was waiting. She began to smile to her in the mirror, then remembered what Edward had said.

'Will that be all, Madam?' the maid asked distantly.

'Yes, thank you,' Lillie nodded. 'Good night.'

'Good night, Madam.'

When the door closed, Lillie laid down her brush and looked at the room. A fire had been laid in the black grate with its tiled surrounds, but had not been lit because no orders had been given. She had been conscious of the large double bed, ever since she came in, and now looked at it. In comparison with her bed at home, it seemed enormous. It had a high headboard of polished mahogany and at its foot was an ottoman couch in dark green velvet. The covers had been turned down on both sides.

Lillie rose and moved to it. Taking off her wrap, she laid it neatly on the ottoman and stood, trying to work out on which side she was meant to sleep. She moved to the side furthest from the door, got into bed and lay down. After a few seconds, she pushed herself up until her back was on the pillows and her shoulders supported by the headboard. The front of her nightgown had ruffles like her wrap. She smoothed them, straightened the line of the bedclothes across her waist and folded her hands, waiting.

All the time, the suppressed excitement inside her had been mounting. She was aware of her body, as never before, and had to curb her breathing. How right Edward had been again, to restrain himself until they were in their own home. The waiting had given her longer to adjust and for her eagerness to overcome her nervousness at what was to happen.

There was a soft knock at the door and Edward came in.

She was surprised for a moment to see he had already changed into a double-breasted, quilted dressinggown over a nightgown and slippers.

He stood still, looking at her. Sitting up against the dark headboard, the light from the lamp catching the red-gold of her hair, which tumbled to her shoulders, she was a vision, tender and bewitching. She smiled uncertainly, excited. 'You – you look very lovely, my dear,' he muttered.

She tensed as he moved forward but, instead of coming to the bed, he went past it on the other side into the dressingroom. After a moment, she heard water running as a tap was turned on, then the sound of Edward gargling. She listened and he coughed twice very loudly, clearing his throat. Then there was silence.

The light went out in the dressingroom and he came back in. Without looking at her, he moved to the dressingtable and turned out the lamp. He turned towards the bed and Lillie smiled again, welcomingly, snuggling down a little. But he still did not look at her. He stopped by the chest of drawers and one by one from his dressing gown pockets took out his keys, his wallet and his loose change which he laid on top of the chest. Although acutely aware of Lillie, he still avoided looking at her.

Listening to him and then watching, her own excitement and expectation had faced. Everything he did seemed deliberately mechanical, crushing any suggestion of loving spontaneity. He paused by his side of the bed, took his watch from his pocket, checked the time by it and placed it meticulously on the bedside table. He slipped off his dressinggown, laid it carefully beside Lillie's on the ottoman and moved back to the bedside table.

All this time, he had not once looked at her, although she had been watching him with wide, uncertain eyes. At last he glanced at her, smiled and turned off the lamp.

In the darkness, she felt him get into bed and the covers move as he lay on his back and pulled them up to his neck. He did not speak. She inched down until her head was on the pillow. In the wide bed, there was space between them and she might have been alone, except that she could hear his shallow breathing. Her eyes were still open. She had seen his tight, nervous smile and her own anxieties returned. The she felt him shift beside her, turning over, and his hand touched her just above the waist. It hesitated, then moved up to squeeze her right breast. It was painful and she gasped.

She was aware of him fumbling with his nightgown, then suddenly he rolled over and was sprawling on top of her. He was grunting and she smelt the reek of brandy. She could not breathe with his weight pressing on her and her mouth opened. Then his wet mouth covered hers, his moustache rubbing against her lips, and she moaned, twisting her face away.

Her moan seemed to send him into a frenzy. He was shifting and squirming on her, bearing down, and she felt his hand between them, wrenching at her nightdress. She was not ready for him, not nearly ready, and she tried to protest, but his panting mouth closed over hers again. She had been pushing at his chest. Instead, she forced her arms between his and his body, clasping them round him. She wanted to pull him off her, to roll him over so that he would lie beside her and she could touch him and help him and give herself a chance to relax before receiving him. But it was too late. His squirming weight forced her legs open. There was a moment's blinding, unendurable pain. Even as her scream strangled in her throat, his whole body stiffened and gave one convulsive spasm. His mouth trailed across her cheek and neck and dropped to her shoulder. She heard him sob. He pushed himself off her and fell on to his back, panting. After a minute, he turned away from her, wriggling as he pushed the nightgown down over his hips and stomach, tugging the covers up over his shoulder.

She lay completely motionless, listening as his ragged breathing stilled. Her knees were turned outwards and the ache had become a dull, throbbing pain. Her breasts and ribs hurt, as though she had been kicked and beaten. She was afraid to move, in case he turned to her again.

# CHAPTER FOUR

Lillie came awake. She lay on her side, her hair over her face. Drowsily, she drew up her hand to push it back, then stopped herself as the events of the night came back to her. She did not want to waken Edward.

She had felt only pain and nausea, the first time he had taken her. She had tried to fight him off, but, while he lay asleep beside her, a change had occurred in her body. She did not know how long she lay, but, as the ache slowly subsided, she had begun to feel a return of the excitement she had experienced earlier. Only now it was stronger. Even the pain in her body added to it, a total, physical longing that overwhelmed her. She pressed her thighs tightly together, breathing in short, dry gasps, until it lessened, leaving her faint and exhausted.

She had just been drifting off to sleep, when she felt Edward touching her again. This time had not been so brutally urgent. When he crawled over on to her, she had even been able to shift into a more comfortable position, so that she was not so crushed. When he kissed her, she had returned his kiss, touching his head, putting her hands on his shoulders. The pain had not been so great, but, as soon as she began to move under him, he had stiffened again, as before. His body had jerked, and it was over. He had fallen asleep, almost at once, leaving her feeling bruised and frustrated again.

None of it had been how she had imagined it would be. She knew instinctively there must be more to it than the discomfort she had suffered. But she had no standards by which to judge. Yet anticipation could not always be so delusive. Otherwise, people would never make love. It could not be Edward's fault, she knew. If anything, it was due to her gaucheness, her lack of ability to attract and satisfy him.

She was ashamed and wanted to make amends, so that he would forgive her. Strangely, her body did not hurt any more. She felt relaxed and supple. Even as she thought about it, there came a stirring of excitement and hunger. She smiled and turned over.

The other half of the bed was empty. She was anxious and sat up. It was morning, and even though the curtains were drawn, the room was light enough to see. His gown had gone from the ottoman.

Just then, Edward came from the dressingroom, wearing his shirt, cravat and trousers. He was buttoning his waistcoat with one hand and carrying his boots in the other. He paused, seeing her. 'Good morning, my dear,' he smiled.

'I couldn't think where you were,' Lillie said.

He pushed one curtain back and light streamed in. 'You were sleeping so peacefully, I hadn't the heart to waken you.' He sat by the bed and put on his boots.

She watched him as he began to tie the laces. 'What are you doing?'

He laughed. 'What do you think? Getting dressed.'

'Come back to bed,' she said quietly. He looked up, blankly. She knew he was being gentlemanly and making it clear he did not blame her, but she wanted to show him that she could be everything he wished. Daringly, she threw down the bedclothes. Her nightdress had ridden up and her legs and long, sleek thighs lay uncovered almost to her hips.

'Lillie! . . .' he exclaimed, shocked.

She slipped out of bed and came to him. 'I'm sorry, Edward.' He gazed at her as she knelt at his feet, stopping him from tying his lace. Her nightdress was unbuttoned at the neck, falling open. She looked up. 'I'm sorry about last night. I – I didn't please you.'

'But you did,' he told her, embarrassed.

'I disappointed you.' She was tender and eager, very desirable. 'I'll make it up to you, I promise.'

He was staring at her. 'Lillie, what are you – ? Everything was normal. You have nothing to reproach yourself with.'

She moved her hands on to his knee. 'But I – '

'Please! Lillie . . .' he cautioned. He rose, pulling her up with him. 'The servants.'

'They won't come in here,' she smiled, moving closer.

'It is morning,' he said sharply and turned partly away. 'Cover yourself.' She stepped back from him, hurt, drawing the nightdress together. 'I – There was nothing – I was perfectly satisfied,' he stammered. 'If I did not show my gratitude sufficiently, I am sorry. It is not something one talks about.'

Lillie turned from him and sat on the edge of the bed.

He was priggish and pompous in his embarrassment. 'I excuse you,' he said, 'because you are – not experienced in these matters. I assure you, I have no complaints. Now, please, let us have no more unnecessary demonstrations.'

She watched him, unblinking, as he finished tying his bootlaces. He put his wallet, keys and loose coins in his pocket, then his watch in his waistcoat and went into the dressingroom. The door of her affectionate and passionate nature had been open to him, and he had just slammed it shut. The realisation that he was wholly satisfied with his crude, fumbling performance during the night was numbing. He came out again, putting on the jacket of his tweed suit.

'Stay in bed, if you wish. I'll have Evans send up a tray.' She shook her head. 'As you please. After breakfast, I am going out.'

'Where to?'

'I have some business to attend to. May take some time.' He smiled. 'Now, you have a restful day, and I'll see you later.'

He went out and Lillie still sat, without moving, watching the door. He had made her eagerness and excitement seem unclean. She knew she should have been ashamed, but she was not.

He did not come home until the evening. She had never felt so alone.

In the morning, she had bathed and dressed, then went on a tour of the house. She told Evans she would not take lunch until Mr Langtry returned, but he did not. She sat in the drawingroom, waiting. At home, she would have gone to the kitchen and gossiped with the cook, or helped the gardener, and would not have been lonely. After Edward's warning, however, she was not sure how to speak to them properly and tried to avoid them. As the afternoon lengthened, she went upstairs and lay on the bed with a book, until it became too dark to see the pages. As she lay thinking, she heard the sound of the front door.

Edward was lighting the mantles of the gaslamps by the fireplace, when she hurried in. He had been over to the shipyard at Buckler's Hard to see the work being done on his racing yawl, *Gertrude*. He had no inkling that she might have been lonely or anxious.

'I couldn't think where you were,' she told him.

'And you were worried about me?' He chuckled and kissed her on the forehead. 'There, there.' He moved to the sideboard and poured himself a glass of brandy. 'She's looking quite promising. I'm having her cutter-rigged, plan to race her a bit this summer.'

'Why didn't you take me with you?' she asked.

'A shipyard's no place for you.' He smiled. 'And what have you been doing with yourself?'

'Waiting for you.'

'All day?' He frowned. 'Well, I mean, I'm sorry. I naturally assumed you'd have things to do about the house and so on. Early days yet, I suppose.' He took a drink. 'That's better . . . Now, what's for dinner?'

'I wasn't able to get anything,' she confessed, upset. His head turned to her, surprised. 'I couldn't go out. I didn't have any money.'

He began to chuckle. 'Didn't have . . . ? Oh, my sainted Aunt!' He collapsed into a chair, laughing. 'Oh, no . . .'

At least, he wasn't annoyed. Lillie smiled. 'What?'

'This isn't Jersey,' he spluttered. 'Ladies don't go out to haggle in the market for meat and fish! You tell the servants what you want. They get it and the tradesmen send a bill at the end of the month.'

Her mouth was open. 'I didn't know.'

'You goose!' he laughed. 'Well, I daresay there'll be something in the house. Wait till I tell them . . .'

As he started to rise, she moved to him quickly. 'No, Edward, please – you wouldn't tell anyone. Please . . .' She sat on his knee to cajole him. 'I didn't know.' He was still chuckling. She kissed his cheek and he sat back.

'What am I going to do with you?' He patted her hand. 'Well, well – we can work out a routine for you, when we get back.'

'From where?'

'From our trip. We'll set off next week.'

He had only been teasing her! He was going to keep his promise after all. 'To London?' she asked, eagerly.

'No, no, no,' he chuckled. 'To Belfast. It's high time you met my family. And mind you're on your best behaviour. I want them to like you.'

At the end of the following week, they crossed to Ireland on *Red Gauntlet*.

The Langtry's lived in Fortwilliam House, an old, Georgian mansion, set in its own grounds on the outskirts of Belfast. They were a Quaker family and strict in their observances. Edward's elder brother Richard, who had run the shipping firm since the death of their father, was a serious, hard working man. He had been troubled in case Edward had chosen someone too young and lightminded to be fitted for the responsibilities of marriage, but he was won over by Lillie's modesty, her beauty and the commendable way in which she considered her husband's wishes first in all things. He agreed with their mother and sister, Agnes, that Lillie was just the kind of quiet, sensible girl to settle Edward down. Agnes adored her for the youth and gaiety she brought back to the old house. The visit was extended and they were all sad when it finished.

When they returned to Cliffe Lodge, Edward was even complimentary and told Lillie she was worth her weight in gold. It did not stop him, however, from spending most of the next few weeks supervising the overhaul of *Red Gauntlet* and his other ships, the sixty-ton cutter, *Bluebird*, the eighty-ton *Gertrude* and the fast, little *Ildegonda*, with which he had won many prizes. Knowing no one and with no socal life, Lillie had nothing to do but read, take short walks and watch from the upper windows the shipping passing down Southampton Water.

She was not so lonely in the evenings, when Edward was at home, although he had no conversation except about his yachts and, occasionally, fishing, his other consuming interest. She tried to enter into his enthusiasms, but it was difficult, since she was excluded from them apart from the times he took her for trial runs on the *Gertrude*. The uncomfortable and unsatisfying performance in bed had not improved, only became less frequent, for which she was grateful. She did not blame him. She had realised that he was shy and unhibited in his lovemaking and that, perhaps, she could have helped him, if he would let her. But she did not want to any more. She looked on it as the price she had to pay for a secure marriage to a rich, if rather boring man. She had the distraction of learning how to run the household and cope with the servants, and tried not to think of the hopes she had once had of travelling with him, of the fascinating places they would visit and the wonderful parties they would give.

As they finished dinner one evening, alone in the panelled diningroom, Edward remarked casually that he wanted to go through all the household bills and get them paid before he went off.

'You're going somewhere?' she asked.

'Well, I do have four yachts, all in prime condition,' he replied. 'I have to keep them in trim, get ready for the International Race at Le Havre, then Cowes. Not to mention the Thames Race.'

Lillie was alert at once. 'To London?'

'No, no,' he said, tetchily. 'Can't you get off that damned hobby horse? It doesn't go that far, thank Heavens. Only from the Nore to Erith.'

When she went to bed, Lillie was still thinking about it. It was clear from what he had said that he planned to be away for most of the summer. She could hear him clearing his throat and spitting in the dressingroom. He came out in his nightshirt and dressinggown and turned off the lamp on the table. Going through his nightly ritual, he laid out his wallet, keys and loose coins on the chest of drawers. She watched him as he came to the bedside table, took out his watch, checked the time and began to wind it up.

'Edward?' she asked. 'When you go sailing – may I come with you?' He was surprised. 'May I?'

'Not possible, my dear,' he grunted.

'Why not?'

He sighed. She always wanted explanations. 'It won't be a pleasure cruise. It's a hard sport – dangerous, even.'

'I'll be with *you*,' she said quietly.

'Yes, but – ' He laid the watch down carefully and took off his dressinggown. 'I'd planned to sail the *Gertrude* most of the time. She's only half the size of *Red Gauntlet* – hardly any cabin space.'

She knew exactly what he meant. He would be too self-conscious to sleep with her on board. 'I don't mind,' she told him.

'But I've explained! I'd be skipper. We wouldn't really be together.' He moved round to drape his dressinggown beside hers on the ottoman.

'I don't want to be left here on my own. Please – ' she pleaded. 'If it doesn't work out – if I'm a burden to you, you could let me off at Jersey, to stay with my parents.' He paused on his way back to the bed. 'I've never been alone. I couldn't stand it. Please . . .'

She is really very keen, he thought. Perhaps it would be for the best, if she were with her people on Jersey. Certainly save some money. He got into bed and turned off the light.

He felt her hand touching his chest. 'Please,' she whispered.

'We'll see,' he said, and turned towards her.

That summer and early autumn were the happiest of their marriage. They sailed all the yachts in turn, cruising in *Red Gauntlet* even as far as Lisbon. Most of their competition sailing, however, was done in the *Gertrude*, which proved to be a champion. She only lost the Thames Race through a stupid technicality. Edward was inconsolable for days.

With the other yachts in dock, these last six weeks on the

*Gertrude* seemed magical to Lillie. The cabin space was more cramped, as Edward had warned her, but she hardly ever wanted to go below, anyway, and was on deck in all weathers. Captain Merritt and the crew would have jumped overboard for her. In the smaller space, she could not keep apart from them and was soon lending a hand to lash the sails and haul on the lines, something which Edward never did, as owner. He did not approve, but finally gave up objecting to it. Encouraged by her, the men worked better. She laughed when high waves broke over the bows and drenched her to the skin with flying spray. In the cold dog-watches before dawn, she would come up from the galley in a seaman's oilskin, bringing steaming mugs of tea. Merritt taught her the finer points of rigging and how to box the compass. Each day was an adventure.

In the closing stage of the International Race, the *Gertrude* sliced through the water back towards Le Havre on the French coast. A fierce wind was driving them and spray spumed high into the air along both sides. Edward, after a day and night on deck, had gone below for half an hour's rest.

Lillie stood with Merritt behind the helmsman. She was exhilarated, her eyes alight with the speed and the tension of the race. She had steered the yawl before, but never at such a moment, and asked Merritt's permission. The had to shout to make themselves heard. 'Only for a minute! Just to feel it!' she promised.

The captain hesitated, then nodded to the helmsman who stepped aside, waiting until she had taken hold of the spokes of the wheel, before letting go and standing by her shoulder. The yawl gave a slight lurch as she took over. 'Hold her steady, ma'am!' Merritt yelled.

But Lillie had her under control, her arms strongly braced but responsive, feeling the insistent tug of the waves against the rudder, the quiver of the planks under her, the crack of the sails and hiss of the ropes, the bounding motion and rushing speed, all as part of her and the controlling wheel which seemed alive in her hands. It was the feeling she dreamt of, to which her body and mind responded, yet never as much as this. Her mouth opened to the bite of the wind.

Edward came hurrying to the helm. The brief shudder in the yawl's frame at the changeover had snapped him out of his rest. He was horrified. 'What's the meaning of this?' he shouted to the helmsman. 'What are you playing at? Get the wheel!'

'No, please, Edward!' Lillie begged. 'Let me!'

'It's too important!'

'No harm, sir,' the captain said. Edward swung round to him. 'No harm,' Merritt repeated. 'By my calculation, we've passed the marker buoy. We're clear of them all!'

Edward ran to the side and gazed back at their wake. He turned, exulting.

From his expression, Lillie knew it was true. 'We've won!' she laughed. 'We've won! We've won!'

In another minute, they could see the Race Stewards' vessels ahead and smaller boats bright with flags, bobbing on the water. Edward ran to the stern and pulled the lanyard of the signal gun, announcing their arrival. When the answering boom of the Stewards' gun reached them, he came back to stand beside Lillie and the crew cheered in jubilation.

The prizegiving and reception at Le Havre thrilled Lillie. Everyone wanted to meet Edward and her, to congratulate them and to marvel at her, the only woman in the race. She told everyone she planned to enter every possible race from now on. For two days they were feted and then they sailed home in triumph to Jersey. Edward only stayed ashore for an hour. He had brought her to visit her parents as he had promised, before sailing for Portsmouth.

Lillie was happy and excited to be home, waving to everyone as her father's carriage trotted up St. Saviour's Hill. At the Deanery, a special surprise was waiting for her. Her brother Clement was at home, wearing civilian clothes. He had decided to give up the army and was at Oxford, studying Law. She was delighted to see Reggie, too. She had fully forgotten the coolness between them and ran to him. He hung back, but let her kiss him, even smiling when she decided he was more handsome than ever.

She had so much to tell them all, she hardly let anyone else speak, interrupting her own questions with others she had remembered about Cliffe Lodge and the Langtry's and the sailing trips. Over tea in the drawingroom, she told them about the Le Havre race and unforgettable moment of victory.

'An achievement, indeed,' the Dean nodded.

'You must have been very proud of Edward,' her mother said. 'Though I don't know how he could allow you to risk yourself like that! He shouldn't have allowed you to come with him.'

The Dean smiled. 'I should imagine, if Lillie wanted to go, she'd find a way to convince him.'

'Very true, Father,' Reggie agreed, drily.

'Cooped up on a small boat for weeks on end,' Mrs Le Breton went on, 'with all those sailors.'

'I've no doubt Lillie managed,' Reggie commented.

There was something unpleasantly ironic in his voice. As Lillie glanced at him, Clement cut in quickly, 'It's wonderful to see you.'

'And you, Clem,' she smiled. 'I'm grateful to Edward for bringing me to Jersey, so I could visit you all.'

'He was coming here, anyway,' Reggie said. 'Or didn't you know that?'

Again, there was something in his tone. Lillie saw both her father and Clement look at him warningly.

'Isn't it time someone told her?' he countered, and turned to her. 'Why do you think Clem's here? He's studying Law. Doesn't that suggest anything to you?'

'Reggie, that's enough!' his father ordered.

Reggie was lounging by the fireplace. He pushed himself upright and shrugged. 'Very well. The barking dog bows to Sir Oracle. If you'll excuse me – '

He went out, leaving Lillie more puzzled. She looked at the others in turn, seeing that they were uncomfortable.

'Pay no attention,' her father said. 'It's only his habitual insolence. Your brother is becoming quite ungovernable.'

'But what did he mean?' None of them answered. 'What

did Reggie mean about Edward coming here, anyway?'

'You really don't know?' her mother asked worriedly.

'Well, you're bound to hear,' the Dean said. 'For the past month or so, Mr Langtry has been advertising his yachts for sale.'

Lillie's eyes widened in shock. 'For sale?'

He coughed. 'It appears that, for some time, he has been living beyond his means – considerably beyond. Now that he also has a wife to support, his creditors will not wait.'

'His family owns a shipping line!' she protested. 'His father left him money.'

'All spent years ago,' the Dean explained. 'I've asked Clem to look into it, with a firm of lawyers. To protect your interests.'

'All Edward has left is a small allowance, not nearly enough for you both to live on,' Clement said. 'That's why he took you to Belfast, hoping his brother would agree to an increase. It has not yet been confirmed. The yachts have to go.'

She could no longer disbelieve what they were saying. 'Not *Red Gauntlet*?' she whispered.

'She's already been sold,' the Dean said. 'With luck, that should cover the most outstanding debts.'

'The sale of the others should see you all right for a while,' Clement added. 'However, since he has no profession – '

'He was at Oxford!' Lillie exclaimed. 'He studied Law like you.'

'Unfortunately, he took no examinations. So he has no qualifications,' her father told her. She gazed at him. His voice seemed to be coming from a long distance to her. 'I am afraid that he has misrepresented himself rather, both as a scholar and as a man of wealth. Still, you will have enough to live on, provided you are careful. But his days of extravagance are over.'

Lillie heard the rest of what they said, but could scarcely take it in. She had to excuse herself and leave the room.

Her heart was beating wildly, her mind in a turmoil. She

kept seeing Edward's superior smile, the offhand manner with which he dismissed the things that interested her. The man she had married. A failure as a lover and as a companion, his one saving grace had now also vanished. He was not even rich!

She had walked blindly and discovered that she had gone automatically to the schoolroom. Instinct had led her, the need to feel again the safety and assurance of her childhood. Yet even as she realised where she was, she saw her name scratched on the bottom righthand windowpane. She had scratched it there with her engagement ring. She turned abruptly to leave, but stopped herself.

Her eyes were smarting and she fought back the tears. She would not cry for herself. Certainly not for Edward. Her mind had cleared again. She had no alternative, she realised, except to make the best of it. It would be too shaming to admit she had made such a mistake, to leave him and become a dependant of her father's, living at home. She would have to wait and see how bad the situation was. Perhaps everything was not lost. Edward . . . , she thought. The fool! Well, she had deceived herself as much as he had. She deserved him.

She still could not face her family and went out on to the terrace. As she walked slowly, thinking, she saw Reggie leaning back against the wall, with his arms folded, watching her.

'Well, well, well . . .' he smiled. She was silent. He seemed amused, but there was tension and bitterness in him, very near the surface. 'So young Lochinvar turned out to be the Old Man of the Sea.'

'I don't know what you mean,' she said evenly, and sat in the cane chair by the terrace table.

'Oh, my dear sister – but you do,' he murmured. 'You married an oaf, an unworthy, boring oaf. I warned you, but you wouldn't see it – only his beautiful yacht. And now it's sunk without trace.'

'That's not kind, Reggie.'

'The truth is seldom kind. You sold yourself.' She stiffened and looked away. He left the wall and moved round so that he could see the effect his words had. 'Sold yourself to a pompous bore, because you thought he was going to carrry you magically o'er the foam to London, to romance and gaiety and fortune . . . Ah, how you sighed for London.'

'That's enough!' she snapped.

He laughed. 'You, too? . . . No, Lillie, I take that from Father, because I'm still living under his roof. Not from you.'

She could not bear the coldness in his voice. 'We were friends once.'

'Friends! . . .' he repeated, stung. 'I'd have died for you.'

'Then why do you hurt me now?' She was nearly pleading.

'You have no idea what it means to be hurt,' he said quietly. 'You were the sun and the moon. The only light in the universe. The island was our world – but you couldn't wait to leave.' He turned away.

'Reggie – try to understand,' she urged. 'It's different for you!'

'How?'

'You're a man! You can do as you please, go where you choose,' she told him. 'For you the island isn't a cage – because you know that whenever you like, you can just leave.'

'I'd never have left you,' he said flatly.

She was becoming upset and rose, moving towards him. 'Oh, you would have – one day. And I'd have been alone. Don't you see? . . . The only way for me to escape was to marry.' She was close to him now and touched his arm. 'At least, Edward seemed kind, and gentle.'

'And rich.'

'Please . . .' she begged. She put her arms round him from the side and leant her head against his shoulder, hoping he would comfort her.

The contact was unbearable for him and he thrust her away roughly. 'Don't touch me!' She was shocked, gazing at him. 'I . . . I – Keep out of my sight!' he sobbed. He broke from her and went quickly into the house.

She did not move for a long time. She was still shaken, realising at last the depth and nature of her brother's feeling for her.

The next morning, she heard that he had taken his horse and ridden off at speed, before she was up. She was concerned about him and Clement agreed to help her look for him. Often, he went riding over to Portelet to see Arthur Jones. They took the little train to St. Aubin and, purely by chance, met Arthur as they came from the station. He hadn't heard from Reggie and was concerned, too, to learn that he was in one of his moods. When they were on him, he would ride breakneck, often along the edge of the cliffs, as near as possible. It was damned dangerous, but the only thing that seemed to calm him.

Arthur was pleased to see Lillie and insisted on Clem and her coming back with him to Portelet House, where Viscount Ranelagh was staying with his younger daughter, Alice. Ranelagh, with his beak of a nose and full beard, dyed a dark brown, welcomed Lillie. He glowered, seeing Clement, but permitted him to call, provided Lillie would promise not to leave him for a single moment alone with Alice. Lillie laughed when she went down to walk on the beach below the house with Arthur, Clem and Alice, but then discovered that Clem had switched to studying Law entirely to increase his suitability as a husband, if he were successful, and that Alice had promised to wait for him. Arthur drew her away from the other two, to give them a few minutes of privacy.

'After all, we're not really leaving them alone,' he reasoned. 'We're all on the same beach.'

He was smiling and Lillie smiled back. 'Clem never let on,' she whispered. 'I hadn't the faintest idea. I just didn't know.'

'I daresay there's quite a few things you don't know,' he said. But he would not explain what he meant.

A week later, Edward arrived back on Jersey in the *Gertrude*. He would not discuss his financial affairs with Lillie. 'As my wife,' he informed her, 'it is sufficient for you to know that I am in a position to support you adequately.'

He told her to pack, as they would be sailing as soon as his business here was settled.

He was not nearly so overbearing, when he was alone with Clement and the Dean. His brother had settled ten thousand pounds on Lillie, which would go to her in the event of Edward's death. It was invested and the small yearly income from it was to be added to his allowance, provided he remained married. With the allowance and what was left of the sale of the yachts, they would have enough to continue living in Cliffe Lodge for the foreseeable future. All the yachts had gone, except the *Gertrude*.

'I have to maintain a certain standard!' he blustered. 'I couldn't bear to part with her.'

'But can you afford to run her?' the Dean asked him.

'That's why Lillie and I are leaving. I shall pay off the crew as soon as we get back to Southampton, then lay her up. When circumstances improve . . .'

'If you could find work,' Clement suggested.

'Work?' Edward laughed. 'I'm a gentleman. I can't go out looking for work.'

'I suppose not,' the Dean grunted. 'Your allowance is just sufficient for the moment. But what if you have children?'

'Ah. Yes, that would do it,' Edward agreed. 'My family would be more amenable, then. They'd do the right thing.'

As he stood, thinking, Clement exchanged a look with the Dean. That was not at all what had been meant.

They were interrupted by Mrs Le Breton. 'I can't think what's happened to Reggie,' she complained. 'He's disappeared again. And I particularly wanted him not to be late, since Lord Ranelagh's coming.'

Ranelagh brought Alice and Arthur with him and it was like old times. While they walked in the arbour after lunch, Lillie almost laughed at the deferential way Edward treated the viscount.

'Sorry we can't have a longer chat, Mr – uh . . .' Ranelagh said. 'Understand you're leaving.'

'This evening on the ebb tide, your Lordship,' Edward told him, bowing.

'Ah, yes – yachting man, aren't you?' Ranelagh was not impressed. Pretty Lillie could surely have done better for herself?

Lillie hung back with Clement. 'Does he know about you and Alice?' she whispered.

'Not yet. Not till I've passed my Bar exams,' Clem confided. He paused and smiled. 'The old devil . . . He's so protective about his daughters. But they're not the ones he takes with him to Paris. Different daughters every year – and they always get younger.'

'Clem!' Lillie said reprovingly, and they laughed. As they moved on, she said more seriously, 'Reggie went riding again before breakfast. He's done that every morning. And he doesn't come home until night. I haven't seen him for days!' Clem nodded, troubled. 'We're leaving. Surely he'll at least say goodbye?'

Clement stopped. He seemed to be examining some little, crimson Jersey lilies that grew along the path of the arbour. 'He felt very strongly about your wedding, you know,' he said carefully. 'He – he took it badly. If he liked Ned more, perhaps – '

'I know.'

He turned to her. 'He wants to see you, I'm sure – more than *wants*. But not with him. You understand what I'm – ? It's hard to explain, Lillie.'

'You don't have to,' she told him.

He was relieved. 'Then, you must realise that it's better for you not to meet, at the moment.'

She was biting her lip. 'If there was some way I could help him . . . I can't bear the thought that he's hurt, and that it's my fault.'

'It's all in his own mind,' Clement reassured her. 'He's turned missing you, like we all do, into – But he's young, he'll come to his senses soon.'

'Will you tell him I'll write?' she asked.

As Clement promised, Edward came back to them. 'What are you two conspiring about?' he smiled. 'You'd better sneak away and finish your packing, Lillie. Mustn't miss the tide.'

To be back at Cliffe Lodge was to have exchanged the prison of the island for another. Only now there was nothing to look forward to. Edward would feel humiliated, he said, if anyone guessed that their circumstances had altered. He would not consider dismissing any of his servants, nor change their outward style of life. Everything went to maintain the house, although he found that even keeping the *Gertrude* in dry dock cost money he could not afford. It meant no more trips nor visits home, no new clothes for Lillie. He had bought her two day dresses and one evening dress, when they were first married. They would have to last.

Without the yachts to occupy him, Edward spent whole days sitting morosely, staring into the fire, while Lillie read. His only conversation was about how much he had lost since he married her, how idyllic his first marriage had been. Occasionally, he went for walks down to the shore and came back as bored and irritable as he had left. His complaints, his pretence in front of the servants, his nightly undressing ritual especially made Lillie want to scream. She would lie turned away, with her eyes closed, but could still hear the click of the coins and keys being laid down and the winding of the watch. When he spoke to her or touched her fumblingly, she pretended to be in a deep sleep.

In the long evenings, when she could not get him to play cards or chess or even to talk, he began to empty the wine-cellar, which he had stocked when the house was built. In an inspired moment, Lillie reminded him of his other interest, fishing. He has all the equipment, lines and rods and flies. There were many places he could fish where it would cost nothing or very little.

In one way, it worked splendidly. He responded and was soon out of the house most days, sometimes all weekend. He was an expert angler, with his long, brooding patience, and having a demonstrable skill gave him back his pride. But with that his air of superiority returned. She knew now that he was an extremely shy man and was no longer taken in by the veneer of masterfulness and pompous complacence with which he concealed it. To have to defer to him still to keep the peace was increasingly difficult and depressing.

Fishing became a mania with him. He could speak of nothing else. Not being diffident about talking to people with the same interest, he began to be known locally and to join in small fishing parties. One day, he announced he had invited two guests to dinner, a local GP, Dr Lewis, and Harrison, a well-to-do businessman. They were their first visitors in over two months and Lillie was delighted.

She took extra care when she dressed that evening, wearing her only evening gown, simple but attractive, revealing by provincial standards. She wore her hair in its heavy coil, twisted round to lie over her left shoulder. Fortunately, the cook was able to produce an acceptable meal at short notice and the two guests were appreciative. Dr Lewis was a friendly, capable, fairly sensitive man in his forties, with prematurely white hair. Harrison, she did not like so much. He was more distant and formal. She had looked forward to acting as hostess, but Edward did not give her a chance to shine. He dismissed nearly everything she said, keeping the conversation at his end of the table and almost entirely about angling.

Dr Lewis was conscious that she had been silent for most of the last hour of the dinner and tried to make up for it, as they moved into the drawingroom. 'That was a delicious meal, Mrs Langtry,' he assured her. 'Thank you.'

'Not at all, Doctor,' she smiled.

'Yes, I don't know how you ladies do it,' Harrison agreed. 'To have guests sprung on you at the last minute and yet produce something so perfect.'

'If it had been left to Lillie,' Edward said, 'I imagine all we'd have had would have been boiled eggs.'

As he laughed, Dr Lewis saw that Lillie was hurt. 'Oh, come now, Edward,' he put in. 'Surely not?'

'It's a fact,' Edward stated. He rang the bell by the fireplace. 'Always got her nose in a book. But not the Household Accounts. Never seen such a muddle.' He chuckled.

'I expect you've always had someone else to take care of

such things, Mrs Langtry,' Harrison said gallantly.

'Yes. My mother – ' she began.

'Wonderful woman,' Edward interrupted. 'Runs the Deanery like clockwork. You'd never guess they didn't have two pennies to rub together. Teaches the island girls thrift, though. Lillie's the exception. My first wife, now – Jane, she was a wonder at running a home.'

He was unaware of the awkwardness his words caused. Harrison looked bland. Lewis saw how Lillie withdrew behind a pose of indifference. The pause ended as Evans came in.

'Ah, yes – the brandy,' Edward ordered. Evans crossed to the drinks cabinet. 'I thought of getting in another few days trout fishing,' Edward went on, 'before the weather breaks. Either of you care to join me?'

'Nothing I'd enjoy more,' Lewis admitted. 'But I'm afraid my patients wouldn't appreciate it.'

'Yes, we can't all be gentlemen of leisure – more's the pity,' Harrison said. It was a faintly envious compliment to Edward and they laughed. 'I might manage some days later in the month, though.'

'I'll keep you to that, Harrison,' Edward promised. 'I've been working on a couple of new flies I want to try out. Thought you might like to see them.' He moved to a side table on which was a flat, walnut case. Lewis and Harrison followed him, interested, as he opened it to show a collection of hand-tied flies.

Lillie was left alone. She saw Evans reach them with three brandy glasses on a tray. 'If you'll excuse me – she said. Lewis was the only one who heard and looked round. 'I only wanted to say goodnight.'

'You're not going to deprive us of your company, my dear?' Edward asked.

'I think I should have an early night.'

'Well, if you must,' he said crossly.

'I'm afraid we've been neglecting you, Mrs Langtry,' Lewis apologised.

Harrison bowed. 'Thank you again for a very fine dinner.'

'. . . Cook will be pleased,' she said. 'Good night.' She headed for the door, which Evans had already reached and held open for her.

Behind her, she heard Harrison confide, 'You're a lucky man, Edward. You have a very lovely wife.'

As she went out, Edward said complacently, 'Yes, she is rather. You should have seen my first wife, though'

Through Harrison and his wife and Lewis, who was a widower, they met more people in the district. 'The right people,' Edward said. That was important. They paid calls. The calls were returned, and gradually a circle of acquaintances was built up.

At first, Lillie was glad of the break in the monotony of her life. After those months of loneliness, she had hardly ever exchanged more than a few words in any day with her disagreeable maid, to have other women to talk to was much more than welcome. Paradoxically, at her first teaparty, she was so excited and anxious for it to go well, she could hardly speak. The other ladies, wives of local notables, were all older and took her silence for attentive respect. Since she was also the wife of a gentelman of leisure and the daughter of a Dean, she was unanimously approved.

A routine became established, coffee mornings, teaparties, visits after Sunday morning church, encouraged by Edward. As newcomers, it was important for them to be accepted in the district he said.

As the months passed, however, Lillie began to realise that a new kind of monotony had taken the place of the other, more insidious. Edward had developed among his male acquaintances the reputation as a wealthy, experienced sportsman and man of the world, able to deal with any situation, which he like to project. They looked on his pretty wife as merely another symbol of his success. The only one who took trouble to talk to Lillie was Dr Lewis, who had wider interests than fishing and local politics, himself, and found his short conversations with her increasingly enjoyable.

Half ignored by the men, she felt even more isolated among the women. Mostly middleaged, they considered any opinions other than their own to be worthless or improper. They patronised Lillie as coming from the remoteness of the Channel Islands. Any attempt she made to speak about books or the theatre or the fashions she had seen in the illustrated magazines was squashed. Subjects for conversation and permissible interests for ladies were strictly limited. Even to someone as inexperienced as Lillie, their horizons were pathetically narrow.

She had become twenty-one just after their return from Jersey. When she reached twenty-two, she saw the pattern of her whole life to come beginning to be laid down, an endless vista of coffee mornings, Church bazaars and whist parties, in a drab, provincial atmosphere. Another Christmas passed and, in the New Year, she revolted against the confines of her life. She escaped back into reading and dreaming. It became a struggle to be polite to the boring women and the offhand men who looked up to Edward and asked his advice and drank his wine. He noticed nothing, since he asked for nothing from her, except for her always to be there to welcome his guests, to take a correct and inconspicuous place in the community and, at very rare intervals, to submit to his easily-satisfied, sexual needs.

One February night, he brought home a group of friends after a fishing trip, including Harrison and Dr Lewis. Lillie excused herself after an hour of listening to them and went upstairs. She had had a headache all day and felt unwell and depressed. Edward had accused her of moping because Reggie had answered none of her letters. She wrote regularly to him and had never received a reply. But it was not that. She had a constant, sick feeling.

She had hardly reached the bedroom and begun to undress, when Edward followed her in. He had been drinking a little and was cross and aggrieved. 'I am thoroughly tired of you marching out whenever I bring friends home!' he protested. 'Hang it all, they want to see you!'

She shook her head and sat on the ottoman. 'I don't feel well enough, Ned.'

'It's your way of paying me back, is it?' he demanded.

'Just because I've been away for a few days.'

'I'm not – I really don't feel well,' she told him.

'You're as strong as a horse,' he snorted. 'What kind of not well?'

'I have a headache I can't get rid of. I can't sleep. Nausea.'

'You've not been eating?' he asked, seeing she was not pretending.

She leant forward, pressing one palm to her forehead. It was hot and damp. 'I try to, but I can't keep anything down.'

'You've been sick, you mean?'

'Last night,' she panted. 'And again this morning.'

Edward had a brief sense of alarm, which had changed to excitement. She looked up and saw that he was smiling. 'Well, now . . .' he said. 'Well, well. We'd better have the doctor look at you.'

'I'll be all right,' she whispered.

His smile broadened. 'I'm sure of it. Why didn't you tell me before?'

'What do you mean?'

'Oh, come on, Lillie!' he laughed. 'You're not so naive.'

She was startled, realising what he meant. 'No, I don't think it's – '

His voice was soothing. 'There, there, nothing to worry about. It's all perfectly natural.' He kissed her forehead. 'Clever girl. Wait till I tell my family! This is what they've been waiting for.'

He patted her cheek and left. Lillie sat back on the couch, troubled. She felt another wave of nausea. She panted, touching her throat, then moved her hand to her stomach. What Edward thought . . . if it were true . . . If it was really true, she was trapped forever.

In the drawingroom, the gentlemen waited for their host and hostess to return. 'Took Langtry over an hour to land it,' Harrison was saying. 'A full ten-pounder.'

'He certainly has a knack,' Lewis confirmed. 'I'll say that.'

As the others murmured in agreement, Edward came in with his butler. He was very pleased, rather self-important,

118

when he asked Lewis to examine his wife, as a favour.

'Is something wrong?' Lewis was concerned.

'She's a little under the weather,' Edward smiled. 'But that's quite normal, I imagine. I'd appreciate it, if you'd have a look at her.'

Lewis hesitated. 'Now? Well, I don't have any of my things with me – but certainly. Is her maid with her?'

'H'm? Oh, yes, of course,' Edward nodded. 'Evans will see to it. He'll take you up.' Lewis went out with the butler and Edward turned to the others. He had lowered his voice only slightly and they all heard. 'Well, gentlemen,' he announced, 'we may have some news shortly.'

Dr Lewis and the maid found Lillie already in bed. She was pale and sweating and seemed to have difficulty in breathing. Whatever it is, Lewis thought, it's developing very rapidly.

He looked at her eyes and felt for the glands at the side of her neck under the jawline. He raised Lillie's arm and touched her wrist lightly. While he took her pulse, her eyes closed. He watched her head move from side to side. Her breath was panted.

Edward was in high good spirits. None of them suspected how precarious his financial position was. For any improvement, he depended on Lillie. His mother would put pressure on his brother Richard to increase his allowance, if he had children. Agnes would back him, too. He poured fresh brandy, himself, for the others, who had all congratulated him.

'What do you hope for?' Harrison asked. 'A boy or a girl?'

'A boy, of course,' Edward told him. 'Immaterial, really. My family'll be equally pleased, either way. Old Quaker stock. Set a lot of store by grandchildren.' He broke off, eagerly, when Doctor Lewis appeared at the door.

'Can I see you a moment?' Lewis asked.

'It's all right,' Edward smiled. 'We're all friends.'

The doctor came further in. 'There's no cause for alarm yet,' he said seriously. 'The fever will take some time to develop.'

119

'Fever?'

'I shall go home and fetch her a sleeping draught. She'll need to conserve her strength.'

'Yes, yes,' Edward agreed. 'But when's it due?' Lewis looked at him blankly. 'The child. She's going to have a child.'

'No, there's no sign of that,' Lewis told him. 'None at all.'

'Are you sure?' Edward demanded, angrily. 'But I naturally assumed – ' He stopped, completely thrown. She's let me down! he thought.

Behind him, Harrison exchanged a sardonic smile with the others.

'Well, I – well, now,' Edward muttered. 'What's all this about fever?'

'You must prepare yourself,' Dr Lewis warned him. 'It will undoubtedly be severe. I am very much afraid, it may be typhoid.'

The guests left almost at once, partly out of respect, partly through fear at being in a stricken house.

The disease came on rapidly. Lewis had to presume that Lillie had already been suffering for several days, since her temperature rose so quickly. Always in the morning it was lower, but by evening it had climbed higher than the day before. Her tongue was furred. She was flushed and restless and, by the end of the week, having short bouts of delirium.

Edward had no experience of sickrooms and the maid proved useless, so Lewis brought in a nurse to sit with her at night, when the fever was at its height. Lillie's belly became swollen and painful, and her chest and back were marked with oval, light-red spots. In spite of the pain and nausea, she tried to stay cheerful, but she was afraid of the attacks of delirium, the raving and sweating and mindless fear.

Lewis thought her brave and touching, and did all he knew to help her. He was conscious that it was deplorably little. No cure had been discovered for typhoid and no treatment was generally accepted. All he could do was give her abdominal injections of antiseptics and try to keep her as cool and comfortable as possible. He came to see her at least three times a day.

The first crisis passed at the beginning of the second week, leaving her spent and exhausted. Any attempt to eat caused vomiting and Lewis would only allow her barley water or boiled milk. The nurse and he took turns in sponging her to try to reduce her temperature. Most of the time she spent in a dazed state, only half awake. When her mind focussed on anything, it was on memories of her father and of Reggie. She wanted her father to save her, to take away the fever, but knew he could not. She wanted Reggie to be with her, to hold her hand. Why hadn't he answered her letters? . . .

In the first days, Edward looked in during the mornings. In the evenings, the doctor had told him, any noise or disturbance was dangerous. There were no callers at the house. The very word, typhoid, kept them away. Eventually, he grew tired of waiting for news and had to get out, himself, as often as he could.

By the middle of the third week, the delirium was almost continuous again, and Lewis and the nurse scarcely ever left Lillie's side. She was emaciated and feeble, unable to hear them or recognise them. Only the last of her strength was holding off a final collapse. Lewis knew that another crisis was approaching. If she survived it, there was a chance. If it was too long delayed or too violent, there was no chance at all.

She lay in bed, trembling and muttering, her head, her legs and arms twitching as her muscles jerked. Her whole body was slick with sweat, her stomach and breasts and shoulders flecked with the reddish marks, her face gaunt and shadowed. The raving was endless, words, broken sentences, just audible. 'No – no, please. I dont – don't want – Father, no – not true – Michel – Michel, never – never see him – up – over the waves – waves – Oh, no – please God, no – Father, no – I don't – Where's – where's Reggie? Not my fault! – Not – I won't leave! – won't . . . no, no . . .'

Dr Lewis and nurse watched her from a distance. The door was opening. As Edward appeared, Lewis moved towards him, signalling to him not to close it loudly. 'There's little change,' he said quietly.

'It's been weeks now!' Edward whispered. 'Can't you do something?'

'Only keep her as quiet as possible.'

Edward stared across to where Lillie lay shaking and muttering and gasping for breath. The curtains were drawn to shield the bed from the light, but he could make out her matted hair and discoloured face. Her ravings frightened him and he stepped back to the door, going out. Lewis closed it gently behind him.

Two nights later, Lillie lay naked on the bed, except for a wet, folded sheet covering her from bust to hips. Only the farthest lamp, on the dressing table, was lit. The raving had ceased, but her head twisted and her body jerked with continuous, muscular spasms. Dr Lewis was sponging her neck, shoulders and arms, while the nurse sponged her legs.

The spasms in her body became more uncontrolled, the trembling reaching a peak, her breathing a desperate, hoarse panting. Lewis stopped sponging and looked worriedly at the nurse, who had also stopped. When he turned back to Lillie, he saw that her trembling was fading. Her arms dropped limply by her sides and her ragged breathing died away. She lay deathly still.

Lewis was dismayed. He pulled the sheet down and bent to listen for her heart. He listened for a long moment, puzzled. When he glanced up, he saw Lillie's cracked lips move and her tongue try to wet them. He took a glass from the bedside table and raised her head, trickling a little water on to her lips. She sighed, without opening her eyes, and fell into an exhausted sleep.

He covered her again with the sheet, smoothed the damp hair away from her face and forehead and stood back. 'Thank God . . .' he breathed. 'Thank God.'

It was another week before he could state definitely that she would recover. But it would be a long, slow convalescence. For months to come, there would still be a possibility of a relapse.

Lillie could not remember even having seen the nurse before, a quiet, broadfaced young woman. She was grateful, however, when she learnt how much she had done for her. And still did, in the days that followed, when she was too weak to do anything for herself. The nurse washed her and fed her and read to her, and every day Dr Lewis called. He was amazed at how rapidly her strength seemed to be coming back.

Soon she was sitting up and, one afternoon, the nurse told him she had had to stop her getting out of bed.

Lillie lay propped up by pillows, in her nightdress. Her hair was spread out around her. She was pale, yet, incredibly, more lovely with the contours of her face fined down. 'Well, I'm tired of lying in bed,' she complained.

'I can't leave her for a second, Doctor,' the nurse said.

Lillie scowled. 'She's worse than gaoler!'

He was glad they were only joking and laughed with them, sending the nurse off to get herself a cup of tea.

'Are you sure, Doctor?' she asked, rising.

'Yes, yes. Off you go. I'll sit with Mrs Langtry for a while.' The nurse smiled and went out, and he moved to beside the bed. As he considered Lillie, she lay looking back at him, completely relaxed, her expression affectionate and trusting. He had to confess that she fascinated him, making him feel protective and very masculine. 'Are you really feeling better?'

'Much,' she smiled.

'Your eyes are a lot clearer. Tongue?' She put out her tongue. 'Uh – huh. Any more headaches?' She shook her head. 'How about the rash? Fading?'

'It's gone,' she said.

He was surprised. 'I don't believe it.' Her ruffled nightdress was partly unfastened at the neck. She undid another button and drew both halves aside, revealing her throat and breasts. Her skin was smooth and unblemished, taut and creamy on the full globes of her breasts, the nipples a pale pink shading into rose. He had seen her naked many times. But then, she had been a patient. Now he realised he was looking at her as a woman and said abruptly, 'Yes, that's much improved.' He turned and sat in the nurse's chair by the bed, composing himself. 'I'd hoped to have a word with Mr Langtry today.'

'He's gone out, I expect,' Lillie said. 'Some days I don't see him at all. Nobody except Nurse and you. I'm so grateful to you for coming very day.'

'You're my – ' He interrupted himself. He had nearly said, favourite. 'My prize patient.'

She smiled. 'How long will it be before I'm really better?'

'You've made a remarkable recovery, as you know,' he told her. 'But it will be quite some while before you're properly fit again. You'll have to stay in bed for a time. Then you can get up, as long as you stay indoors.'

She was horrified. 'Indoors?'

He was trying to avoid looking at her directly. She had not buttoned the neck of her nightdress, only pushed it together. 'It's been a very severe winter,' he said. 'You mustn't risk going out.'

'With no one to talk to?' she protested. 'I'd go mad.'

'You have your husband for company,' he reminded her.

'He's worse than no one. He even enjoys my being ill. It means he doesn't have to make conversation.'

He shifted uncomfortably. 'You shouldn't say things like that, you know.'

'But it's true. I thought you understood?'

'Well . . . You have friends.'

'No one. No one here – except you,' she said softly. 'You are the first person who has been kind to me, since my marriage.' He was drawn by her voice and had to look at her. Her eyes were fixed on him, trusting. 'I have never been so alone. I never knew what it was to be lonely, until I came to this house.'

'Well, perhaps it might do you good to get away for a while,' he admitted, making himself matter-of-fact. 'Do you both good. When you're fit enough, you might go to stay with your parents in Jersey.'

'No,' she whispered. 'Edward would only complain. He has spoilt that, also. Help me . . . Help me?'

She held out her hand. Lewis hesitated, then took it. It

was warm and firm in his. 'I . . . would do anything I could,' he faltered. 'But – '

'There is only one place I could get better,' she said. 'If I stay here – I never shall. I know it!'

She was leaning forward and the unfastened neck of her nightdress had fallen open. He would never know if it was deliberate. Her voice, her hand in his and her eyes gazing at him made it impossible for him to think clearly. 'If you tell your husband – ' he began.

'He wouldn't believe me!' Her hand gripped his tighter. 'But if you spoke to him – '

He was confused. 'I would have to be sure.'

She made him bend towards her by drawing up his hand, until she could lean her cheek against it. The gesture was suppliant and, at the same time, provocative. He was more than ever aware of her warmth and nearness and beauty. 'I have no one else to turn to,' she said simply. 'If you don't help me, you might as well have let me die.'

Edward was pleased to find Dr Lewis waiting for him, when he got home later. He had wanted to have a chat, but his pleasure changed to indignation. 'London? You can't be serious!' he exclaimed. 'It's the worst possible place, I'd have thought, for anyone to get back their health!'

'In Lillie's – Mrs Langtry's case,' Lewis said, 'it is not merely a question of air and rest. But of distraction.'

'She's harped on about it ever since we first met!' Edward snapped.

'Precisely. She has convinced herself it is only there she will recover. And indeed, the milder weather and stimulating environment could prevent a serious relapse.'

Edward needed a moment to collect himself and poured himself a whisky from the smaller decanter. He felt more in command with something in his hand. 'Well, now I'll tell you what I told her,' he growled. 'I've no money to spare to go jaunting off for weeks to London.'

'It's not a matter of weeks, but of months,' Lewis told him calmly. 'Perhaps even permanently.'

Edward was thrown by the doctor's balanced and professional manner. 'Do you know what you're saying? . . .'

he spluttered. 'I'd have to sell this house, and furniture – give the servants notice. Do you expect me to give all this up?'

'It depends how much you value her,' Lewis said. Edward stared at him, but he did not back down. 'Rightly or wrongly, she feels you have neglected her during her illness. Indeed, at times, you have been conspicuous by your absence.'

'I had things to do,' Edward muttered. He turned away, taking a drink. 'I didn't want to get involved.'

'I beg your pardon?' Lewis asked, not sure he had heard rightly.

Edward felt he had to explain. He did not wish to give the wrong impression. 'My first wife, my Jane, died only three years ago,' he said slowly. 'Consumption – most distressing. I thought Lillie would – I didn't want to go through all that again.'

It was a minute before Dr Lewis could trust himself to speak. He was apalled by Langtry's self-absorption and totally determined now that Lillie would have what she wanted. 'I am speaking for your own good as well as hers,' he said categorically. 'If you do not move, I am afraid that your wife's life very probably, and your marriage most certainly, are in danger.'

Angrily, Edward swallowed down his drink.

It was late spring in London. Mr and Mrs Edward Langtry booked into Brown's Hotel, a good, but unpretentious, establishment in Half Moon Street, near Piccadilly Circus. Edward was reluctant, complaining at the expense. It was only for a day or two, however. Lillie scoured all the morning and evening papers for promising accommodation and soon found what she wanted, 'Furnished Apartment, suitable for Discriminating Married Couple, Meals Provided On Request,' in Eaton Place, Belgravia. The district could not be more perfect.

When their hansom cab trundled over the cobbles of Eaton Place, a newly-built, double row of tall, terrace houses behind fashionable Eaton Square, Lillie felt as if she were coming home. She could swear she recognised

Number 25 before the cab swung in to the kerb outside it. When Edward climbed out and helped her down, she was radiant.

There were several steps between railings, leading up to the front door, which was set back between pillars, with a rounded fanlight above it. She walked up the steps and stood by the door, smiling, while the cabdriver handed their travelling cases down to Edward.

It had taken her over two years of marriage, but she was here at last.

# CHAPTER FIVE

The apartment was on the second floor. It had two bedrooms, a bathroom, a drawingroom, a small diningroom and its own entrance hall off the landing outside. The house was owned by a Mrs Jennings, who kept a maid to answer the front door and a cook, who did the meals, 'on Request'. Lunch and dinner were brought up by Mrs Jenning's maid. Lillie made breakfast and tea, herself, in the tiny pantry off the diningroom. A great saving, she explained to Edward.

Remembering the fiasco at the Suffields', she would not contact any of the acquaintances she had made in Jersey. Her mother had her address and was authorised to pass it on to any visitors who enquired after her. A few did, but she heard from none of them. Their only caller in the first six months was Clement, passing through from Oxford.

Edward disliked every moment of the first two months, since they had to stay in the apartment for much of the time, because Lillie was still convalescing. He did not care to go out on his own. The sheer size of the city overwhelmed him. It soon became apparent that, in spite of the way he had talked, he had no knowledge of the city and knew no one. It was a great disappointment to Lillie, who had depended on him. She urged him to make friends, but he flatly refused to go introducing himself to strangers. He had achieved a certain standing in Southampton where his yachts were remembered and his style of life envied. Now he had nothing with which to impress new acquaintances and he resented it. He sat in the apartment, sluggish and morose, often in the diningroom, where he could lay his pots and hooks and boxes out on the table and pass the hours mending and fashioning fishing flies out of brightly-dyed, little feathers.

Lillie never had a moment of boredom. She loved the apartment, especially the drawingroom, which she filled with flowers, whenever Edward would let her. It was much smaller than the one in Cliffe Lodge, but brighter and more cheerful. The furniture was good quality, covered with brocade. The windows had frilled net curtains, which caught the sunlight and under one of them was a polished writing table, at which she could read and write her letters home. She still wrote to Reggie, only not so often, since he did not reply. But she lived in hope that he would come to visit them, as she had suggested.

She could spend hours at the window, watching the people going by in the street. It would have been even better to meet some of them, but it did not matter. Just to be *here* was enough.

Although Eaton Place was not very grand, it was in the centre of one of the best areas, just round from Belgrave Square and separated only by a mews from the gardens of Eaton Square, where the rents were ten to twenty times more than they paid. Many of the people whose social lives were reported in the papers lived there and in other streets and squares nearby. They were within an easy walk of the river at Chelsea, and of Hyde Park Corner. Just over the houses to the right was Buckingham Palace. 'Might as well be on the moon, for all we'll see of it,' Edward muttered.

It was better when Lillie could get out more. Even he sometimes enjoyed it, although he complained that in a few weeks she had dragged him round every museum, church and art gallery within twenty miles. But her curiosity and excitement were infectious. They went out walking every day, although he did not like to go too far, because they sometimes lost themselves and had to spend money on a cab home. They did everything that was free, or nearly free. They climbed the Monument, watched Punch and Judy shows and listened to concerts in the parks. Once he took her rowing on the Serpentine lake and, sometimes, they mingled with the strolling crowd on the walks by the bridle path in Hyde Park at the fashionable hour, when the circuit was nearly jammed by ladies and gentlemen riding or taking the air in their carriages, a gorgeous display of exquisitely turned-out equipages, landaus, victorias, gigs, curricles and barouches, drawn by some of the most superb horse-flesh in the country. The Prince of Wales had just returned from a state visit to India. They had heard that he rode here every day with Princess Alexandra, but they saw neither of them. Lillie recognised many famous faces from their photographs, but had not one glimpse of even minor Royalty to write home about.

She would like to have hired a horse for an hour one day, but Edward said there was nothing to spare on inessentials. He had become extremely careful about money. He had managed to rent out Cliffe Lodge, rather than sell it, although for much less than they were paying at Eaton Place. It was still there, if they needed it, he kept telling her.

She had one unforgettable experience. After a long, wearisome campaign, she managed to talk him into taking her to a theatre. They decided to go the the Lyceum in the Strand, where the new leading actor, Henry Irving, was presenting *Hamlet* to great critical success. All society had flocked to it and the production was said to be in the most sumptuous, yet refined, taste. Edward still did not approve, but Lillie argued that Shakespeare was as respectable a part of the national heritage as the Queen or Westminster Abbey.

She did not really know what to expect. To enter a theatre was like going into church of another religion, where one had no idea of what attitude or customs were observed. In fact, it was just like going to a concert, except that the interior of the Lyceum was more magnificent than any concert hall. Edward was grumpy and self-conscious, but she forgot him as soon as they took their seats.

From where they sat, fairly high in the Upper Circle, she could see the boxes and front rows of the Stalls, with gentlemen in eveningdress and starched white fronts, ladies in lowcut dresses, their hair upswept and crowned with diamond tiaras, their throats and arms glittering with jewellery as they moved. There was movement between the boxes, gentlemen greeting one another and kissing the ladies' hands. In some only one silent couple sat. Others were crowded and she could see ice buckets with champagne. The rich dresses and jewellery, the peep into that secret, elegant world was worth the price of their tickets. She was clutching her programme and gave it to Edward to hold, in case she should spoil it. The chatter and motion around them and the deepening hush as the theatre's footmen turned the gaslights down raised her suspense to the heights. The crystal gasolier over the auditorium dimmed, then the huge, red curtain rose on the dark ramparts of Elsinore.

It was a revelation. The realistic setting, gorgeous costumes and swirling action ravished her eyes. From the first eerie moment, she was lifted out of herself, mesmerised, following every word, every thought, devouring every gesture, the development of the characters as the plot unfolded, the sinister Claudius and winsome, pathetic Ophelia, poor, bumbling Polonius. To hear the lines she had recited so often with her father, the great speeches she knew by heart, spoken by living actors, swept her into a state that was almost like a trance. And over all was the tall, gaunt figure of Irving, with his hawk's profile and harshly magnetic voice and strange, stalking walk. And that hypnotic quality of stillness, when the stage was filled with colourfully-dressed courtiers and ladies and soldiers, yet all one could see was the motionless, brooding figure of Hamlet in his doublet of black velvet.

She relived every second of it for days afterwards. She knew the programme by heart, the name of every member of the cast and stage management, even the advertisements. She read and reread the play, with the programme in front of her, visualising every scene. Edward would not take her again, but it kept her content for so long, he considered every penny had been well spent.

They had still not met anyone and had spoken only to occasional shopkeepers and to Mrs Jennings and her maid. As December began, the town seemed deserted by the higher classes. Many houses in Belgravia were shut, their owners having moved to the country for the shooting season and for Christmas. Everywhere, in shopwindows and churches, there were signs of preparation for the festive season, but there were no preparations made at Eaton Place.

'Be a bit different, if we were at Cliffe Lodge,' Edward grumbled.

Anything is better than that, Lillie thought. 'I don't mind,' she smiled. 'I feel so much better now.'

'It's the only reason we're here,' he reminded her. They sat opposite each other at the fire. He was reading an article on freshwater angling in The Times and it made him discontent. 'All right for you.'

She did not want another argument. 'I'm grateful, Edward,' she said. 'Really grateful.'

'You might show it.' He lowered the paper. 'If you're feeling so much better, isn't it about time you started being my wife again?' He smiled slightly. 'You know what I mean.'

It was a question she had been avoiding. 'Soon. When I'm really better,' she told him. She rose to get away from him, but as she passed him he caught her hand. 'Soon,' she promised, and smiled.

'Well, that's something,' he muttered. He let her go.

She heard the rustle of his paper behind her, as she moved to the window. With the longer evenings and bad weather, they were not able to go out so much. It was going to become more difficult to avoid his fumbling attempts to make love. You cannot *make* love, she thought. She had tried. 'Shall we go for a walk?' she asked.

Just then, there was a knock at the door to their hall outside.

'Mrs Jennings, I suppose,' Edward sighed. 'I'll get it.' He put down his paper and went out.

He smoothed his hair at the mirrored hatstand in the little hall and opened the door. Mrs Jennings, the landlady, was waiting, a plump, genteel woman in her fifties. 'This has just come,' she said. She was holding a telegram envelope which she gave to him. 'I brought it straight up. For Mrs Langtry.'

'*Mrs* Langtry? . . . Ah – thank you, Mrs Jennings.'

Lillie turned at the window, hearing the door close again. 'What is it?' she called.

Edward came back in, opening the envelope. 'A telegram – for you.' He unfolded the form and began to read. 'It's from your father.' She saw at once that something was wrong. 'Your brother, Reggie – he's had a riding accident.'

She tensed. 'How bad is it?'

Edward hesitated, sorry he had to be the one to tell her. 'Lillie – ' he said and held the telegram out towards her. 'He's dying.'

She flinched as though he had struck her.

She took the earliest train in the morning to Southampton, where she caught the first ferry. But it was two days before she reached Jersey. She prayed that she would be in time to see him alive, but she was stricken, when her cab from the harbour reached the Deanery. All the blinds were drawn.

Her father and Clement led her into the study. She felt too faint to climb the stairs to the drawingroom. She had not cried, since she was a child, and still would not. Not like her mother, who had wept herself into exhaustion and was asleep. Strange, Lillie thought. In her grief, her whole mind felt empty.

'I'm sorry, Lillie,' her father said. 'The funeral could not be delayed.'

'Did he suffer?'

'Not towards the end,' Clement told her quietly.

Reggie had gone out riding as usual. Racing along the cliffs, too near the edge, his horse had taken fright, stumbled and thrown him. In falling, his horse had rolled on him, crushing from the waist down. He was brought home on a shutter, unconscious.

'It was a miracle he survived,' the Dean said. 'Even for a few hours.'

Lillie had to fight not to break down. 'If only I'd seen him . . .' she breathed.

'He asked for you,' her father said. 'You were the only one he asked for. But it was not to be.'

She closed her eyes.

Later, Clement found her in the schoolroom. It was growing dark. She had been sitting alone for a long time, thinking and remembering the childish days, the difficult days of growing up and Reggie's bitter pain, when she told him she was to marry. 'Was it an accident?' she asked quietly.

Clement hesitated. '. . . Of course.'

'He was too good a horseman,' she objected. 'How can you be sure?'

'Because we must be, Lillie,' he told her seriously. 'Whatever happened, he wished it on himself. It was no fault of yours.'

'I'll never forgive myself for leaving.'

He sat beside her on the windowseat. 'If you'd stayed in Jersey, it would only have been worse.'

'It's like losing a part of myself,' she said, bleakly. 'You and Reggie are the only ones close to me.'

'There's your husband. Why didn't he come with you?'

As she looked at Clement, her eyes slowly filled with tears. For once, she could not hold them back and she clung to him, weeping at last.

It was a cheerless Christmas. Clement left soon after. Mrs Le Breton was over the first shock, but Lillie wrote to tell Edward that she felt she should stay with her, until she had fully recovered.

To her surprise, he arrived on the island within the week. He had not come with her, saying he could not afford two fares. However, he had realised this was a heavensent opportunity. The cost of living was much lower in Jersey and he could again take his place as a man of some standing. He would not live at the Deanery, where he did not feel at home. Instead, he rented the fairly imposing, stone-built Noirmont Manor, on a height overlooking little Belcroute Bay. It had once been a Le Breton manor and Lillie could not resist a sense of pride at being its mistress. It was a well-conceived plan of Edward's to make her happy to remain in Jersey, where she could call on her mother whenever she pleased and he could once again become a gentleman of leisure.

Even servants could be hired quite cheaply, to come in during the day. He was not pleased, yet could not refuse, when Mrs Le Breton insisted on Lillie having a maid of her own, to live in. Mrs Le Breton had even chosen one, Dominique, the Italian girl who used to work for the dressmaker, Madame Nicolle, and was now seeking a position as a lady's maid. She was a blackhaired, round-faced young woman with a quick smile and a lively intelligence. Lillie remembered her and liked her again when she came for an interview.

'Well, if your mother chose her . . .' Edward said grudgingly. 'You got her reasonably enough, I suppose?'

'Three pounds a month,' Lillie told him. He was startled. 'I know I could have offered her less,' she went on, 'but she's very willing. She'll be such a help.'

Dominique proved to be more than a help. She became indispensable. The daughter of a ship's carpenter who had left the sea to work in the shipyard in St. Helier, she had looked after a large family of brothers and sisters from the age of ten. For years she had admired Lillie and quickly became devoted to her. She took care of her clothes and helped her dress, washed, ironed, sewed, mended and even cooked, on occasion. In no time, she was as good as running the house, and she was excellent company, when Edward spent the afternoon or evening drinking with old yachting friends.

Apart from its Corinthian portico and elaborate, iron entrance gates, another charm of Noirmont Manor to Lillie was that it was in walking distance of Portelet House. Young Arthur Jones, the only real friend she had left on the island, lived there and could come over to see her or she could meet him halfway. Artie had been close to Reggie, too. Together, they had had a reputation for wildness, although with Artie it was more highspirits. He had been sobered by his friend's death and, often, Lillie and he walked in silence. He was so like Reggie, Lillie thought, and sometimes fancied, on the cliff paths or the beach, that she was with her brother again. It was not all solemn, though. Artie could be recklessly funny, jumping from rock to rock on the cliff edge and capering like a demented seagull, until she begged him to stop, half afraid for him and half helpless with laughter, or running into the waves fully dressed to fetch her a handful of seawater, because she had said she was thirsty. He had nearly made her drink it. Sometimes, they chased each other like children and laughed through a whole afternoon. But sometimes, he was as moody and distant as Reggie had been. Like Reggie, he did not care very much for Edward.

Lillie had to think very carefully. She had been back on the island for nearly two months, and enjoyed it, although she was still saddened by her brother's death. Yet she could see the old pattern of her life emerging, only shifted from Cliffe Lodge to Noirmont Manor, and when Edward began to talk of extending the lease, she told him it was time to go back to London. He blustered and argued, but her parents supported her. There was still a problem with her health, they said. He would be responsible, if she fell ill again.

Her mother had a quiet talk with her, shortly before they left. She was convinced that Lillie was right not to remain. To an extent, it was the Dean's fault. In his sixties, he was still pursuing women and it was better for Lillie and her husband not to live in Jersey, if a scandal broke which could lead to the whole family being ostracised. To Lillie, she said she had not given up her dream of making a social success in London, the only achievement possible for a woman, since none of the professions were open to them. Lillie had told her that her life with Edward was not altogether unhappy. Aimless, rather. Empty. At least, in London there were distractions, places to go. 'But I saw you being invited to all the grand balls and receptions.'

'So did I,' Lillie smiled. 'But reading about them in the Illustrated News is the closest I've been to an invitation. Probably just as well.'

'Why?'

'I've nothing to wear,' Lillie explained. 'Ned doesn't believe in wasting money on clothes. I only have this dress and one other. And the evening gown I had when I was first married.'

They were on the terrace at the Deanery. Mrs Le Breton rose. 'That's why I wanted to see you,' she said. 'You're

136

coming into St. Helier with me. To Madame Nicolle's.'

'But why,' Lillie asked, rising.

Mrs Le Breton was wearing black. Lillie wore a black crepe band round the sleeve of the short jacket of her blue suit dress. 'I know you are upset at not having any proper mourning,' Mrs Le breton said. 'Madame Nicolle still has your measurements. I had her run you up a little, black dress that will do for any time of day.'

Lillie was touched, but protested. 'Mother, you can't afford – '

Mrs Le Breton put up a hand, stopping her. 'It's nothing elaborate. Just a simple dress you can wear for a month or so – in remembrance of Reggie.' Her eyes were wet.

Lillie hugged her. Having no mourning dress was something that had, indeed, upset her deeply. Ladies of any standing wore mourning for at least six months, if not a full year, after the death of a near relative. She had seen people looking at her oddly, and it had hurt her to appear to be slighting Reggie's memory. 'Dearest Mother,' she said, and kissed her.

Mrs Le Breton was prim with embarrassment. 'If you start to thank me,' she declared, 'I shan't give it to you.'

Mrs Jennings was delighted to have them again at Eaton Place and impressed that they now had their own maid, for Lillie had refused to part with Dominique. She was installed in the smaller bedroom and came to help with the unpacking, having put on her apron and lace cap. Lillie had decided against a traditional maid's uniform, as Dominique was really a personal lady's maid, and she really looked very fetching and continental with the little apron over her fawn, check dress.

She was almost comically tearful and happy at them having brought her and Edward told her to stop snivelling or he would send her back. He had joined a small sporting club in Victoria during the weeks he had been alone and he wanted to call round there. 'Of course, if you'd rather I didn't,' he said.

'No, no,' Lillie told him. 'It's important for you to meet people with the same interests.' She was pleased. It had always been up to him to make friendly contacts. As a woman, she could not, or only to the most limited extent. When he left them alone, Dominique swore that she was so grateful she would have worked for Lillie for nothing. 'Don't tell Mr Langtry,' Lillie murmured.

She had worn her blue suit and cape for travelling and, when Dominique unpacked the new black dress, she thought she would try it on again. Madame Nicolle had cut it to her measurements as a girl and it had seemed very tight. Satin soon stretches, her mother had assured her, but it still felt tight and Dominique had some difficulty fastening it. It was simple and square-cut with a white collar, the kind of dress Lillie had seen a hundred times at funeral lunches in Jersey. She bent her knees, trying to get an impression of it in the mirror on her dressingtable. She was glad she had insisted on Madame replacing the collar with a wider one of white lace and adding white cuffs. The slight bustle effect was also an improvement.

'It . . . it looks very nice on, Signora,' Dominique said, doubtfully. 'Are you going to wear it all the time?'

Lillie smoothed the material over her waist. 'Only when my husband and I go out.'

The next weeks were the most tedious Lillie had known in London. She was seldom able to talk Edward into taking her anywhere. He was deliberately neglecting her and spent a large part of each day at the club he had joined, an all male club, to which he could not have taken Lillie, even if he had wanted to. It was his way of punishing her for making them return to London.

She was thankful to her mother, again. At least, she could talk to Dominique. Even so, she could not go on outings with her maid, only on infrequent shopping expeditions or on pretext of showing her something of the city. She could not count the hours she spent by herself, reading, or seated at her dressingtable brushing her hair and trying it in different styles.

On a rainy afternoon in March, she lay on her bed in her wrap, turning the pages of an illustrated magazine. She was listless and bored. The drawings and photographs of society balls, celebrities, garden parties and royal functions seemed a mockery of her own uneventful life. There was a map of the Balkans, showing the territories over which Russia and Turkey had recently been at war. A Peace Conference at Constantinople had just ended in confusion and it was obvious that, unless Disraeli's government could force terms more favourable to its Turkish ally, the Russians would take control of the entire eastern end of the Mediterranean. There were two pages of designs for printed fabrics by William Morris, with matching wallpaper, and she briefly imagined how the drawingroom would look, done up like that. It was pointless. Edward would never agree to it.

Dominique brought in a tray of teathings, which she set down on the dressingtable.

'Is it still raining?' Lillie asked.

'Si, Signora.' Dominique poured a cup of tea and put it on the bedside table. When Lillie pushed herself up to sit, some pages of the magazine flipped over, lying open at a drawing of a lovely, young woman, her fair hair swept up in layered coils, higher at the back. 'Lady Dudley is very beautiful, isn't she, Signora? Molto bella . . .'

'Yes,' Lillie nodded, glancing at the magazine. She looked up, surprised. 'You know her?'

Dominique laughed. 'Only from the photographs. All the society ladies, the beautiful ones, you see their photographs everywhere – Mrs Wheeler, Lady Helen Vincent, Mrs Cornwallis West, Lady Aylesford, I know them all.' Lillie laughed with her. 'I read all the social columns, and the gossip, especially about the ladies,' Dominique confessed, and added daringly, 'They are all very friendly with the Prince of Wales.'

'So one hears,' Lillie said, guardedly. Even in Southampton there had been rumours of the Prince's escapades with ladies. He seemed to have a very roving eye, in spite of having and incomparably beautiful wife.

Dominique leant forward, confidentially. 'Sometimes I think he should see you, Signora.' She was sure her mistress was just as lovely as Lady Dudley. Well, almost. No one could rival Lady Dudley

'Dominique . . .' Lillie warned, reproving her. She really should not encourage her, yet she smiled at the thought.

Dominique had been chastened for a moment, but brightened when Lillie smiled. It was so sad. Often she looked so pale and lonely. 'It is a pity you do not go out more, Signora,' she sympathised. 'For weeks you hardly go out.'

'Mr Langtry is so busy,' Lily said. 'And anyway, I still have to rest.' She turned another page of the magazine to change the subject. It showed the picture of a building with a plain facade, crowned with a triangular, Greek pediment. 'What's that?' she wondered.

'The new aquarium,' Dominique told her. 'The Royal Aquarium. Prince Leopold opened it last month.'

Lillie mentioned the aquarium to Edward later that evening. It was a considerable entertainment centre, in fact, with a theatre and musichall, Summer and Winter Gardens with orchestras, on the corner of Tothill Street, Westminster, and she was very keen to see it. She led up to it by reminding him that it would soon be their third wedding anniversary.

'So it is,' he marvelled. 'Well, I say . . .'

'Let's go somewhere,' she suggested. 'Somewhere special. I know! You can take me to the new aquarium in Westminster.'

He had begun to look dubious, but sparked up at the word. 'Aquarium?'

'It's all the rage,' she assured him. 'As well as all sorts of fish, they have alligators, an octopus, even. You'll like that.'

He was definitely intrigued. And nodded. 'H'm . . .'

The entrance hall of the Royal Aquarium was tiled, with several exhibits, including a large, stuffed swordfish, mounted on the walls.

Edward marched out past them with Lillie on his arm. He was disgusted. 'Well, that was a waste of time!' he declared.

'At least, we've seen it,' she said.

He snorted. 'Seen what? If there was an octopus in that tank, I couldn't make it out.'

The aquarium *had* been disappointing and she was anxious in case it spoilt the whole outing. She had been looking forward to it. 'There's lots more to look at,' she told him. 'There's a fire-eater, and sideshows. There's an ice fountain in the Winter Gardens. Let's go and see that.'

'No, no,' he grunted. 'We're going home.'

She was upset as he turned her towards the main exit, but could not argue with him in public. Because it was their anniversary, she had taken extra trouble. She wore her black dress and had made a hat to go with it, buying a little, black-glazed straw bonnet and winding a black-dyed ostrich feather round the brim. It tied with a black bow under her chin. She knew she looked smart. Several gentlemen had seemed to notice her.

One was passing, a bearded, elderly gentleman, in a glossy tophat and tightly-buttoned frockcoat, walking with a cane. He paused and said, 'Bless my soul! It's pretty, little Miss Le Breton.' It was Lord Ranelagh. There were two girls behind him, well dressed, but with rather bold looks, over made up. They did not expect to be introduced. He tipped his hat, when Lillie turned and smiled, recognising him. 'No, it's something else now,' he reminded himself. 'Longtree, is it?'

'Langtry,' she laughed. She had always enjoyed meeting him on his visits to Jersey. 'Edward, you remember Lord Ranelagh.'

Edward bowed.

Ranelagh nodded to him. 'How d'you do?' He noticed that Lillie was wearing black. 'What's this? Not one of your dear parents, I hope?'

'My younger brother,' she said quietly.

'Ah.' He remembered the rascal, friend of Arthur's. As a connoisseur of women, he could not help noticing that Lillie looked remarkably fetching. She was turning into a stunner . . . The black satin dress was high-necked, long-sleeved, very fitting to the hips, hugging her full bust and narrow waist. It was relieved with a wide collar of white lace and white lace cuffs. With her pale skin and reddish gold hair caught back loosely under the black bonnet, she was really – He coughed. 'Well, what a surprise to see you here.'

'We're living in London now,' she told him.

'Are you, indeed? Well, well . . . I suppose you're pretty busy.'

'Not really,' she smiled.

'Well, you'll have to pop over to my place at Fulham some time. We keep open house every Sunday for tea – on the lawn, if the weather's decent.' He lowered his voice. 'Unfortunately, my daughters aren't at home just at the moment.'

Lillie saw the girls behind him smile. 'What a pity,' she said. 'But it's kind of you to invite us.'

'Not at all,' he chuckled. 'Any Sunday you're free. You keep in touch, now.' He raised his hat again and headed off down the hall, followed by the two girls.

Lillie had come alive again. 'Wasn't that a nice surprise?' she said.

'A bit rum,' Edward muttered. 'Were those two young ladies with him or not? And why didn't he introduce us?'

Lillie laughed. 'He's very absentminded.'

Fulham was a pleasantly rural district, only beginning to be built up. It was just over half an hour's hackney carriage drive from Belgravia. An unwarrantable expense, considering they had had no real invitation, Edward said. Lillie insisted it would be insulting to her parents and to Arthur, if they did not go.

The next Sunday afternoon, they arrived at Ranelagh's house in Fulham, a creeper-covered mansion surrounded by acres of gardens, with a wide, tree-shaded lawn, sloping down to the Thames. The afternoon party was already in progress, the atmosphere light, aristocratic and relaxed. It was a mild, sunny day and white-painted, wrought iron tables and chairs were set out on the terrace and down the sides of the lawn under the trees.

For a second, Lord Ranelagh seemed surprised to see them, then welcomed them warmly. 'Well, how splendid you could come! Lots of interesting people here. Now, you come and meet everyone.'

He introduced them to one of the groups, 'Mr and Mrs Langtry – young friends of mine,' and left them to circulate. Edward was wearing his most formal, dark suit with stiff, high collar and pearl cravat. Lillie was in her little, black dress and the hat with its ostrich feather. After a few impersonal greetings, the people they had joined carried on talking about a houseparty at which most of them had been guests. Lillie and Edward listened and smiled politely, but the conversation meant nothing to them and, when the group split up, they were left alone.

Ranelagh came across to them again and took them to meet another group, where Edward was asked his opinion of the recent appointment of the Duke of Marlborough as Viceroy of Ireland. After a long moment, he nodded and said he understood it was quite an honour. From a long reactions Lillie observed, it was not the correct answer. When the group moved on, they were again left alone.

Edward wanted to leave at once, but Lillie made him walk slowly down with her to the boathouse at the river and back up the path at the side through banks of spring flowers. She hoped that Lord Ranelagh would return to find them. Apart from waving to her once, however, he was too busy.

When they reached the upper lawn again, footmen were setting out tea on the little tables and the strolling groups and couples beginning to converge on them, laughing and animated. It seemed wrong merely to move in amongst them. There was an unoccupied table to the left of the terrace and Lillie made for it. It would be better, if they were seated and others came to join them. Then conversation would start more naturally. She sat at the table and Edward came to stand behind, a little to her right, leaving three empty chairs. After some minutes, a footman brought a pot of tea. The gentlemen were intended to fetch whatever else the ladies requested from a long buffet table, but she was not hungry. She poured tea for herself and Edward, and waited.

Although quite a few people were still standing, including some to whom they had been introduced, no one joined them. She poured another cup for Edward and filled the teapot from the silver hotwater jug. Edward was bored and irritated. 'This is intolerable!' he fumed.

'Please, Edward . . .' she begged him, not looking at him and not raising her voice. Her hand holding the cup trembled and she rested the cup and saucer on her lap.

'I told you he wasn't really expecting us,' he went on. 'But no, you had to come. Well, I for one don't enjoy being treated like a poor relation!' When she did not reply, he lapsed into a resentful silence.

Lillie was upset by their being ignored. She had prayed that, at last, through this party, they would meet pleasant people, ladies on whom she could call afterwards and exchange visits. It was so possible . . . if only she could take the first step. Surely there was nothing about Edward or herself which marked them immediately as outsiders? If so, perhaps he had been right all along and they should go back to Southampton, or Jersey. The easy conviviality of the people circulating and seated at the other tables was like a direct insult. No other couple was alone. She would not let her feelings show and sat straighter, surveying the scene with her old, protective expression of faintly amused detachment.

'Five more minutes,' Edward said.

On the edge of one of the groups by the buffet table, an energetic woman in her late thirties, wearing a loose 'aesthetic' dress in green flower print and a straw sunhat, touched Lord Ranelagh's arm as he passed. She was Lady Sebright.

'Can I fetch you something, Olivia?' he asked.

'No, thank you,' she said. Her voice was very clear and expressive. 'Who's that exquisite creature over there, with the unhappy man?'

'H'm?' He squinted round. 'Oh, it's Mrs Langtry. Her father's the Dean of Jersey.'

'Charming.'

'Yes,' he agreed. 'Lovely girl. No conversation, though. And her husband's a frightful bore. Would you care to meet them?'

Lady Sebright smiled. 'I've seldom heard such a resistable invitation.'

'Be doing me a favour, actually,' Ranelagh admitted. 'If you'd talk to them for a couple of minutes.'

As they approached, Olivia Sebright decided that the young woman was even more bewitching than she had thought, pure Rossetti. No . . . rather, one of those mystic Arthurian heroines that Edward Burne Jones loved to dream of and draw, only brought to life. He would faint at the sight of her. And so aloof. So clearly above this mundane bunfight of Ranelagh's . . .

'I *so* wanted to meet you,' she told Lillie, when Ranelagh introduced them. Edward bowed stiffly. Lillie made to rise, but Lady Sebright stopped her. 'No, no, my dear.' She drew a chair slightly nearer and sat, handing her cup and saucer to Edward, without looking at him.

Edward would have had either to lean over her or to move round to put it on the table. He stood selfconsciously holding both hers and his own.

Lady Sebright was studing Lillie. 'You are from the Channel Islands. That is obviously where you get your complexion.' Lillie smiled fleetingly. 'I've been watching you. You clearly find this gathering very dull.'

Lillie was a little overawed by this strange woman, plain, but with striking eyes, heavily outlined with brown mascara. She kept her detached expression. 'Not at all,' she said, evenly. 'It's rather amusing.'

Lady Sebright laughed. 'You mustn't be too critical. They can't help being philistines.' Lillie smiled faintly again and Lady Sebright nodded, smiling back. 'I think we have a lot in common. I give a small supper party on Sundays for a few artist friends – painters, writers, and so on. You must come.'

Lillie inclined her head. 'We would be delighted, Lady Sebright.'

'Not this evening. I'll send you a card,' Lady Sebright said, and studied her again. 'You're really very pretty, Mrs Langtry. You ought to be seen by people who appreciate that sort of thing.'

Lillie was thoughtful, in the cab on the journey home. According to Lord Ranelagh, Olivia Sebright was a highly rated amateur artist, whose rich husband indulged her taste for collecting modern works. A discriminating patroness of the arts, she held concerts and amateur theatricals, in which she was a spirited performer, and on Sunday evenings her home became a kind of salon for the artistic set. 'Meet all sorts. there,' he told Lillie. 'Not my cup of tea, but you might find it amusin'.' To Lillie, it sounded fascinating, just the kind of parties she had once dreamed of giving, where there would be interesting talk in which ladies could join freely. At Lord Ranelagh's, as an unknown couple, convention decreed that the opening of any conversation should be directed to Edward, who had replied awkwardly and not continued the conversation, although she had thought of many things to say. But at Lady Sebright's . . .

Beside her in the cab, Edward was seething. 'I've never been so humiliated! Virtually ignored, except by that insufferable woman!'

'She was very kind,' Lillie said.

'I could scarcely make head or tail of what she was saying half the time,' he complained. '"Artistic" conversation, I suppose. And the way she patronised you!'

'I liked her,' Lillie said.

He let out a short, scoffing laugh. 'Oh, yes – anyone who pays you compliments.' He sat in offended silence for the rest of the journey.

In the days after, she did not mention Lady Sebright to him again, nor even talk about her to Dominique. The invitation had been impulsive, then quickly qualified by saying she would send a card. If she forgot or changed her mind, that was the end of it. There had been so many disappointments. Lillie did not show anything and tried not to hope, yet the tension inside her became almost agonising.

On Thursday, when Edward came back from buying his daily paper, he saw that she was excited as she showed him an invitation card, written in a flowing, sepia script. 'Lady Sebright's card has arrived,' she told him, smiling. 'For

Sunday.'

'Well, you can tear it up,' he said, dismissively. 'Don't imagine we're going.' He turned away, opening his paper.

Her smile had faded. 'But I'd like to go, Ned.'

'To be humiliated and patronised again – by a riffraff of scribblers and artists?' he demanded, loudly. 'I won't expose myself to that again. So you can throw that on the fire.' When she did not move, he looked at her commandingly.

'No,' she said.

'Lillie – ' he threatened.

'I'm not a fool. I know what you've been doing,' she answered, her voice cool and level. 'You thought if our life here was so dull and wearisome it became unbearable, that I'd agree to come back to Southampton.'

'It's our home!'

Her voice still did not rise. 'I'm not leaving here.'

'You'll do as I say!' he ordered, angrily. 'You'll write to that Sebright woman and tell her you are unwell.'

'No,' she said. 'I haven't waited all those months to turn down the only invitation we have had. I am going on Sunday – even if I have to go alone.'

She was so controlled, so completely determined, he flushed, choking for words to reply, and watched her cross the room and leave. When the door closed, his bluster was pricked like a balloon. The drinks tray was on the sidetable near him. He snatched up the brandy and poured himself a glass.

Dominique was nearly as excited as Lillie, and showed it far more. She assisted eagerly with Lillie's preparations. These were limited, since she had almost no choice in what to wear. The evening would not be rigidly formal, so she could wear her black dress. That was appropriate, anyway, as she was still in mourning.

As the time for which the cab had been booked drew nearer, Dominique was pressing the dress with a flatiron, for the third time. She was watching Lillie, who sat at the dressingtable in her camisole vest with narrow shoulder-straps and long, muslin underskirts. They had cut photographs of some of the society beauties from the magazines, the ones showing their hairstyles, and they were propped up against the mirror. All day, Lillie had been trying different styles, pinning and unpinning her hair, but it was so heavy and glossy it would not stay up in an elaborate chignon and, layered on top like Lady Dudley's, it made her face look far too long.

She had plaited her hair into a thick rope again and held it wound round her head. 'It just won't stay up,' she said, and lowered it.

'If you fastened it with a piece of jewellery, Signora,' Dominique suggested.

'I don't have any.' Not a brooch, not a bracelet, not a single row of pearls. Only her wedding and engagement rings. Deciding, Lillie twisted the coil of her hair once round her head, then into a loose figure-of-eight knot at the nape of her neck and tucked in the end.

'Where did I put the pins?' She took a long hairpin from the table and skewered the knot with it, then another. She examined herself in the mirror from side to side, quite pleased with the effect.

'You are going like that, Signora?' Dominique asked, troubled.

'If it stays up,' Lillie smiled. 'It'll have to do.' She rose as Dominique came to her with the dress.

'For the evening, ladies should wear a corset,' Dominique told her.

Lilllie glanced at the silhouette of her figure in the mirror. 'Well, I shan't,' she said. 'Not till I need one.'

The Sebright's townhouse in Lowndes Square was less than five minutes' drive and the cabby was sarcastic, which irritated Edward. He had accompanied Lillie only under protest and only after she had threatened again to go alone. He gave in, because it was unthinkable for a lady to go out in the evening unaccompanied by her husband, as they both knew. But also because privately he hoped for another abortive fiasco which would teach her a final lesson.

The house was more elegantly formal than Lillie had pictured it, although the main drawingroom was bright and its walls so covered with paintings, watercolours and sketches by all the modern giants, Ford Madox Brown, Holman Hunt, Millais, Burne Jones, Whistler, Woolner and others, that it gave the impression of an art gallery.

Lady Sebright greeted them effusively. She was wearing a colourful, loose evening gown, with amber beads twined in her upswept hair and more amber round her throat and wrists. 'Mr and Mrs Langtry! . . . How nice of you to come to my little party!' she enthused, and clasped Lillie's hands. 'Now, let me see – who do you know?'

'No one, I'm afraid, Lady Sebright,' Lillie smiled.

'You shall call me Olivia. We're quite informal here. My husband's around somewhere. Yes, there he is. There's John.' She beckoned to a quiet, serious man who was speaking to someone and took no notice. 'Oh, well, you'll see enough of him later.'

Lillie smiled more fully, liking her. A footman approached with a tray of champagne, which seemed to be the only thing anyone in society ever drank. Edward and she took glasses.

'There we are,' Lady Sebright said. 'Both of you just enjoy yourselves.' She was looking round as she spoke. More guests were coming up the stairs, among them a tall, athletic-figured man, strongly handsome. 'How simply wonderful!' she exclaimed. 'Will you excuse me? Make yourself at home. I'll be back in a moment.' She hurried to the head of the stairs.

Lillie had begun to relax, even Edward was smiling, and it was a shock to be left along so brusquely. Lady Sebright was welcoming the incoming guests, volatile and animated, taking them off to inspect the bronze statue of a nymph in the hall outside.

Lillie was aware of Edward stiffening. She glanced at the spacious drawingroom filled with strangers, most of them the same kind of people who had been at Lord Ranelagh's, only wearing eveningdress, the ladies in vivid satin and silk, powdered skin displaying their jewellery, the gentlemen polished and assured, all of them part of an exclusive world to which she did not belong. Now that Lady Sebright had gone, no one paid them any attention. Once again they had been shuffled off.

They were too exposed, standing alone near the door. Ignoring everyone in the room, Lillie walked calmly across to the far corner, where there was a single, highbacked chair. Edward followed her stoically and stood beside her, while she sat. Her hands were twisting in her lap. She forced herself again to sit erect and cool, hiding her bitter disappointment behind the aloof, slightly amused expression.

'Are you satisfied?' Edward murmured. 'How soon do you think we can leave?'

The broadshouldered, craggily handsome man, whom Lady Sebright had greeted so excitedly, was John Everett Millais. He looked more like a farmer or sportsman than one of England's leading artists, the man who had caused a national sensation by carrying off John Ruskin's virgin wife, Effie. He nodded, listening to Olivia Sebright. A frequent guest and a sociable man, he knew most of the people present and was trying to spot Leighton, the painter-sculptor with whom he wished to discuss the arrangements for this year's Royal Academy Summer Exhibition, when his eye was caught by someone sitting at the other end of the room, a young woman. Some people between them moved and he could see her more clearly. More than just a young woman. Much more. It was not merely her colouring, which was exquisite, the pale, almost translucent skin contrasting with the blackness of her dress, the auburn halo of hair framing the strong oval of her face. There was something remote about her, unworldly, a quality of watchful stillness that was irresistibly intriguing and challenging.

'You know everyone, I expect,' Lady Sebright remarked.

'Not quite. Who is the Grecian Goddess in the corner?'

Lillie sat perfectly still as Lady Sebright brought the tall, smiling man to her. She merely raised her head slightly, keeping the cool, detached expression.

'Mrs Langtry, may I present Mr Millais?' Lady Sebright said. 'You may have seen some of his work.'

Lillie was glad she had prepared herself not to react. Otherwise, she might have blushed or gawped like a schoolgirl. Millais . . . He had been one of the first Pre-raphaelites. She had read about him and seen his signature on so many wonderful things on her months of touring the galleries. 'At last year's Autumn Exhibition,' she replied, her voice as controlled as her features, 'I talked of nothing else for days.'

'But not to me,' Millais smiled. 'How cruel.'

There were other people in the room whom Lillie might have recognised, if she had not been deliberately avoiding looking at any one person. Millais was not the only one who had spotted her and wondered who she was. Seeing him being introduced, some of them began to move forward.

Lillie glanced to the side. 'Mr Millais – my husband, Edward.'

Edward bowed curtly, determined not to show himself up by currying favour like Lillie.

'How d'you do?' Millais said, and forgot about him, concentrating on Lillie, who was even more breathtaking closer to. That complextion was natural, the face and neck without a trace of powder. And the posture of her seated body was queenly. 'I particularly asked to meet you,' he confided, 'not only because your beauty shines like a beacon in a dark landscape, but because of the bond between us.'

'And what is that?' she wondered.

'I am of a Jersey family, myself, and frequently return there.' He saw he had caught her interest, and was gratified. 'So you see, I am your countryman. Though how, if you are the daughter of the Dean, I never met you on such a small island, I cannot conceive.'

Her smile was just visible. 'Perhaps if you had gone to church more often, you would have, Mr Millais.'

Millais and the two other gentlemen who had joined them laughed delightedly. The unknown charmer was not merely beautiful, but promisingly amusing.

On the edge of her sight, Lillie had seen a young man of about her own age take some paper and a pencil from his pocket and begin to sketch her profile. Without seeming to achnowledge him, she kept her head steady, while Millais

151

introduced the first of the other two men, bearded, round-shouldered, with a high forehead. All the time, she was forcing herself not to look at the second man who was hanging back, as she desperately wanted. Tall and ascetic, his sloping pince-nez glasses attached to his lapel by a black ribbon and perched on his unmistakable, aquiline nose. It was Henry Irving.

'This is Frederick Leighton,' Millais said. 'Mr and Mrs Langtry.'

Again Lillie was grateful for her carefully schooled poise. Many thought Leighton the greatest painter in the country, in the classical tradition, likely to be the next President of the Royal Academy. He was leaning towards her, smiling. 'You mustn't let Millais monopolise you, Mrs Langtry. Besides, he could never catch your colouring.'

'Perhaps not. But I'm going to try,' Millais announced. He had been planning a painting to illustrate a scene from Scott's novel, *The Heart of Midlothian*, in which the heroine, Effie Dean, says goodbye to her outlawed Highland lover. She had exactly the quality he wanted, tender, yearning, yet spiritual. 'May I have the honour of being the first to paint your portrait, Mrs Langtry?'

'It will be a pale likeness,' Leighton joked. 'I hope you will also sit for me?'

Lillie looked from one to the other and could not prevent herself smiling. 'Why, yes . . . The honour would be mine.' Her fuller smile entranced them for the moment it lasted.

The intense young man who had been sketchng her stepped in from the side. The paper he was holding was an envelope he had torn in half. He bowed. 'I hope you will remember that, while they were in dispute, I was the first to capture you.' He raised the torn envelope, showing his delicately lovely sketch of her.

'That's really very good,' Leighton approved, like a schoolmaster. 'Frank Miles, Mrs Langtry.'

Miles bowed again. 'And your devoted admirer.'

'Already?' Lillie smiled.

'And forever,' he vowed, handing her the sketch. 'Will you accept this as my first tribute?'

'I couldn't take it,' Lillie teased him, 'since it obviously means so much to you.'

'Ah, but you see – I've already made a copy,' he said, taking the other side of the envelope from his pocket. They laughed.

There was no other topic in the room now, except the ravishing young woman in the simple, black dress. Some of the ladies were piqued and criticised her as insipid and not by any means becomingly dressed. The men, however, could not take their eyes from her and several had clustered round Lady Sebright, demanding to be told more about her. Lady Sebright was bemused by the unprecendented success of her little discovery and frantically wished there was more she could tell them.

The most insistent was the noted, American artist, James McNeill Whistler. An arresting man in his early forties, short, wiry, with sharp, black eyes in a lined, oddly handsome face, he was holding a monocle to his right eye. 'But who is she?' he barked. 'She can't just have sprung from nowhere, like Venus from the foam?'

Irving had, at last, stepped forward. He had waited while Abraham Hayward, William Yardley, and his fellow actor-manager, the urbane Squire Bancroft, had been introduced to Lillie. He had been studying her, both as a man and as an actor, and appreciated the poise with which she had accepted a wealth of extravagant praise and compliments with dignity and quiet good humour. He was a keen observer, yet even he was deceived. He thought the poise was natural.

The others gave back out of respect as he approached and bowed. 'Since no one is going to present me, I must do it myself,' he said, in the unique, staccato voice she remembered so well. His manner, as always, was scholarly and courteous.

Her heart was pounding. An hour ago, to have seen him even pass in the street would have thrilled her immeasurably. She was not certain she could speak and inclined her head slowly to give herself a second or two longer. 'You need no introduction, Mr Irving,' she said, levelly. 'My husband – ' Irving bowed to Edward and his piercing eyes swung back to her. 'We saw you recently in "Hamlet" at the Lyceum.'

That's it!, Millais thought. That's where I've seen that effect before, the motionless black figure among all the gaudy dresses.

'Were you impressed?' Frank Miles laughed.

'. . . Beyond words.'

'I am flattered,' Irving smiled. 'Hamlet is a role which every actor wishes to attempt.'

'I had never seen it before,' she confessed. 'In fact, it was the first time I had been to a theatre. So you are, and will be, my only Hamlet.'

There was the faintest gasp of admiration round them at the gracefulness of the compliment.

Irving seemed tense. 'You make me aware of a great responsibility, Mrs Langtry,' he said quietly, and paused. 'I trust you will allow me to assist your theatrical education, by being my guest at the Lyceum, whenever you choose.'

In the hush that followed, Bancroft said quickly, 'You're more than welcome to come to the Haymarket, too.'

But he was robbed of his laugh, when Whistler pushed his way aggressively through the group that had formed round her and demanded, 'When they say you're from Jersey, do they mean New Jersey? Are you a countrywoman of mine?'

'No, of mine, Whistler! You can't claim her,' Millais told him. 'James Whistler.'

'James McNeill Whistler,' Whistler corrected. He had not stopped looking at Lillie. 'You're going to sit for me, aren't you?'

There was a chorus of protests. Lillie was intrigued by this abrupt, little man with his curly, shining black hair, except for one snow-white lock that fell over his forehead, wearing a flowing tie, frockcoat, checked trousers and yellow spats over his shoes, instead of evening dress. 'I've already promised these gentlemen,' she said.

'That's what they are – gentlemen,' he scoffed. 'You need someone who can see beyond the classic features to the eternal woman.'

'Which you can?' Leighton asked, drily.

'Now that you mention it.' They laughed, but Whistler was not entirely joking. 'I'll call on you, Mrs Langtry, if I may – when we won't be interrupted by this rabble.'

Lillie responded to the twinkling friendliness of his eyes, which contradicted his fierce expression, and smiled to him, through the amused protests which had broken out again.

The group was parting for Lady Sebright, who had a wedge of other men behind her. 'Lots of other people want to meet you, my dear,' she announced to Lillie, 'but it will have to be after supper. We're going in now.' She glanced round, wickedly. 'Who's going to escort Mrs Langtry?'

There was a profound silence as Lilie rose. Edward stepped forward.

'No, no.' Lady Sebright waved a hand. 'Not husbands.'

'May I?' Frank Miles asked swiftly.

'If I might have the honour?' Irving echoed him.

'Let her choose,' Whistler rasped, crooking his arm for her.

Lillie looked round at the gentlemen, who all waited hopefully, eager for her decision. Which arm was she to take?

'Can't have that,' Millais declared, helping her out. 'She's to sit for me first and I'm her countryman. So I claim the privilege.'

Lillie smiled to him and laid her hand on his arm as he held it out. He led her through the group and across the room towards the door. Lady Sebright followed next on Irving's arm and the others, stimulated and lighthearted, collected their ladies quickly and fell in behind, like a triumphal procession.

Disgruntled and overlooked, Edward brought up the rear

# CHAPTER SIX

It was like a dream. When she wakened in the morning, she was half afraid it *had* been a dream, but there was the little sketch of her on the envelope. And later, a letter from Millais was delivered by hand, requesting her formally to sit for him and inviting Edward and her to lunch.

She had been too tired to tell Dominique, when she got home, but as she described the evening over breakfast, her maid's eyes grew as round as new pennies. And it was true. It was all true. First four or five, then a dozen, then twenty or thirty men, all of them wellknown, some famous, they had all gathered round her, admiring her, asking her opinion on everything from poetry to spiritualism, laughing, scoring off one another and showing off for her benefit, just like the young men at the promenade concerts and the Garrison Balls in Jersey. For a time, they had even seemed to be testing her by mentioning all sorts of obscure subjects, but she had read and listened and thought so much that she was never once caught out.

The only part she had not liked was when they had left the gentlemen to their brandy and cigars after dinner. Alone with the ladies in the drawingroom, she had been made to feel uncomfortable. Many of them had been openly disapproving, except for Olivia Sebright and Lady Wharncliffe, a tall, forthright woman, who had told her the rest were only jealous. Then the gentlemen had cut short their drinks and come to join them. It was only because they missed her, they swore, as they crowded round her and it had all begun again. 'I shall never forget it,' she vowed.

'Neither shall I,' Edward grunted sourly. 'Can't understand why everyone made such a fuss of you.' He had not enjoyed people looking right through him, while they laughed and marvelled at every trivial thing Lillie said. He knew it would be weeks, if not months, before she got over it.

When they returned from their walk that afternoon, Mrs Jennings was waiting for them. She was agitated, holding a bundle of cards, letters and printed invitations which had arrived for them. A stream of gentlemen, footmen and messengers had been delivering them ever since they went out. Even as they hurried up the stairs to their apartment, the bell rang again.

When Edward and she began reading through the invitations, she tore open the envelopes, exclaiming at each one. They had been asked to lunches, dinners, receptions, visits to the Opera, garden parties . . . 'Look . . . Look!' she said. 'Lady Wharncliffe – Mr Leighton – Mr Whistler.' She paused. 'Lord and Lady Manners? . . .' Sorting quickly through the cards, Lillie discovered that some were from people she had not met, but who had already heard of her astonishing success at the Sebrights'.

She was kneeling by the sofa with the cards and letters spread out along it. Bending over them, Edward was bewildered. 'Dinner – ball – dinner – ' he read. 'It would take us months to get through all these. What are we going to do?'

'Accept them.'

'Which ones?'

'All of them – even if it means being in three places at once!' she laughed.

'What do you mean, "all of them"?' Edward demanded. 'How can we accept thirty-seven invitations from people we don't even know?'

She swept them into a pile and rose, carrying them across to the writing table. 'Quite simply,' she told him. 'We write to say thank you very much, we'd love to come.'

'Don't try to be clever with me!' he spluttered. Much of his irritation came from the feeling he was being rushed. 'I mean – hang it, we have to discuss this! Some of these people are the cream of society. Why have they asked us?'

'Does it matter? They've heard about us and want to meet us.'

'Yes, but don't you see? There's been some mistake. We

won't – we won't fit in.'

'Perhaps there has been a mistake,' she said quietly. 'They may be as disappointed in us, as we in them. But I don't intend to slip back into the crowd, until I find out.'

She was so positive, so completely determined that he was silenced. He watched her as she sat at the table, beginning to sort out the invitations into dates. 'So your mind's made up,' he muttered, lamely. 'We're to accept hospitality from strangers.' She did not react. 'When we arrive, they won't even know who we are!'

'I've thought of that. I'll accept the invitations from people we met at Lady Sebright's first. Tomorrow we've been asked to dinner at the Wharncliffes'.'

'Tomorrow!' he protested. 'And they just expect us not to be doing anything?'

She looked at him. 'Are we?'

'. . . No,' he admitted. If she had laughed, he honestly believed he would have hit her.

Lillie wrote a short note of acceptance to Lady Wharncliffe, but did not know where to send it. All she knew was that the Wharncliffes lived in Curzon Street. In the morning, she walked with Dominique to Mayfair, where a policeman directed her to a long, low house like a country mansion set back in its own garden, Wharncliffe House. She waited out of sight, while Dominique delivered her note. It was an odd feeling to think that in a matter of hours she would be entering that house as a guest.

When Dominique rejoined her, they went through an arched alleyway into the jumble of small streets of Shepherd's Market where the ancient May Fair used to be held. Once notorious for its gambling dens and brothels, it was now outwardly more respectable, with a quaintly eighteenth century air. Dominique paused outside a stationer's shop, looking through the little panes of the window at a collection of prints and photographs, framed and unframed, all sizes. They were all of royalty and society beauties and Dominique had joined the craze for collecting them. 'Look, Signora,' she said. 'The Duchess of Manchester, Mrs Wheeler – Mrs Cornwallis West – Lady

Dudley.' Lillie nodded and moved on. It was not an area in which unaccompanied women should linger. 'Signora!' Dominique exclaimed, and she looked back, surprised by the urgency in her maid's voice.

Dominique was staring at a corner of the window. In the corner was a row of four or five small prints of the profile sketch of Lillie. It seemed incredible. Her mind racing, she gave Dominique a shilling to go in and buy one of the unframed prints. She could not even remember the name of the artist. Was it Wyles or Miles? She would not discuss it, until they were home and she unwrapped the print and saw it was nearly identical to the one on the torn envelope.

'I'm so proud of you, Signora!' Dominique told her, her eyes shining. 'It's wonderful! You have only been to one party – and already you are a P.B.'

'A what?' Lillie laughed.

'A Professional Beauty. Like Mrs Wheeler and Lady Dudley and Lady Randolph Churchill. Ladies of society whose only profession is beauty.' It was beneath these ladies to charge a fee. They posed merely to gratify the public's passion for collecting their photographs, nine or ten of them becoming the idols of millions who had never actually seen them. 'And people will buy this one of you,' Dominique sniffed. 'I'm so proud.'

Lillie was touched and excited. But also worried at what Ned would say.

There was a knock at the door outside and Dominique hurried out to answer it. Lillie took off her little, black bonnet and smoothed her hair. As she looked at the sketch and print, she posed subconsciously, raising her chin.

Dominique hurried back in, flustered. 'Signora – he is here to see you. The artist, Mr Miles.'

Quickly, Lillie took off her coat. Under it, she was wearing the long-sleeved black dress, with the white lace collar sewn again round the neck. 'See if Mr Langtry is at home.' she ordered. 'If he is, call him in four or five minutes. But show Mr Miles in first. Give me a moment,' Throwing Dominique her coat to take out with her, she slid the print under the envelopes on the table, chose an armchair near the window and sat, her face partly turned so that the sunlight caught her profile.

As she composed herself, Dominique showed in the young, fair, goodlooking artist. He wore casual day clothes and a flowing tie, and carried a cane and a wide-brimmed hat. Catching sight of Lillie, he stopped short. 'Mr Miles, Signora,' Dominique announced and left them. Lillie turned her head slowly and smiled.

'Signora . . .' Miles breathed. 'What a perfect way to address you! Sitting there with the light turning your hair into a golden halo, you are the image of a Raphael Madonna.'

'Compliments already, Mr Miles?' Lillie smiled. 'When you have not yet even said good day.'

'A good day? . . . It is a glorious, a sublime day! But till this moment, it has been grey and empty.'

'Please – ' Lillie protested gently.

'No, I must tell you!' he insisted. 'For two nights I have hardly slept. The first I spent drawing and sketching you from memory. Then all yesterday I ran from one to the other, saying "Tell me – is this not the most beautiful vision you have ever seen?" All agreed, but some said, "Yes, she is a vision. You could only have imagined her." So last night, the black thought came – was it true? Had I invented you? And today I couldn't rest until I had seen you again. Yet I was afraid.'

'Of having your illusions shattered.'

'How was I to know the reality would far transcend the vision?'

Lillie inclined her head. 'That is a very pretty compliment, Mr Miles.'

'A simple statement of fact. You see?' He held out his right hand. 'How I am trembling? I can scracely control myself.'

'Oh, I sincerely hope you will,' Lillie said demurely. 'My husband will be here any moment.'

Miles laughed boyishly. 'You need have no fear, Mrs Langtry. I shall observe the proprieties.' He sat on the sofa and laid his hat and cane on the floor beside him. Lillie had learnt the custom in London. If a male guest was invited, he handed over his hat, gloves and cane at the door. If uninvited, he laid them on the floor beside his chair, to show that he did not presume to stay long. When she laughed, Miles jumped up, taking a flat package wrapped in tissue paper from his inside coat pocket. 'Forgive me – I had forgotten my excuse for calling. To ask you to accept this.'

Lillie unwrapped the package to find a copy of the print drawing she had bought, although this one was signed. She could see him waiting anxiously for her verdict. 'It is very flattering, Mr Miles.'

'Oh, no – much less beautiful than the original.'

'You really should not pay me such compliments,' she told him. 'I am not used to them.'

'Then you will become so,' he smiled. 'The first person I showed this to was a friend of mine, just down from Oxford. He said, it made him understand at last how Helen's beauty could have caused the Trojan War.'

Lillie laughed. 'He sounds as much of a poet as you.'

'Oh, more, much more,' he assured her. 'He is a real poet. You must meet him. Yet he is practical, too. It was he who advised me to take this sketch straight to my printers. And they rushed out five hundred copies immediately.'

'Why so many?'

'For the shops,' he explained. 'They'll be kicking themselves. They're almost sold out already. That's another reason I am here – to ask if you will pose for me properly, as soon as possible. In a few days, people will be clamouring for any picture of you they can get. I want to be ready – and I want mine to be the best.'

Lillie had promised to pose first for Millais, but that was for a portrait which would take some time to complete. Sketches like this would take almost no time and might be the answer to another problem. 'How can people "clamour" for any picture of me,' she asked carefully, 'if they do not know who I am?'

Miles followed her thought and smiled. 'How very true, Mrs Langtry. I shall make sure that your name is on every print of mine that is sold. Then you will sit for me?'

'You must first ask my husband.' She had rewrapped the print in its tissue paper and handed it back. 'In fact, it might be as well to give this to *him*.'

How very astute she is, Miles thought. Beautiful enough to set pulses dancing, yet so cool and balanced. The body was superb. So superb he had to force himself not to think of it or his thoughts would be bound to show. Her husband was coming in. Medium height, round faced with a fairly long nose, goodlooking really. A full moustache hiding a rather weak mouth. Superior expression. Miles had only the haziest memory of him from the Sebrights'. 'Yes. Yes, I remember. How d'you do?' he was saying.

Miles shook hands with him. 'I hope you'll forgive the intrusion, but I wondered if you, and Mrs Langtry, would care to visit my studio.'

'Studio?'

'On the corner of Salisbury Street, just off the Strand. It's quite informal. People just drop in.'

'We'd love to, wouldn't we, Edward?' Lillie prompted.

'Most kind,' Edward nodded. 'We must arrange that.'

'By the way,' Miles said, 'I wonder if I could ask you to accept this, Mr Langtry?'

Edward unwrapped the print and looked at it in some puzzlement. 'I say . . .' he observed at last, 'that's a bit like Lillie.'

Miles controlled himself and smiled. Now he knew why he had had difficulty in remembering him.

Edward did not really care for Frank Miles. He was not like Millais, not even a real painter, and he was a sight too pushy. Still, he had filled them in on the Wharncliffes. The family had apparently been pretty impoverished, then coal had been discovered on their estate in Yorkshire and Wharncliffe had slaved for years, building up a private industry. Now he was worth a fortune and he and his wife were great patrons of art and artists. Edward resigned himself to another evening of artistic twaddle. But, at least, dinner should be good and, according to Miles, they had some of the best trout fishing in England on their place in Yorkshire.

Edward was trying to see himself in the mirror on the dressingtable, as he tied his white tie. Lillie was sitting at the table, her arms and shoulders bare, in a white camisole top and underskirts. Her arms were raised, repinning the figure of eight knot at the nape of her neck and he had to dodge from side to side. 'This Miles fellow. It's all a bit rum, isn't it?' he said. 'D'you know, I've a shrewd idea he only invited us to his studio so he could do some more sketches of you.'

Lillie smiled to him in the mirror. 'Really?'

'Transparent!' he snorted. 'Well, he needn't think he's hoodwinked me. If he tries sending a bill in, he'll get a nasty surprise.'

Lillie began to tease into place the little curls that lowered her forehead. 'Oh, I don't think it's money he wants,' she murmured.

'Well, I don't think we should encourage him,' Edward said. He put on his tailcoat. 'That's me ready. How do I look?'

'Very . . . debonair,' she told him.

He tugged down the points of his white waistcoat, pleased. 'You're not going to be long, are you? I hate waiting about.'

As he made for the door, he heard Lillie say, 'I shan't be long. After all, I don't have to worry about which dress to wear.'

He swung round, bridling at once. 'You have a perfectly adequate evening gown!'

'It is three years out of date.'

'Well, I can't afford to keep buying you clothes,' he told her stiffly. 'If you feel you are not dressed grandly enough for your new friends, then I am quite happy to stay at home.'

'I'm not going to quarrel with you, Ned,' she said quietly. 'I don't intend to miss this evening.' Before he could reply, there was a knock at the door and Dominique came in. Lillie turned back to the mirror. 'I'll be ready in ten minutes.'

Dominique bobbed nervously as Edward stalked out past

163

her. She had brought the black dress. She had carefully removed the collar from it and pressed the neck. 'It is done, Signora,' she said, holding it up for Lillie to examine. 'But it is a pity you have to wear it again. Ladies of Society appear in a different dress at every party.'

'Well, I shan't,' Lillie said. 'I'll wear the same one.'

'All the time? But if we keep taking the collar off and sewing it on again, it is bound to leave marks.'

Lillie had been considering it critically. 'Yes. I want to cut down the neckline, anyway. It still looks too like an afternoon dress. We can leave three or four tabs to sew the collar to. For tonight, I'll just fold the neck down and pin it.'

'Lower, Signora?' Dominique objected, shocked. 'It will show the camisole.'

'That's quite simple,' Lillie smiled. 'I shan't wear one.' She slipped off the ribbon shoulder straps of her camisole and rose, beginning to unfasten its little pearl buttons.

Among the elaborately and colourfully gowned ladies in the great drawingroom of Wharncliffe House, the provocative simplicity of the long sleeved, figure-hugging black dress, its neckline lowered to reveal even more of her shoulders and deep bust, again made Lillie conspicuous. Some people had heard of her debut at Olivia Sebright's and were keen to see her. They were not disappointed. Again she was quickly surrounded by an admiring group of men, drawn by her faintly enigmatic, faintly challenging smile to outdo one another for her approval. Again Edward found himself standing to the side behind her, largely ignored.

Lord Wharncliffe, a tall, expansive man, was amused by the effect she had on Edward Poynter. Poynter, full-bearded, a serious Academician in his forties, was famous for the meticulous draughtmanship of his paintings of historical and classical subjects. Normally restrained, even grave, in public, he was showing all the enthusiasm of a rackety art student, striking himself over the heart with his clenched fist, when he heard Lillie had arranged to pose for Millais. 'It is a plot,' he declared. 'A plot! He knew I was looking for someone exactly like you. I've been searching everywhere.'

'Only one thing for it, then, Mrs Langtry,' Wharncliffe suggested. 'You'll have to agree to sit for Poynter, too.'

'But I have already promised Frederick Leighton and Frank Miles,' she told them.

'Then I am fourth in line? . . .' Poynter gasped. 'This is too much!' The others laughed at his mock tragic face. Edward smiled stiffly. It was all going rather too far, he felt.

Many of the ladies watching were not amused, either, Lady Wharncliffe noticed. She was more than pleased at the effect her new guest was creating. Every leading hostess vied with the others in providing sensations at their parties, inviting royalty or eminent men of letters, engaging the foremost singers and musicians. None of these had been invited to this routine dinner party so early in the season, but the unknown Mrs Langtry was turning it into an event that would be talked about. She had asked two of the reigning Professional Beauties, too, and they were virtually ignored.

One of them, the petite, enchanting Mary Cornwallis West, known as Patsy, was with Lady Wharncliffe observing the knot of men round Lillie. Twenty-five, with her light chestnut hair worn short and close to the head in a style all her own, she was vivacious and highspirited. Lady Wharncliffe, by contrast, was older, with a commanding presence, nearly as tall as her tall husband, her hair unashamedly dyed golden blonde and her face brightly made up. They were joined by a striking man in his late twenties, with intense, bulging eyes and a full, handlebar moustache, Lord Randolph Churchill.

He was disappointed that Lady Wharncliffe could only tell him Lillie's name and that she came from one of the Channel Islands. 'But where's she been hiding?' he demanded. 'Do you know her, Patsy?'

'No, but James Whistler came to tea today,' Patsy told him, with a charming trace of an Irish brogue. 'He was full of her – barking on in that Yankee way of his about flesh tones of cream and amber.'

Churchill's mouth twitched. 'Do I detect a touch of the

green-eyed monster?'

'Well, it's no fun to have one of your admirers raving on for two hours about someone else,' Patsy confessed. 'How do you think Jennie would like it?'

Lady Wharncliffe had a sudden picture of Jennie, with her raven hair and black, sloe eyes. 'Lady Churchill would not appreciate it, I'm sure,' she said. Churchill chuckled, shaking his head. 'But in spite of all the artists being after her,' she went on, 'it doesn't seem to have turned Mrs Langtry's head. I'd say she was fairly modest and intelligent, with enough of a sense of humour not to take it too seriously.'

'What a pity,' Patsy sighed. 'Just when I was all prepared to detest her.'

One of the men round Lillie had asked her how she had spent her time, since coming to London. 'Well, my husband and I have done a great deal of sightseeing.' Edward nodded and coughed in agreement.

'Have you been to the Academy in your sightseeing?' Poynter asked.

Lillie smiled. 'You mean, did I see your painting, *Atalanta*, in the Exhibition? Yes, I did, Mr Poynter.'

Poynter looked an apology as the others laughed. 'And?'

'The proportions worried me at first,' she admitted. 'But then I was struck by the tension between the desperately running man and the stooping figure of the girl, eager to win the race, yet fascinated by the golden apple.'

'But that's exactly what I was trying to convey!' Poynter exclaimed. 'And what the critics did not see.' He looked round the group and back to Lillie, with a new respect.

Lillie made to rise, when Lady Wharncliffe came to them with Patsy West. Lady Wharncliffe waved to her. 'No, no, my dear. It is the gentlemen I want to send packing.' She laughed, as the gentlemen protested. 'Shame on you. I haven't had more than a few words with Mrs Langtry since she arrived. Now go and make yourselves agreeable to the other ladies for a while. Mrs Langtry will still be here after dinner.'

'We are half afraid she will vanish again,' Poynter said,

as suddenly as she appeared.' He and the others bowed to Lady Wharncliffe and Lillie and left reluctantly to circulate.

A tall, very slender woman had joined Lord Randolph Churchill. Her head was quite small, her features clearly marked and delicate. She was the second of the PBs who had been invited that evening and she was clearly annoyed, when Churchill bowed and left her alone. Lady Wharncliffe stopped her husband. 'Take Mrs Langtry to meet Mrs Wheeler, will you, my dear? She's not used to being ignored. She looks rather cross.'

'I daresay,' Wharncliffe murmured, then tapped Edward's arm. 'Come along, Mr Langtry. Let me introduce you to some of the others.' Edward stiffened with embarrassment as his host led him across the room.

Lillie had recognised Patsy at once from Dominique's pictures of her, when Lady Wharncliffe introduced them. 'Thank you for coming to rescue me,' she said.

'You looked as if you were enjoying it,' Patsy observed.

'One must,' Lillie said. 'When gentlemen are trying so hard to be amusing, one must at least look interested.'

Patsy laughed. 'How lightly she throws away a secret that has made some women enchantresses – from the beginning of time.'

Lord Randolph had hurried to catch Edward Poynter alone. 'What do you think of her?' he asked.

'Perfection,' Poynter said. 'And as intelligent as she is beautiful.'

'Intelligence in a woman being, of course, a relative matter.'

Poynter's eyebrows rose. 'I'd say she's as perceptive as any man I've ever met.'

'With a body of a young Amazon,' Churchill breathed. Lillie had risen to speak to Patsy and he watched her turn, laughing. 'Intriguing. Look how she moves.'

Poynter nodded. 'Her figure is exquisite.'

'Which that dress is designed to reveal. I'd be prepared to bet there's nothing much under it except Mrs Langtry.'

'I don't think I'd take you up on it, Lord Randolph,'

Poynter smiled. 'Besides, how is it to be proved?'

'Fortunate, indeed, the man who could . . .' Churchill did not take his eyes from her.

Lillie watched, fascinated, as Lady Wharncliffe took a cigarette from an ivory box on the table and lit it from a match held by a footman. She had never seen a lady smoke before and tried not to look shocked.

'It's my vice,' Lady Wharncliffe said. 'My one little vice.'

'Half the ladies in London might wish that was all they had to reproach themselves with,' Patsy commented.

'As usual, Patsy speaks for herself,' Lady Wharncliffe told Lillie, and they laughed. 'I must tell you, Edward Poynter is doing a series of panels on Greek mythology, for the hall in our place at Wortley, near Sheffield. What's holding him up is finding the right models.'

'He hasn't asked me,' Patsy complained.

'It's not Irish mythology,' Lady Wharncliffe said drily. 'You look about as Grecian as the Blarney Stone.' Patsy chuckled. 'Would you consider modelling for one, Mrs Langtry?' When Lillie said she would be honoured, Lady Wharncliffe summoned Poynter back and told him she had done his work for him.

'I am – I am overwhelmed,' he stammered, gratefully.

'What do you see her as?' Patsy asked.

'Nausicaa,' Poynter said instantly. 'The island princess who enraptured the wandering King, Ulysses.'

'Well, now . . . Is he being fanciful – or prophetic?' Lady Wharncliffe whispered to Patsy. Lillie heard and saw them smile as if they shared a secret, but did not understand.

'I'd like to start as soon as possible,' Poynter was saying.

'We can arrange it all later,' Lady Wharncliffe said. She had seen her butler come in and stand by the doors. 'I think we can go in to dinner. You're promised to my husband I believe, Patsy.' She beckoned to Churchill, who was hovering near them. 'Mrs Langtry, may I present Lord Randolph Churchill?'

Churchill advanced and bowed. 'This is a moment I have been waiting for.'

Lillie's mind went blank. She had read of Lord Randolph

as a fiery young Member of Parliament, a younger son of the Duke of Marlborough and married to the lovely American heiress, Jennie Jerome. A dedicated Tory Democrat in the tradition of his party leader, Disraeli, she had read reports of many of his speeches. He and his wife were close friends of the young Prince and Princess of Wales, members of the Marlborough House set. If there was any woman she envied, apart from Lady Dudley, it was Jennie Churchill for being married to a man with such an exciting future. She smiled her half smile and inclined her head.

'Well, I suggest you take Mrs Langtry in, Randolph,' Lady Wharncliffe said.

Lillie felt herself flushing, when Churchill assured her he would be honoured and offered her his arm. Lady Wharncliffe signed to her butler and two footmen opened the doors to the diningroom.

Edward was standing alone by a side table. All he had got from the lovely Mrs Wheeler was an icy 'How do you do?,' then she had drifted away. Seeing the movement towards the diningroom begin, he gulped down his sherry and looked round for Lillie. He was just in time to see her on Lord Randolph Churchill's arm, following Lord Wharncliffe and Patsy West out.

The first invitation he really enjoyed was when Lillie and he had lunch with Millais and his Scots wife, Effie, on Sunday. Their large, new house at Palace Gate, Kensington, was roomy and elegant, without being overpowering. Effie was pretty and charming and Millais, himself, turned out to be an expert salmon fisher. Broadshouldered, ruddy complexioned, wearing a belted, tweed jacket, he looked more like a country squire than a distinguished artist. By the time they moved to his first floor studio for coffee, they wre all relaxed and as friendly as could be.

Millais was amused by Edward Poynter's reaction to Lillie. The evening had been another success for her and resulted in another flood of invitations. 'And you were seated next to Randolph Churchill?' he nodded. 'What did you talk about?'

'I didn't,' Lillie said. 'I let *him* talk.'

Millais laughed. 'Very wise. Well, what did *he* talk about?'

'Education – the Irish Question – Mr Disraeli moving to the House of Lords. Relations with America, mostly.'

'That's something he should know about,' Effie smiled.

Millais saw that Edward was puzzled, when they laughed. 'He has quite a few relations in America,' he explained. 'Through his wife.'

'She wasn't there?' Effie asked.

'Unfortunately, no, Mrs Millais,' Lillie said.

'Please, call me Effie.'

Lillie smiled to her. There was a genuine warmth about Effie and her husband that appealed to her. She saw that even Ned was responding. She had not seen him so relaxed before in company.

'His wife is very beautiful,' Millais was saying. 'Quite a different kind of beauty from you island girls, with your warm clear skin and summer colouring. But I think I prefer the island girls.' He chuckled. 'You obviously agree, Mr Langtry.'

It was an opening to lead Edward back into the conversation and also an opportunity for him to repay Effie's compliment by suggesting Millais used first names. They waited to give him the chance. 'Oh, yes. Yes,' he nodded. 'My first wife was from the Channel Islands, too. I wish you could have seen her. She was *really* beautiful.'

Millais felt a surge of impatience at the man's boring smugness and noticed Lillie look away in pretended indifference to a remark that had obviously become hurtful through repetition. 'Effie,' he suggested, rising, 'perhaps you'd like to show Mr Langtry the garden, while my model and I make a start.'

Effie smiled and rose. Edward hesitated, not certain about the propriety of all this. 'Come along, then,' Effie said to him. 'Don't worry about Johnnie. He won't bite,' Edward rose selfconsciously as Millais and Lillie laughed. 'We'll see them again at tea,' Effie told him. She took his arm and led him out.

Millais advanced until he was standing over Lillie. 'At

last, we are alone,' he intoned, dramatically. When she smiled, he gave her his hand. 'Up,' he ordered. 'Up and let me look at you.' He led her to the posing dais under the huge windows that bathed it in light. She stepped up and turned, uncertain, aware of him watching her.

There was a throne-like wooden chair at the rear of the dais. 'Would you like me to sit?' she asked.

His eyes were intent on her. 'No, just stand there. And try to relax.'

'I am,' she assured him.

'No, you're not.' He took his unlit pipe from his pocket and sucked on it. 'You give the impression of being poised and cool, very sure of yourself and the world. But inside you're as uncertain as a lost child and scared as a cat.'

She gazed at him, for a moment almost angry. But he was right. 'You are very perceptive,' she said.

Millais shrugged. 'I am a painter.' He moved back to his large, revolving easel and swung it round to show her the sketch outline he had already made of the young man representing her kilted, outlaw lover. The figure of Effie Dean was suggested by an arrangement of lines, triangles and ovals. She was leaning over a style, saying goodbye, he explained. 'We'll turn the chair and you can kneel on that, leaning over the back.'

When he finished for the day and the Langtrys had gone, he was amazed at how much he had achieved. The whole basic shape was there. He had only changed one of his original thoughts. He had meant to show Effie Dean partly in profile, looking sadly down, but that would have been a waste of his new model. He had caught Lillie full face, her lips lightly parted, her eyes raised beseechingly to her faithless lover. 'She is a marvel,' he told his wife. 'A marvel.'

Effie, who was named after Effie Dean, had been his first choice as a model, but the scandal they had lived through made the subject too delicate. 'So you are pleased with her,' she said.

'Pleased? She is quite simply the most beautiful woman I have ever seen.'

'Should I be jealous?' Effie teased.

171

Millais kissed her. 'Of course, not, my dearest.' Then he added, 'But don't trust me, if I'm ever left alone on a desert island with her.'

The next morning, Dominique was almost speechless, when she opened the door to one of her idols, Mrs Cornwallis West.

Patsy looked delicious in a pale blue afternoon dress and hat, carrying a blue parasol. She swept into the drawing-room at Eaton Place, smiling at Lillie's surprise. 'I hope you don't mind my dropping in?' she said. 'But since we're such near neighbours – We're at Number 49. Just down the street.'

Lillie really was surprised to see her, and pleased. 'How nice.'

'That's what I thought,' Patsy laughed. 'What a relief to have a kindred spirit within walking distance.'

'Yes,' Lillie agreed. Patsy was her first visitor. It was exciting, almost worth it just to have seen Dominique's pride as she announced her. 'Do sit down.'

'Thank you.' Patsy sat and leant her parasol against the side of her chair. 'Though don't be surprised, if I bob up again. I can never sit still for two minutes together. My husband says I'm first cousin to a Mexican jumping bean.' Lillie smiled. 'I tell him he's descended from a long line of turnips.'

They laughed. Lillie remembered her husband at the Wharncliffes', a physically large, but gentle and reserved man, at least twenty years older than his wife. 'Colonel Cornwallis West is very distinguished,' she said.

'So much so,' Patsy agreed, 'there are times I could hit him, if I didn't get out of the house. Though I'll confess, it's as much to get away from the children.'

'Are they very demanding, Mrs West?' Lillie asked.

Patsy broke in. 'No, please call me Patsy. I was christened Mary Adelaide Virginia Thomasina Eupatoria Fitzpatrick. But all my friends – and I'm sure you're going to be one – call me Patsy. Can you wonder?'

Lillie smiled. 'I am Emilie Charlotte – known as Lillie.'

'Much better,' Patsy nodded, and rose, looking round.

172

'Are you comfortable here? These houses are so small and dark.'

'We only have this floor,' Lillie explained.

'Very sensible. But then, you don't have children to clutter the place up. It's not so bad at our house in the country, Ruthin. It's an old castle, so they can go and get lost in the dungeons.'

'How many do you have?' Lillie asked.

'Three – two girls and a boy. And that's quite enough. I made sure I had them all before I was twenty-one, so they wouldn't muck up the rest of my life.' Patsy, from an old Irish family, had married at sixteen and a half and produced three children in the next five years. The boy, heir to the family name, came last or she would have stopped sooner. And he arrived a month early, after she had chased the gardener all round the grounds with a hose, when she was eight months pregnant.

'Will you bring them round one day?' Lillie invited her.

'No, you can come and see them in their nursery,' Patsy said. 'I never take out more than one of them at any one time. Well, I don't want to go round looking like a fertility symbol.' She laughed with Lillie, then said casually, 'You seemed to be getting on well with Lord Randolph the other night. Did he say how Jennie was?'

'No. Only that they'd enjoyed their trip to America – and that she was staying with his parents in Dublin.'

'. . . Yes,' Patsy nodded. 'They'll stay there for a while, I expect.'

Lillie was intrigued. Patsy had evidently been fishing for something, but before she could phrase a question, Dominique knocked and came in. She bobbed excitedly and handed Lillie a visiting card. 'There's a gentleman to see you, Signora. A photographer gentleman.' It was almost too much for Dominique. She had barely recovered from meeting Patsy.

'Which one is it?' Patsy asked.

Lillie read the card. 'Alfred Ellis.'

'Oh, he's very good. He's take some of me.'

'Ask him to wait a moment, Dominique,' Lillie said. Her

173

maid hurried out.

Patsy was smiling. 'Which of the others have been after you?' She seemed surprised when Lillie told her this was the first. 'Oh, they'll be here. Every new face brings them round like flies round a honeypot.'

'You don't mind?'

'Other ladies being photographed?' Patsy laughed. 'Not a bit. Mind you, there's some – Mrs Luke Wheeler, now. She can't stand competition. And Georgiana Dudley don't much like it, either. But I say, the more the merrier. There aren't enough PBs to go round all the different functions as it is. And no party can be a success without one or two.'

'But what's the point of it?' Lillie wondered.

'Does it have to have one?' Patsy replied. 'It gives a lot of pleasure to a lot of people. And being a Professional Beauty means your life is never dull.'

'I suppose not.'

'Of course, it's all very silly – but it's nice to be well known. Everyone makes a great fuss of you. Don't tell me you wouldn't like that?'

After a moment, Lillie smiled. Patsy and she really were kindred spirits.

Patsy had noticed the assorted piles of letters and cards on the table. She moved to look at them. 'Are these your invitations?'

'I should have cleared them away,' Lillie said, embarrassed.

'No, no,' Patsy murmured, reading the ones on top. 'The Harwickes' Ball . . . Are you going?'

'Yes.'

'Good. I'll see you there. Mr and Mrs C. J. Freake . . .' Patsy made a face. 'At least, they have one of the best cooks in London.'

'My husband thinks I'm mad to have accepted so many,' Lillie confessed.

'Oh, this is only the beginning,' Patsy told her. 'The season's just starting.' She saw that Lillie was perturbed. 'What's the matter?'

Lillie hesitated. 'How are we – ? Frankly, we are not in a

position to pay back all this hospitality.'

'That's one of the best things about being a PB,' Patsy confided. 'You're not expected to. And that's the answer for your husband. You get the best of everything, and no obligations. Now, I'm forgetting why I called. Are you going to Lady Wharncliffe's this afternoon?'

'I haven't been asked,' Lillie said.

'Anyone just drops in for tea,' Patsy explained. 'It's a way of saying thank you for the other night. I'll be there.'

Lillie wanted to meet Patsy again, and Lady Wharncliffe. They had not yet settled when she was to pose for Edward Poynter. There had even been some talk of Ned and herself being invited to the Wharncliffe's house in Yorkshire. That would be exciting. 'I'd love to come,' she frowned. 'But I've promised to visit Frank Miles' studio.'

'Come along after,' Patsy said. She was partly turned away. 'I'm going to call on . . . a friend. So if anyone asks, the two of us spent the day together.' She looked at Lillie. 'All right?'

Lillie paused only for a second. 'All right,' she agreed.

'Fine,' Patsy smiled. 'Do the same for you one day. Now, that poor man's waiting for you. I'll be off.' She headed for the door and paused. 'Till later, then, Lillie.'

Lillie opened the door. 'Till later . . . Patsy.'

Patsy ran back to pick up her parasol, laughed and was gone.

Lillie moved towards the table with its piles of invitations. 'Only the beginning.' She was pleased at the start towards a friendship with Patsy, although she realised she was to an extent being used. But that, itself, showed trust. It was a glimpse of a wholly different attitude to convention and morality, that she had already suspected. She absorbed from everyone she met, and she could learn from Patsy, merely by letting her burble on. Dominique had told her the gossip columns described Patsy as a favourite of the Prince of Wales. Even closer than a favourite.

She had almost completely forgotten the photographer, until Dominique showed him in, a short, tubby man with an ingratiating smile. 'Mr Ellis, Signora,' Dominique said,

175

proudly.

He stepped forward. 'Most kind of you to see me, Mrs Langtry,' he bowed. 'My attention has been drawn to a likeness of you by Mr Frank Miles. I wonder it you would consider sitting for a photographic portrait?'

Miles lived on the corner of Salisbury Street, between the Strand and the River Thames. It was a rambling house full of beams and leaded windows, with high, pointed gables, so old it might be Jacobean. Lillie found it quite easily. There was no reply at the front door, which was latched open. She went in and made her way up the narrow, twisting stairs. They were very dimly lit and she paused, just as she reached the second landing.

The landing was partly lit by a shaft of light from a high skylight. A man was standing in the light, gazing up towards its source. He was quite young, very tall and well built. His face was pale and long, oddly handsome with its large eyes and finely sculptured mouth, his brown hair swept back and poetically long. He wore tight, light-coloured trousers and a loose, Byronic shirt. His expression intense, he seemed to be searching for something in the light.

Lillie hesitated as she came up the last step. She was wearing her black dress and the little black bonnet, now with a sweeping white ostrich feather wound round the crown. The young man's head turned towards her and his eyes fixed on hers. They were the most expressive she had ever seen. 'You emerge from the darkness like one of the spirits of faery who ensnared the hearts of men, when the world was young,' he said, in a rich, perfectly modulated voice.

'Excuse me?' Lillie smiled.

'My lady,' he smiled, 'I would excuse you anything. But which particular absolution did you have in mind?'

She could not decide whether to smile back or to seem offended. 'I am looking for Mr Miles' studio,' she answered coolly. 'Is it on this floor or the next?'

'The next, fair lady. Art must always lie closer to Heaven.' He gestured towards the door beside him. 'I, myself, inhabit this lower region.'

'Thank you,' Lillie said. She was very conscious of his size and strength as she walked past him on the narrow landing, and was genuinely relieved when she turned to go up the next flight of stairs.

'Never doubt the power of prayer,' he said behind her.

She started and looked round. He had not moved. 'I beg your pardon?'

'He doubted you would come,' the young man exlained. 'I told him he should have faith. And did you not materialise from the motes of light, in answer to my silent invocation of the Aten, the golden disc of the sun?'

'No,' Lillie said flatly. 'I came by cab from Eaton Place,' She bowed her head slightly and moved on. She could hear him laughing delightedly, as she went up the twisting stairs.

Frank Miles was agitated. He had been sure she would come. In fact, he had sworn it. He stood by his easel on which was an unfinished outline from memory of Lillie's head and shoulders. The short, compact James McNeill Whistler sat watching him, but he was more conscious of a narrow-featured, pale young woman who was also seated, watching. She was Princess Louise, Marchioness of Lorne, the most artistic of Queen Victoria's daughters, a frequent and honoured visitor to his studio. An older lady-in-waiting stood behind her. With her was the elegant Lord Rosslyn, an almost foppish man in his forties, a noted connoisseur. Nearer the door, crosslegged on a cushion, was a waiflike, pretty girl of fourteen or fifteen, known as Miss Sally. She was dressed in Pre-Raphaelite style, in a long, flowered smock and a chaplet of flowers round her loose hair.

'Why don't you finish it?' Whistler asked.

'I long to, Jimmy,' Miles sighed.

Princess Louise smiled. 'Then, why don't you, Mr Miles?'

'I think you're teasing us, Frank,' Rosslyn drawled, when he shrugged in reply. 'Still, I must admit, I find it quite effective as it is.'

'Yes, but tantalising,' Princess Louise agreed. 'I don't believe this mysterious discovery of yours exists.'

'Oh, she exists, all right,' Whistler confirmed. 'I, too, have seen the vision. But I don't know why Frank's claiming to have discovered her. I was introduced to her a full five minutes before him.'

Princess Louise joined in the laughter. 'Well, if she doesn't arrive soon,' she said, regretfully, 'I'm afraid I must be going.'

Just then, there was a knock at the door and Sally rose to open it. Lillie came in, but paused in the doorway, surprised to see so many people. She had not known what to expect, perhaps that Frank Miles would be on his own, and had been half prepared for an adventure.

'At last!' Miles greeted her and hurried to take her hand, leading her forward as if exhibiting her.

Lillie had a confused impression of the studio. It was very different from Millais's, dusty and cluttered, full of odd angles. The room was partly panelled, on its many shelves a jumble of bric-a-brac, props, pieces of armour and many pots of flowers. There was a large, sloping window over the posing dais and easel, an odd mixture of oriental and period furniture. There were drawings and portraits on all surfaces.

'Your Royal Highness,' Miles was saying, 'may I present Mrs Edward Langtry?'

Lillie was startled only for the briefest moment and gave a small curtsey. Whistler smiled, admiring her composure. He rose in tribute.

'I'm so glad you are here, Mrs Langtry,' Princess Louise said. 'We were beginning to doubt your existence.'

Lillie smiled, then inclined her head as Miles introduced the lady-in-waiting, Mrs Maberly, and Lord Rosslyn. He waved a hand. 'James Whistler you already know.'

Rosslyn wore a monocle. He adjusted it as he bowed. 'Up till a moment ago,' he declared, 'I'd have wagered that Frank and Mr Whistler were playin' a game with us. Now I can only admire their restraint in describin' you.'

'Where are the words to describe perfection?' Miles asked him.

Lillie could tell that the rather strained young woman

addressed as 'Your Royal Highness' was watching her reaction. 'Please,' she begged. 'Too much praise is bad for anyone . . . so soon after lunch.'

The laughter was dominated by Whistler's sharp bark. The girl, Sally, was seated again. Miles signalled to her. 'Sally, fetch some tea.'

'Not for me,' Princess Louise told him. 'Mrs Maberly and I are expected at Clarence House.'

Sally rose and went out.

'My carriage is outside, Ma'am,' Rosslyn said. 'May I have the honour to drive you?'

Princess Louise thanked him, then smiled to Lillie. 'I hope you will help Mr Miles to finish his pencil portrait of you, Mrs Langtry. We are, all, most anxious to see it completed.'

'I shall try, Ma'am,' she promised, copying Rosslyn's form of address. 'But life has become so hectic, I do not know how I shall find time to pose.'

'How much time will you need, Mr Miles?' Princess Louise asked.

'Only about eight hours a day,' Miles replied innocently.

'So what d'you say?' Whistler chuckled, when the laughter died. 'Are you going to let Frank declare a monopoly?'

'I'm afraid it's against my principles,' Lillie told him. 'You see, I was brought up to believe in Free Trade.'

The laughter was even louder. Princess Louise sighed. 'I wish I didn't have to go, but I'm late already.' She rose. 'I have enjoyed meeting you, Mrs Langtry. I hope we may see each other again soon.' Lillie curtsied and Whistler bowed, as she headed for the door which Miles hurried to hold open for her.

Rosslyn paused by Lillie. 'I trust I may have the pleasure of invitin' you and Mr Langtry to dine?' he said.

Lillie smiled. 'We should be delighted.' Rosslyn bowed to her and followed out Princess Louise, her lady-in waiting and Frank Miles. Lillie looked round the studio, aware of Whistler examining her openly. Although she had gained enormously in social poise, she was still not used to being alone with strange men and his examination disturbed her. Finally, she looked straight at him, challenging.

'A cat can look at a Queen,' he grinned. She could not stop herself smiling back. There was something puckish about his lined, cynical face and shrewd eyes, under that black, oily, curled hair with the one snow-white lock over his forehead. He wore a suit of fairly loud, brown and white checks, with a nile green cravat and a matching handkerchief in his breast pocket, a canary waistcoat. 'Which reminds me,' he added. 'Did you know who that was?'

'. . . No,' she admitted.

'I thought not. I must say, I commend your composure. People usually either get dithery or stiffen up, when they're brought face to face with royalty.'

'Who was she?' Lillie asked.

'The Queen's daughter – Princess Louise.'

'. . . Oh.' She was puzzled. 'She comes here?'

'Like half the fashionable world,' Whistler told her. 'Sometimes you can't scratch yourself for titles in here. Frank's little, coloured sketches are quite the rage. Of course, they're a lot cheaper than mine.'

He grinned again and Lillie decided that she liked him, in spite of his abrupt manner and fairly harsh voice. 'Are yours so terribly expensive, Mr Whistler?'

'It's Jimmy,' he said, 'and they are. Of course, so few people buy them I can afford to make them as expensive as I like. It doesn't affect the sales.' She laughed and sat in the armchair in which Princess Louise had been sitting. 'Nowadays,' he went on, 'people are preoccupied by reality. They want to see every leaf on the tree, every hair on the dog's tail. That's not art, it's illustration. What interests me is beauty and inner reality – pure beauty. Which is why, one day, I shall paint you.' To his surprise, Lillie frowned. 'Have I said something wrong?'

She seemed almost uncomfortable. 'It's just that I'm not used to comments on my – There! I nearly said it, myself. My "beauty". I was brought up with six brothers.'

Whistler smiled. 'You must've been thoroughly spoilt.'

'Far from it!' she assured him. 'They lost no opportunity

180

of impressing on me what a miserable handicap it was to be a girl.' He laughed. 'I was certainly never encouraged to think very much of myself.'

'I guess not.'

'So you see,' Lillie confessed, 'it's very flattering to be paid so many compliments – but sometimes I wonder, are they really talking about me?'

Whistler had a reputation as a destroyer of egos. He would quite gleefully have pricked any bubble of conceit he had found in her, if it suited him, and he was touched that she had confided in him. 'The golden rule is,' he said slowly, 'when you are paid a compliment, accept it. Above all, never disagree.' She smiled. 'Beauty is in the eye of the beholder – do not throw the dust of doubt into the eyes of your admirers. I say you are beautiful, naturally and by nature. But your beauty is still in bud. It needs warmth and cultivation to come to bloom. Accept all the tributes, every act of homage, however fanciful. Enjoy, absorb, believe as the chorus of praise swells around you – and by the end of the year, you will be the most beautiful woman in London!'

Lillie gazed at him. In his way, he was a spellbinder and his black eyes burned with conviction.

The moment was broken when Frank Miles came back in with Sally, who was carrying a tray of teathings. 'I hope we weren't too long,' he said. 'How have you been getting on?'

'Lillie and I have been discussing the nature of beauty,' Whistler told him.

'Lillie?' Miles queried. There was more than a hint of possessiveness.

Whistler smiled. 'You'll pardon my transatlantic bluntness. But my democratic spirit rebels against formal titles in informal surroundings.'

Lillie nodded. 'I agree.'

'There you are. Queen Lillie's first Act of Parliament.'

Miles bowed. 'As a loyal subject, I can only obey.'

While they laughed, the door opened and the tall young man she had met on the landing came in. He was now fully dressed. Over his shirt and light trousers, he wore an embroidered waistcoat, a white silk cravat secured by an amethyst tiepin, a black frockcoat with only the lower button fastened. He was carrying a pair of pale lavender gloves, which he used to emphasise his gestures. 'Frivolity in the Temple of Art?' he wondered. 'I thought I would find nothing but hushed reverence and the busy scratching of pencils.'

'I haven't had a chance to begin,' Miles told him. 'Princess Louise was here.'

'Ah – poor Louise,' he sighed.

'Why poor?' Whistler asked.

'She married to escape the dreariness of life with the Widow of Windsor, and woke up to find herself in bed with the most boring man in England.'

They laughed.

Miles turned to Lillie, smiling. 'This is the friend from Oxford I told you about – Oscar Wilde.'

Oscar advanced and bowed, handsome, magnetic, sure of his personal genius. When Lillie held out her hand, he raised it and kissed it. 'Mrs Langtry and I have already met,' he said. 'She caught me en deshabille, at my devotions.'

'Queen Lillie has already approved an Act of Parliament, Oscar,' Whistler cut in. 'It's first names here.'

'That sounds like sacrilege,' Oscar protested. 'I thought we would observe the custom of those Eastern religions where it is forbidden to utter the secret name of the Divinity?'

'But since the Divinity, herself, decrees,' Miles said, 'what can we do but submit?'

Oscar raised his arms eloquently, submitting. He sat on the chair nearest Lillie. She found his personality fascinating already. The minute they had spent together on the stairs seemed to have linked them in some secret manner. She could tell he felt it, too.

The girl, Sally, brought her a cup of tea. Lillie had not noticed her before and smiled at her elfin appearance, the loose, filmy dress and the flowers circling her head. 'You haven't met our Miss Sally,' Miles said. She smiled radiantly to Lillie, thinking her beautiful. In spite of her waif-like, slightly pinched look and thin, undernourished arms, she was an uncomplicated, sunny child of nature. While she took tea to Whistler, Miles explained quietly about her. Oscar and he had found her one wet night, starving and filthy, huddled against a wall in Victoria Station. Nominally, she was the daughter of one of the flower women, a woebegone creature who pocketed the shillings they gave her and made no objections when Miles lifted the child and carried her home to be cared for. 'Cleaned up, she turned out to be quite delightful, as you see.'

'A fawn, lost in the metropolitan jungle,' Oscar commented.

'And she lives here?' Lillie asked.

'It is as much her home as mine now,' Miles answered simply. 'I could not turn her out again to the life of the streets.'

Sally brought tea to Oscar, then curled up at his feet. 'Too many birds of prey with sharp talons and cruel beaks lie in wait for little singing birds like her,' he murmured.

Lillie watched him as he fondled the girl's hair. 'Are you an artist, too, Oscar?'

He smiled to her. 'I strive to be, but the pictures I paint are with words, not pigment.'

'I told you,' Miles said. 'He's a poet, His poetry is exquisite.'

'It's exquisite, all right,' Whistler grunted. 'Doesn't always make much sense, but it's exquisite.'

They laughed, Oscar as much as the others. Miles moved to his easel and turned it. 'Carry on talking,' he said. 'I must make a start.'

'I'm afraid I can't stay much longer,' Lillie told him.

He was disappointed. 'Is your husband expecting you?'

'No, he is at his Club. I am engaged to have my photograph taken this afternoon.'

She had not imagined Miles would be so disturbed. 'By whom?' he demanded.

'A Mr Ellis. Then by a Mr Downey, and afterwards, I've promised to go to the Wharncliffes. Then at five-thirty, I have to sit for Mr Millais.'

'The Wharncliffes I accept,' he said stiffly. 'Millais, I can forgive. But those photographers are intolerable!'

'I've promised.'

'Jimmy – talk her out of it,' he appealed.

'No.'

'Oscar!'

'No, Frank.'

'But don't you see?' Miles complained. 'Those photographers will swamp the market with cheap prints. Her face will be known to everyone with two pennies to spare!'

'Precisely,' Whistler nodded.

Oscar spread his hands. 'We are the Apostles of a new religion and each print will win us a new convert. What more could we ask?'

'Your drawings are aimed at another section of the public, Frank,' Whistler said reasonably. 'And the more she is known, the more they will sell.'

Oscar smiled to him. 'Besides, you always work better for a little competition. I personally shall escort our Divinity to Mr Ellis's studio and to Mr Downey's. And help to arrange her poses.'

Miles was calming down. He jerked his shoulders irritably. 'Very well,' he conceded. 'But you owe me at least twenty minutes, Lillie. Keep looking at Oscar. That is your punishment for denying my rights as your discoverer.'

Lillie was about to retort, but stopped herself. She looked at Oscar, who smiled and raised an eyebrow very slightly at the temperament of artists. She smiled back and he settled lower in his seat, gazing at her with his great, dark eyes.

# CHAPTER SEVEN

Only ladies were present at the informal buffet tea at Lady Wharncliffe's. She was seated with the slender, haughty Mrs Luke Wheeler and the statuesque Lady Dudley. In her early thirties, Georgiana Dudley was blonde, imperiously beautiful, her manner deliberately remote.

'They say she has only one dress to her name,' Mrs Wheeler smirked.

'Poverty is not included among the cardinal sins,' Lady Wharncliffe remarked.

'No, but no one seems to know anything about her – or her husband, for that matter.'

'Well, Patsy West has been seeing quite a bit of her,' Lady Wharncliffe said. She looked round. 'Patsy, is it true that Mrs Langtry's father is the Dean of Jersey?'

Patsy was standing behind them, talking to Violet Lindsay. She had no idea what to answer, but nodded brightly. 'Oh, yes. He's an intimate friend of the Archbishop of York. At school together.'

'And Mr Langtry?'

'Now, what was it he said? Something about sailing? Yes, shipping – he has shipping interests, I believe.'

'How apropos,' Lady Wharncliffe murmured and rose. She had just seen Lillie coming in.

Lillie was still smiling. Oscar had kept his promise and accompanied her to the photographers' studios, insisting on supervising the angles from which she was taken. 'I grant you Mrs Langtry's right profile is a sonnet,' he told Alfred Ellis. 'But her left is an ode to immortality. The left profile, please.' Normally, Lillie disliked being photograhed. The long process of setting up and focussing, then having to hold a rigid pose for the seconds the lens was uncovered made her unnaturally stiff and she usually did not care for the results. But Oscar had kept up a flow of such amusing talk that she had laughed and relaxed, enjoying posing for the first time.

Mrs Wheeler had been put out by what Patsy had told them and Lillie's arrival made her more cross. 'I still say it's not right,' she protested quietly. 'The Beauties have always been ladies of some standing and impeccable breeding. If just anyone is admitted, it will cheapen the whole thing.'

Lady Dudley sipped her tea. 'It is all quite vulgar, anyway,' she drawled. She observed Lillie as Lady Wharncliffe brought her to them. So that was what all the fuss was about. Pretty enough, and the black dress was certainly cut daringly tight, though scarcely in the height of fashion.

'Georgiana, I don't think you've met Mrs Edward Langtry,' Lady Wharncliffe said.

Lillie smiled. 'How do you do?'

Lady Dudley inclined her head a fraction, discouraging closer acquaintance.

'Of course, you know Mrs Wheeler,' Lady Wharncliffe said.

When Lillie smiled to her, Mrs Wheeler copied Lady Dudley's brief acknowledgment, even more icily.

Lady Wharncliffe looked at Patsy in a quick appeal. All conversation had stopped. Everyone had noticed that the newcomer seemed to be being snubbed. 'You've been spending the day with Patsy, I hear,' Lady Wharncliffe said loudly.

In case Lillie had forgotten their pact, Patsy cut in quickly. 'Yes, we gossiped for hours. What a pity you had to rush off, Lillie! Who was it you were going to see?'

Lillie suddenly realised she had the perfect answer. 'Her Royal Highness Princess Louise.' Patsy nearly giggled, when she saw how Mrs Wheeler started.

'At . . . home?' Lady Wharncliffe enquired.

'No, at Frank Miles' studio.'

Lady Wharncliffe was eager to hear more. 'Do come and have some tea, Mrs Langtry,' she urged. 'Or may I say, Lillie? You must call me Susan.'

Mrs Wheeler was mortified as she watched them cross to the buffet table. 'You see?' she complained.

Lady Dudley glanced at her and away. 'People run after one or two new faces every season,' she drawled. 'They never last. In a few weeks, no one will even remember her name.'

Edward was annoyed when Lillie reached home and apologised for being late. Millais had kept her longer than she expected, and they were going to the Hardwickes' ball. Edward had been dressed for an hour. 'I will not make an exhibition of myself by arriving late,' he told her. 'The cab is arriving in six minutes. If you are not in the hall, I shall send it away.'

Dominique was waiting in the bedroom. Lillie did not even take off her dress. She only unfastened it, so that Dominique could detach the collar and tuck in the concealed tabs. She sat at the dressingtable to retie the figure-of-eight knot at the nape of her neck and pin it more securely for dancing.

She was thinking of Georgiana Dudley. One of the Queens of Society, Millais had called her, the doyenne of the Professional Beauties. 'Now you've been accepted by her, you can say you have really arrived.' But Lillie knew that Lady Dudley had not accepted her. She had hardly appeared to acknowledge her existence.

When Dominique heard that she had actually met her, she trembled with excitement. She was like her photographs, Lillie told her, and just as cold.

'But was she not lovely?'

'Very lovely,' Lillie said. 'With an unlovely voice.'

'She is the most beautiful woman in England!' Dominique protested, shocked. 'Everyone says so.'

Lillie had pinned the knot and turned her head from side to side to check that it hung evenly. She paused, looking at her reflection. '. . . Do they?' she murmured.

Coming in late at the ball was, accidentally, a piece of brilliant strategy. A considerable number of people had been waiting to see her again or to meet her and had just begun to feel disappointed, when she walked in with Edward. Even those who had only heard her described recognised her at once. She had scarcely greeted her host and hostess and smiled to Patsy before she was surrounded by men, clamouring to dance with her. Edward was pushed aside. Patsy's husband, Colonel Cornwallis West, whom she called Poppets, took pity on him and engaged him in conversation. He was used to not seeing his wife, himself, from the moment they entered a ballroom or party. Sometimes, he admitted, he even went to sleep in an anteroom, trusting to her waking him up, when it was all over. He would gladly have stayed at home, but convention demanded that ladies must be accompanied by their husbands.

Lillie went from partner to partner, for, of course, it was unthinkable that she should dance with anyone more than once. That would give rise to immediate scandal. Quite effortlessly, she became the centre of attention. Everyone wanted to dance with her, to prove for themselves what others had reported. To hold that radiant beauty in one's arms in a waltz or schottische was an unforgettable experience. Especially, the first heady moment when one placed one's gloved hand on her waist and felt not the rigidity of steel strips or whalebone, but the yielding softness of her uncorsetted body, masked only by a few layers of cloth. And as one danced, the whole universe became bounded by her dazzling, blue-green eyes, her bewitching smile and the warm and supple movement of her waist under one's hand.

During one polka with the elegant Lord Rosslyn, the other couples stopped dancing for several minutes and formed a circle to watch them. There was sharp competition for who would partner her in the supper dance and lead her in. Their hostess resolved it by deciding that she should be escorted again by Lord Randolph Churchill, whose wife was still, regrettably, in Ireland.

The next few weeks brought a total transformation in Lillie's life. Invitations poured in. So many, in fact, that Mrs Jennings had to borrow Dominique during the day to help her own maid answer the door.

Yet it was not only the apparently unending round of lunches, dinners and parties. Soon all London knew her, when the photographs of her began to be displayed in the shops. She, personally, was not too happy with them. The primitive lighting could not suggest her real colouring and only a few caught her unique quality. Oscar agreed. 'The camera has the miraculous ability to turn wine into water,' he said. Yet the public bought them in their hundreds, then thousands, and a demand for them rose all over the country. Her mother wrote to tell her they were even on sale in King Street, in St. Helier. From being only one of the Professional Beauties, in a very short time she became one of the leaders, with Lady Dudley and Patsy, and before long her photographs were outselling even theirs. Her rivals went to extraordinary lengths to think of new, eyecatching poses to maintain their popularity, being photographed in hammocks, on horseback, in skiffs on the river, in historical costumes. Once, Patsy let herself be talked into posing in an artificial snowstorm, seated on a rock and wearing an ermine coat and muff. After Lillie had been shown, looking sadly at a dead bird she held, one of her rivals unwisely copied her pose and was reproduced gazing at a dead fish.

Nothing could slow the sale of Lillie's photographs and Frank Miles' enchanting sketches of her. Women began to adopt her hairstyle. All over the country it became smart to wear one's hair in The Langtry Knot. People began to point her out in the street and Edward and she could not linger anywhere on their walks or they were soon surrounded.

Then Millais' painting, *Effie Dean*, was exhibited at the Marsden Galleries. Some of Frank Miles' pen and pencil sketches had suggested Lillie's colouring with a delicate touch of watercolour, but suddenly it was fully revealed by Millais, the golden brown hair tinged with auburn, the glowing, almost translucent skin and melting, blue-green eyes. Crowds came to see it and many, many replicas were sold. The cult of her beauty reached the vast, prosperous middle class. One night shortly after the painting was shown, Lillie went to the Haymarket Theatre with Edward. When she appeared in the box, applause began in the stalls and spread throughout the auditorium. Edward sat quickly, startled and embarrassed. The applause only ended, when Lillie responded to it with a slight bow and sat, turning her eyes to the stage curtain.

At Frank Miles' studio, she met other painters and poets, Rossetti, ailing and addicted to chloral, and the strange, passionate Algernon Charles Swinburne, whose paganism shocked and titillated the entire literary world. And William Morris, the poet and designer, a former disciple of Rossetti's, who saw in her the living personification of his idealised mediaeval maidens. Violet Fane, the poetess, notorious for her immodestly unrestrained verses. And Lillie's favourite, Irving's new, young leading lady, the adorable Ellen Terry, who became a friend. And for most of the time, to Edward's annoyance, Oscar was with her, a constant visitor and companion, her adoring apostle, as he styled himself.

One day, she received a huge bouquet of flowers from Millais. The note with it thanked her for her part in making *Effie Dean* so successful, and went on to say that, in his opinion, its only fault was that the painting was not of her, alone. Many famous people wished him to do their portraits, but more than anyone else he wanted to paint Lillie's. As well as sitting frequently for Frank Miles and her for photographs, she had begun to pose now for Edward Poynter, Henry Weigall and Frederick Leighton, yet she owed Millais such a debt and his note was so flattering that she could not refuse. He was overjoyed, when she arrived at Palace Gate that very morning. 'When would you like to start?' she asked him.

'What's wrong with now?' he laughed. 'Unless you're busy.'

While Effie rang for coffee, he studied Lillie, sucking on his pipe. She was used to it by now. Sometimes, he would just stand and look at her for a quarter of an hour without moving, analysing some technical problem. 'You are the most exasperating subject I have ever painted, you know,' he said at last. 'For fifty-five minutes out of sixty you are just beautiful, but for the other five . . . you are amazing.'

She had listened to Whistler's advice. Instead of protesting as she would have done until recently, she merely smiled, accepting the compliment.

When they moved to the studio and she was once more standing on the dais, he studied her again, walking slowly round until he faced her. 'Do you want me seated this time?' He shook his head. 'What would you like me to wear?'

'Just what you have on.' She was wearing her black dress with its lace collar. She glanced down at it, seeming troubled. 'Are you disappointed?'

'I thought you'd want me in classical robes,' she said, 'or a cloak or – '

'Something to hide behind? No. I want to paint *you* . . . Turn to your right a little. Look over there.' Lillie turned slightly, looking past Millais' left shoulder. He moved back to his easel, still watching her. 'When people see this portrait, I want them to stop and gaze, to have the same sense of shock as I did the moment I first saw you, at seeing a creature so rare – fragile, delicate, lovely, proud, wistful, yet eager . . .' He smiled. 'So you see, we have quite a lot to do.'

Lillie looked at him, responding to his smile, half seduced by his voice.

He took up a large sketchbook and a charcoal pencil from his paint table. 'Keep looking at the corner,' he ordered. 'And as you value your immortal soul, for the next ten minutes – don't move!' She composed herself, looking past him, and he began to make the first quick strokes of his preliminary sketch.

The portrait took shape swiftly. Millais worked in concentrated bursts, punctuated by long periods of thought, or sometimes he would draw her out to talk about her childhood. He was particularly fascinated by the attempts she had made in her early teens with two girl friends to contact the spirit world. The table they had used for their seances had shaken or spun round, scaring her but leading them on to further attempts, until one moonlit night when the sofa on which all three sat began to move and they clung to one another as it rolled from one end of the drawingroom in the Deanery to the other, while the air seemed filled with the rustling of wings. People usually laughed, when she told them of it now, but Millais did not.

One afternoon, she looked round on the dais to see a short, severe, old man watching her. His eyes were quite piercing, his nose prominent under beetling, dark eyebrows, his hair receding and grey, but worn long at the back as if to compensate. He was dressed in black, except for his white shirt with its old fashioned, upstanding, pointed collar. It was the former Liberal Prime Minister, William Gladstone. To her embarrassment, she found that he was one of the people whose portraits Millais had postponed to be sure of finishing hers in time for the Summer Exhibition. Gladstone would not let her apologise. Having met her, he said, he fully understood the artist's keenness and was happy to wait. He questioned her about the economy and history of the Channel Islands. 'Let me see,' he said, 'when did we take Jersey?'

'Take Jersey?' Millais laughed. 'I'm afraid, sir, you mean, when did we Normans conquer England.'

'At any rate, we may put down this year as the one in which Mrs Langtry subjugated London,' Gladstone said, giving her one of the rare, sweet smiles which transformed his stern face.

He had always been one of Lillie's heroes and she could not accustom herself to the thought that he was really quite short. With his athletic build and upright carriage even at nearly seventy, in his pictures he seemed much taller. 'He's rather conscious of it,' Millais told her. 'He always has himself shown alone or, if with others, either he or they are seated.' That someone as great and powerful as Gladstone should not be above such simple vanity seemed strange to Lillie, but she did not believe Millais, when he told her he was sure the old man had only made the unnecessary trip to Palace Gate out of curiosity, hoping to meet her. Yet she had seen how warmly he responded to her, and filed it away.

At their next session, she arrived late, with Oscar.

Oscar accepted the blame. He had insisted on Lillie coming with him to a jeweller's shop in Bond Street, to show her a tiny Greek portrait head in lapis lazuli set in a ring, which he had discovered, with a remarkable resemblance to her. While they were examining it, people began to gather outside. Someone had spotted her going in and, as word spread, more and more faces appeared at the windows. 'Until there were a hundred or so, all jostling and jabbering. We felt like exhibits in a Gothic aquarium.'

Effie had brought them in. 'What did you do?' she asked.

'They'd have torn her to pieces, if she'd gone out.' Oscar told her. 'So the owner of the shop let us out the back door. We could hear the mob shrieking with frustration.'

'And we ran all the way to Berkeley Square!' Lillie added.

Millais laughed and forgave her. 'It's those photographs, he said.

Oscar smiled. 'And Frank's sketches of her.'

'Yes,' Millais admitted. 'I only hope they'll like the portrait as much. If it's ever finished.'

Lillie had moved up on the dais. She began to smile, then realised that he was serious. 'What's wrong?'

Millais was standing by the easel, looking at the partially completed portrait. 'There's just something – I don't know. Something.'

'Perhaps she should wear another dress,' Oscar proposed.

Lillie shrugged. 'I don't have anything suitable.'

Millais shook his head. 'No, it's not the dress.'

Effie was leaving and paused in the doorway. 'It's the hands,' she said.

All three turned to her, then Millais nodded. 'And of course, you are right, my dear.' She smiled to him and went out.

'I will not have a word said against the perfection of those hands,' Oscar objected.

Lillie was puzzled. 'What did Effie mean?' she asked.

'All those weeks you have been posing for me and you have not yet fully relaxed,' Millais told her. 'Your hands give you away.' Made aware of her hands, Lillie became selfconscious and could not think where to put them. 'Perhaps you should be holding something.'

L.—G

'A flower,' Oscar suggested.

'Perhaps.'

Oscar was wearing a white gardenia in his buttonhole. He plucked it out and stepped forward, presenting it to Lillie. 'A gardenia for my lady.' She smiled and turned to face Millais, holding the gardenia with both hands.

He considered her. 'Yes . . . But it's all black and white. I n't there a little, red flower? There's a crimson flower they grow on our island, isn't there?'

'The Jersey lily.'

'How long would it take to get some?'

Lillie thought. 'Two days, if they were sent express.'

'It should be summer in the island. Could you ask your mother to send three or four, just in bud?'

'Yes,' Lillie agreed. 'But it's quite a small flower. Nothing remarkable.'

'Send for it,' Millais decided. 'And we shall see.'

When they told Frank Miles about the delay, he was jubilant. 'You know why he's in such a ferment, don't you?' he chuckled. 'He wants it ready for the Summer Exhibition at the Royal Academy. I have an absolutely brilliant idea! Why don't I do a portrait of you?'

Lillie was helping Oscar and him to water all the plants in his studio, a drop or two to each pot. She stopped in surprise.

'Why not?' he laughed. 'I work in oils, too – and a lot more quickly than Millais.' His excitement was growing as the idea took hold. 'I would have it ready in eight to ten days. It would be a sensation! The first "official" portrait. It would scoop all the Members of the Academy.'

Lillie was troubled. She was grateful to him and liked him, although there was not the rapport between them which she had once expected. She did not feel nearly so close to him as to Oscar. 'No, Frank,' she said.

'You don't have to worry about Millais. He's had so many successes.'

'I didn't mean that,' she said levelly. 'You are not the artist he is. I want my first portrait to be by him.'

He was brought up short, as if she had slapped him.

There was a silence in the room, while he stared at her.

Oscar was listening and he, too, winced at her directness. He was that she regretted it now, yet it had been spoken. 'An oracular truth, Frank,' he said smoothly. 'She means your art is of a different nature. More delicate, and more ephemeral. You concentrate on pen and pencil, since you are partly colourblind. A considerable handicap, you must admit, since colour is the essence of portraiture.'

Lillie glanced thankfully to Oscar, when Miles turned away from them both, his face set.

Sally was sitting crosslegged on the floor by a huge blue and white bowl, filled with fruit. She had eaten some grapes and reached for an apple. 'Miss Sally, if you keep on eating so much you will grow fat,' Miles snapped pettishly, 'and I shan't worship you any more!' Sally dropped the apple and lay back on the floor on her elbows, grinning.

When the package arrived from Jersey, Lillie opened it to find it lined with waterproof paper and packed with damp moss. In the moss were three or four branched lilies, with small, crimson flowers. They must have come from the path by the Deanery. She lifted one out and held it up to catch the light from her bedroom window. It was fragile and pretty and unpretentious, just a little flower, but she knew instinctively that its choice was perfect.

Millais invited over a hundred guests to his Show Evening, when the portrait was completed. There was much anticipation and many of the guests brought friends who had not received invitations, so that his studio was crowded, even though it was such a large room. Edward was impressed to be presented to Princess Louise and stammered when she asked him how he felt about the way his wife had captivated the artistic world. Quite truthfully, he could say he had not thought much about it. Lillie was unaccustomedly nervous, and so was Millais. 'It's quite a simle portrait,' Effie said, 'but he's put a lot into it.'

'We are all most intrigued,' Princess Louise told them.

There were several canvasses already on view, landscapes like his famous *Chill October* and one or two Biblical subjects. Lillie's portrait stood on the dais on an easel, covered with a cloth, still to be unveiled, and was the centre of speculation.

While she circulated, making conversation, Lillie found the waiting almost unbearable. She could not drink any of the champagne that was offered to her. She paused briefly in a group that included Lady Dudley, Lord Randolph Churchill and Edward Poynter. They were intrigued by Oscar, who was with them.

'Which college were you at, at Oxford?' Churchill asked.

'Magdalen, Lord Randolph.'

Poynter had heard of him as one of the coming men. 'I'm told you won the Newdigate Prize for poetry.'

'Yes,' Oscar said. 'The adjudicators showed great powers of judgement.'

They all laughed, except for Churchill, who turned away, thinking him a conceited puppy.

As Lillie turned to leave, too, she came face to face with Lady Dudley. Their paths had crossed several times at balls and parties and now, as before, she was conscious of the older woman's assessing eyes fixed on her. 'Tell me, Mrs Langtry,' she said bluntly, 'why do you always wear black?'

'Out of respect for my younger brother, Lady Dudley,' Lillie replied quietly. 'He died last December.'

Lady Dudley's expression did not change, but her voice was gentler. 'I do beg your pardon,' she murmured.

Effie Millais was waiting and touched Lillie's arm, leading her to the dais.

Across the room, Mrs Wheeler and her wealthy husband had been talking to Whistler and Frank Miles. 'You do not have a Show Day for your latest offerings, Mr Whistler, do you?' she observed. 'Why not?'

Whistler shrugged. 'Because I do not ask for other people's opinion on my work.'

'Nor accept it, if it is given,' Miles added, smiling.

'It does seem like begging publicly for approval,' she agreed disdainfully. 'I cannot think why we have come here, when we could have waited to see this "famous" portrait in the Exhibition.'

'I presume, Madam,' Whistler growled, 'you are here

because, like myself, you are consumed with curiosity.' She did not at all care for his tone, nor for the way that her husband and Frank Miles laughed.

Edward was standing by *Chill October*, a painting of a small lake with windswept grasses and reeds, bleak and forlorn. He had been listening to Patsy and Lord Rosslyn and the others around him discuss it. It was like a foreign language. His mind went blank, when Colonel Cornwallis West turned to him. 'I think Millais' later work shows much more depth. Don't you, Mr Langtry?' Edward muttered and nodded.

'Which of his pieces do you like?' Rosslyn asked.

'Some things.'

'But which in particular?'

Edward had not paid much attention when Lillie and he had gone round the galleries, and even less when she chattered on about what they had seen. '. . . Some things,' he said.

Patsy ended the uncomfortable pause by asking him, 'Are you doing anything special this Season?'

'It doesn't really start till later,' he told her.

Her eyes opened. 'I'm sorry?'

'The trout,' he explained.

'Ah.' Rosslyn had understood. 'The trout fishin' season. Yes . . .' He glanced at Patsy and her husband, while Edward waited for them to continue the conversation. They were saved from embarrassment by a general move forward and turned eagerly with the others towards the dais on to which Millais had just stepped.

He held out his hand to draw Lillie up to stand opposite him on the other side of the draped easel. Facing it, she tensed as Millais pulled off the cloth covering her portrait. It showed her in her black dress, her right arm by her side, her left crossing her body and holding the little, crimson lily that made the only small splash of colour. Even the background was plain and muted. There was nothing to distract the eye from the pale beauty of her face, looking to the right, her expression calm, poised, yet alight with secret anticipation, just the shadow of a smile. Oscar's gardenia was tucked into the lace of the front of her collar, and so toned with it to be almost indistinguishable. Behind her, she heard a gasp of appreciation. A pause followed, then when the startling simplicity of the portrait began to make its impression, there were murmurs of admiration and applause.

She turned to the crowd and the admiring comments and applause increased, until Millais held up his hand. 'Your Royal Highness, my lords, ladies and gentlemen,' he announced. 'The Jersey Lily.'

Oscar raised his glass and called loudly, 'The Jersey Lily!'

Those who had glasses raised them, others applauded as the name was repeated with laughter and appreciation. Flushed and smiling, Lillie stood by her portrait, responding with Millais to the applause. No one seeing her there, so cool and reserved, could have imagined the fierce exultation that filled her.

Oscar was making his name. He was already known as one of the most promising young men at Oxford, a disciple of John Ruskin and Walter Pater, and was acceptable nearly everywhere, being the younger son of the eccentric, widowed Lady Wilde, the revolutionary poetess who had taken the name 'Speranza'. Born in Dublin, he had already won prizes and medals at Trinity College before moving on to Magdalen, where he had taken a First Class in the Honours Finals. Now his student days were over and he had to admit the necessity of earning a living in the wider world.

His father, Sir William, a noted surgeon, had died two years before, leaving him a small property on which he managed to raise some money. That and occasional gifts from his mother and his elder brother, who was a practicing lawyer, were all he had to support him. Fortunately, he had used his four years at Oxford wisely, impressing visiting celebrities and making friends in literary and artistic London during the vacations. He was not sure what he would do, perhaps some journalism, perhaps write poetry, but it had to be something spectacular. He had to be talked about. He saw that to get into the best society, one had either to feed people, amuse people, or shock people. He could only do the first on the most modest scale, which left the last two possibilities, both of which he was superbly equipped by talent and temperament to carry out. Like Disraeli, on whose style and wit he partly modelled himself, he also saw that society was ruled by women and that no man could be a real success without their backing. His one major piece of luck was in being taken up by the extremely rich Duchess of Westminster, whose brother, Ronald Gower, had been a student friend. With her help, he met everyone and, although some were offended by his apparent affectation and pose of indolence, many others responded happily to his charm and gentle nature and irreverent, impish sense of humour. His sayings were quoted and his hilarious, inconsequential stories repeated and repeated.

Then two things happened to him. He realised that he lived at the centre of a Movement, undefined and unorganised, a revolt of many writers and artists against the philistine standards and moral humbug of the day. Art did not have to 'serve a Higher Purpose'. Art was art and existed for and of itself. It was primarily an aesthetic revolt and he set himself to embody and champion it, allying himself firmly with iconoclasts like Whistler and Swinburne and William Morris.

The second thing was Lillie. He adored women, not least because they proved highly susceptible to his unusual mixture of athletic physique and poetic temperament. Part actor himself, he was especially fascinated by actresses and formed fairly close relationships with several, including Ellen Terry, Mrs Bancroft and the Polish Helena Modjeska. But his feelings for Lillie were quite different. They amounted more to an obsession. Attracted first by her looks and flattered to be seen with the new, rising Beauty, he had soon discovered the almost masculine sharpness of her mind and delighted in the laconic wit, which was often above the understanding of the admirers who clustered round her. He watched her astonishing rise with wonder and the revelation of her ability to deal brilliantly with any situation. They were so alike he realised, nearly sharing the same birthday in October, although he was exactly a year younger. Schemes and plans and ambitions were driven from his mind and she filled his waking thoughts and disturbed his dreams.

He rose one morning, dressed with much care and walked up to the flower market in Covent Garden. He had only a few shillings in his pocket, so had to be very selective. Finally, he chose one perfect amaryllis, enthusiastically assisted by the market porters once he had told them it was for Lillie.

Carrying it reverently before him, he crossed back down to the Strand and walked through Trafalgar Square, up to Piccadilly and along to Knightsbridge, Belgravia and Eaton Place. Many of the people he passed stopped and stared at him, some smiling, some disbelieving. He bowed slightly to them in passing. Going up Lower Regent Street, he heard one pompous gentleman declare, 'There goes that bloody fool, Oscar Wilde.' He paused and bowed to him, saying, 'For all your possibly justified superiority, I am carrying this to Mrs Langtry. Would you not gladly change places?'

Reaching Eaton Place at last, he presented it to Lillie in her little drawingroom on one knee.

'Thank you, Oscar,' she said, touched. 'And you carried it all the way here?'

He rose solemnly. 'All the way – on foot. It was like a royal progress.'

She smiled. 'One day they will send for a doctor to certify you.'

'The only thing certifiable about me is my genius,' he told her and she laughed. 'No, my Lily, I give you this as a simple tribute to the triumph of your portrait at the Exhibition. Did you know it has been chosen as Painting of the Year?'

*The Jersey Lily* had been an amazing success. The reaction of the public to it was so great that it had to be roped off and guarded to prevent it from being damaged. It was now almost impossible for Lillie to walk in a street by daylight. Her appearance caused a kind of immediate hysteria. A young woman with colouring vaguely like hers, who happened to be wearing a black dress, sat down to rest one Sunday afternoon under the Achilles statue in Hyde Park. As soon as she was noticed, people rushed towards her and, when police forced a passage through the mob that formed round her, they found her unconscious and suffocating and she had to be taken by ambulance to St. George's Hospital.

'How does it feel?' Oscar asked. 'In a few short weeks, you have become the heroine of the illustrated papers, the toast of all the town. The other Beauties could vanish overnight and no one would care – as long as you remained.'

She was radiant, unable to maintain her poise. And with Oscar it did not matter. 'It feels . . . I can't – Is it true – really?'

'Thou hast conquered, O pale Aphrodite. You only have to hear the comments of the thousands who crowd into the Exhibition every day.'

'Every day?' she laughed.

'I can vouch for it,' he said quietly. 'For I go there to gaze at it every day, myself.'

She had stopped laughing, and smiled to him, tenderly.

Encouraged, he said, 'Shall I tell you my secret, what draws me there? It is that none of them has seen, just peeping from under the frill at your throat, my little gardenia – resting on your breast.' His voice was rich and warm. His hands had reached out and his fingertips just raised the lower edge of the frill of her lace collar. For a moment, they were motionless, gazing at each other. And Lillie felt the first stirring of feelings she had not known for three years.

They moved apart as the door opened and Edward came in and paused, seeing Oscar. 'Look what Oscar has brought me,' Lillie said. Edward eyed the single lily bleakly and nodded. She moved round to the window to place it in a vase with some smaller flowers.

'My congratulations on the success of the portrait,' Oscar bowed.

201

Edward grunted. 'Thank you. Most kind. Sometimes, I think the town's gone mad.'

'A divine madness,' Oscar smiled.

'I don't know about that,' Edward commented, distantly. 'It makes it hazardous even to go for a walk. People forget themselves.'

'I tell her, she owes it to herself and to us to drive daily through the Park,' Oscar said, 'dressed entirely in black, in a black victoria drawn by black horses. With "Venus Annodomini" emblazoned on her black bonnet in dull sapphires. But she won't do it.'

Edward stared at him. 'I sincerely hope not!' he choked.

'As it is,' Oscar went on, 'I have come to invite you both to supper. Nothing elaborate, alas, a simple repast prepared by my own hands.'

'Oh, I'd love to, Oscar,' Lillie assured him, 'but we can't. Irving has given us a box for his new play at the Lyceum.'

Oscar was disappointed, yet smiled at her. 'How nice of Henry. And how wise. If the audience does not enjoy his performance, they can always watch you.' He nodded to Edward, '. . . Sir,' and headed for the door.

Lillie went with him and touched his arm. 'I'm sorry about this evening.'

'Oh, we shall foregather another day,' he promised her. 'To see you, as Disraeli says somewhere, is absolutely necessary to my existence.' He took her hand, kissed her fingertips, and left.

'I don't like that fellow,' Edward said. 'I don't understand what he says half the time. I don't like him hanging around.'

Lillie looked at him. 'He's a friend.'

'Only because it suits him!' Edward snorted. 'Because we are in the public eye, he hopes some of it will rub off on him. It's bad enough all this – all this celebrity, without dandified Bohemians like him cluttering up the place. People notice. I don't want tongues to wag.'

'I don't see how they could, Edward,' Lillie said flatly. 'Since you are always here.'

She rarely saw him during the day now. In the evenings,

he was needed to accompany her, but her days were so fully occupied that she was free of him. Edward spent a considerable amount of time at his club or with men who cultivated him, hoping it would lead them closer to Lillie. He had come rather to enjoy his own touch of celebrity, as husband of the reigning Beauty. They dined well and were on familiar terms with most of the best people. When his sister Agnes came to see them, she was staggered by the names on their visiting list. Most of all, although they did not have much of a home life, he enjoyed the strange, secret feeling of leaving a party or dinner with her, knowing that every man envied him in his heart for taking her home to bed. The fact that he had not made love to her since they came to London occasionally gnawed at him, yet it was not the be all and end-all of existence, he told himself. Both of them were usually so tired. When she decided she had had enough of gadding about and wanted to raise the children his family kept asking for, their sexual life could begin again.

Although she frequently complained of headaches and exhaustion to Edward, when he seemed likely to make demands on her, Lillie was never tired. Day after day, she did the rounds of visits in the morning, lunched with someone, visited an exhibition, posed for photographs, then a portrait, in the afternoon, went to the Opera or a theatre and on to dinner, or attended two or three parties or balls, dropping in for an hour or two at each and dancing till dawn, then rising after a few hours sleep to begin again. Her energy and enjoyment simply seemed to increase and she showed no sign of strain. Even Patsy, with whom she had become inseparable, could not keep up with her.

The number of portraits of her continued to mount. Edward and she spent a luxurious two weeks in Yorkshire with the Wharncliffes, and Poynter, at last, had all the models for his vast murals, Susan Wharncliffe herself, the lovely Violet Lindsay, and Lillie as Princess Nausicaa in flowing draperies. They went on to have a short holiday with John and Effie Millais in Perthshire, where Edward fished for salmon, while Lillie explored Macbeth's Birnam

Wood and Millais drew endless sketches of her on any piece of paper that came to hand. Effie gathered them all up and had them framed to hang in her own boudoir. Prudent and Scots, she pointed out, 'These will be verra valuable one day.'

A special honour came with the request for her to pose for George Frederick Watts, the most revered painter of the time, whose perceptive portraits and allegorical canvasses like *Hope* and *Love Fighting Death* were considered unsurpassable.

She wondered what to expect, on the drive to his Queen Anne villa in semi-rural Holland Park, where he lived very much like a hermit. His housekeeper met her and showed her into his imposing studio, resembling a museum with its statues, old masters and many of his own works with which he would not part. She knew that he had been briefly and unhappily married to Ellen Terry, when she was only seventeen. Even then, he had been an old man. Now he looked venerable, particularly in the black skull-cap and gown he wore in tribute to his idol, Titian, his long white hair and white, pointed beard.

He lived for colour and his paintings blazed with it, yet, like Millais, he saw Lillie in black, with no ornament to detract from her naturalness. He insisted on painting her as he first saw her, in her black coat, with the frill of her dress just visible at the neck, and her little black bonnet, from which he tore away the white ostrich plume in spite of her protests. Again, like Millais, there was no background and he posed her looking to her right, in profile. The resulting portrait, *The Dean's Daughter*, showed his vision of her as more resolute and more warmly feminine than the hesitant young woman pictured by Millais. Opinions varied on the relative merits of both paintings, but she had another enormous success.

Watts was captivated by her and immediately set about a second portrait of her, to show her as the personification of Summer, in gold and purple draperies, carrying a basket of roses, against a cloudless, blue sky. Like many others, he was astounded by the quickness of her perception. She, herself, liked to draw and shyly showed him some of her sketches. He was charmed by them and often, when he should have been painting, would talk to her instead in his soft, gentle voice about the mysteries of art. For hours, they would both be absorbed as he took her through the development of the principal Italian schools, from the early Renaissance to Leonardo and Titian, illuminating her understanding. Although she gave him over forty sittings, the second portrait, *Summer*, was never finished.

One Saturday afternoon, she and Oscar had gone to Wharncliffe House. The ladies welcomed Oscar delightedly and he was stretched out on a chaise longue, wearing a white lily in his buttonhole, with them seated all round him. Lillie sat with Susan Wharncliffe, listening. 'The day after Narcissus the shepherd was drowned,' he told them, 'the wood nymphs who had all loved him came and knelt by the little crystal pool, weeping. "Why do you weep?" the pool asked. "For Narcissus," they replied. "He was so fair." "I weep, too," the pool said. "For as he leant over me, I could see the reflection of my beauty in his eyes . . ."'

The ladies sighed in appreciation. While they begged him to tell another story, Lady Wharncliffe heard the door open and Patsy Cornwallis West came hurrying in. Lillie and she were surprised to see Patsy, who had gone with her children to the country for a week.

She apologised to Lady Wharncliffe, took Lillie by the hand and drew her away. 'Dearest Lillie!' she exclaimed. 'Thank Heavens you're here! I've been looking everywhere.'

'What is it?' Lillie smiled. 'I thought you were in Wales.'

'We have been – and they still are. It's looking lovely. I've only come down for tonight.'

'What's the matter?' Lillie asked.

Patsy had returned in answer to a special invitation to go to the Opera with Lady Dudley, only to find when she arrived that her maid had forgotten to pack any of her evening gowns. She wanted to know if Lillie was going out that evening. By chance, Lillie was not and Patsy hugged her in relief. 'Well, I thought, what a marvellous stroke it would be, if I borrowed your dress, your little black dress. Can you imagine the effect – me appearing in your dress? With Lady Dudley? All my admirers, and yours, would realise at once!'

'Yes,' Lillie said, doubtfully.

'Then you'll let me borrow it?' She touched Lillie's sleeve, already imagining herself in it.

Lillie hesitated. She did not wish to seem unhelpful nor overcautious, but she knew Patsy was quite liable to forget and go off with it to Wales. 'Of course,' she answered. 'But it is a little the worse for wear.'

'Oh, don't worry,' Patsy assured her. 'I'm a trifle fuller in the hips than you, but I shall take the greatest care of it. You're an angel! It will be wonderful!' She kissed her and went to say hello to Lady Wharncliffe.

Oscar had risen and overheard. 'It would be even more of a sensation,' he murmured, 'if you appeared at the Opera with Lady Dudley.'

'She's hardly likely to ask me,' Lillie said.

He sighed. 'Well – at least, your dress will have the honour.'

Late the next morning, Lillie was still in her white wrap, when Dominique showed in Patsy, who was returning her dress wrapped in tissue paper. Patsy was sparkling and lively. 'It was an unforgettable evening! I just haven't been to bed.'

Lillie smiled. 'You look very well on it.'

'I'll sleep on the train and suffer for it tomorrow,' Patsy said and handed the package to Dominique. 'And here's your dress.'

Lillie was relieved to have it back. 'Did it have the effect you wanted?'

'Oh, my dear, I can't tell you! Everyone raved about it. Of course, they all realised whose it was. I went on to a ball afterwards and I've never been asked to dance so often!'

'I'm glad,' Lillie laughed.

Patsy hesitated. 'There is one thing . . . It was a little long for me, after all. And we were playing some silly game and I caught my foot in the hem. And as I was dancing, I kept catching it!' She laughed. 'It was very amusing.'

Lillie managed to keep smiling.

Patsy kissed her. 'Nothing to worry about. Now, I must dash or I'll miss my train. Thank you again. See you soon.'

Dominique saw her out and Lillie waited, a little perturbed, until she came back in, still carrying the package. 'Is she not lovely, signora?' Dominique smiled. 'So sympatica.'

'Let me see it,' Lillie said urgently. 'The dress, Dominique.'

Dominique unwrapped the tissue paper and held up the black dress. Both she and Lillie gasped. It was ripped badly near the hem at the front. Lillie hurried to it and opened the skirt out, 'Oh, no . . .' Dominique breathed. It was torn in several places. 'And under the arm, Signora.'

Lillie gazed at it, upset. The seam under the right arm had given way. 'How could she? . . .' she muttered. 'How *could* she?' It was a disaster. Lillie had absolutely nothing else to wear in the evenings.

'She has so many dresses herself, she would not think it important,' Dominique said. Lillie ran her hand under the tears. It was not possible for them to be mended. She looked up to see her maid smiling shyly, even pleased. 'Now Mr Langtry will have to buy you something new – and you will be like the other ladies.'

But Edward was less than sympthetic, when she showed him. 'More fool you for lending it to her,' he grunted. And he was annoyed when she told him they would have to send their excuses to Lord Rosslyn who had invited them to dinner. He had been looking forward to it and would not accept her statement that she had nothing to wear. 'We've been through this before!' he snapped. 'That evening gown you had in Southampton –'

'It is dowdy and provincial,' she told him. 'For better or worse, what I wear now is important. Our clothes must be right for the world we live in. Before, it didn't matter. Now it does.'

'It's all because of that damned black dress!' he fumed. 'It's a kind of talisman. You only wear it because it gets you noticed!'

'I wear it because people respect mourning, so it is suitable for every occasion,' she said evenly. 'Without it, nothing that has happened would have been possible. And without it, we can forget these past months and sink quietly back into the crowd. No more invitations. Is that what you want?'

He knew she was challenging him, but he, too, had become used to their new life. 'The prices these London dressmakers charge are ruinous,' he complained.

She breathed more easily. He had given in. 'I shall write to Madame Nicolle in Jersey,' she decided. 'She has my measurements. If I tell her it is urgent, she can make up an identical dress, say, by the end of next week. We shall only have to cancel invitations till then.'

'Very well,' he agreed reluctantly. 'She should be reasonable. Better get her to use a stronger material.'

They were in the bedroom. When he left, Lillie sat down at the dressingtable immediately. She took pen and paper and began to write to Madame Nicolle, but she had scarcely started when the door opened and Dominique hurried in. Her eyes were wide and her mouth worked, although no sound came out. 'Yes?' Lillie waited. 'What is it?'

Dominique swallowed. 'She's here! Signora – Lady Dudley . . . She's here – in the drawingroom.'

Lady Dudley, dressed in a gorgeous pink confection, all frills and tucks with a full bustle, a coquettish birds' wing hat, was inspecting a framed sketch of Lillie by Frank Miles. She turned as Lillie came in with Dominique. She was still in her wrap.

'Do forgive me,' Lillie apologised. 'I haven't dressed yet.'

'You must forgive *me*, Mrs Langtry,' Lady Dudley answered, 'for calling so unexpectedly.' She would not take tea, saying she had only looked in.

In her excitement, Dominique had quite forgotten herself and stood gazing. 'Very well, Dominique,' Lillie said. Dominique blinked, bobbed and went out, but could not resist a last look back at the door as she closed it.

Before Lillie could speak again, Lady Dudley smiled. In contrast to her manner on any previous occasion, it was open and friendly. 'You must also pardon me, Mrs Langtry, for not having got to know you before this. I have wished to very much, but there have always been so many people claiming your attention. I would have called, but did not wish to intrude since you were in mourning.'

With surprise, Lillie realised that Georgiana Dudley was very different from how she had imagined her. She was friendly and charming to those she liked. 'I should have called on you,' she said.

'I wish you had,' Lady Dudley informed her. 'The reason for my coming here today is that King Leopold of the Belgians is shortly to visit London, as you may know. We are giving a reception and ball for him. My husband and I would very much like you to be there.'

Lillie's elation faded as quickly as it rose. 'Thank you, but – we have had to cancel all engagements for the next eight or nine days.'

'Our ball is not till a week on Saturday,' Lady Dudley told her.

Lillie worked out the dates quickly. It left just enough time for Madame Nicolle. 'That should be possible. I – we would love to come.'

'Good,' Lady Dudley smiled, then added after a pause, 'And I promise, you shall not be taken in to dinner by Lord Randolph Churchill.' Lillie was puzzled and Lady Dudley went on. 'If you do not know, then a word of warning. Since Lord Randolph insulted the Prince of Wales, or more accurately, Her Royal Highness Princess Alexandra, the Prince has said he will attend no function at which Lord Randolph is present, nor will he receive anyone with whom he is intimate, until he apologises fully. His wife Jennie, very sensibly, is staying in Ireland with his parents for the time being. Those hosts who have protected their friends by ensuring that he partners you, when he shows himself, have displayed great lack of consideration for a newcomer. Watch out for them.'

Many things had become clear to Lillie. Remarks about

Jennie Churchill staying away, about Randolph's father, the Duke of Marlborough, accepting the position of Viceroy of Ireland so unexpectedly, the four or five times she had been seated next to him. 'Thank you, I shall be more careful,' she said. She had a sudden thought. 'Will the Prince be present at your ball?'

'Unfortunately, no,' Lady Dudley regretted. 'He's in Paris. Well – we look forward to seeing you.'

'I am delighted to be asked,' Lillie said sincerely. To have Georgiana Dudley as an avowed friend would make her position immeasurably more secure.

Lady Dudley smiled to her and moved towards the door. 'Oh – there is one small point,' she mentioned, turning back. 'My husband is of advancing years and has a morbid fear of black mourning. He will not allow me to wear it, nor anything of that colour to be in the house. I would appreciate it, if you could lay aside your mourning just for that evening. Frankly, that is why I have not been able to invite you before.'

Lillie smiled back, but her mind was in turmoil. It was a bombshell.

As soon as she had shown Lady Dudley out, she changed quickly into a blouse and the skirt of her old blue travelling suit and took a cab to Salisbury Street to find Oscar.

He was as understanding and sympathetic as she had known he would be. In his shirtsleeves, writing an article on the reform of architecture, he gave it up at once to concentrate on her problem. The answer was basically simple, he told her. Edward would just have to spend some money for once.

'For a dress I'll be able to wear three or four times at most?' She shook her head. An evening gown, especially made and designed for her, could cost hundreds of pounds. Ladies of fashion needed at least four or five completely new gowns each year, as well as morning and afternoon dresses, clothes for the country, for riding and sailing, not counting hats, capes, coats, shoes and all the other accessories. The Beauties were tacitly excused from entertaining, because for them it was even more expensive. They were seen night after night and were expected to dazzle, to appear constantly in something new and more gorgeous. Lillie had not exaggerated when she said that, for her, without the black dress none of it would have been possible. She was resigned to having to miss the ball at Dudley House. When the copy of her black dress arrived, she would be able to continue for a while as she had done, but only for another month or so, until it would no longer be credible for her to wear mourning. What would happen then, she would not let herself think.

Oscar had taken her hand. 'My poor Lillie,' he sympathised. 'If only I possessed the riches of the East! I would pour them at your feet – rubies and emeralds, pearls the size of pigeons' eggs and diamonds like your eyes.'

She smiled as he kissed her hand. 'It's only another reception.'

'You might as well have said to Wellington, "It's only Waterloo,"' he declared. To have come so near . . . 'There must be something!' he snapped his fingers. 'Borrow a dress from Patsy.'

'She's in Wales,' Lillie reminded him.

'Write to your Madame Nicolle and ask her to make you something of a different colour, in a different style.'

'I daren't. Not without being there.'

'Tell her you want something Grecian, classically severe in line, embroidered with pearls,' he suggested seriously. Lillie had a quick vision of the garment Madame Nicolle would turn out, given these directions, and laughed. Oscar drew her down on to the settle sofa and sat on the floor at her feet. He rested an arm across her knees and she caught her breath at the contact. He did not seem to notice and she was glad. Her feelings for him had risen closer to the surface and she knew that she would find it difficult to resist, if he made advances. He looked up. 'The only other answer is to order something from one of the fashionable dressmakers, like Mrs Stratton.'

'How could I pay for it?'

'They don't send in their bills for months,' he pointed out. 'When they do, order something else. It could be years

211

before they realise you can't pay for any of them.'

'That sounds rather dishonest,' she objected.

Oscar sighed. 'How shall I ever convince your Puritan conscience that honesty is the worst policy?' She smiled, then became grave as he gazed up at her. He rose slowly to his knees, facing her. He took her face gently in both hands. 'Oh, my dear,' he whispered, 'one day you and I will commit a great folly . . .'

Lillie spoke to Edward, who was doubtful at what she proposed, but finally gave her permission at least to try. She wrote to Madame Nicolle and, at the same time, to society's leading dressmaker, Mrs Stratton, who called at Eaton Place the very next day.

Mrs Stratton was middleaged and shrewd. She took in the modest decoration and furnishings of the apartment and listened attentively, nodding, while Lillie explained why she had asked to see her. 'The reception and ball for King Leopold, at Dudley House. Yes, I have made gowns for several ladies who'll be there.' She was controlling her own keenness. It would be something of a coup to add The Jersey Lily to her list of clients. 'There is just enough time, and it would be a real pleasure to dress you, Mrs Langtry.' She hesitated. 'Although I understood you always wore mourning.'

'Other colours are suitable for mourning besides black,' Lillie said.

'Oh, indeed. Silver, white, mauve.'

Lillie felt tense, now the moment had come. 'There is the question of cost.'

'I'm sure we can arrange something,' Mrs Stratton said warily.

'I am limited by a fairly strict budget,' Lillie told her.

'Perhaps I didn't – ' Mrs Stratton began, then smiled. 'What I mean is, for someone like you, my cost would be negligible, almost non-existent – if you would agree to say now and then who made the dress for you?'

It was even better than Lille had hoped, but she hid her surprise. She had been prepared for some bargaining. 'It would have to be something I designed myself,' she insisted.

'. . . Within reason,' Mrs Stratton conceded.

Lillie could already see it in her mind. 'Something Greek, classically severe, embroidered with pearls.'

Mrs Stratton's eyebrows rose and she nodded. 'That should be possible. If you are not too busy, perhaps I could take your measurements now.'

Dudley House in Park Lane was one of the most superb houses in London. The rich Earl of Dudley had married Georgiana, daughter of a Scots baronet, when he was nearly fifty and she still in her twenties. It was an arranged marriage, not a love-match. Although they had grown to care for each other and she had borne him six children, they were not emotionally attached. Following the rigid custom of the day, in spite of his infidelities, she had remained completely faithful to him, until after the birth of their son and heir. For a time, she had been the chosen favourite of the Prince of Wales, a satisfying and courtly romance with no risk of further complications, which had confirmed her standing as one of the leaders of civilised society.

Dudley House was a fitting setting for a royal reception, as sumptuous as a palace all the long way from the marble entrance to the impressive ballroom, ablaze with a spangled mosaic of lights, dresses, jewellery and uniforms, with footmen in powdered wigs and livery spaced out along the rose marble walls. Lady Dudley in a deep-cut gown of dark green satin, statuesque, resplendent, wearing her celebrated double rope of matched pearls was greeting the handsome Russian Ambassador, Count Schouvalov. With her was her aged, very aristocratic husband. They stood near the opened doors of the ballroom to greet their guests who were led forward by the majordomo. The circulating guests already inside kept a casually interested eye on each new arrival. Their conversation made a low hum against the Mendelssohn selection being played by the orchestra.

After Schouvalov came Sir Charles and Lady Elphinstone, then the majordomo announced, 'Mr and Mrs Edward Langtry.' The buzz of conversation increased noticeably in volume but suddenly was cut off, when Lillie appeared. The only sound was the light, tinkling music.

In advance of Edward, she paused deliberately just in the doorway, before moving forward to Lord and Lady Dudley. She wore no jewellery. Her dress was of pure white velvet, classically simple except for the ruched pout of its bustle. Down its front, from the neckline to her white, satin slippers were two rows of tiny pearls. Her arms were covered with long, white gloves. With her auburn colouring and the creamy swell of her breasts above the low neck, the effect was sensational. All eyes went to the slenderness of her waist and the revealed shape of her thighs against the straight front of the dress, as she came forward. The crowd began to edge nearer and a murmur of astonishment and admiration grew at the dramatic transformation of her appearance.

Glancing round, Georgiana Dudley saw that some people seemed actually amazed and had so far forgotten themselves as to stare. She smiled to Lillie. 'I am so glad you could come, Mrs Langtry. You are looking especially lovely tonight. My husband – '

Lord Dudley bowed, utterly captivated. 'My dear Mrs Langtry . . . I shall never forgive Georgiana for hiding you away,' he swore. 'Now, you must come with me, I'm afraid. I've had strict instructions to present you the minute you arrive.' He bowed to his wife. 'Forgive us, my dear.' He offered Lillie his arm as they turned to the room.

Millais and Effie were there with Lord and Lady Rosslyn and moved forward with the crowd, which split apart to form an avenue. Lillie advanced between the lines of excited, whispering people on Lord Dudley's arm. She walked gracefully, with her faint hint of a smile, her head raised. People on the outskirts began to push forward, craning their necks. No one could remember anything like it. As the fever spread, women, some quite elderly, climbed on to chairs to have a better view.

Millais and Rosslyn gazed around, staggered by the reaction. Rosslyn saw Mrs Wheeler staring in disbelief and smiled, when she turned, chagrined, and sat abruptly, facing away from Lillie's triumph.

Edward walked down the avenue several paces behind Lillie and Lord Dudley. He felt abominably self-conscious, yet need not have worried. Hardly anyone noticed him. He stopped, when they stopped. Ahead of them was a short, stocky man in his forties, wearing evening dress, talking to three or four men in uniform. When one of them said something, he turned. He was heavily bearded, wearing the star and ribbon of the Order of the Garter. His raffish, assessing eyes widened as he caught sight of Lillie.

Lord Dudley bowed. 'Your Majesty, may I have the honour to present Mrs Edward Langtry?'

As Lillie curtsied, King Leopold's eyes swept over her. He stepped forward and held out both hands to raise her up, retaining both her hands in his. 'I did not know England possessed so rare a jewel,' he said, his voice strongly accented, guttural. 'This is worth coming so far.'

When Lillie presented Edward, the King nodded affably and then ignored him, as he did everyone else, speaking only to Lillie. The ball was about to begin. By etiquette, he should have danced first with his hostess. Instead, holding Lillie's right hand, he led her out on to the floor and bowed to her. At a signal from Lord Dudley, the orchestra began to play the opening waltz and Lillie and King Leopold began to dance alone. The applause was started by Lord and Lady Dudley.

Lillie could have laughed with happiness. The results had been even more striking than she had dared to hope. As she spun, she saw Lord Dudley and Georgiana begin to dance and, gradually, the other guests watching from the sides joined in, until the whole ballroom was spinning with dancers. King Leopold was smiling to her, his eyes fixed on hers, his hand gripping firmly at her waist.

# CHAPTER EIGHT

It was not long after eight on a summer morning. The curtains in the bedroom were closed and Lillie and Edward were in bed, asleep. Lillie came awake at a soft but urgent knocking at the door. Beside her, Edward grunted in protest.

The door opened a crack and they heard Dominique whispering, 'Signora . . . Signora!'

'Come in!' Lillie called.

Dominique opened the door and stopped, embarrassed to see them together in bed. She turned away as Edward sat up in his nightshirt, fumbling for his pocketwatch on the bedside table. 'What the devil's the time?' he complained.

Dominique was flustered. 'Scusi – scusi, Signore, Signora. Ma – '

'What is it, Dominique?' Lillie asked.

Her maid swallowed. 'The King!' she blurted. 'The King is here.' Lillie and Edward stared at her. 'King Leopold – of the Belgians.'

Edward's mouth gaped. 'It's not half past eight yet!'

'He's called to see the Signora,' Dominique shrugged. 'Alone.'

'What – what have you done with him?' Lillie asked.

'He is waiting . . . in the drawingroom.'

'Oh, my heavens,' Lillie gasped and slid quickly out of bed.

King Leopold was wearing a dark frockcoat and trousers and carrying his tophat and gloves, which he beat slowly against his thigh as he looked round the little drawingroom. He turned swiftly when Lillie came in.

She had put on a housedress in soft, lightly tinted chiffon, the skirt very full and gathered behind, the neck round and deeply cut. Her arms were bare, but her shoulders were covered by a short cape of the same chiffon material, which

216

tied in a wide frill round the neck. The dress clung to her figure when she moved and gave a teasing impression of being almost transparent. Her hair hung behind in a thick, braided coil, reaching to her waist. Dominique closed the door behind her and she curtsied.

King Leopold gave her his hand to raise her. His gaze travelled over her figure and slowly up again to her face. 'You are even more beautiful than I remembered,' he breathed.

'You must forgive me for not being ready to receive you, Your majesty,' she said. 'But I had no idea – '

'It is I who ask forgiveness, madame,' he assured her. 'I gave way to impulse – an irresistible impulse to see you again before another day had passed.' He was still holding her hand and released it with a touch of reluctance.

'I am honoured,' Lillie murmured. It was two days after the Dudleys' ball and all London was ringing with the story of how she had entranced the royal visitor, but she had not expected to see him again. Certainly, not at Eaton Place. She moved away, turning instinctively just where the light from the windows caught her hair and the translucent folds of her dress.

'You are a thief, Mrs Langtry,' Leopold declared.

'Sir?'

'You rob a man of breath. And of words. I cannot remember a single one of the pretty speeches I made up on the journey here.'

She inclined her head slightly, over her surprise. 'I am forgetting,' she apologised. 'May it please you to sit? May I offer you some coffee?'

'No, no. I regret, chère madame, that I cannot stay. I have meetings with your Colonial Office and Foreign Office, then I dine with my respected Cousin Victoria, at Windsor.'

'You lead a crowded life, sir.'

'That is why I am here at this unearthly hour,' Leopold smiled, 'the only time I have to spare. I keep remembering the moments I spent in your company at Lord Dudley's. That memory drew me back like a bee to a rare and delicate blossom.'

Lillie smiled. 'You have remembered your pretty speeches, sir.'

He moved nearer. 'By heart, and from the heart,' he said. 'I wished to renew our acquaintance in less formal surroundings – and to beg the privilege of calling on you again.' He held out his hand. When Lillie gave him hers, he raised it to his lips.

Later in the day, Patsy looked in, dressed for walking. She was agog when she heard the news. 'And so saying, he left? Like the Demon King in the pantomime! And before breakfast, too. What did Mr Langtry say?'

'He just turned over and went back to sleep,' Lillie laughed. 'We didn't get home from Lady Manners' party till four this morning. Anyway, the King never even asked if he was at home.'

'No, he wouldn't,' Patsy said. 'When royalty call, if it's only you they want to see no one else can come into the room – unless they're invited.'

'No one?'

'Not even husbands,' Patsy told her. 'That's what got the Prince of Wales mixed up in the Mordaunts' divorce. He used to call and spend an hour or so with Harriet, when Sir Charles was at the House of Commons. And of course, none of the servants could go in, unless they were sent for.' She smiled. 'They never were.'

After a moment, Lillie smiled, too, understanding. 'People always think the worst.'

Patsy's eyes twinkled. 'The trouble is – they're usually right.' They laughed. 'And now, the King of the Belgians comes calling on you before breakfast. All the ladies in London will be mad with envy.'

'After what you've just said,' Lillie murmured, 'I'm not sure I want them to know.'

'Well, don't ask me to keep it secret,' Patsy protested. 'It's far too good a story.'

The dress from Madame Nicolle had been delivered, to Dominique's regret, a perfect replica of the one that had been torn. She thought that Lillie's triumph would lead to a whole wardrobeful of new gowns. Lillie explained to Patsy that she was still, officially, in mourning. 'Yes,' Patsy sympathised. 'And besides, it's so distinctive. Wearing it, one could hardly fail to be recognised.' In some things, they understood each other perfectly.

The point was proved an hour later, when they went for a walk in the Park. It was the fashionable hour, relaxed and elegant. Ladies and gentlemen strolled by the sides of the bridle path. Older ladies sat on painted chairs, watching the passing scene as impeccable horsemen and ladies in riding habits, sitting sidesaddle, rode by. As soon as Lillie appeared, there was a shift of interest among the spectators.

She paused in her walk along the path, acknowledging the gentlemen who had raised their hats. Patsy had dropped back to speak to one of the riders, who had dismounted by her.

He was Moreton Frewen, in his mid twenties, only a little older than Lillie and Patsy, tall, handsome, with a light moustache. His tight coat and breeches revealed an aggressively masculine physique. When Patsy beckoned Lillie over to introduce her, she was surprised to find they had already met.

'Last night, at Lady Manners',' Frewen told her, and bowed to Lillie. 'I'm still trying to think of an answer.'

'To what?' Patsy asked, intrigued.

Frewen paused. 'I was placed next to Mrs Langtry at table. She looked straight at me and asked, "What are your spiritual beliefs?"'

Patsy just stopped herself from laughing out loud. 'And what did you reply?'

'Nothing,' he admitted. 'It shut me up throughout the whole dinner.'

He had been so superior and male, talking down to the little woman, that Lillie had been unable to resist deflating him. 'Perhaps we can discuss the subject again some time, Mr Frewen,' she suggested innocently.

'I'd be more than delighted,' he said quickly.

Patsy saw him glance to the side, where his friends were waiting, and excused him from staying any longer. He remounted reluctantly, raised his tophat and rode on. Patsy could laugh at last. 'Spiritual beliefs, indeed! Lillie – really . . . You might as well ask an aborigine for his opinion of the Pre-Raphaelites.' They walked on. 'Why didn't you tell me you'd met him?'

'It wasn't at all important,' Lillie said.

'Not important? He's one of the most elegible bachelors in London. Oh, not as far as money goes. He hasn't a penny. But he has other qualities.'

'Yes,' Lillie smiled.

'I thought you'd notice,' Patsy murmured. They spoke quietly, responding to the greetings of ladies and gentlemen as they passed. 'I protest I'm not going to introduce you to anyone else – particularly not to any more of my admirers, or potential admirers. It's the surest way to lose them.'

Lillie was surprised all at once to find herself ignored. Everyone had begun looking beyond Patsy and her, the older ladies rising from their chairs. Patsy and she stopped and turned.

Coming up the bridlepath at a brisk pace were three riders, one ahead of the other two. He wore a short, clipped beard. At thirty-five, his figure in a few years could become stout, but he was still compact, physically powerful. He was not conventionally handsome, but the air of command and authority which enveloped him made him enormously attractive. Lillie had never seen him before, though she had seen many drawings and photographs of him. In any case, the broad, red headband of his horse identified him at once as Albert Edward, Prince of Wales.

Of the two riders following him, one was an equerry, the other she recognised as the famous Arctic explorer, Sir Allen Young. The Prince was faultlessly dressed, wearing a hat with a lower crown than the standard tophat. He touched the brim occasionally in greeting as the gentlemen on the paths raised theirs and the ladies curtsied.

Lillie was excited to see him smile and touch his hat to Patsy, as he passed. 'Do you know him?'

'The Prince of Wales?' Patsy laughed, then bit her lip and nodded. 'Quite well. We're old friends.'

Lillie gazed after him as he rode away.

Oscar's livingroom was deliberately bare, painted white. One section of the wall seemed to be decorated with an arabesque scrawl. Closer to, one could see that it was, in fact, covered with the signatures of dozens of notable people who had visited him. The few objects the room contained were in perfect taste, mainly bowls and vases of blue and white china. There was a Japanese flower print on one wall. On the surfaces were several, strategically placed floral arrangements, but the centre pieces of all the arrangements were lilies. One superb amaryllis stood alone on a pedestal table under a pen and ink portrait of Lillie, herself.

She had spent the whole day with Patsy and was now seated on the settle next to Jimmy Whistler, watching Oscar rearrange a display of pale, lemon-coloured single roses. They were sipping tea from tiny, blue porcelain bowls, which Oscar paused to refill from a blue and white teapot that stood on a trivet by the fire.

'It seems our Divinity has had an eventful day, Oscar,' Whistler observed.

Lillie smiled. 'You must not mock me for being impressed.'

'Perish the thought, my dearest Lillie,' Oscar protested. 'Were we mocking, James?'

'By no means. After all, a day which begins with being awakened by the King of the Belgians and ends with one's first glimpse of the future King of England cannot be called entirely uneventful.'

'And what did you think of him?' Oscar asked.

'The King or the Prince?'

'The King.'

'I've an idea he thinks his divine rights extend a little further than I'd be prepared to admit.'

Oscar and Whistler laughed. 'And the Prince?' Whistler asked.

'He rides like a gentleman,' Lillie said. 'I think I might be a little afraid of him – though Patsy says he's approachable.'

Oscar raised an eyebrow. 'Well, she should know.'

It was just sufficiently pointed for Lillie to want to ask what he meant, but before she could do so, the door opened and Ellen Terry came in. Warmhearted, beautiful Nelly, with her shining, golden hair, tilted nose and generous mouth. She was thirty, but looked much younger, her figure lean and tall. She wore a dress of brown silk, with a sealskin jacket and cap, and had called in on her way to the theatre. Frank Miles had taken her up to show her his latest portrait sketches of Lillie. 'They are exquisite,' Nelly told her. 'Exquisite!'

Oscar bowed to Lillie. 'Praise not the artist, but his inspiration.'

Miles had followed Nelly in, his arms round the shoulders of Sally in her loose draperies. 'I happen to think they are some of the best things I have ever done,' he said, piqued.

'Which only goes to prove my point,' Oscar stressed. 'You were awaiting a subject which lit the divine fire in your soul and touched the tip of your brush with magic.'

'Thank you, Oscar,' Miles said. 'At least, I think I thank you. I assume that is a compliment.'

'It is safer to assume so,' Whistler grunted, and they laughed.

'You will now take tea, Nelly,' Oscar insisted. 'Chinese – my own blend.'

He beckoned to Sally who fetched him a white porcelain container and removed the stopper. Ceremoniously, Oscar took two pinches of tea from it and dropped them into the teapot, topping it up with boiling water from the kettle at the fire. Sally returned the container to the sideboard and came back to kneel beside Lillie.

'Now we leave it for two minutes to release its flavour,' Oscar explained.

'How charming!' Nelly exclaimed. 'Is that the way they make tea in China?'

'If not, it's the way they should,' Whistler commented.

Lillie was the only one who did not laugh. She had not really been listening. Nelly looked at her. 'You're very quiet, Lillie.'

222

Lillie stirred. 'H'm? . . . Yes, I'd love some more.'

The others laughed, but Oscar was slightly disconcerted. 'You haven't heard a word we've been saying,' he accused.

'I was – sorry, I was thinking about something else,' she confessed.

'Are we to hear what it was?' Miles asked, and she shook her head.

'Then we must guess,' Oscar proposed.

'She was wonderin' if you 'ad any biscuits,' Sally said, her accent a rich, unmistakable Cockney.

In the laughter, Lillie ruffled her hair. 'Forgive me, Miss Sally,' Oscar apologised. 'They are in the blue barrel over there.' Sally rose and found the china biscuit barrel. She brought it back and squatted, starting on the tea biscuits.

'She was wondering what to wear for the ball at the Russian Embassy,' Nelly guessed.

Lillie shook her head.

'She was wondering . . . how to stop us wondering what she ws thinking,' Whistler said.

Lillie smiled to him. 'Thank you, Jimmy,'

'No truly,' Oscar decided, 'if I were asked to consider the daydream of the Lily, I would say she was thinking . . . about love.'

Lillie was too surprised for a moment to deny it. Seeing her reaction, Miles chuckled.

Nelly was interested at once. 'Who is it?'

Lillie had to answer. 'If you must know,' she said slowly, 'I was thinking about my husband.'

It was fairly late, when she reached home. In the drawing-room, the gaslight was turned down low. She moved round to look at the highbacked chair by the fire.

Edward lay sprawled in it, in a drunken sleep, his stiff collar wrenched open. The brandy decanter was on the wine table beside him, empty, and he was still holding an empty brandy glass loosely in his lap. She took the glass from his hand and set it on the mantelpiece. He had begun to drink too much at Cliffe Lodge, but, until recently, it had seldom had any visible effect.

She glanced again at him expressionlessly and turned out

the light.

She was alone in bed when she came awake as Dominique touched her shoulder. It was morning.

'Signora!' Dominique said urgently, 'he is here again, King Leopold! I told him you were asleep, but he said he would wait.'

Lillie pushed herself up, her head clearing. 'Where's Mr Langtry?'

'Asleep,' Dominique reported, disapprovingly. 'On the sofa in the diningroom.'

Lillie got out of bed, shrugging off her nightdress, trying to think. 'Help me dress,' she said. 'Then make some coffee. Bring it into the drawingroom in ten minutes – and stay to serve it.'

King Leopold was seated by the fire. He rose and crossed to meet Lillie as she came in. She made to curtsey, but he caught her hands, preventing her. 'No, no,' he chuckled. 'No need for formality between us.' He looked at her appreciatively. She was again wearing the loose, chiffon housedress with its small cape over her bare arms and shoulders. 'Enchanting – as ever.' Still holding her right hand, he stroked the skin of the back of her hand.

'I am overwhelmed Your Majesty should visit me again so soon,' Lillie said.

'I could not stay away.'

She did not withdraw her hand, but began to move towards the fireplace and he had to let it go. 'I hope my husband may have the honour of meeting Your Majesty this time,' she said.

His voice was flat. 'I have already met Mr Langtry, at Lord Dudley's.'

'Will Your Majesty be seated?'

'It is you who must sit.' He smiled. 'You see? I am learning the English manner – which is more democratic.' He was suddenly quite charming. Lillie sat in the smaller armchair by the fire. 'Ravissante!' he professed. 'I have longed to see you seated by your own fireside.'

'You are used to far grander surroundings, sir,' she smiled.

'I weary of them,' he said quietly. 'Of what value is a marble palace, if it does not contain the only object one desires?' He moved nearer.

Lillie had known this could be awkward, but his tone was so courteous, deferential almost, that she was reassured. She was used by now to gentlemen swearing devotion to her, and had learnt how to handle them. 'Are your days still so busy, sir?' she asked, conversationally.

'Hélas . . .' he confirmed. 'Otherwise, I would beg you to keep the afternoons for me.'

'I would not presume to take up so much of your time, sir.' She became aware of him standing over her. 'And I am sure you have many other calls to make. It might cause resentment that –'

'How should it?' he broke in. 'If we keep my visits here a secret – between us. H'm?' She stiffened as his hand touched her shoulder. 'Who needs to know?'

'My husband may not understand that you –'

Leopold chuckled, his hand fondling her loose hair. 'Si douce . . . si lisse, ta chevelure. And your skin, so soft . . .' The back of his hand caressed her cheek.

'Please –' Lillie entreated. She rose and stepped away. She had been mistaken. King Leopold would not let himself be put off easily. Subtle men she could deal with, but he was much more direct. She could hear him laughing quietly.

'There is no need to be coy,' he chuckled. As she moved further away, he followed her. 'You are a realist. I can tell. And you are beautiful – but poor. That can change. You understand?'

It would soon be too late and Lillie prayed that Dominique would arrive. Her whole newly won place in society was in the balance. She had to appeal to him. 'Sir,' she began, 'if I have said or done anything to make you think –'

He caught her arm, pulling her round to face him. 'Your eyes told me everything I needed to know, the moment we met.' Her drew her to him and kissed her. His arms were incredibly strong. Other men had snatched kisses from her and she had reproved them, laughing and forgiving them. She stood perfectly still, letting him kiss her without responding, but his mouth was greedy, forcing hers open. She twisted her head away. He did not let her go, but nuzzled her neck, pawing her. 'You are – You must let me! Je te desire . . . tu comprends?'

They were nearly at the small sofa and he dragged her down on to it. She had managed to get her hands between them to keep him from pressing against her and could not prevent him throwing the cape back to bare her shoulders. 'Comme tu es belle! Et blanc comme le lys! . . . The Jersey Lily . . .' he chuckled, caressing her arms and shoulders, his hands dipping towards the swell of her breasts. Lillie felt no excitement, only an icy revulsion at his crudity. She struggled against him, not violently, just enough to stop him pulling down the top of her housedress. His left arm was round her, his right squeezing and tugging at her breasts which he could feel, soft and unprotected, under the chiffon. 'Say what you want,' he muttered. 'Whatever you want, it is yours! Jewels – clothes – whatever you –'

'You mustn't!' she pleaded. 'No, please – I beg you.'

His left arm moved up, going round her neck, forcing her head towards him, silencing her as he kissed her again. His right hand dropped to her upper thigh, gripping it tightly, and she lowered one hand to thrust it away. He laughed and his arm went round her waist, crushing her against him. It had been a feint. 'No,' she protested. 'No, please!'

He laughed. 'Struggle – yes, struggle! It is better, hein?' He kissed her, openmouthed, forcing her back on the sofa, overpowering her as he climbed on to her with his full weight. Her neck was bent forward painfully against the arm of the sofa. For all her own strength, she was helpless. Her senses swirled as she felt his hard masculinity rubbing insistently against her thighs. Then his hands were between them, snatching at the skirt of her dress, pulling it up to uncover her knees. She felt his fingers scrabbling between her legs and twisted sharply, trying to roll him off her, but he only pressed down more heavily, his fingers clawing at the buttons of his trousers.

The first knock at the door was soft, she barely heard it. She sobbed, when it was repeated. Then it came again, louder. Leopold stopped pawing at her and looked round, angry, panting. 'Who is – ? Send them away,' he hissed. Lillie was silent. 'Send them away!'

The door opened slightly and he pushed himself off Lillie quickly, sitting back on the sofa, fighting for breath, his lips drawn back. Lillie drew away from him and rose, her skirt tumbling down to cover her legs again. She pulled the cape round over her bust and shoulders. Controlling her own breathing, she called, 'Yes?'

The door opened fully and Dominique came in, carrying a tray with one cup and saucer, a silver coffeepot, milkjug and sugar basin. She bobbed. 'The coffee you ordered, Signora.' Her voice trailed way as Leopold glared at her.

He stared incredulously, when Lillie explained that a photographer would be arriving in ten minutes and excused herself to get dressed. She curtsied and went out, leaving Dominique to pour him a cup of coffee.

Frank Miles and Oscar looked in later. When Lillie told them what had happened, Miles laughed, but Oscar was angry at the thought of anyone, even a King, pawing at Lillie.

She had not told Edward. If he learnt the truth of the King's behaviour, she did not know how he would react.

'Yes,' Miles chuckled. 'One can hardly throw visiting Royalty down the stairs.'

Oscar knew it was worse than that. Lillie could not risk insulting Leopold. If he persisted and she did not give in to him, he could destroy her in Society. It would only take a word or two from him in the right place. 'You'll have to be very careful next time he calls,' he warned her. 'For he'll be back. You realise that? So what will you do?'

'I'm not sure,' Lillie said. 'But I know one thing. If I'm to be raped, I'd prefer to choose who does it.'

Again, it was only Miles who laughed.

The next morning was cold and wet, with rain beating on the windows of the bedroom.

Lillie had wakened early. She rose and put on her wrap. While she was making tea with Dominique in the tiny pantry, they heard knocking at the front door, downstairs.

She sent Dominique to answer and took a cup of tea back for Edward, who was sitting up in bed. She sat at the dressingtable to brush her hair, the long regular strokes of the brush helping to steady her nerves.

Dominique knocked on the door and came in, unable to hide her excitement. 'It *was* him, Signora.'

'You said what I told you to?'

'Si, Signora. But he insists on seeing you.'

'Then tell him again,' Lillie said. 'I am not yet dressed and am not available. He is not to be allowed in.'

'Si, Signora.' Dominique bobbed nervously.

Edward had been listening, puzzled. When Dominique left, he asked, 'What is all this? Who's not allowed in?'

'King Leopold,' Lillie told him calmly.

'King – ? And that stupid maid of yours left him standing on the doorstep?' he yelped. 'It's pouring out there! Call her back!'

'No.'

'But he's the – !' Edward nearly spilt the cup out of his saucer in his agitation. He laid it on the table and scrambled out of bed in his nightshirt. 'What are – ? You've done all this to get into Society – and you're sending the king away!'

'He called once too often,' Lillie said.

Edward ran to the window. He drew the curtains apart a chink and squinted down. Lillie was not nearly so calm as she appeared. For a second, she paused, showing her uncertainty, then went on brushing her hair.

From the window, Edward could see the top step outside the front door in Eaton Place. King Leopold was standing there in the pouring rain, in his tophat and frockcoat. He looked up and Edward shut the curtains.

King Leopold was certain he had seen movement. He stared up at the curtains, then at the front door, which was closing. When its lock clicked into place, he turned away. In one hand he carried a large bouquet, in the other a furled umbrella. He glanced up at the windows again and threw the bouquet down. Wet and chilled and furious, he shook out the umbrella, raised it over his head and stumped down the steps to the street.

It was nearly four o'clock before Lillie could get to Salisbury Street. Oscar was waiting, impatient to hear. 'I have never heard of anything so gloriously daring!' he laughed. 'So sublimely audacious.'

'And suicidal,' Lillie added.

'And suicidal,' he agreed. They were both partly excited, partly apprehensive at what she had done. 'To send a king packing . . . Oh, my dearest dear, I could hug you!' Oscar took Lillie by the shoulders and they smiled into each other's eyes. She expected him to embrace her and was ready to yield. Instead, he kissed her on the forehead and broke away, chuckling. 'One can only imagine how he felt. For the first time in his life, to have someone say "No" . . .'

He realised as clearly as Lillie that she had taken a very dangerous step, one that might make her no longer socially acceptable. So far she had only told Patsy, but, as he said, if she knew, by lunchtime half London would have heard. Lillie usually had several callers in the early afternoon. That day, no one had come. It might mean that already it was considered ruin to be seen with her. 'On the other hand,' Oscar comforted her, 'it may not mean anything. A few doors may close. A few invitations may be cancelled. But they can hardly send you to the Tower.'

As she smiled to him, troubled, Frank Miles joined them. 'Well, he's here,' he announced. 'Coming up the stairs.'

'Who is?'

'Leopold,' he told them, blandly. Lillie and Oscar were shaken, and Miles laughed at the success of his joke. 'Don't worry. It's not the king. It's the Prince.'

Lillie did not understand, but Oscar gasped, relaxing. 'I hope you're aware you nearly gave us both heart attacks . . . He means Prince Leopold, the Queen's youngest son.'

'He calls now and then. Like Princess Louise,' Miles explained to Lillie. 'Do come up to my studio and meet him.'

The door behind him was opened by Sally. 'They're in 'ere,' she called back.

Lillie was still recovering from the shock and had barely time to compose herself and curtsey. Miles turned in some confusion and Oscar and he bowed, as Sally showed in a pale, slim, young man of twenty-four, Prince Leopold. Quite handsome, with a thin moustache and short pointed beard just covering his chin, he was very intelligent, with gentle, perfect manners. A sufferer from haemophilia, his health had always been delicate, yet he refused to lead an invalid's life. With his very fashionable, older gentleman-in-attendance, he bowed in return. 'I trust you will forgive the intrusion? Lord Suffield and I were passing and thought we would like to see your latest work, Mr Miles.'

Lillie was startled, but hoped it did not show. It was the gentleman with the Prince to whom she had reacted. The urbane, elegant Lord Suffield, whose ball she had attended with her mother on that disastrous evening nearly eight years before.

Miles could see that Prince Leopold and Suffield were both intent on Lillie. 'Your Royal Highness, may I present Mrs Edward Langtry?' he said.

Lillie curtsied again and Prince Leopold smiled. 'You have no idea how keenly I have wanted to meet you, Mrs Langtry. I have heard so much about you from my sister Louise.'

'Her Royal Highness is very kind,' Lillie curtsied.

He gestured. 'May I present Lord Suffield?'

'If you'll pardon me, sir,' Suffield said with a bow, 'it is I who should have carried out the introductions. For after all, I am Mrs Langtry's oldest friend in London.'

Oscar and the others were surprised. Up till that moment, Lillie had never known how she would react if she met any of the Suffields. She smiled. 'I was not sure you would remember.'

'How could I ever forget?' Suffield exclaimed. 'You see, sir – gentlemen – my family and I have known this young lady since she was a mere child, in Jersey. And the first time she visited London, she came to visit us.'

'I have never forgotten that evening,' Lillie said smoothly, after a faint pause. 'It was the first ball I ever went to.'

Oscar was intrigued. 'I don't think you've ever told us about it.'

'What a delightful meeting,' Prince Leopold observed. 'We must not eavesdrop on old friends, gentlemen. Let us give them a moment.' He moved away and Frank Miles followed him. Oscar lingered to listen, but the Prince went on, 'I believe these are your rooms, Mr Wilde,' summoning him.

Left alone, Suffield took both Lillie's hands. 'Lillie, Lillie, Lillie . . .' he marvelled. 'I can't believe it. You're married?'

'For three and a half years now.'

'Bless me! And your parents are well?'

'Very well, thank you.'

'We should never have got out of touch,' he said. 'Of course, about the time you must have married, I went off with the Prince of Wales on his tour of India. After that, he sent me on a . . . private mission to St. Petersburg. When I returned last month, everyone was talking about the new beauty, Mrs Langtry. I saw some sketches and I must admit I wondered – '

'But you did not think it could possibly be me,' Lillie finished for him.

'How could I?' he laughed.

He has no inkling of how hurt I was that night, Lillie thought. He did not notice. Possibly, no one did. 'It would seem rather far-fetched,' she said.

Suffield considered her. She had become very poised, very different from the naive, pretty girl he remembered. She was undeniably lovely. He knew she had caused some stir, yet had not grasped its full extent. 'Look here,' he began, 'I don't know how many people in London you've met – '

'Quite a few.'

He smiled. 'What I meant was that we're giving a small concert at home tonight. Rubinstein is playing for us. And Madame Patti has agreed to sing. I should like – no, I insist on Mr Langtry and you joining us. We're still at the same place, Upper Grosvenor Street. My wife will be so pleased.'

Lillie inclined her head, with a faint smile. 'And so shall I be, Lord Suffield.'

'We have given you long enough, Lord Suffield,' Prince Leopold called.

Suffield bowed. 'Your indulgence, sir. I shall surrender the lady at once.'

As they moved forward, Lillie paused for a moment by Oscar. 'Prince Leopold obviously hasn't heard anything about this morning yet,' he told her quietly.

'Neither had Lord Suffield,' Lillie answered. 'He has invited me to a party tonight.'

Oscar was worried. 'It would be a disaster, if people snub you in public.'

'There is only one way to find out.'

'You'll go?' he asked her, surprised.

'I must,' she said. 'Or people will think I am afraid to show myself.'

The Suffield's ballroom was fairly crowded. They were popular hosts and Patti and Rubinstein a tremendous draw. Yet there was really only one subject of conversation.

Lord and Lady Suffield were told by Sir Allen Young, an inveterate gossip. Suffield was concerned. 'Leopold of the Belgians? I had no idea there was any connection.'

'Apparently, he had been most attentive.'

As a courtier, Suffield saw immediate and embarrassing complications in having invited Lillie and her husband. He could tell that his wife was upset. 'We must just hope, at least for tonight, that no one has heard.'

But it was too late. Everyone by now had been told some version of how Lillie had refused to receive King Leopold. Patsy was surrounded by a whole throng, agog to hear the details. 'It is true. Every word,' she assured them.

'I can't believe it!' Moreton Frewen declared.

'Neither could I at first,' she admitted. 'I asked her why. All she said was, "He did not behave like a gentleman, so I showed him the door."'

The coldly beautiful Mrs Wheeler was listening with Jimmy Whistler. 'It proves what I have always thought,' she remarked. 'That there is no place in Society for people who do not really know how to behave '

Whistler looked at her, screwing his monocle into his eye. 'I presume you are referring to the Belgian person.'

'You are not serious, sir,' she gasped, shocked.

'But I am. You see, to me it proves that kings, short of their royal trappings, may turn out to be mere mortal men.'

Mrs Wheeler wrote him off, finally and forever.

There was a surge of excitement in the room. Suffield heard his wife draw in her breath and turned. Lillie was coming in, holding Edward's arm. He could not hide his apprehension. She was wearing the new white dress which she had worn only once before, at Lady Dudley's. She was pale, but perfectly composed. Many memories swept in on her, as she saw the white and gilt ballroom with with its row of giant chandeliers. She paused just inside the doorway, aware of a tense silence and of everyone looking at her.

'Oh, dear . . .' Lady Suffield breathed, anxiously.

Suffield decided that he must just greet Lillie and her husband and try to act as if nothing had happened. Most people would take their cue from him, as host. As he took his wife's arm and started forward, there was a simultaneous movement of many of the other guests towards Lillie. Edward and she were coming forward and, within seconds were completely encircled, the gentlemen bowing, the ladies smiling, hoping to be noticed by her.

For a minute, the Suffields could not get through. They heard applause and watched in amazement as ladies on the edge of the crowd climbed chairs to see Lillie over the heads of those in front.

Lillie kept her poise in the crush, but was grateful when Patsy reached them, with Frewen. Patsy kissed her. 'My dear, you have never been so admired!' she said loudly. 'Everyone who is anyone is completely on your side.'

'May I add my admiration, Mrs Langtry?' Frewen asked. He nodded to Edward. 'Good evening, sir.'

Edward nodded back. He did not pretend to understand, but evidently, for some reason, these people approved of Lillie's treatment of their royal visitor.

Suffield and Lady Suffield managed to get to them. Lillie smiled. 'I'm sorry if we are a little late.'

'Not at all, Suffield assured her. He was as puzzled as Edward by the buzz all around them. 'My dear, you remember . . . Lillie?'

'Of course,' Lady Suffield said. She needed time to match the queenly young woman in the white gown with the awkward girl of her memory. 'Although, I might not have remembered you.'

Lillie smiled. 'I have merely left girlhood behind, Lady Suffield. My husband, Edward.'

Edward bowed and Suffield shook his hand. 'You are a fortunate, fortunate man, sir.'

'Yes, I – I am,' Edward replied.

Suffield chuckled, thinking he was being amusing. When nothing more came from Edward, he turned. 'May I introduce Sir Allen Young?'

Edward showed a trace of real interest. He had read all about Young's voyages of exploration. He was by way of being a popular hero, tall, spare, with restless, grey eyes.

Young bowed. 'Good evening. I have hoped to meet you before this, Mrs Langtry. But our paths never seem to have crossed.'

'How could they, Sir Allen?' Lillie smiled. 'You are always in the Arctic, searching for the North Pole, are you not?'

'Searching, but not finding,' Young conceded. 'Indeed, I have just returned from my latest expedition.'

'But without – uh?' Edward put in.

'Without success, sir, as you say,' Young nodded. 'Still, I shall not give up.'

'I'm afraid it is high time for the concert to begin, if you'll excuse us, Alleno,' Lord Suffield said. He offered his arm to Lillie. 'Now, you must sit with me. I'll introduce you to some of the others later.'

Lillie smiled demurely and took his arm. She was still glowing with the success of her dismissal of the King. She had not merely escaped from an embarrassing situation, but had won golden opinions for modesty and propriety. When they moved towards the dais at the far end of the ballroom, the other guests parted for them and Suffield was amazed by the obvious interest they all took in Lillie and by her wide acquaintance.

Whistler was standing foursquare in their path, one hand on his hip. Suffield paused and introduced them, then blinked when she said, 'Oh, yes. Hello, Jimmy.'

'Ravishing as ever, my Divinity,' Whistler admired. 'I am here only to gaze on you.' He touched his fingers to his lips in a kiss and stood aside.

Beyond him, an exotic figure was staring at Lillie. A lean man, with hair so long it heaped in curls on his shoulders and was secured by a leather headband round his forehead. He had a close-cropped beard and wore a fringed leather shirt, buckskin trousers and mocassins. 'May I introduce a countryman of mine,' Whistler barked, 'a distinguished poet – Joaquin Miller.'

Lillie had heard of the backwoodsman poet, really from San Francisco, whose deliberately simple verses had created something of a literary sensation during his tour of Europe. 'Good evening, Mr Miller,' she said.

Miller was silent, as if he had seen a vision, but as she made to move on, he bowed low. 'I beg your pardon. Humbly.'

'There is no need,' she told him.

'Oh, but there is!' he broke out. 'Where did you get those eyes? Those blue eyes . . . I have watched you since you came into the room, devoured you. Trying to frame a glittering fabric of words to greet you. But I am speechless.'

'You seem to be doing very well, Mr Miller,' Lillie said.

There was light laughter from those around. 'Oh, do not mock!' Miller cried passionately. 'I have seen the power of the lodestone, the irresistible homing instinct of the birds. But until this moment, I never knew what it was that drew me to these shores.'

'You should put it all in a poem, sir,' Allen Young suggested drily.

Miller shook his head, sadly. 'I cannot. I have never written a poem to a living woman. It is a rule.'

'Then, pray do not break it on my account,' Lillie told him gently. She moved round him with Suffield, as he bowed again.

On the dais where the orchestra normally sat, a grand piano was already in position. Sofas and small, gilt chairs were placed seemingly at random facing the dais. Suffield led Lillie to one of the little sofas for two and sat beside her. Lady Suffield sat in the sofa next to them with Sir Allen Young. Edward stood, uncertain what to do, until Whistler pulled him down on to a chair next to him.

Suffield saw Young smiling to Lillie and, beyond Young, he spotted Joaquin Miller take up a position, leaning back against a pillar, where he could gaze at her. 'My dear Lillie,' he muttered, almost dazed, 'I had no conception that your acquaintance in such a short time was so – nor of the effect you have on people.'

Lillie had to admit that she had been showing off a little for his benefit. 'I have met one or two,' she said. Suffield noticed her slight smile and chuckled.

They joined in the applause as the Russian pianist, Anton Rubinstein, stepped on to the dais, reached the piano and bowed. Lille had been conscious of Joaquin Miller watching her. She glanced at him again. He had taken a letter from his shirt pocket and was tearing off the lower, blank half of the paper. When he began to write on it with a stub of pencil, she was inevitably reminded of Frank Miles and again there was a faint trace of a smile, as she looked back at the dais and Rubinstein thundered out the opening bars of a Beethoven sonata.

The next day, Lillie had promised to pose for Frank Miles. Oscar joined them to hear more about the Suffields' concert and she was flattered when Prince Leopold turned up again, shortly followed by Sir Allen Young. Both had come hoping to see her and the Prince, who had by now heard of her difficulty with his royal namesake, was relieved to learn that the evening had been an enormous personal success for her.

'One poor man tried very hard to impress Mrs Langtry last night,' Young told them, 'but got all tangled up in his own metaphors.'

'The Californian poet?' Miles chuckled. 'Jimmy Whistler said he laboured like a furnace and brought forth only a few sparks.'

They laughed, but Prince Leopold objected, 'I have read some of Joaquin Miller's verses, and liked them. I am sorry he did not write something for you.'

'But he did, sir,' Lillie said. They were astonished, when she took from her bag the torn piece of paper on which Miller had been writing. 'He gave me this at the end of the evening.'

'How dare he!' Oscar growled.

'May we hear it?' Prince Leopold asked.

Lillie hesitated. 'Well . . . if someone will read it.'

Oscar rose with bad grace and took the paper from her. 'To the Jersey Lily,' he read out.

> 'If all God's world a garden were,
> And women were but flowers,
> If men were bees that busied there
> Through endless summer hours,
> O! I would hum God's garden through
> For honey till I came to you.'

He paused as he finished, considering the piece of paper distastefully. 'This is a poem?'

'It rhymes,' Miles pointed out.

'I thought it simple – but charming,' Prince Leopold decided.

Lillie smiled, 'Thank you, Your Royal Highness. I was touched by it.'

'Touched . . . !' Oscar protested, indignantly. 'By this scribble? This backwoods jingle? Lines to you should burn with fire and sing to the heavens! This is no poem for you.'

'Then I'll say to you what I said to him, Mr Wilde,' Allen Young put forward. 'Why don't you write one?'

'Yes,' Sally agreed. 'You're always talkin' about it.' She sat on the floor by his feet, eating grapes, all legs and arms. Her interruption was so unexpected that they all laughed.

'How very true, Miss Sally,' Oscar conceded. 'Yes, I shall produce something more worthy of her – my tribute to

237

the Lily.'

'Bravo!' Leopold applauded.

Frank Miles was signing his initials on the portrait sketch. 'While you talk about your tribute, Oscar,' he murmured, 'I have finished mine.' He swivelled his picture round on its stand so that they could all see it. It was an etherialized, full-faced study of Lillie, with a budding lily in her hair, more the essence of her than a portrait. For all his moodiness and quirks, Miles had a touch of genius.

'That is . . . captivating,' Prince Leopold said softly.

'Her tenderness exactly,' Oscar added.

Miles was looking at Lillie for her verdict. 'I think, this time,' she said sincerely, 'the praise is the artist's.'

Miles smiled to her. He was really very proud of it and had sometimes been hurt lately that she seemed to prefer Oscar's company to his.

Prince Leopold had risen and moved closer to examine it. 'What will you do with it, Mr Miles?' he asked.

'Offer it to a gallery, sir. We shall have reproductions made.'

'I should not like it to be reproduced,' the Prince said shyly. He glanced at Lillie and back. 'I should like to have it for myself.'

Lillie was as surprised as the others, and touched.

Miles bowed. 'I'd be honoured, if you would accept it, sir.'

'No,' Prince Leopold insisted. 'Since it was my wish, I would like to buy it. As a reminder of being here at its creation.' He smiled to Lillie.

Allen Young accompanied Lillie home, in his carriage. Unexpectedly, she found Edward in the drawingroom with Patsy and Moreton Frewen. 'Entertaining our guests, my dear,' he explained.

'Most kind,' Patsy muttered. She was acutely bored. He and Moreton had spent the last half hour talking about angling.

'I thought you'd be at your Club,' Lillie said.

Edward took the hint gratefully. It had been torture to him to have to make conversation. 'Just off,' he nodded.

'I'm sorry you have to rush away, Mr Langtry,' Young said. 'We must have a chat some time.'

Edward brightened up. 'I – uh – I look forward to that,' he told Young. 'Well, if you'll excuse me.' He bowed awkwardly and left.

'He leads such a busy life,' Lillie said, to cover his abrupt departure. None of them was deceived. 'Now, please sit down,' she smiled. 'I'll ask Dominique to make something for tea.'

'I'm sorry, dearest Lillie. I must dash.' Patsy apologised, and added, 'I'm invited to tea at Marlborough House.' The statement had the effect she had intended. 'And I'm sorry again, but I'm going to ask one of these gentlemen to escort me. I mustn't ask you to choose which one, Lillie – so I shall.' She considered Frewen and Young, both bachelors, both attractive. Moreton had annoyed her by carrying on the angling conversation and deserved to be pushished. 'Sir Allen,' she decided. To her mortification, she saw that Moreton was pleased to be staying and Young showed a flash of disappointment at being chosen.

'I'd be charmed to accompany you, Mrs West,' Young said.

She smiled sweetly to Frewen. 'You will forgive me, Moreton.'

'By all means.'

The odious man had the impudence to grin! Patsy consoled herself with the thought that he would be given short shrift by the inexplicably faithful Lillie, who could have transformed her life by being a little more discreetly accommodating to King Leopold.

'Now, we must be off. You won't forget you're coming to lunch tomorrow?' she reminded Lillie.

'No,' Lillie smiled.

'Good. My husband would be inconsolable.' She inclined her head coolly to Frewen and made for the door, which Young opened for her.

He looked back to Lillie. 'I'm just getting my house in order. When it is, I hope that you and Mr Langtry will come to dinner?'

'I'd like that,' Lillie said.

He bowed and left with Patsy.

Frewen could scarcely believe his luck. For a week or so now, he had been unable to think of anything but Lillie. And here he was, alone with her. 'You might almost think Patsy had arranged it,' he said.

'What?' Lillie asked innocently.

'Well . . . she knows how much I've wanted to talk to you.'

'About what?'

Frewen was disconcerted. 'Oh – nothing. And everything. Just to . . . have you to myself for a minute.' He smiled. 'Provided you don't try to make me talk about anything serious. I was sent down from Cambridge, because I can't take anything seriously.'

'So you're not a philosopher,' Lillie commented, teasing.

'Good grief, no!' he laughed. 'Horses, fishing, hunting – that's about it. Though I'm good with animals.' He stopped himself. 'You wouldn't be interested.'

Lillie sat on the sofa. She liked him more now. He was attractive and open, if still a little too overbearingly masculine. 'Why not?' she asked. 'I thought you rode very well, when I saw you in the Park.'

'I was brought up on horseback,' he shrugged. 'I haven't seen you riding in the Row.'

'No. I rather envy people who can.'

'Would you like to?' he asked, interested.

'Very much,' she smiled. 'But first, one must have a horse.'

Frewen saw his chance, but not that she had carefully given it to him. 'Oh, that's no problem! It's easy enough to borrow a hack.'

Lillie was exhilarated. Of course, he was right. For her, it would be easy. Yet . . . . 'I suppose one would have to ride sidesaddle,' she said, doubtfully.

'Oh, Lord, yes. Look, here,' he proposed, 'Hyde Park is not exactly the least public place in the world. But early in the morning, there's not many people about. If you like, I'll teach you. She was startled. 'How to ride,' he explained.

She seemed amused by the thought. 'You'll teach me?'

'There's nothing to be afraid of,' he assured her. 'I have a spare horse. He's very well behaved. So all you'll need is a dress of sorts, whatever ladies wear. Leave the rest to me.' He was very confident and encouraging. 'What d'you say? Shall we have a shot?'

Lillie looked at him with the faintest trace of a smile. 'I think I might rather enjoy it,' she said slowly.

There was a problem. She could have a riding-habit made by Mrs Stratton or one of the other couturiers anxious for her custom, at very favourable rates, but she could not expect them to supply all the accessories that would be needed. Yet to be seen riding in the Park was an important step in her campaign.

Mr Downey of Bond Street, the celebrated photographer, called at Eaton Place the following morning, by appointment. Downey, a very proper, middleaged man, was rather embarrassed to be received by Lillie in her chiffon housedress, a garment which appeared peculiarly revealing.

'It was your own idea, Mr Downey,' Lillie said. 'A series of photographs of me At home, in a more natural setting.' She sat at her writing table and took up a quill pen. 'Don't you think a photograph, perhaps writing in my diary, might be effective?' As she leant forward on the table, her bare arms and bustline under the lace cape were subtly emphasised.

Downey saw the possibilities at once. 'Why, yes,' he coughed. 'Very intimate, and striking.'

She looked round, smiling. 'It would also help you to steal a march on your competitors.'

'Yes, indeed,' he nodded.

Lillie turned on her chair and smiled more fully. She was bewitchingly lovely and Downey could not help responding. 'I have been more pleased with your photographs than any others taken of me,' she told him. He bowed. 'In fact, I was thinking of offering you the exclusive right to photograph me.'

Downey had been gratified. It was swamped by excite-

241

ment. 'I – I am overwhelmed,' he stammered.

'It would be of value to you?'

'Inestimable!' he gasped. 'No one's portraits are in such demand as yours, Mrs Langtry. And to be able to control the number and sale of prints . . .' Even to have her pose for him was worth much. To have the exclusive right to her, he could make a fortune!

'There is one thing,' she mentioned casually. 'The other ladies who are photographed have extensive wardrobes to draw on. I, alas, do not. Might I suggest, for each master print selected, a fee of fifty pounds?'

Downey's smile faced. He felt a distinct sense of shock. 'But ladies of Society are not *paid* for . . .' he began. He drew himself up. 'I – I find the subject embarrassing to discuss, distasteful even,' He waited, but Lillie was silent, watching him, and he knew instinctively that her mind was made up. He coughed. 'May I suggest . . . twenty?'

'Yes, the subject is distasteful,' she agreed coolly. 'So I shall not discuss it. I take it you would prefer me to speak to some other photographer.' She laid down the pen and prepared to rise. Downey capitulated at once.

'There will be no need, Mrs Langtry,' he said, resigned.

The gate of the cobbled mews was closed. A groom held two horses, one a grey, the other a superb chestnut. It was early morning and they pawed the cobbles, impatient to be moving.

Impeccably turned out, Moreton Frewen turned, when he heard the door in the heavy, wooden gate open. Lillie was coming through, stunning in a gleaming, black tophat and a black riding-habit, cut so tight it seemed moulded to her figure. Frewen hurried to meet her and took her hand. 'My word,' he breathed, 'you really do look . . . quite the perfect horsewoman.'

It was a fairly strange compliment, but Lillie smiled. 'Thank you, Mr Frewen.'

'Oh – Moreton, please,' he begged. 'Since we're to be stablemates.' She laughed and he led her forward to the chestnut. 'Now, this is Redskin,' he told her. 'He'll be yours. He looks pretty big, but don't worry. He's very well trained.' He gentled Redskin's nose. 'There's a good boy . . . Come and stroke him. He won't bite.'

'Hello, Redskin,' Lillie said softly. The stallion's coat was glossy, a deep, dark russet, his mane and tail a shade lighter. She reached out and touched his nose, running her hand down it.

'Fine,' Frewen praised her. 'Very good. Now he knows you, you see. Here – we use this for getting up into the saddle.' He led her round to a wooden mounting block by Redskin's stirrup. He was fitted with a side-saddle. 'Don't worry if it seems a bit far off the ground at first,' Frewen reassured her. 'I'll stay close.'

Lillie raised the skirt of her riding-habit slightly and Frewen handed her up on to the mounting block. He glanced sharply at the groom, whose eyes had flicked involuntarily to Lillie's ankles in their smooth, black riding boots. She reached for the saddle. Lifting herself, she appeared to lose her balance and fell back. Frewen caught her and, for a second or two, she lay in his arms, their faces quite close. Her eyes were apprehensive and he smiled, his arms tightening round her yielding weight.

Damn the groom, he thought. 'Up we go!' he said and lifted her easily into the saddle. As she settled herself, he fitted her feet into the stirrups and stood back.

Lillie reached for the reins. 'No, don't bother about the reins just yet,' he ordered. 'Get the feel of it first.' She smiled to him.

For several minutes, he watched the groom lead her round and round the mews, calling out instructions to her how to sit. Her back was good and straight and he was relieved that she did not seem nervous. 'Good! Very good,' he called, and mounted the grey. There was a short halter rope attached to Redskin. He rode up and took it. 'Now, don't be nervous,' he said. When the groom opened the gate, he rode out, leading Redskin.

The streets were quiet, almost deserted, as they rode through, and Lillie was thankful. They entered the Park by the Albert Gate and he led her through and on to Rotten Row. They ambled along at walking pace.

'Enjoying it?' he asked.

'Enormously,' she smiled. The air, the motion, just to feel a horse under her again, even in the strange posture of the side-saddle, was wonderful. It did not allow the same control, but felt reasonably secure. She had taken up Redskin's reins.

'Good. That's right,' Frewen said, pleased. 'Hold the reins very lightly.' It was a joy to teach her. She had a natural aptitude.

'Do you think you could let him go for a moment?' she asked.

'Well . . .' he hesitated. 'If you're sure.'

'Just for a moment.'

He looked round. There was no one coming up fast who might make Redskin skittish. The only other riders were far off to the right, through the trees. He released the halter. 'Hold him steady,' he warned. Smiling indulgently, he fell back to ride beside her.

She smiled to him, kicked Redskin smartly with one heel and clicked her teeth. The big chestnut started forward.

'Wait a minute!' he said urgently, to her back.

Lillie urged Redskin on and he picked up speed, breaking into a trot.

Frewen was alarmed. 'Hold on!' he called. 'For heaven's sake – Lillie!' He spurred to catch her up, but Redskin had taken off and was racing away along the bridle path. 'Hold on!' Frewen shouted frantically. 'For pity's sake, hold on!'

Smiling, glorying in the power of the stallion under her and the speed, Lillie galloped up the path, straight for the Albert Memorial whose topmost spires she could see above the trees ahead. She heard Frewen shouting to her and the drumming hooves of the grey as he tried to catch her up, but she did not slow down until she was reaching the end of the Row. Where the path widened for the turning circle, she eased Redskin again to a trot, turned him round and brought him to a halt.

Frewen galloped up in a state of high alarm, cursing himself for not taking more care. At least, miraculously, she was safe! How could he have expected her to take off like

244

that? She was bent over Redskin's neck and he prayed she would not fall off, until he could get to her. As he reined in and reached for the halter, he saw that she was not faining, but speaking quietly to Redskin, patting his neck. The chestnut whickered in pleasure and she straightened, smiling.

As she sat there, looking at Frewen, the truth began to dawn and his anxiety was replaced by astonishment, then by outraged pride. 'You . . . You devil!' he swore. 'You said you couldn't ride!'

She shook her head. 'Only that I wanted to.'

'But you were worried!'

'Only because I've hardly ever used a side-saddle,' she smiled. 'I started bareback.'

He glared at her, indignantly. 'And you got me to – ! I hope you're satisfied!'

To his amazement, she laughed instead of apologising. 'I'm loving it, Moreton,' she said happily. 'Come on – race you back to the Gate!' She kicked her heel and Redskin started off again.

Frewen watched her go, offended. Then all at once, he saw how she had let him delude himself. And after all, he had what he wanted – she was here with him. And he had never seen her so relaxed and happy. He began to smile. She looked round for him and he laughed. He rode after her and they galloped away down the bridle path together.

# CHAPTER NINE

It was late, when Edward reached home. He had been at his club, stayed longer than he meant and was slightly tipsy. It was fairly dark and he was careful going up the steps from the street to the front door. Even so, he nearly tripped over a figure lying across the front step, his back against the door jamb. 'What the – what on earth – ?' he muttered. He peered down and, to his astonishment, saw Oscar Wilde.

Oscar lay motionless, his coat collar turned up, his arms wrapped round himself against the cold. 'No cause for alarm,' he said quietly. 'Pass on – pass on.'

'Mr Wilde . . .' Edward exclaimed. 'What's wrong? You'll freeze!'

'I am on fire,' Oscar revealed. 'In an incandescent dream.'

'I beg your pardon?' Edward asked, perplexed.

'An artist must stay as close as possible to the warm source of his inspiration,' Oscar told him patiently. 'My dear sir, do go in. My Muse is timorous and may steal away at the sound of voices.'

Edward gave up and went on in, banging the door behind him.

He found Lillie sitting up in bed, reading. She did not follow him at first and he had to repeat it. 'Curled up over the doorstep like a hibernating bear!'

'But why?' she wondered.

'To keep warm, he said. Or something.'

She made to get out of bed. 'I'd better ask him in.'

'You'll do nothing of the kind!' Edward snapped. Lillie at back, surprised by his anger. 'If he chooses to catch neumonia and make an exhibition of himself, that's his ffair! What's he doing here, anyway? That's what I want to now.'

Lillie smiled. 'He's started writing a poem to me.'

246

'What next? . . .' Edward protested, disgusted. 'As if it isn't bad enough having him hanging about here day in and day out! And that Frewen fellow. *And* Young.'

He was working himself up and Lillie said quickly, to calm him, 'You enjoy talking to Sir Allen. You have a lot in common.'

Edward was flattered. He had to admit that he had been jealous of Young, but had seen nothing ungentlemanly in his attitude to Lillie. Of course, Young was not rich and depended on the support of others to finance his expeditions. For that he needed publicity and it was only natural that he would wish to be seen with the toast of the season. 'Well – he's a cut above the others,' he said grudgingly.

'And Mr Frewen has invited you to go fishing with him,' Lillie reminded him.

Edward took off his jacket and untied his stock. Frewen was really quite a decent sort, too. 'I'd like to see Wilde try to land a ten pound salmon,' he muttered.

Lillie was worried about Oscar. She had not seen or heard from him for days and when she called at his rooms in Salisbury Street, he was not there. Not to see him left a gap which no one else could quite fill. When she asked Frank Miles where he was, all he said was, 'I thought you might know that better than anyone. He's obsessed by the poem he is writing to you. Nothing else exists for him.'

On Sunday morning, she went as usual to Whistler's Breakfast as he called it, at his studio. The White House, in Tite Street, Chelsea. He had designed the house himself, with his friend, the architect, Edward Godwin, for whom Ellen Terry had left Watts. It was a jumble of narrow passages and oddly-shaped rooms with low ceilings. The walls were mustard yellow, the floors covered with mats, faintly Japanese, and very unlike any other house she had ever been in. The furniture was low and sparse and the ornaments again showed the love of Japanese art which so influenced his painting. The blue and white china bowls in the diningroom had shown Lillie the source of Oscar's liking for them, but he was not there and Whistler had not seen him.

247

Usually, she enjoyed the Breakfasts. Whistler had learnt his cooking in America from his mother, to whom he was devoted, and the corn muffins, buckwheat cakes and pop-overs were delicious. But that day she felt unsettled, even though she was the centre of attention as always, with Swinburne curled up on a cushion at her feet like a pet monkey and Abraham Hayward, the essayist, sitting opposite her, each vying with the other in a contest to produce the perfect simile to express the essence of her beauty. With all the other guests applauding, she presided like a mediaeval Queen of Love and Whistler judged the contest. He, alone, realised that Lillie was only joining in with part of her mind and, when Hayward, Swinburne and the others left, satisfied, swearing eternal fidelity, he asked her what was wrong and was surprised when she told him. 'But Oscar spends most days and half the nights wandering round Belgravia, to be near you. Didn't you know?'

'No,' Lillie said. 'I've never seen him.'

'Well, you wouldn't,' Whistler told her. 'He watches your house, follows you from afar. He says, if he actually met and spoke to you just now, reality would spoil the ideal image he is creating. He neither eats nor sleeps. But . . . is a willing martyr. He answers to no name, except The Apostle of the Lily.' Whistler paused and frowned. 'To which, I must confess, I take exception. I had always considered him to be *my* Apostle. Disciple, at the least.'

Lillie smiled. 'Will you tell him I have been looking for him?'

'No.' He saw she was hurt, and smiled. 'I wouldn't give him the pleasure of knowing you miss him.'

'Please, Jimmy.'

Whistler would not promise. 'Shall we finish the buck-wheat cakes?' he suggested, blandly. 'By the bye, he has seen you riding in the Park with your White Knight in attendance. What on earth do you see in him?'

'Moreton? He's charming and attractive.'

'And physical. Is that enough? I thought you told me he was too masculine and arrogant.'

'He's more manageable now,' Lillie said demurely.

Whistler barked his short laugh. 'When will those gentlemen learn not to underestimate you?'

Lillie was honoured when Prince Leopold called at Eaton Place. She had sensed a rapport with him on the occasions they had met in public. It was even stronger, when they were alone.

The Prince's shyness disappeared and he was able to talk to her, in a relaxed and friendly manner. He confessed, himself, that he was not confident with women, especially beautiful ones. He had just had a sobering experience. His mother, Queen Victoria, had chosen a wife for him, Lord Rosslyn's stepdaughter, Frances, known in the family as Daisy. Lillie remembered her, a ravishing, highspirited girl of seventeen. The first time Edward and she had dined with the Rosslyns, she had noticed Daisy sitting on the stairs to watch her as she came in and had stopped to speak to her. Daisy had been invited to Windsor, approved by the Queen and presented to Prince Leopold. But she had turned him down, to Victoria's utter disbelief. Privately, Lillie thought that he was well out of it. He was reserved and in constantly poor health. Daisy would have run him ragged in months.

As they talked, Leopold told Lillie that he had had a silver frame made for her portrait and hung it in his room at Windsor.

'It must look out of place in such surroundings,' she objected.

'Oh, no,' he smiled. 'The private rooms at the castle aren't really very grand, you know. Certainly not as comfortable as this, nor so relaxing. Of course, that is larely due to the company.' He paused. 'I hope you do not mind my inviting myself?'

'I was honoured,' she told him, sincerely.

'I know convention makes it difficult, if not impossible to refuse,' he said hesitantly.

She understood. He needed reassurance. 'You are welcome for yourself, sir,' she smiled. 'The fact that we have so many interests in common, art, literature, the theatre, makes it even more of a pleasure.'

He was grateful. 'It is a relief to find someone to whom one may talk openly . . . without always being on one's guard.'

He rose. Lillie rose with him and rang the bell-pull by the fire. When she turned, she was concerned to see him leaning for support on the back of his chair. 'Are you quite well, sir?'

'A little tired, that's all,' he panted. 'I hope I may come again?'

'Please. Whenever you choose.'

'I must be careful not imitate the example of my Belgian cousin,' he said quietly. It was a subject that had never been mentioned between them and Lillie tensed, as he continued. 'His presumption went beyond the bounds of acceptable behaviour. We are all relieved it went no further – for, if he had given you any stronger grounds for complaint, it could have caused a serious diplomatic scandal.'

She realised that he knew there was more to the Leopold affair than had come out. Indeed, that this was the chief purpose of his visit. He was asking if she were prepared to be discreet. 'Whatever grounds there may be, sir,' she answered carefully, 'I would not wish to expose His Majesty, King Leopold, to censure, as a guest in this country.'

He had been watching her intently, and was well satisfied. 'My family and I are indebted to you, Mrs Langtry,' he bowed. 'I look forward to our next meeting.'

When Dominique had shown him out, Lillie put his teacup and hers on the tray and sat again, looking at the fire, thinking. She had confessed only to herself that she had been tempted, not by King Leopold, but by what he offered. Patsy had told her how he kept a mistress in Paris, who lived in absolute luxury. Edward and she had less money than ever and it was undeniably tempting to imagine herself being pampered, smothered in jewels and waited on by a troop of servants. She could have that, if she wanted, she knew. All kinds of men, many of them very rich, had made proposals to her, which she pretended not to understand. Some had even sent her gifts, which she had scrupulously returned. It was not through faithfulness to Edward, but knowing that every move of hers was observed as minutely as it had been, when she was a girl in Jersey. The rules had been set by the Prince of Wales, and were simple. Faithfulness was respected, but those who did not wish to be faithful were allowed any excess, provided it did not become public and bring Society as a whole into disrepute. Already, she had heard stories which would have rocked the country. She knew scandal about many of the people who kept such a strict watch on her. Yet the fact remained that, as a newcomer and in the artificially eminent position she had attained, she was peculiarly vulnerable.

She heard the door behind her open and close. Dominique had come to clear away the tray. 'Has he gone?' she asked.

'I passed the sorrowful Prince in the hall,' she heard. It was Oscar's voice. She spun round, rising. He was standing by the door. She smiled radiantly and stepped forward.

'You look pleased,' he said.

'Pleased? . . .' she repeated. 'Oh, it's been too long!'

'At times, it seemed an eternity,' he agreed softly. 'Now, only a moment.' He was paler and appeared to have lost weight. There were lines round his eyes.

Her joy at seeing him surprised even her. 'And the poem?' she asked. 'Frank and Jimmy said you wouldn't come to see me, until it was finished.'

'They were right.' He smiled at her reaction. 'Yes, it is done. Completed. This morning I wrote "Finis." Ave atque vale.' She could not hide her eagerness. 'No, you shall not see it, until it is printed – and perfect. It has been torn out of my living flesh and will be a holy revelation!'

'Oscar, you are – you are unique!' she laughed.

'Have you only just realised?' he murmured and came to her. She held out both hands and he took them, kissing each in turn. 'Now that I have returned from the twilight, what shall we do? Say the word, tonight is yours!'

There was a pause, while he gazed down at her. 'Oh, my dear . . . I can't,' she told him, stricken. 'We are going to a reception at Devonshire House. The Marquess of

251

Hartington's.'

She saw his eyes harden and he released her hands. 'Your final test,' he said bitterly.

'What do you mean?'

'Before you become a fully-fledged "Professional Beauty."'

She was wrung by the pain and resentment in his voice. 'I don't understand.'

'Oh, surely,' he scoffed. 'The Beauties all conform to one type. Fair, young, married, the type most admired by the Prince of Wales. Those he specially favours become his mistresses. Lady Filmer – Lady Aylesford – Patsy.'

'Patsy? . . .' Lillie whispered.

'You must have known? Society chooses you and pampers you and dangles you before him – to entice him to their homes.'

'How can you say that?' she demanded. 'I've never even met him!'

'But you will,' he assured her. 'You are beautiful and intelligent. You have proved you are discreet. You have been vetted by his aides, Allen Young and Suffield. And tonight, you will be inspected by his closest adviser, Hartington – Harty-Tarty!'

What he had blurted out had explained many things. The cult of the Beauties . . . Patsy . . . But none of it applied to her. Or did it? She thrust the thought away. 'Oscar, that's nonsense!' she protested.

'Is it?' As he gazed at her, all at once, the bitterness flooded out of him as suddenly as it had appeared. He was overcome with tiredness, felt for the chair next to him and sat. 'Oh, my dear . . .' he muttered. 'Pay no attention. I have been through such . . .'

The lines of strain in his face showed themselves more deeply etched and she was concerned. 'What is it?'

He looked away. 'How can I tell you? These past days, weeks – seeing you in the distance, laughing with others, your lighted window, your voice in my heart . . . I have known such jealousy.' She moved to him and touched his bent head. 'But now, it is over,' he sighed.

'There was no need,' she said gently.

His head lifted and he smiled faintly, comforted. 'No. And my tribute to you is finished.' He had lived through an agony of creation, his mind fixed on her, poised between despair and exultation, and partly terrified that his words might not capture what he felt. He rose again, as excitement took over. 'Edmund Yates is going to publish it,' he told her. 'For years he has been waiting for a major work from me. Destiny! That my hymn to you should make my reputation.'

'Yes,' Lillie breathed.

'And your copy will be special – bound in white vellum – inscribed with my duty, and my love.' He took her face in his hands and kissed her, very softly. 'But tonight you go to Devonshire House.'

After nearly two weeks without him, she wanted nothing more than to be with him, to hear his voice and laugh with him, especially now that the bond between them was even stronger. She could not bear to hurt him again, yet Hartington was a leading politician and had sent her a personal invitation. 'It is a grand, diplomatic affair,' she explained. 'I shall arrive and leave – unnoticed.'

The celebrated marble staircase in Devonshire House was lined with footmen in splendid liveries, one every four steps. Past them, ladies and gentlemen of the fashionable, political and diplomatic worlds, in eveningdress, uniforms and decorations, ascended slowly in twos.

Lord Hartington received his guests in the space between the head of the stairs and the doors of the main reception room. He was head of the Liberal party and of the Opposition in the House of Commons, elected unanimously after Gladstone's impetuous resignation after Disraeli's resounding victory in the last election. The heir to the immensely rich Duke of Devonshire, Hartington was a tall, sleepy-eyed man with a long face and straggling beard. He paid so little attention to dress that visitors to his country estate had been known to mistake him for the gardener. Slow to think and act, he had a fund of commonsense that amounted to genius and made him greatly trusted in the country. His long-standing affaire with Louisa, Duchess of Manchester, was an open secret. Stately and aloof in public, in private Louisa was a frolicksome, madcap charmer, addicted to gambling, and the two of them were constant and welcome visitors to Marlborough House.

Lillie mounted the stairs of Edward's arm. They were both slightly awed by the grandeur of the house and the solemnity of the occasion. Conversation was very muted and the sound of faint, formal music from the reception room above added to the dignified, processional atmosphere. Looking up, Lillie saw a vista of backs, in black, in scarlet, blue or grey uniforms, of swaying bustles and the trains of ladies' gorgeous gowns held over their arms, ostrich feathers and tiaras. She, herself, having worn the new white dress three or four times had gone back to her new little, black dress and wondered, briefly, if she had made a mistake. Perhaps, she should have called in Mrs Stratton again.

She saw movement among the people ahead, some agitation as they stood or were brushed aside by someone coming down the stair. Then she recognised the unmistakable, flowing hair and fringed buckskins of the Californian poet, Joaquin Miller. She heard Edward beside her mutter, 'Oh, no . . . ,' and Miller stopped a few steps above them, bowing down to her, holding a large, upturned sombrero in the crook of his left arm, flourishing with his right. Edward was appalled and embarrassed. Everyone had stopped and was turning to look at them.

As Lillie smiled to him, Miller cried loudly, 'Fairest of ladies – Queen of the Night!' From the sombrero he scooped a handful of rosepetals mixed with violets and scattered them on the steps at Lillie's feet. 'Be these your path through life!' he intoned. 'May rosebuds and violets ere sweeten the path you tread!'

All up and down the stairs, the murmur of astonishment grew. Edward was rooted to the spot. Holding his arm, Lillie nudged him and they carried on up the staircase. Edward did not know where to look, but Lillie continued to smile slightly, graciously, losing none of her poise, as Miller preceded them walking backwards, scattering petals on each step ahead of her and repeating the incantation, 'Be these your path through life!'

Hartington was genuinely bored by ceremony. He stifled a yawn, nodding and shaking hands with his guests as they passed. He had heard the murmur of surprise and seen heads turning in the line of ascending couples. As more people turned to look down, he could not resist his curiosity and moved to the head of the stairs. For a second, he was as astonished as the others, seeing Miller casting his petals at Lillie's feet as she climbed up, calmly and serenely. What amused Hartington was the discomfort of the stolid man with her whom he took to be her husband and the way in which the people around them were trying to look as if it were an everyday occurrence.

When they reached the top step and Joaquin Miller, with a final flourish, tossed the last contents of his sombrero into the air so that they drifted down, settling on Lillie's hair and shoulders, Hartington applauded and offered her his arm.

His other guests were forgotten. It was extraordinary. Leading politicians were there, minor royalty, visiting ambassadors. Hartington led Lillie into the reception, presented her to the principal guests, then walked back out with her. She had merely said the house looked magnificent and she would like to see it properly one day. He took her on a complete guided tour of the palatial rooms, pointing out some of his treasures. A footman followed behind them, carrying a silver tray with a bottle of champagne and two glasses.

They came down some carved stairs into a stone court, lined with huge, Attic vases. In the centre of it was a marble pool, in which waterlilies floated. Footmen appeared, ready to open the doors leading off.

Lillie's head was spinning with it all. When Hartington paused to refill their glasses, handing hers to her, she searched for words. 'It is all . . . superb, Lord Hartington.'

'Glad you like it,' he said.

She turned slowly. 'The sculpture, the paintings . . . Everything is – it's like a Renaissance Palace!'

'I suppose it is,' Hartington chuckled. He could understand the furore she'd created. She made him think of a garden in spring. 'Its been a great pleasure showing you round. I've never noticed half the things, myself.'

'I'm very grateful,' she smiled, then hesitated. 'Should we be getting back?'

'What for?'

'Your other guests will be wondering – '

'Let them!' he declared. 'You know, I haven't enjoyed one of these do's so much for years.'

They put their empty glasses on the tray and moved on. Lillie stopped, seeing the coloured waterlilies in the marble pool. 'Oh – aren't they lovely!' she exclaimed.

'You like them, Mrs Langtry?' he said.

'More than anything, almost.'

'Right – you shall have some,' he decided. He left her and went to the pool, stooping to pluck up one of the waterlilies. He could reach the outer leaves, but not the flower. 'Oh, hang it!' he grunted, and stepped into the pool, the water reaching to his knees. The footmen were dumbfounded.

'Lord Hartington – ' Lillie warned, starting forward.

He looked round, grinning. 'Which one would you like? That one? How about that one?' He plucked up two of the lilies, offering them to her.

His smile was so infectious, she had to laugh. 'Either – I don't mind.'

He was enjoying himself. 'You must have more than one.' He started to pluck up more lilies, trailing great, green leaves, soaking himself, chuckling.

'No, please – please!' Lillie laughed. 'That's enough!'

'No hang it!' he declared. 'Have the lot!' He clicked his fingers to the two nearest footmen. 'Here! Here!' They came to the edge of the pool. His eyes alight, laughing with Lillie, Hartington splashed round the statue of a mermaid in the middle of the pool, scooping up armfuls of lilies and throwing them to the footmen, who stood stoically with water dripping down their plush breeches.

He excused himself afterwards to change his trousers, but for the remainder of the evening his guests kept noticing the stains of green scum on his sleeves and the starched, white front of his shirt. Whenever his eyes caught Lillie's, they burst out laughing, until they could control themselves.

Edward could think of no reason for the hilarity. Neither could Sir Allen Young whom, fortunately, he had found to talk to, during her absence. All was explained when they got into their cab to leave and footmen marched up, bringing bundles of waterlilies which they laid on the seat beside him and thrust on to his lap until he was banked by them, holding them with both arms.

The cab was lit by a tiny hanging lamp and, as they started off, Lillie could see his outraged expression. She tried very hard not to laugh.

'Did you see those footmen? Did you?' he fumed. 'They just dumped these things on top of me!'

'Lord Hartington was most thoughtful,' Lillie said gravely.

'Thoughtful? . . . I'm soaked through!' he protested and she gurgled. 'It is not in the least funny! This cab smells like a cesspit!'

'He only meant it as a gesture.'

As he glared at her, she could not stop herself from laughing. 'Is that so?' he shouted. 'Well, I'll show you a gesture!'

He wrenched down the cab window and began to pitch the waterlilies out into the road. It did not have the effect he intended. It was only just after midnight and there were still people in the street. Someone recognised Lillie and called out her name. Men started to pick up the waterlilies, cheering and running after the cab, begging for more. Soon they were fighting for the flowers and the cabbie had to whip up his horse to get away before they were mobbed.

Lillie was still bursting with suppressed laughter when they reached Eaton Place. Edward followed her into the bedroom and stood indignantly, while she turned up the oil lamp. Seeing him in the mirror, incensed, rigid with annoyance, she giggled.

'It is no laughing matter!' he spluttered. 'I am wet – I am

wet through and smelling like an old duckpond!' She laughed out loud and he tore off his tailcoat and threw it down. 'If you think I'm going to stand here – Will you stop laughing?' She sat on the chair at the dressingtable, biting her lip, but could not stop. Edward turned on his heel and stalked out.

After a while, Lillie controlled herself. She picked up his tailcoat and shook it out.

Edward marched into the drawingroom. The brandy decanter was nearly empty, but there was another bottle in the cupboard. He got it out and wrenched off the cork. Seething with resentment, he poured himself a glass and drank it quickly. What did she think he was? His hand steadied as he drank another glass. Her attitude to him lately left a great deal to be desired. Getting above herself. He drank again, pulled his white tie undone and tore his collar open.

Strange . . . The whole business about Lillie. He had thought the storm over her would blow itself out, but it had only increased. She was so confident now. Nothing threw her. And she had ripened, become more lovely . . . Friends? They had hundreds of friends. Hardly a moment to themselves. He thought more about that. How long was it since he last sat down and talked to her? Since he had kissed her? It was a mockery that he was envied. People like Wilde and Rosslyn and Whistler got more smiles from her. And dammit, she was his wife! She'd be nothing, it it wasn't for him. Married to some farmer or clerk on her boring little island.

The light in the bedroom had been lowered again and Lillie lay in bed, nearly asleep. She heard Edward come in and swear under his breath when his knee struck the corner of a chair. 'Lillie . . .' he said quietly, 'Lillie are you asleep?' She did not answer. 'Come on!' he said louder. 'Don't pretend you're sleeping already!' He reached the bed and sat on the edge, heavily. She turned over on her back and looked at him. His face was flushed and he squinted at her in the dim light. 'I'm sorry,' he told her. 'I was – was angry earlier. I spoilt your evening.'

'It doesn't matter,' she said.

'I don't know how you do it,' he muttered. 'Those parties. You always have something to say to everyone. The right thing. You smile at the right time. I never know what to say.' He shook his head. 'Half an hour after someone's spoken to me, I can think of what I should have answered. But I just – I don't enjoy it much, you know.'

She felt sorry for him. He sounded lost. It was unheard of for him to admit he was inadequate in any form or manner. 'Don't think of it as being so important,' she advised him gently, to help him. 'Don't worry about what people think. If you let them see you as you –'

'I don't need any advice from you, thank you very much!' he broke in roughly, angered by her tone which he considered patronising.

She looked at him for a long moment and turned away.

He laid his hand on her leg through the bedclothes and moved it slowly up, his fingers beginning to squeeze her thigh. 'No,' she said, shifting away.

'Please . . . I need you,' he pleaded. 'It's been months now, Lillie.'

The whine of his voice and the probing of his fingers high up on her thighs revolted her. She moved her leg sharply. 'I'm tired.'

'Your're always tired,' he grated and threw himself forward.

She tensed when his body landed on hers, crushing her on to the bed, but forced herself not to truggle, even when she smelt the sick sourness of the brandy on his breath. For a few seconds, he took her lack of movement for consent and pawed at her through the bedclothes, pulling them down from her shoulders, kissing her bared neck. He glanced up at her, grinning, and stopped in shock, seeing her impassive, dead expression. 'No, Edward,' she said tonelessly. 'I'm tired and you are drunk.'

He reared up from her, his face dark, and for a moment she thought he was going to strike her. Breathing heavily, he pushed himself off her to stand by the bed, leaning over her. 'You – you're not a decent wife any more,' he said thickly. His voice rose. 'You're a – do you know what you are? You're a . . .' Unable to think of a word, he snapped his fingers in her face. 'That's what your are!'

Still completely expressionless, she watched him turn and walk unsteadily out of the bedroom. She breathed out slowly and closed her eyes.

Oscar brought his poem to her.

She sat at her writing table, reading the special edition which he had promised her, bound in white vellum. It was longer than she had expected, a hundred lines in the form of an ode, split into sections. Oscar waited by the window with a suggestion of nervousness, watching her as she read. It was hers. He had wrought it for her and no one else's opinion mattered. He desperately wanted a cigarette. Something to do with his hands. Her bowed head reading was so inexpressibly lovely. He was certain his words had failed.

She finished it and closed the pages. She sat for a time in silence, not looking up.

'Well?'

'I – I don't know what to say.'

His heart seemed to lurch. 'You're disappointed?'

She looked up at him at last and could not hide that she had been deeply moved. 'Oh, no . . . How could you think that?' she faltered. 'It is so beautiful – I don't feel worthy of it.'

'Oscar panted sharply in his relief. He smiled. 'I will not have my Goddess renounce her divinity. If it succeeds, it is only because it catches something of your mystery.'

She gazed at him. 'I am so touched, I . . .'

'No, please,' he insisted. 'Accepted it for what it is. A tribute – to Helen, formerly of Troy, now of London,' He moved closer, when Lillie smiled. 'I have called it "The New Helen". You really like it?'

'Much more than like it.'

'All of it?' he asked. 'Or some lines more than others?'

'All,' she told him. 'But some parts are –' She opened the bound pages. Each section had a separate page and she riffled through them, stopped and began to read quietly.

'The Lotus leaves which heal the wounds of death
Lie in thy hand; O, be thou kind to me,
While yet I know the summer of my days;
For hardly can my tremulous lips draw breath
To fill the silver trumpet with they praise,
   So bowed am I before thy mystery,
So bowed and broken on Love's terrible wheel,
   That I have lost all hope and heart to sing,
Yet care I not what ruin Time may bring,
   If in thy temple thou wilt let me kneel.'

The words died away, yet the echo of her clear, expressive voice still seemed to fill the room. They were both moved. 'To read – to have words like that written to me just now . . .' she whispered.

He could see that she was upset. 'What is it, my dearest?'

'Edward and I, we – ' she began, but broke off and rose, moving away. 'I should not be saying this.'

'Tell me.'

Lillie heard his concern and knew it was not fair, neither to herself nor to him, not to speak. 'My marriage . . . is a sham. Edward and I appear together in public. In private, we have nothing to say to each other. Nothing that draws us together.' She paused. 'It is my fault. I cannot, cannot bear him to touch me. We have not been . . . man and wife now for over a year.'

'My – my poor darling,' Oscar murmured. She was on the point of breaking down and he moved to her, holding her in his arms. She leant her head on his chest and he stroked her hair. 'Cry. Cry if you want to.'

'I never cry,' she said. She looked up at him. 'I'm sorry. I shouldn't have told you.'

He smiled gently. 'Who else could you tell?' He let her go and she steadied herself. 'How does Edward feel?'

'Resentful,' Lillie said simply. 'He says it is all due to my . . . coldness.'

'Your coldness!' Oscar objected indignantly. 'You are a creature of fire!'

She looked at him. 'No, Oscar. I'm just a woman.'

'No!' he protested. 'You – '

'A woman – with natural affections. Who needs sympathy and companionship. With everything that's happened these past months, my head has been in a whirl.'

'You have been like a rock, against which adoration beats – but have not changed,' he told her proudly.

'Adoration,' she repeated. 'What does it mean – if there is no one who really loves me?'

'You are surrounded by men who worship you!' he declared. 'And there is – there is me.' She was suddenly taut. She had been waiting, hoping for him to speak more personally, to come into the open. 'You must know how deeply I feel for you,' he went on.

'I have felt closer to you than anyone,' she said quietly.

'Because we are twin spirits.'

She felt happiness seeping through her. 'I have never been so happy,' she confessed. 'So at ease, as with you.'

'Because you know that I love you – totally,' Oscar said.

It had been spoken at last and she caught her breath. 'Oscar – '

Instead of taking her in his arms as she wanted, he seemed to hesitate. His eyes were troubled. 'Yet – it is your pure perfection that I love,' he told her. 'Which must remain inviolate, untouched by desire.'

He was hedging. The joyful expectation which was trembling in her, was snuffed out. She gazed at him, hurt. 'What you mean is . . . it is all a pose. Nothing you have said is true?' She could not accept it.

'What is truth?' he asked softly. He had to make himself look at her, ashamed. 'The truth is – I really do love you. Yet the curse of my nature is that I can desire, but not possess, beauty. It must always be just out of reach.' There was yearning and sadness in his voice. 'I have wept for you – and for myself.'

Lillie's eyes searched his face. It was not a pretence. He as genuinely stricken. 'If you let me,' she promised quietly, 'I would show you that I am more real than the goddess you imagine.'

She moved closer to him and they both had a strange sensation as if the air between them was charged. 'That is the one truth I am afraid of,' Oscar whispered.

Just then, the door opened and Edward came in. He was in a fairly good humour, but it evaporated noticeably when he saw Oscar. Neither Lillie nor Oscar moved, although they looked at him. 'Didn't realise you were here, Mr Wilde,' he said.

Oscar paused. 'I brought Lillie her copy of my poem.'

'Look forward to reading it,' Edward coughed. 'Offer you a drink?'

'No, thank you. I think I may already have . . . outstayed my welcome.'

'Of course, not,' Lillie said quietly.

Oscar tried to smile to her. 'Well, I hope you'll forgive me, if I . . . run away.' He turned from her. 'Good day, sir.'

'Good day,' Edward nodded.

Oscar bowed slightly and left. Lillie was distressed, but Edward did not suspect it. 'And good riddance!' he snorted. 'Come on, Lillie. We'd better start getting ready.'

'For what?'

'We're going to the Opera with Allen Young tonight.'

'I don't feel like it,' she told him.

'Oh, don't you?' he jeered. 'Well, you just remember the times I've had to go to places because of you! Young's an interesting chap – real sportsman. Not like those artistic Johnny-come-latelies. He's asked us to the Opera and to supper after, without fail – so we're going!'

The drawingroom of Sir Allen Young's house in Stratford Place off Oxford Street was not large, but in very good taste. He was not wealthy and his supper parties were usually fairly select. Tonight there were only ten guests, among them Lord Suffield, Patsy and Mrs Wheeler. Lillie was wearing her black dress. She was unusually quiet, pale, but composed. Still thinking of Oscar, she had hardly noticed the opera, Meyerbeer's *Dinorah*, and could remember nothing of it.

She stood with Edward, Young, Patsy and Lord Suffield. They had been waiting for some time, but there was no sign of supper being announced.

'I think Madame Patti sang wonderfully,' Patsy said.

'Such a pure voice,' Suffield agreed.

'Do you enjoy Opera, Mr Langtry?' she enquired.

Edward started. 'H'm? Oh, yes, Yes.'

She enjoyed teasing him and continued. 'Which is your favourite?'

'Ah – well, d' you see?' he fumbled. 'I can never remember their names.'

'That's because they're all in Italian,' Young said, helping him out.

'Exactly,' Edward nodded, gratefully.

'Yes, it's so difficult,' Patsy agreed innocently. 'Aida – Norma – The Barber of Seville.'

They laughed and Young chided Patsy, smiling. 'Now then . . . Edward's like me. He'd rather be up to his waist in a trout stream than half asleep at Covent Garden.'

'Absolutely,' Edward said with feeling.

Lillie saw Young glance at his fobwatch.

'Get much fishing these days, Mr Langtry?' Suffield asked.

Edward shook his head. 'Not much, no.'

There was a pause. 'Excuse me,' Young muttered. His butler had come in and he moved to him. They went out quickly.

Mrs Wheeler turned to speak to Patsy, ignoring Lillie. 'I expected to see you at Lottie Manchester's.'

'We were in the country,' Patsy explained, turning to her. 'I was so sorry to miss it.'

Suffield had moved with Patsy. Momentarily uninvolved, Lillie crossed to the open fireplace with its carved, Adam surround. With her back to the room, she could let her mask drop briefly. The evening had had a tinselled emptiness for her. She could still see Oscar as he left, trying to be jaunty, but desolate. If only they had time. If only he would let himself surrender.

She became aware of someone beside her. It was Edward who had followed her. 'Can't imagine what's holding supper up,' he grumbled. 'I'm starving.'

As Lillie turned, they heard a deep, resonant voice outside say, 'I'm afraid I'm a little late, Alleno.' At the sound of it, the room fell silent. There was a surge of excitement.

Young came to the doorway. 'Not at all, sir,' he said, bowing. 'We are just ready to go in.'

With him was a broad-chested, smiling man with dark gold hair and a clipped, slightly lighter beard, the Prince of Wales. Albert Edward, known to his family as Bertie, had been to a reception for his Russian sister-in-law, the Czar's daughter, Grand Duchess Marie, Duchess of Edinburgh, and was dressed in a tailcoat and knee breeches, with the blue ribbon of the Order of the Garter across his breast. He was glad to have escaped and was affable and expansive as he strode in.

For once, Lillie was almost panic-stricken, realising why Young had been most insistent on her being present. 'It's the Prince of Wales!' Edward whispered nervously. She nodded tightly. Involuntarily, Edward straightened his tie.

Bertie knew everyone else in the room. He advanced with Allen Young, shaking hands with the men, who bowed, and smiling to the ladies, who curtsied, greeting favourites. 'Good evening – good evening. Good to see you, Suffield.' He paused by Patsy, who smiled as she curtsied. 'My dear Mrs West, how very charming you look tonight.' Mrs Wheeler curtsied. 'And Mrs Wheeler – how nice to see you.'

He had nearly reached Lillie and Edward. She stepped to the side, almost giving way to an absurd impulse to escape, but he had halted and was looking at her. His eyes were a clear, light blue, warmed by appreciation.

'Your Royal Highness, may I present Mrs Edward Langtry?' Young said.

Lillie curtsied quite slowly, with great poise. Bertie held out his hand and their fingers touched for a second. 'I have seen your portrait, Mrs Langtry,' he smiled. 'It does not do you full justice.'

She very much wanted to make an impresson, but could think of nothing witty. 'Mr Millais is a very fine artist,' she replied seriously.

'I didn't mean Millais,' he told her, then chuckled. 'I

meant the one my brother, Leopold, has on the wall of his room.'

His rumbling laugh was warm and friendly and, in spite of her effort to stay poised, Lillie smiled back. The smile lit her up.

'Mr Langtry, sir,' Young said.

'How d'you do, Mr Langtry?' Bertie nodded. Edward bowed stiffly and Bertie and he shook hands. 'You're a yachting man, I hear.'

'I do do,' Edward stammered. 'I have sailed, yes, sir.'

'Good. We must have a race some time, eh?'

Edward bowed again jerkily, instead of answering.

'Would you care to go in to supper, sir? Young suggested.

'By all means , Alleno. Mustn't keep everyone waiting any longer.' Bertie smiled to Lillie and turned away. 'Patsy,' he said loudly, 'I believe I have the honour?'

Patsy curtsied and took his arm. As they moved off, she could not resist a tiny, triumphant glance at Lillie. The other guests prepared to follow.

Lillie and Edward were left alone by the fireplace. She felt a definite sense of anticlimax. Many people had speculated on the result of a meeting between her and the Prince. It had been anticipated for months. Now is had happened and had led to nothing. She could tell that Mrs Wheeler was delighted.

Edward was merely thankful that he no longer had to try to think of anything to say. 'Well! . . .' he marvelled. 'I'd no idea it was him we were wainting for.'

Near the door, Bertie had paused to murmur to Allen Young, who came back down the room and bowed to Lillie. 'May I take you in, Mrs Langtry?' he requested. 'Perhaps you would care to sit on His Royal Highness's other side.'

Lillie straightened and smiled. She had not been passed over, after all, and Patsy would have to work much harder. She laid her hand on Sir Allen Young's arm and they went out, following Patsy and the Prince.

# CHAPTER TEN

Lillie was thoughtful when they got home, realising that in the excitement she had quite forgotten Oscar. At the thought of him, her uncertainty returned. He had been her anchor. The man against whom she measured all others.

She was only half conscious of Edward, chuckling, congratulating himself. 'Well! Who'd ever have imagined even a month or so ago that we'd have supper with the Prince of Wales, eh?'

She slipped out of her dress and sat at the dressingtable, beginning to unpin the heavy knot at the nape of her neck. 'Sir Allen might have warned us he was expected.'

Edward laughed. 'When he walked into the room, I thought you were going to faint. I've never seen anyone so tonguetied.'

It was true. For a dizzying moment, she had wanted to escape up the chimney. She had seen that the Prince had the same effect on others. It was more than simple respect that made them defer to him. There was an aura about him. No matter how friendly he tried to be, it was there, not only a sense of royalty, but something more dangerous. Seated next to him at supper, she had been content to respond like the others and not try to sparkle. Patsy had kept him interested and amused. The Prince and she were completely at ease with each other, old friends and lovers. Their looks and little remarks to each other were not difficult to interpret, when one knew.

Lillie wondered how she would behave, if it were her.

She had no illusions about herself. One day she would be unfaithful to Edward. Nearly every man she met wished to become her lover. She had only held back because, after the mistake of her marriage, next time she gave herself she had to be absolutely sure. Of them all, the only one she would have chosen was Oscar. She had dreamed of him for a while, but had been chasing a will o' the wisp. Dazzled by his wit and charm and physique, she had thought him self-reliant, a tower of strength. He was even more weak and uncertain than she was. She had been searching for love. What was love?

'Did you hear me?' Edward said sharply. 'You let me down.' She had teased her hair out on to her shoulders, and paused. 'If the Prince takes a fellow up, he's made!'

'You expect him to take you up?' she asked, surprised.

He was winding his watch and laid it on the bedside table. 'It's not impossible,' he said huffily. 'Hang it, you could have interested him! Got him to take some notice of us. He paid more attention to Patsy Cornwallis West.'

'She makes him laugh,' Lillie said, and picked up her brush.

He was working himself up into a temper. 'Well, why didn't you? You'll flutter your eyes at any Tom, Dick or Harry till they think you're the cat's whiskers. But the one time it could have been really important, you seize up!'

'I didn't want him to think I was trying too hard.'

'You didn't try at all! I was depending on you, and you made no effort.' He sat on the bed, disgustedly.

Lillie went on silently, rhythmically, brushing her hair. She remembered how the Prince had looked at her, when he bowed goodnight. Nothing had been said, but she was absolutely sure she would see him again.

The next day, Bertie went to lunch with his sister Helena and her husband, Prince Christian of Schleswig – Holstein, at Cumberland Lodge. En route, he called in on his youngest brother at Windsor Castle.

Leopold's room was quite small, with space for little more than a single bed and locker, a writing bureau and chair. The wallpaper was sombre and the whole effect always reminded Bertie of a monk's cell. The only touches that spoiled the impression were the red despatch box lying on the open desk shelf and the silver-framed sketch of Lillie with the lily in her hair that hung above it. 'Attractive,' Bertie commented.

Leopold was proud of it. 'Oh, much more than that, I'd

say.'

'What would you say?' Bertie smiled. Leopold was uncomfortable. 'Are you smitten?'

'She's a married woman, Bertie,' Leopold protested.

'Ah, yes, of course,' he nodded, amused. 'I'll confess, when I was told that Leopold had made an idiot of himself over her, I thought they were talking about you – having heard you called on her occasionally.'

Leopold was partly embarrassed and partly flattered. 'He behaved disgracefully.'

'Thank heavens you managed to hush it up.'

'I did nothing. Lillie – Mrs Langtry – had no wish to cause a scandal,' Leopold assured him. 'No one could be more discreet.'

'Indeed?' Bertie murmured. He glanced again at the portrait. He had been fishing carefully, confirming other reports. And now he knew also that his brother was not involved with her to any great extent. He was fond of Leopold, although because of the difference in their ages they had never been very close. And he was sorry for him. He was not so priggish as he seemed, but had few opportunities to enjoy himself. Any exertion, even riding or dancing, could bring on a severe bout of illness, so their mother kept him on a very tight rein. 'Have you heard from Mama?'

'Daily,' Leopold smiled. 'I might as well have gone to Balmoral with her. You?'

Bertie shrugged. 'The usual lectures. Oh, and her latest hobbyhorse. She wants me to insist that Alix cuts short her holiday in Greece and comes home immediately.'

'It might be wise. This trouble between Russia and Turkey –'

'Could involve us all, I know,' Bertie said. 'Not if we act firmly.'

Leopold hesitated. 'I have promised Mama I wouldn't discuss it.'

'With me?' Bertie did not press him for an answer. He did not need to, after so many years of being deliberately denied any responsibility by his mother. The only duties he was allowed to fulfil were purely ceremonial, accompanied by his Danish-born wife, Princess Alexandra. The Queen had never forgotten his adolescent revolt against the strictness of his upbringing and the revelation of his first sexual adventure which had so shocked his father, Prince Albert, shortly before he died. She had never forgiven him and could not see that, by denying him any opportunity to serve her, she herself had forced him to lead the life of pleasure which she condemned. His limitless energy needed release and he had become the unquestioned leader of international society, the First Gentleman of Europe, arbiter of manners, dress and elegance, the Prince of Sportsmen and of Hearts, a compulsive collector of fair women after the honeymoon years with Alexandra were over. And he found ways to serve his country, calming political storms through his friendships in both main parties, opening channels of communication and resolving diplomatic difficulties through his many contacts in foreign courts and embassies. Yet it had all to be done in secret, with others taking the credit for what he had achieved. It could have been so much more, but the Queen even made cabinet ministers promise never to discuss government decisions with him, until they had been announced in the newspapers. The wisest of them found means to ask his advice indirectly and, from time to time, sought his help, but only when they needed him. Throughout the whole war and diplomatic struggle between Russia and Turkey over the Balkans, he would have been invaluable. However . . . 'Yes,' he nodded. 'My wife's brother is the King of Greece and her sister is married to the Czarevitch, so I am supposed automatically – and wrongly – to be on the side of Russia.' He realised it was not fair even to talk about it. Leopold had been sworn to silence. But he could not hide his bitterness. 'She dislikes my way of life, my friends, my opinions. Most of all that I am not an imitation of Father. So, although my only wish is to serve her and my country, I am not trusted. Unlike you.'

He touched the lid of the despatch box and Leopold tensed. Their mother had recently made him her personal assistant and entrusted him with a key to the government despatch boxes, but only on condition that he never divulged their contents to his eldest brother. 'I only act as Mama's secretary,' he pointed out, uncomfortably.

The box was locked and Bertie would not force Leopold to break his promise. '. . . Only,' he said quietly. 'If you knew how much I envy you even that. I have begged her to let me do some useful work. Anything.' He shrugged. He moved to the door and paused, touching the handle. He looked back with the very faintest of smiles. 'Still – having no responsibility does leave one free for other pursuits.'

Lillie's friends were astonished to hear that Edward and she were moving. It was a fairly sudden decision, taken by Edward. Puffed up by their new social eminence, he had grown dissatisfied with the style in which they lived, contrasting their cramped apartment with the mansions they visisted. He was ashamed to invite people to their rented accommodation. The solution came from the millionaire manufacturer, C. J. Freake. A selfmade man and determined social-climber, he had recently founded the Royal Academy of Music to win social approval. Seeing Lillie's rise to fame, he made sure of her attendance at his parties and dinners by cultivating Edward, whom he advised on short term investments bringing quick returns. The illusion of prosperity pushed Edward into making his decision and they moved to a larger apartment, a maisonette on two floors in Norfolk Street, off Park Lane. Mrs Jennings was not too upset to see them go. She had liked Mrs Langtry, but had had to engage an extra maid to answer the door to her callers and, from now on, life would be much more peaceful.

Oscar did not meet Lillie for several days after the evening at Allen Young's. He avoided her and she did not seek him out, spending more of her free time with Moreton Frewen. They became a regular pair in the morning or early evening parade in the Park, with her mounted on Redskin, although many men begged the favour of accompanying her and they were usually followed by an escort of gentlemen riders, to Frewen's annoyance. With her husband and numerous admirers, it was almost impossible ever to get her alone, but the more attached she became to Redskin, the more confident he was of eventually taking her to bed.

She saw Oscar again at lunch at Patsy's. He arrived late, wearing a high-buttoned velvet jacket over a lavender waistcoat and light trousers, a heavy overcoat draped over this shoulders with a huge collar of brown fur and more fur at the wrists, nearly to the elbows.

Colonel Cornwallis West was an accomplished amateur artist and had a studio built at the rear of his house. Patsy and her guests had waited there. When she pointed to a little, ormulu clock, expecting an apology, Oscar waved his lavender gloves towards it. 'My dear Patsy, how can that tiny clock know what the great golden sun is doing?' His arm swept up in an arc.

They laughed and forgave him.

'Oscar,' Whistler barked, 'stop masquerading as a Kodiac bear. Take off that garment and rejoin the human race.'

As he bowed and took off his coat, Lillie remarked, 'Surely it's too warm for it?'

'He wears it to be noticed,' Frank Miles told her.

'To be noticed is a necessity of life,' Whistler agreed, 'but that is altogether too excessive.'

Oscar smiled. 'In life, as in Art, nothing succeeds like excess.'

He could not relax with Lillie. The link between them was cut and she thought him mannered and artificial. She had never noticed before how stained his fingers were with the incessant cigarettes he smoked, and his teeth. His hand fluttered constantly in front of his mouth to hide them, when he laughed. All society had been breathlessly awaiting the outcome of her meeting with the Prince of Wales and were robbed of sensation when it had come and gone with no result. Oscar remarked on it, that the most eagerly anticipated explosion of the season had fizzled out like a damp squib. From then on, Lillie cut him.

The coolness between them lasted for two weeks, during which she moved to Norfolk Street. Then one night at the theatre she looked down from her box, hearing a commotion in the stalls, to see Oscar overcome with grief at the sight of her, weeping and sobbing, being helped out by Frank Miles. She summoned him to visit her and forgave him. Their relationship began again, Divinity and devoted Apostle – but now she knew that it was a game.

Oscar was grateful to be received back into the fold, to be her closest confidant again, yet even he was aware that she was less open than she had been. He discussed it with James Whistler.

'Yes,' Whistler nodded. 'Our Divinity is becoming devious. She says just enough to each. Tells everything to no one.'

'In that way, the Sphinx keeps her mystery,' Oscar said. 'And her secrets.'

'What do you mean?'

'I mean,' Oscar smiled, 'I have cause to believe the Lily is ripe for adventure.'

As soon as he could, Whistler called at Norfolk Street. It was a small redbrick, terrace house, not at all spacious, but Lillie was thrilled with it and showed him round, proudly. Upstairs were three bedrooms and a bathroom. Downstairs, there was a narrow, panelled hall, with the front door, a door to the terracotta-painted diningroom and another, opposite, to the drawingroom. At the rear was a door to a small study and, under the stairs, the entrance to the servants' quarters in the basement.

Whistler was not overimpressed, but was 'pleased she was pleased,' as he put it. 'It feels like a palace after that rabbit hutch at Eaton Place,' she told him.

'Yes, I often wondered whether to bring you flowers, or a lettuce leaf.'

She laughed. 'Now, you see, I can entertain properly at last. And Ned can have his own study and – and bedroom.'

Whistler noted the hesitation, and the information, as he was meant to. Well, well. Another step in the emancipation of the Lily. She was showing him into the drawingroom and he stopped still, looking round. It was really tiny, its walls painted a plum colour and divided by swathes of dark purple velvet. It had a carved, tiled fireplace and with its blackened oak, antique furniture had a funereal atmosphere, not relieved by innumerable photographs and knick-knacks. The only good thing about it was the strong sunlight coming from two muslin-draped windows.

'Don't you love it?' Lillie said.

'It is rather . . . bijou.'

'It's like living in a doll's house,' she smiled. 'But I'd rather have rooms than space. Besides, the servants have to have somewhere to sleep.' Again he noted the hesitation and the plural. 'Isn't it marvellous?' she laughed. 'Ned says we're to have a butler. And another maid to help Dominique. We even have a stable down in the mews.'

'Do you have a four-footed friend to put in it?' he asked.

'Not yet. One day, perhaps.'

She had hesitated again, although this time it was not explained. Whistler moved slowly round, absorbing the room. He was not enchanted. 'Lillie, my dear,' he murmured, 'don't you think this furniture is just *un peu* too heavy for the size of the room?'

'We were very lucky with it. It's antique.'

'It's fake.'

Her smile faded. 'Fake?'

'Fake,' he said flatly. She did not know whether to laugh or be upset. 'And who chose the, uh, draperies?' He indicated the purple swathing.

'It was my idea,' she told him. 'I thought they would . . . add something.'

About to be scathing, he bit it back and nodded. 'Most original.'

She was relieved and smiled again. 'Then you like them?'

He was saved from the difficulty of answering, when Dominique showed in Moreton Frewen, handsome, self-assured, dressed for riding. They had met before and Whistler had not cared for Frewen's proprietorial attitude to Lillie. 'Have you been riding?' he asked him.

'Just about to,' Frewen drawled and turned to Lillie. 'Unless you've forgotten I was to pick you up.'

'Oh – I'm so sorry!' she said.

Her pretence at remembering did not deceive Whistler,

but Frewen frowned. 'I've brought Redskin for you. My man's holding him.'

The third hesitation was explained. 'What a pity. You could have left him in the stable,' Whistler suggested blandly. Lillie's smile was just for him. 'Don't let me detain you, my dear,' he bowed. 'I merely came to inspect the doll's house. I must run – or skip, as the mood takes me. Stir not. I shall see myself out.' He blew a kiss from the tips of his fingers to her, bowed to Frewen, and was gone.

'He's a funny little chap,' Frewen chuckled.

Lillie controlled herself. Compared to Jimmy, Moreton was a pygmy, although a fine figure in his own world. 'Will you excuse me?' she said, and made for the door.

As she passed him, Frewen caught her, smiling. It was a moment for which he had waited a long time and he exulted at the warmth of her in his arms. He bent his head to kiss her and she raised her hand between them, so that he kissed her wrist, instead. She eased back as he tried to hold her more tightly and seemed about to swoon at his nearness. 'I have to change,' she whispered.

Frewen laughed quietly and released her, like the gentleman he was. She smiled faintly to him as she left the room. He was excited by his success with her. He had shown her that he could be trusted and also that he could be masterful. He stuck his thumbs in his waistcoat pockets and laughed to himself again, thinking how close he was to becoming the most envied man in London.

In her black riding habit and black tophat with a bow of lavender chiffon round the crown, Lillie looked stunning.

Riding slowly beside her in the Park, Frewen watched the supple sway of her figure. 'Whistler was right, you know,' he said. 'Now that you have your own stable, why don't I leave Redskin there for you?'

Lillie's head was turned from him. She smiled to herself, then looked round as though surprised. 'Leave him?'

'Wouldn't you like to borrow him?' Frewen smiled. 'My groom would take care of him for you. And I'd pop in as often as possible.'

It was what she had hoped for. But there was still a

problem which only he could solve. 'What would my husband say?'

'Oh, Ned won't mind,' Frewen drawled. 'I'll take him off fishing for a couple of days. Tell him what a favour he's doing me.'

'Moreton . . .' she chided, gently.

A rider was coming towards them, Lord Lonsdale, suave and elegant. He touched his hat to Lillie. She smiled in greeting and Lonsdale wheeled to take up a position just behind her, on the opposite side from Frewen. Frewen glanced round, annoyed, and blinked. Without his realising it, other riders were already formed up behind them, making a small cavalcade. Lillie had been aware of them ever since she had entered the Park and laughed, riding on faster.

The strolling promenaders were amused and whispered to one another, 'Here they come – Langtry's Lancers.' Lillie acknowledged their greetings with a smile, trotting past at the head of her escort.

That evening, Edward and she were supposed to be dining with Lord Ranelagh, who was now extremely proud of his connection with her, claiming, with more justification than most, to be her discoverer. She also particularly wanted to remain friendly with him, since Clement had just finished his Bar examinations and was more determined than ever to marry Ranelagh's daughter, Alice. However, Edward had been drinking and, coming down the stairs after they had changed to go out, tripped, missed the handrail and slithered to the bottom on his back. Lillie did not realise how drunk he was, until she hurried down to help him to his feet.

The new butler had arrived, Simmons, a stout, red faced man. She sent for him to carry Edward up to bed, then to take a note of apology to Fulham. She felt humiliated and angry, but there was nothing else to do. She could not go on her own. She changed into her housedress. Dominique brought her some sandwiches on a tray and she settled down in the drawingroom to read Swinburne's *Songs Before Sunrise*, a copy of which he had specially dedicated to her.

She had been reading for some time, when she heard the jangling of the outside doorbell. She was certainly not expecting any callers and was surprised when Whistler was shown in. He was wearing his waspwaisted frockcoat and check trousers, his extra high tophat with the flat brim, a long pink handkerchief flowering from his breast pocket. He carried his artist's case with his palette and paints and Dominique followed him in with a large, tissue-wrapped parcel and a paper bag he had brought. He swept off his hat and bowed. 'Your maid tells me you are not going out this evening.'

'No,' Lillie replied, puzzled.

'Splendid!' He set his case down on the table and signed to Dominique who laid down the parcel and paper bag and went out, closing the door, as intrigued as Lillie. 'Now, instead of merely leaving this impedimenta,' Whistler said, 'we can get to work.'

'On what?' Lillie asked. 'What is that, Jimmy?'

He was opening the artist's case, then the parcel and paper bag with an air of mystery. 'I have been unable to stop thinking of your sanctum sanctorum here – and of its purple draperies. The suggestion is almost of the Arabian Nights Tales. Yet – there is something missing.'

'But what is it?'

'Palm leaf fans.' He lifted a feathery palm frond from the parcel and a pot of paint from the bag. 'And gold paint. We pin them to the walls. By the application of one to the other, we shall turn this funeral parlour into *quelque chose d'extraordinaire*!'

Seeing him hold the palm leaf in his left hand and the pot of paint in his right, twinkling to her, an ageing faun, Lillie smiled and began to laugh.

It was one of the funniest evenings she could ever remember. Whistler stripped off his coat and demonstrated to her how to pin the palm leaves like a frieze round the room in the spaces between the draped velvet and how to gild them with the little brush he gave her. He, himself, dragged the oak table to the corner which would be most brightly lit by the windows, climbed on to it and, with a charcoal pencil, quickly sketched on the ceiling an outline of clouds and two long-necked birds flying. When she asked him in astonishment what it was to be, he told her to wait and see. They set to work and he kept up a flow of anecdotes and reminiscences about his childhood in America, then in Russia with his engineer father, his hilariously inept days as a military cadet at West Point and his life as an art student in Paris, where he had shared rooms with George du Maurier and Edward Poynter, who was scandalised like an old maid by the parade of pretty models Whistler was always enticing home. Edward Poynter and Jimmy, what an unlikely combination, Lillie laughed.

Dominique sat on a chair outside the drawingroom door, in case she was needed. She was only summoned once, to fetch some wine. She sat listening to Lillie's gurgles and shouts of laughter and smiled. The Signora had been so solemn of late, it was a joy to hear her happy again. It was two hours later when Simmons came back from Lord Ranelagh's. Dominique was still sitting listening.

Whistler, holding his palette and brush, was putting the finishing touches to his ceiling painting. Lillie was gilding the last of the fans. He had confessed to her that his greatest disappointment was at not having taken part in the Civil War, in which he would have been on the Confederate side. Having trained as a soldier, he saw it almost as a slur on his honour that he had never seen a battle nor fought for a cause in which he believed. 'So having missed the Civil War, I decided to join an expedition to help Chile in her struggle for freedom against Spain. With a boatload of volunteers, I set sail for South America. We were just too late. We reached Valparaiso an hour or two before it was shelled almost out of existence by Spanish gunboats.'

'What did you do?' Lillie asked.

'Got out of town as fast as lightning,' Whistler shrugged. 'The riding was splendid – and I, as a West Point man, was head of the procession.'

His sharp, staccato laughter joined in with Lillie's. She put a final dab of paint on the last leaf and stood back. The frieze of golden fans of palm leaves round the walls between the purple drapes lightened the room and gave a striking, exotic effect. 'There, I've finished,' she said.

'So have I,' Whistler said, and jumped down from the table.

She was able to see his finished work completely at last and her eyes widened. The corner of the room glowed with colour. On the low ceiling, he had painted an impression of blue sky glimpsed through cloud. Across the sky two magical cranes were flying, with outstretched wings. 'Oh, Jimmy . . . It's beautiful,' she breathed.

'Naturally,' he agreed, without false modesty. She could not understand how he had done it so quickly. He explain that it was a harmony in colour. 'An impromptu, if you like. Most artists spend weeks, months, trying to capture a subject in paint. My work is all done in the mind. The actual painting is a tedious, mechanical process. The quicker I can finish it, the more effective, the more alive the result.' He looked round the room and smiled. 'We are making a beginning.'

'I think it's – ' Lillie began, then paused, upset. 'Oh, no! There's paint spattered all over the furniture.'

'Good,' he said. 'For the next step is to get rid of it.'

She looked down at herself. 'And just look at my dress . . . It's ruined.' Her chiffon dress and bare arms were spangled. Seeing that he was spattered, too, she had to laugh. 'There's gold paint in your hair. We're covered in it!'

She stood quite still, as she smiled to him. His hand was reaching out towards her. She had taken off the cape of her housedress earlier. There was a blob of gold paint at the top of the cleft of her breasts, revealed above the low neckline. With the tip of his forefinger, he spread it slightly into a circle, like a golden caste mark. 'See what an artist I am,' he said softly. 'For I have gilded the lily.'

They stayed standing motionless, looking into each other's eyes. Whistler had thought himself immune to Lillie's physical appeal, but he was strongly tempted to kiss her. She waited, wondering if he would and how she would react. His touch had disturbed her.

They heard a knock at the door and Whistler stepped

away, smiling, rubbing his forefinger and thumb slowly together.

The door opened and Simmons came in, his eyes darting round to the new paintwork and to Lillie's gold flecked arms, dress and bust. 'Excuse me, Madam,' he bowed, handing her a monogrammed envelope, 'this has just come. From Lord Suffield.' He bowed again, going out.

Whistler watched as Lillie opened the letter. 'Suffield. You know him quite well, don't you?'

She smiled. 'Ever since I was a little girl. These last months, he's been almost like a father to me.' She read the note. 'He's asked me to tea tomorrow.'

The drawingroom in Suffield's townhouse was in rich, opulent taste, a long, high, L-shaped room. When Lillie was announced, Suffield went to lead her in, himself. She wore her black day dress and her cap-like bonnet without its plume. 'I'm so glad you could come, my dear,' he greeted her, smiling. 'It's a real joy to see you.'

In the drawingroom, she said hello to Sir Allen Young and the shrewd, burly C. J. Freake, who were waiting. There was no one else. 'Isn't Lady Suffield here?' she asked.

'No, unfortunately,' Suffield told her. 'She had to go to the country for a couple of days.'

'How's Edward?' Freake enquired.

'Very well, thank you, Mr Freake,' she smiled.

There was a slightly awkward pause. A footman was carrying in a tray of teathings. He set it down on a stand beside a low table laid with sandwiches, scones, jams and cakes near the sofa. 'Thank you,' Suffield said. 'Now Lillie, my dear, I have one or two matters to discuss with Sir Allen and Mr Freake. Would you excuse us for a minute?'

'Of course,' Lillie said, although she was more than a little surprised.

The three men seemed under some sort of constraint, scarcely looking at her as they bowed and left. How odd, Lillie thought. What am I to do, wait or have tea? How odd to be left alone. She turned towards the table, and realised suddenly that she was not alone. Another man was standing in a shorter side arm of the room, facing its window. Even before he turned and smiled, she had recognised him.

It was the Prince of Wales.

For a second, Lillie was startled and hardly knew how to she controlled herself, remembering to curtsey when he came towards her.

She was even lovelier, cooler and more poised than Bertie had remembered. 'How nice to see you again, Mrs Langtry,' he bowed. 'Well, since our host seems otherwise engaged, perhaps we shouldn't wait.' He indicated the chair by the tea stand. Lillie moved to it. It was exactly as Hartington had said. She moved like an elegant hound set on its hind legs. He saw her hesitate. 'Please.'

He allowed her to sit first, then sat on the chair across the low table from her, watching her. Lillie understood that she was expected to preside at the table. She turned to the tea stand, and paused. As well as the silver teapot, milkjug and sugar basin, it only had plates, cups and saucers for two.

'Please forgive the subterfuge,' he said seriously. It was his voice she had remembered more clearly than anything else about him, deep, intimate, with a faintly guttural r, which almost made him sound as if he had an accent, German or French. 'I very much wanted to meet you again. But I find that, when I call on a lady, she automatically risks losing her reputation in the eyes of the world. You may leave if you wish.'

Many thoughts had streamed through Lillie's mind from the moment she had seen him. What Oscar had warned her of was true. She had been selected, vetted, inspected and had now been delivered. She could leave. From what she had heard of the Prince, he would not be vindictive. He would simply not know her. Hostesses who wished to use her as bait to lure him to their parties would learn sooner or later that he was not attracted and she would quietly be dropped, except by her few genuine friends. On the other hand, if she became a favourite of the Prince, even meeting him in secret, her position was secure. She had still to learn what he wanted of her. Whatever it was, it was not more than any of the other men who tried daily to seduce her. She had accepted that one day she would form an attachment with someone other than her husband. If so, how much higher could she reach than the heir to the throne, the First Gentleman of Europe? 'Since Lord Suffield has gone to so much trouble, sir,' she said evenly, 'and provided such a delicious tea, wouldn't that seem rather rude?'

As Bertie laughed, Lillie smiled and poured two cups of tea.

Lillie arrived home just in time to find Edward showing out Moreton Frewen. He told her he had agreed to let Frewen keep one of his horses, Redskin, in their stable and had arranged that, in return, she might ride it as often as she pleased.

'You are most generous, Mr Frewen,' Lillie thanked him.

'Not at all,' Frewen assured her. 'Professional stabling is ruinously expensive. I trust I'll have the pleasure of seeing you more frequently in the Park.'

She smiled. 'I should think that is very likely.'

'Call any time,' Edward urged.

'I would be charmed to, Mr Langtry,' Frewen said.

'Ned – to my friends.'

'Very well, then – Ned. We'll meet soon.' He bowed to Lillie, with a slightly ironic smile, and Edward let him out.

She was reaching the foot of the stairs, when Edward called to her. 'That's the sort of chap we should cultivate, instead of those namby-pamby poets and artists who're always hanging around. Scroungers.' He snorted derisively. 'Frewen now, he has some very good connections. Asked us down to his place in Sussex for the weekend.' She showed her surprise. 'That got you, didn't it?'

'A little,' she admitted.

He put his hands in his pockets and sauntered towards her with a touch of his old self-importance. 'Don't think that you're the only one that people want to know. He'd heard quite a bit about my sporting days. He's a first class huntsman, himself – and an expert angler.'

'So I should imagine,' Lillie murmured, and went upstairs to change.

She continued to meet the Prince in secret, sometimes for lunch, sometimes for tea, in other people's houses, Youngs, Freake's, Suffield's. He asked nothing more of her than an hour or two of her company. He enjoyed being with her. Her clear, intelligent view of events and personalities refreshed and amused him. Sometimes he held her hand, sometimes he kissed her on parting. She was mystified, having thought he wished to make love to her. Clearly he did, but something held him back.

By discreet questioning of Patsy, she discovered the reason. He, himself, had laid down the rules by which gallantry would be governed. The first was that unmarried girls were taboo, not to ruin their chance of a good marriage. Likewise, married women were considered unapproachable until they had produced an heir. After that, they were free to be courted and to take lovers, if they chose and if their husbands were either kept in ignorance or did not strenuously object. Since most marriages in the higher reaches of society were arranged and not love-matches, husbands and wives frequently agreed to permit each other emotional freedom. Provided the most unbreakable rule of all was observed, absolute and total discretion. Divorce meant instant social ruin for the guilty and could seriously damage the husband or wife who brought the case to court. Nothing might be done which could crack or tarnish the fabric of society.

Lillie at last understood Patsy's rush to produce children in the first years of her marriage, stopping as soon as she had a boy. Georgiana Dudley had given birth to six daughters as well as an heir. The blatancy of it might have shocked Lillie, but life had prepared her for it. Many relationships, hints and allusions among the ladies she knew became explicit. It was not a question of morality, but of finding a means to survive the incompatibility of loveless marriages and yet preserve the good name of the ruling classes, aristocratic, social and political.

According to Bertie's code Lillie could be flirted with,

admired and made much of, but she was sexually out of bounds. In many ways, the knowledge made her liaison with him easier, while it added to her growing sense of frustration.

The Prince's requests for a private rendezvous were unpredictable and she sometimes had to break engagements, without being able to explain. Her friends were the first to realise that she was meeting someone. They hoped it was not Moreton Frewen, who boasted openly that he had the key to her bedroom, with her husband's unsuspecting help. Georgiana Dudley and Lady Wharncliffe thought they recognised the Prince's mode of operating, but Patsy did not believe it could be him. For good and sufficient reasons. In any case, if it was, she said, they would never know unless Lillie told them. He had been so badly burnt over the Mordaunt divorce, he would make no open move. She had not reckoned on his ever increasing fascination with Lillie and his need to see her more often than their stolen meetings permitted.

Only a week or two after the first tea at Upper Grosvenor Street, Frewen and two friends were riding in the early evening in the Park. He reined in and smiled, seeing Lillie trotting towards them, followed by some of her Lancers. 'Here's my little filly,' he announced, 'on the best investment I ever made.'

As he moved towards her, he reined in again sharply, seeing another horseman ride out of the trees, raise his hat to Lillie and fall in beside her. Like Frewen, the Lancers stopped in some confusion, recognising the Prince of Wales, who was followed by his secretary, Francis Knollys, and an equerry.

Frewen stared, dumbfounded. He recollected himself in time to raise his hat as Lillie and the Prince passed. Lillie smiled, the Prince nodded and they rode on, with the strolling ladies curtseying, the gentlemen bowing, gazing after them and whispering in excitement.

As soon as Oscar heard, he hurried to Patsy in Eaton Place. Lady Dudley was already there. Hostesses who wished to invite the Prince sent their guest-lists to Marlborough House for his approval. Already they were being sent back with Lillie's and Edward's names written in, if they were not already there. 'Soon,' Patsy said, 'he will go nowhere, unless she is invited.'

'Is he so predictable?' Oscar wondered.

'Totally. His enthusiasms are temporary, but all-absorbing. And she is the current favourite,' Patsy answered.

'Forgive me,' Lady Dudley remarked delicately, 'I thought you were.'

Patsy raised her hands slightly and let them fall. 'Not any more.'

Oscar was intrigued. 'Do you mind?'

'If it weren't Lillie – possibly,' Patsy smiled. 'To tell the truth, I am quite relieved. Being the royal favourite is very, very exhausting.'

Now that it was out in the open, she had discussed it with Lillie, giving her very valuable advice. She was also concerned about her. Whatever happened, Lillie had to preserve the appearance of her marriage, yet found it more and more difficult to tolerate Edward. Where once he had been excessively cautious with money, now he did not seem to mind how much they spent. He had learnt all he had to do was mention to Freake or Allen Young that Lillie and he might have to leave London, because it was so expensive, and they would immediately suggest another lucky investment on the Stock Exchange.

'She thinks they are . . . arranging for him to be lucky?' Lady Dudley asked.

'They are the Prince's friends and can afford it,' Patsy shrugged. 'At least, it makes it possible for her to accept all invitations and to be suitably dressed. But the thought that he is accepting money from them has killed whatever feelings she has left for him.'

'I can see that,' Georgiana nodded. 'Whether she is genuinely distressed is another matter.' She had noticed Oscar's dismay. 'Don't worry, Mr Wilde. She has not become the Prince's mistress.'

'No,' Patsy smiled. 'He only chooses ladies who have

given their husband a son. Otherwise, he prefers a romantic friendship. It can be ended more easily, with no complications.'

'He is making her the Queen of Society,' Oscar said.

'For a season,' Lady Dudley told him. 'That is as long as his enthusiasms ever last.'

If life had been hectic for Lillie before, it was now a perpetual frenzy. Hostesses who owed their social position to the Prince's favour outbid one another in their efforts to entice her to their homes. Everywhere they met, Bertie did not hide his interest in her, but singled her out. Soon she was automatically placed on his right at table, Edward and she were invited to houseparties, dinner were given in her honour, theatre performances were delayed to give them time to change after riding in the Park, where she and the Prince became a daily sight. While, previously, several of the Beauties had always to be on hand, it was discovered that Lillie was the only one needed. With his restless, inexhaustible energy, he could not stand being bored, not for a minute. In Lillie's company he never was. The Prince has never been so taken, it was whispered. Her fame spread.

And everywhere they went in the evening, Edward accompanied them, always on the guest-list, always in the background with Bertie's friends recruited to talk to him and keep him sufficiently entertained.

Using Edward's newfound money and the unlimited credit given to her by the dressmakers, Lillie was able at last to indulge her taste for extravagant clothes, appearing in creation after creation that she herself helped to design. And her taste was matchless. Langtry hats, Langtry shoes, became the rage. She only had to be seen one day carrying a muff for that ancient style to be readopted by all the women in the country. The modistes and manufacturers marvelled at her clothes sense and hastened to copy whatever she wore.

It was an amazing season, the year of her discovery. By the end of it, she was on a pinnacle of fame which none of the other Beauties had ever attained. Allied to her beauty were legends of her sense of humour, which was nearly as robust as Bertie's. It was a time of practical jokes and many of hers were told over and over. She visited Heron Court, the home of the former diplomat, Lord Malmesbury. An autocratic, old gentleman, he was exceedingly vain about the excellence of his cook. At dinner, at the third course, he announced, '*Gratin a la Grammont* – named after my relative, the *duchesse*. You will like that.'

Lillie was served first to an undistinguished dish of minced chicken covered with cauliflower in white sauce. Malmesbury insisted that she taste it at once. It was so hot it scalded her tongue.

'Well, well!' Malmesbury demanded. 'How is it?'

'Excellent,' Lillie said. 'If it were not so cold.'

Furious at the slur on his chef, Malmesbury took a huge forkful and swallowed it quickly to check for himself. Lillie was quite alarmed at the effect. He nearly had a seizure, from which it took him minutes to recover. But afterwards, he laughed as loudly as everyone else.

She had just returned from a long weekend at the Rosslyns' country house near Dunmow, where she had spent three glorious days galloping over the estate with their beautiful, highspirited daughter Daisy and her sister. Her favourite memory was of Daisy and Bertie, himself, helping her to balance a chamberpot filled with ink on top of the door of the room she shared with Ned, just before he came upstairs to change for the evening. The crash, yell and cursing they had heard, all hiding in Bertie's room down the corridor, had been music to her. Later at dinner, when Edward finally appeared with black streaks down his face that no amount of scrubbing would remove for several days, Daisy and she and their royal accomplice kept bursting into fits of suppressed laughter that startled the company. She had managed to maintain a straight, sympathetic face with him, so he did not suspect her. He could not suspect the Prince. His baleful, accusing eyes fixed on Daisy.

Shortly after their return to London, they went to a supper party at the Suffields' after the theatre. It was relaxed and informal. Suffield and C. J. Freake kept

Edward happy, making sure his glass was never empty. He buttonholed them, slightly tipsy. 'No, I was saying – the outgoings on the house are desperately high. Now that we have a carriage and coachman as well.'

He was hoping that Freake would come to his assistance. Instead, Freake said drily, 'Well, it's nearly the end of the season. You'll find your expenses will drop considerably.'

Lillie was the centre of attention in the group seated round the fire. They had been listening to her stories of trying to contact the spirit world in her childhood and how she gave it up, when the sofa sailed across the room.

'With one of your brothers underneath it,' Bertie remarked.

In the laughter, Lord Ranelagh said, 'Nevertheless, these experiences are something that usually do happen to children, sir.'

'But they *still* happen,' Lillie protested. 'Dreadful things. Even to my butler.'

She was very serious and the others fell silent, waiting to hear.

'What kind of things?' Lady Dudley asked.

Lillie bit her lip. 'Well, our house in Norfolk Street is built almost where the gallows called Tyburn Tree used to stand. Our butler sleeps in the basement – and night after night, he is wakened by shrieks and moaning, to see the gibbet rearing up beside him and the execution block – and the heads of the victims rolling across his bed.'

Bertie puffed on his cigar, frowning. 'Does he vouch for this?'

'He swears to it, sir.' Lillie told him. 'Though I admit, I'd be more inclined to believe him, if he didn't sleep next to the wine cellar.'

Seeing her smile, Bertie began to chuckle. 'You minx!' he roared, breaking into laughter. Everyone joined in.

'That was very unfair, Lillie,' Patsy protested. 'You made me go all shivery for nothing.'

Edward had come to the edge of the group with Suffield and Freake. 'She's right about that house,' he insisted. 'It's pretty gloomy.'

'Well, you'll be glad to get away from it,' Freake said.

'Away?' Edward echoed, puzzled. 'Where to?'

'After the season,' Suffield said.

The others had become aware of them and were listening. 'Have you decided where you'll be going?' Allen Young asked.

Edward did not understand what he meant. Neither did Lillie. 'We hadn't thought of going anywhere,' she smiled.

'There'll be nothing to stay in town for,' Lady Dudley told her. 'No one does. It'll be absolutely dead for the next four or five months.'

It was something Lillie had not thought about. She had enjoyed so much being feted, she had never stopped to wonder what happened at the end of the season. Which was now. 'Will you . . . be leaving, sir?' she asked Bertie, carefully.

Aware of them all watching him, Bertie blew out a puff of smoke. It was unfortunate it had come up like this. 'No reason to stay, once the season's over,' he said shortly. 'After Cowes, my wife and I always take the waters for a month or so in Austria, then go to our place at Abergeldie, near Balmoral, for the shooting. We spend Christmas at Sandringham. Don't get back to town till February or March.'

Suffield could see that Lillie was shaken. He felt sorry for her. So did Patsy and wished now that she had thought to warn her. No one had expected the Prince to dismiss her so bluntly, and in public. Edward looked from Bertie to Lillie and back, nearly in a state of shock.

Sir Allen Young took pity on them and said to Lillie, 'I'd be delighted if you and Mr Langtry would join me for a cruise on my yacht for a week or two.'

Edward brightened and accepted quickly. 'That's very kind of you, Sir Allen.'

'Very kind,' Lillie agreed.

After a pause, Suffield felt he should make a suggestion. 'Somehow, I imagined you'd go back to Jersey, to stay at the Deanery with your parents.'

Dean Le Breton had moved from St. Saviour's to the

L.—K

larger town church of St. Helier. Lillie's childhood home was gone.

'No, the new Deanery is not suitable for . . .' she began, and stopped, still shaken by the abruptness with which the party had ended. She glanced at Bertie. He was smoking, withdrawn, no longer looking at her. Without doubt, he was hoping she would not make a fuss and would not resond, if she did. She had much to be grateful to him for and made herself smile. 'I've just thought of something marvellous!' she exclaimed. 'I shall have the whole Park to ride in, all by myself.'

There was light laughter from some of the others, admiring her unbroken poise. Patsy smiled to her. 'You'll miss your Lancers.'

'Oh, the poor men must be given leave sometimes,' Lillie said airily.

The laughter was louder, the atmosphere becoming relaxed and cheerful again.

'*I* was thinking of going to Jersey,' Ranelagh said slowly. 'Look, I have an idea. I shan't be going there for a month or two yet. Why don't you, Mr Langtry and you, stay at Portelet House for a while?'

Edward was dubius, but Lillie looked up, excited. 'Seriously?'

'It's there,' Ranelagh told her. 'You might as well use it – if you'd like.'

Lillie was radiant. 'Lord Ranelagh,' she said thankfully, 'I can't imagine anywhere I would rather be, nor anything I would rather do.'

Bertie glanced at her, puffing on his cigar.


Lillie's homecoming to Jersey this time was triumphal. Reports in the newspapers, her photographs in the shops and stories told by visitors had made her the most celebrated person in the island. There was a band to welcome her at the quayside and a crowd followed her, cheering when she boarded the little train for St. Aubin.

Arthur Jones, slightly older, more handsome than she remembered him, was waiting at St. Aubin station with an open carriage. She hugged him and kissed his cheek. 'Ned, you remember Artie?' she laughed.

Edward nodded distantly. He was far from happy at returning to this damned island again, and again as a poor relation.

Lillie's mother was waiting at Portelet House and bustled out, when they drove up. She was nearly in tears as Lillie kissed her. 'You're here! Oh, Lillie – oh, my dear . . .'

Edward climbed down from the carriage more slowly, leaving Dominique to clamber out by herself. He bowed formally to Mrs Le Breton.

She was taking off her apron, her happiness damped by his formality. 'Welcome back to Jersey, Edward,' she bobbed.

The house was as pretty as always, on its shelf of land overlooking the little bay. Lillie came into the livingroom, hugging her mother's arm, the veneer of poise she had developed in London vanishing as she saw the remembered room with its large, stone fireplace, the sparse furniture old and mellow. She wanted to kick her shoes off and run down to the beach. 'It hasn't changed. It hasn't changed at all!'

'A bit more dilapidated, maybe,' Arthur said. He had followed them in, carrying their trunk, and Lillie smiled to him quickly.

She saw Edward beyond him, looking round without enthusiasm. She squeezed her mother's arm. 'I expected you to meet the boat.'

'I had to get the rooms aired and see the beds were made,' Mrs Le Breton told her. She and the Dean lived in St. Helier now, but she had insisted on coming over to make certain everything was ready.

Lillie laughed and told them about the band and the crowd. 'And what do you think?' she smiled. 'We've been invited to dine at Government House the day after tomorrow, with the Lieutenant Governor. You and Father, too.'

Mrs Le Breton gasped. 'All the years I've lived here, I've never once been asked to Government House. Your Father, not me.'

'Where is Father?' Lillie asked.

'Didn't he meet you at the quay?' Arthur said.

'No.'

'He was going to,' Mrs Le Breton said, then paused, embarrassed. 'He – he must have been held up on parish business.'

Nothing changes, Lillie thought.

Mrs Le Breton was thankful for the interruption when Dominique came in, carrying bags and hat boxes. 'I'll show you to your rooms,' she said to Lillie. She glanced at Edward who stood with his back to them at the window, and lowered her voice. 'It was *two* bedrooms you wanted?'

'Yes.'

'I'll show you yours.' Mrs Le Breton took Lillie out and Dominique followed them.

Edward had barely listened to what they had been saying. To him, being here was like being in exile. And he did not care for the house, which was too remote. He was slightly cheered by spotting a sherry decanter and some glasses on a table beyond the windows.

Arthur had set down the truck and was watching him. 'You'll be getting some sailing in, while you're here,' he remarked.

'I don't have a yacht any more,' Edward said dismissively.

Arthur thought. 'I daresay I could borrow one for you.'

Edward perked up. 'Really?'

'From one of the fellows at the Victoria Club,' Arthur told him. 'I'm sure they'd like to sail with you. You're a notable.'

'Really? . . .' Edward chuckled. 'Let's have a drink on it.'

Some days later, Lillie was kneeling in the pretty, little walled garden, working with a trowel and clippers. She loved gardening and had never forgotten how she used to tend this one. And the work helped to soothe her thoughts. It was hard to accept having been deposed so unceremoniously. One day the Prince seemed unable to exist without seeing her, and the next he was gone. Various people had hinted it might happen, Patsy, Lady Lonsdale, but she had not listened. By the start of the next season in the new year, everyone would know. Men like Moreton and Lord Hardwicke and the others whom the Prince's attention had kept at bay would come sniffing round her again, not restrained by the niceties of the rules like he had been. She would not be in such demand – except by the men.

She was worried about her father, too. The compulsive lechery, which he could not control, was not so tolerated in the town parish as it had been in St. Saviour's. His many fine qualities ensured him some devoted supporters, but there were more audible voices, questioning his fitness to remain as Dean.

Arthur Jones had been watching her for some time, before she sensed he was there. She was wearing a loose, scoop-necked day dress and a shovel-shaped straw hat, tied under her chin. 'I thought I'd find you here,' he said.

She smiled. 'I always think of it as my special garden. It's how it was.'

'I knew you'd want it to stay the same,' he told her. 'I wouldn't let anyone change anything you'd planted.'

She was touched. 'Thank you, Artie. I remember how you and Clem and – and Reggie used to tease me about it.' She sat back. 'I thought you'd be with Ned.'

'He's at the Victoria Club.'

'Hasn't he gone sailing?'

He shook his head. 'He'd rather drink and talk about it.'

'You mustn't say things like that.' She turned away from him, carrying on working.

'I hate to see you so unhappy,' he said after a moment.

'What do you mean?' she laughed.

'With Ned – your life. With everything.' She swung round, looking up at him. His serious, grey eyes were fixed on her. 'I hadn't realised it till I saw you at Government House. Elegant, complimented, with everyone clustered round you. I began to understand what your other life was like, in London. But you were like an actress, playing her last part.'

She was disturbed by his perceptiveness. She gathered

up a bunch of flowers she had cut, and rose. 'Perhaps it was.'

'How?' he asked.

'I see no point in discussing it,' she said sharply. She left him abruptly, heading for the house.

Indoors, she took off the sunhat. She had placed a vase on the small table by the windows and stood there, arranging the flowers she brought in. Her composure had been shattered by what Arthur had said and she could not stop her hands trembling. She was aware of him coming in and standing by the door, watching her.

'I'm sorry if I upset you, Lillie,' he apologised. 'I had no right.'

She already regretted having snapped at him. He had spoken out of affection for her, one of her oldest and dearest friends. Almost a member of the family. 'I'm only upset because what you said was true,' she confided quietly. 'I'm not happy with Ned. I never have been. I tried to make our marriage work, but – but I gave up. Now it's a pretence. Like everything else about me.'

He came closer. 'You can't say that.'

'Oh, I got what I wanted,' she admitted. 'Everything I'd ever dreamt of. To know all the best people, admiration, fame of a sort. But now that other life, as you called it, is over.'

'Why?'

She had finished arranging the flowers and stood back to see the effect. 'I was the season's novelty,' she smiled. 'It all happened so quickly, I never stopped to think it would end. I don't mean I'll be ignored from now on. But the best is over. It will never be the same again.'

'Have people been unkind?' he asked gently.

'No,' she told him. 'Just the opposite. Though when they look at me, they don't see *me* – only something created by a kind of hysteria.' She hesitated. 'I know it sounds weak – silly – but, for all the men who've written poems to me, tried to seduce me, there is not one person in the whole world who really loves me.'

'I do,' he said and she smiled to him. His eyes did not

leave hers. 'I've loved you ever since we were children.' She could not doubt the sincerity in his voice and his eyes and realised he was serious. 'Why do you think I was at your father's church so often?' he smiled. Then was serious again. 'When you told me you were going to marry Langtry, I don't know how I went on living. If I'd had the money, I'd have followed you. I'd have come to London and – somehow – taken you away from him.'

'Artie,' she whispered. 'Oh, my dear . . .'

'I always knew you'd come home one day,' he said. 'That you'd find the life you wanted was empty, and not for you. And that you'd find me waiting.'

He was so direct and natural, there was no question of not believing him. A moment before, she had felt alone. Now she knew that he loved her completely, just for herself, and so faithfully all those years. There was a tension between them. She remembered how happy she used to be walking and talking with him, running on the sand, sitting in silence, content, watching the slow swell of the waves. Why hadn't she understood then?

They heard the sound of the carriage drawing up outside. 'It's mother and Dominique coming back,' she said.

They were very close. He wanted more than anything on earth to kiss her, but still could not take the step. There was the murmur of voices in the hall and both knew that, for this time, it was too late. She kissed the tips of the fingers of her right hand and touched them fleetingly to his lips. As she did so, she realised it was a gesture she had learnt from Oscar. Her mother and Dominique were coming in and she moved away from him, more perturbed than ever.

# CHAPTER ELEVEN

Lillie was deeply troubled when they returned to London. She had at last been unfaithful to Edward.

She had always been fond of Arthur, almost as another brother, and had had no suspicion of his true feelings for her. Once he had confessed them, though, she began to remember things he had said and done and now could not understand how she had failed to recognise that he loved her. He had not only loved but worshipped her all those years.

He was young, virile and goodlooking. Handsome, really, with his strong, slim figure, regular, rather fine features and clear, light eyes. Being Ranelagh's son, he had breeding, without the Viscount's haughtiness, and more than a trace of recklessness. Brought up on the mainland, he might have been just another arrogant, young man about town, but his island life and education had made him more natural and considerate. Having Portelet House and its home farm, he could have won nearly any girl in the island, even though he had very little money. The end of the season and the bitter knowledge that she had been the season's novelty and nothing else made her want to reject the life she had been living. She was ashamed to think that even a few weeks ago she would not have considered Arthur good enough for her, not rich, nor titled, nor artistic, nor socially prominent. With him, she did not have to pretend, did not have to be poised and always on her guard.

The first time he kissed her, there was no explosion. She had felt no wild passion, only a warmth and contentment at his nearness. She had not been alone with him for two days after he confessed his true feelings. She had not tried to avoid him. The weather had been bad and Ned had not left home. Yet during those two days, she thought about how Arthur had loved her for so long in secret, and loved her real self, not because she was a challenge, the reigning Professional Beauty. They had so many memories, so many interests in common, he was like an extension of herself. If she had not rushed into marriage with Edward, Arthur might now be her husband, Reggie might still be alive and life would be very different.

On the third day, the weather cleared and Ned harnessed the carriage and drove down to the inn at St. Aubin harbour. In the late afternoon, Arthur found Lillie kneeling again in her garden and she rose and kissed him, as easily and naturally as if they had always been lovers.

In the days that followed, they met alone many times, rode and walked together. They were golden days for Arthur, to be able to hold her hand out of sight of the house, to kiss her in a corner of the lane where the tall hedges shielded them, to tell her all the things he had thought and dreamed of them sharing. Edward never realised for a moment what was happening. On most days, he was already fuddled by the afternoon, sleeping it off if they were invited out somewhere in the evening, carrying on to drink more at the inn or the Yacht Club, if they were not. Lillie tried to talk to him about his drinking which was becoming a problem, but he was angry and abusive, insisting that he only drank socially, like a gentleman, and she gave up. Arthur could not understand how she could bear to be under the same roof as him. If they had shared a bed, he was sure he would have gone mad. To hide his feelings became more and more difficult, although there was a peculiar excitement in being with her in public, polite and friendly, knowing that when they were alone he could touch her and she would turn to him, smiling, her lips soft under his.

The limits of their lovemaking were set by her. He sensed a reserve in her, even though she did not draw back nor protest when his hands moved over her, touching her through her light summer dress. A natural reserve, he thought, a lingering guilt at betraying her husband, and he did not try to force her to yield more than she wished. He could not have been more mistaken.

One afternoon, he rode out with Lillie, west from

Portelet, taking the track for St. Brelade's Bay. The tide was out and the sand stretched, firm and golden, for nearly a mile before them. They covered it in one delirious gallop that left them breathless and laughing. Instead of turning back, they went on, winding up to the top of the cliffs again and riding at a walk till they came to a steep, green slope leading down to one of the smaller, enclosed coves. They tied their horses to a bent thorntree and ran down the long slope, hand in hand, to the beach. All the heat of the late autumn sun seemed concentrated in that tiny bay. There were no buildings, no sign of any human beings but them. A haze had risen on the sea and hung like a shimmering curtain between the cliffs that formed the horns of the bay. There was not a sound but the cry of high-flying gulls and the whisper of the water as it rippled in towards the powder-dry sand.

After the gallop and the race down the slope, Arthur felt his shirt clinging to him. Lillie was barelegged. She had kicked off her shoes and run, holding up her dress, to walk along the edge of the water, gasping at its coolness as it washed over her feet and ankles. Arthur turned to her, and caught his breath. She had stepped back from the water and unfastened her dress. As he turned, she was slipping her arms from it and it fell to her hips. She pushed it down, stepped out of it and threw it further up the beach. She was wearing only a loose, linen shift and the sun shining through it showed him the strong curve of her waist and buttocks, the long, sleek outline of her legs. She looked round and smiled to him over her shoulder, then ran straight into the sea, slowing as it reached above her knees and the shift rose, floating round her. With a kick of her legs, she dived and swam out, disappearing into the haze.

Arthur had been gazing at her, unable to move. When she dived, he pulled off his boots and hurried forward, dropping his clothes as he tore them off. The water seemed cold to his naked body only for a moment, then he was swimming in the direction she had taken.

The haze was coming in and soon he could see neither the beach nor the horizon. He was swimming in his own globe of limited visibility and was almost disorientated, becoming anxious for her, when he could not see her. 'Lillie!' he called, and heard her answer to his right. As he moved towards the sound, she swam out of the haze to him and they linked fingers, treading water and laughing at the pleasure of finding each other. They swam back in the path of the waves, side by side, until Arthur's feet struck the bottom. They had reached the shallows. He caught Lillie's arm, drawing her down, and she squealed before her knees touched the sand and she realised that he, too, was kneeling. They stayed kneeling, smiling to each other. Even so, the water did not reach their waists. Lillie's shift was moulded to her, become transparent. Arthur's eyes swept to her waist and back over the high thrust of her breasts to her face. She was still smiling, waiting for him, and he took her hands, drawing her up to stand.

He was naked and she thought him beautiful. The shift was like a slick film of gossamer wrapped round her, hiding nothing of the perfection of her figure. He drew her to him and they kissed, softly at first, then more fiercely as their bodies warmed and he felt the smooth surge of her thighs against his, the yielding pout of her belly and the sharpness of her nipples as her breasts pressed against his chest. His hands slipped from her back to the flare of her haunches and she panted on his mouth, feeling his sudden hardness. Her hand eased between them and she held him tightly, murmuring.

Still linked, oblivious of everything except their need for each other, they stumbled to the shore and sank to the dry, hot sand, becoming one in the same fluid motion. For a long count of heartbeats, neither of them moved. Lillie had never felt so whole, so complete, and when his body at last began to surge slowly over hers, she gasped at a delight, a release of joy such as she had never known.

That was the afternoon, when they rode home, that she told him Edward had insisted they return to London. In the island, he was no longer shown the personal respect he considered due to him and he resented it. They were to sail at the end of the week.

Arthur was shaken. Ranelagh was not due for nearly a month and he had counted on having Lillie until then. Especially now that they had really become lovers, the thought of her leaving was unbearable. Yet he could not keep her. He could not ask her to break with Langtry, until he could support her.

On the evening before they left, Lillie and Edward had dinner with her parents in their new house in St. Helier. She left early to finish packing and Edward went for a farewell drink at the Yacht Club. Arthur was waiting for her at the station to see her home. They went straight to her room, since only Dominique was in the house and Lillie had taken her into her confidence. They made love again, more desperately. Lillie surprised him with her passion. The first time, it had been like the first time ever for her. She had been dazzled by her own reactions, her own pleasures. This time, she thought of Arthur and, when he began to take her gently again, urged him to a demanding frenzy that consulsed and exhausted them both.

She thought of that night often, when she was back in Norfolk Street. Arthur had still been with her, when they heard Ned return, chuckling to himself as he crept unsteadily to his own room, trying to be quiet but banging the door drunkenly behind him. Arthur had dressed quickly and kissed her mouth, her breasts and her belly before he left. Sometimes, alone in bed, she held herself tightly, remembering. Her sensuality had been awakened and whereas, before, she could dismiss it from her mind, now longings came that tormented her. She wrote to Arthur every second day and his letters crossed hers. At times, she thought they were all she lived for and did not know how she would survive until they could be together again. It had not been guilt, nor fear of being unfaithful that had restrained her at first, as Arthur had thought, but awareness of her own nature. She was afraid that if her sexuality was aroused she would be unable to control it.

The town seemed deserted, with most of the houses between Portland Square and Palace Gate shut for the winter, while their owners were in the country. It reminded her only too vividly of the previous year, when she had been so alone. And made her more conscious of the future. Without help from Freake and others, bills were more difficult to pay. Edward took refuge in brandy and visits to his club. Christmas was when most bills would be presented and she simply could not think how they were to be met. Perhaps they could be avoided till the start of the new season but, once the stores and fashion houses realised she was no longer in the leading position she had held, they would press for payment. Edward's elder brother disapproved of their gadabout life and refused to help. She thought more and more of the tranquillity of the island and longed to be there. She would not miss luxuries, if only Arthur had enough money to keep them both. She would leave Edward without a qualm. Yet it was such an irrevocable step. For a few delirious months she had lived in another world, of gaiety and splendour. It had taken possession of her like a drug and she could not bring herself to give it up voluntarily.

She very much wanted to ask someone's advice, yet could not go to Oscar nor Jimmy Whistler, each for their own reasons. Then by chance, she heard that Lord Suffield had been enquiring after her. She sent round a note to Upper Grosvenor Street and a reply came by return, inviting her to call.

Suffield was surprised and very pleased to see her. There were no servants and he showed her into the drawingroom, himself. Most of the furniture was covered with dustsheets. 'The house is closed up, really,' he apologised. 'I've come back to town only for a day or two. I can't tell you how delighted I was to get your note. I thought you were in Jersey?'

'We came back sooner than I wanted to,' she said, tautly.

'How is Edward?'

'It's about him I wanted to talk to you.' She stopped, and Suffield waited, seeing that she found difficulty in going on. 'You know what he's like. Lately it's become worse. With nothing to do, he drinks all the time.'

'What do you wish me to do?' Suffield asked cautiously.

She paused. 'I – I can't stand it any longer. I'm going to leave him.'

It was news, indeed, and Suffield tried to conceal his agitation. 'You realise what it would mean?'

'Yes.'

Suffield had recovered his urbanity. 'Forgive me asking – is there someone else?'

'. . . Perhaps,' she admitted.

'Someone I know?' She shook her head and he was relieved. 'Someone in Jersey?'

It was easier for her to talk now. 'I've known him all my life. He's quite young. Very different from Ned.'

'And you love him.'

That was a question Lillie had asked herself, over and over. 'I don't know,' she replied, honestly. 'I'm happy with him. I don't have to pretend. I don't have to be anything I'm not. He's so alive, so open-hearted.'

Without realising it, she had put Suffield in a very awkward position. 'And you want my advice,' he said slowly. She was looking at him, troubled and lovely, trusting. 'If you go to this young man, no doubt you will have a carefree, happy life, out of the public eye. Having left your husband, you will, of course, be finished in Society – and can never return. You understand that you will surrender for ever the position you have won?'

She smiled briefly. 'I have lost it, anyway. It finished with the season.'

'On the contrary, my dear.' Suffield was seated next to her on the sofa. He rose and moved away, choosing his words carefully. 'I am here on the Prince's business – expressly to contact you. He wishes to see you.'

Lillie sat up very straight, surprised. 'I thought he was in Scotland.'

'He was.' After taking the waters at Homburg and a short visit to Alexandra's parents in Denmark, the Prince and Princess had gone as usual to Abergeldie. In the old castle, Charlotte Knollys, Alexandra's Woman-of-the-Bedchamber and closest friend, had fallen victim to typhoid. 'Her Royal Highness has insisted on nursing her, herself,' Suffield finished. 'And that the Prince should not remain at Abergeldie.'

She saw that Suffield was unable to look at her directly. 'He is coming to town?'

'Incognito. To see you.' He hesitated. 'I should explain – since Lady Mordaunt gave birth to her first child and her husband, quite wrongly, accused the Prince of being the father, he had made it a rule never to enter into a liaison with a childless, married woman. However, he has thought long and deeply about your relationship. He sincerely admires you. He says, in fact, that he cannot live without you.' His voice was toneless. It was a mission he would gladly have refused, but could not. He turned to her at last. She was gazing at him, her eyes huge with disbelief. 'He must have the answer from you, yourself. If it is yes, in return, you will be given a position in Society such as no woman has ever had. You will be the most envied woman in the world. That is what you will be giving up. And that is what you must decide.'

Lillie shut herself in her room when she got home, telling Dominique she was not to be disturbed. She had agreed to see the Prince, but had not given any indication of what her answer would be. Suffield had fully understood.

She unlocked her wardrobe and took out the hatbox in which she kept Arthur's letters. She sat on the bed reading them through, as she had done many times. They were frank and passionate, like hers to him, and usually they brought the image of him very clearly to her. This time, however, other thoughts kept intruding. Her mind was turbulent and she had hoped the letters would calm her and help her to reach a decision. They remained only words. She kept thinking . . . the Prince of Wales . . . She lay back on the bed and found she was excited. Not so much by the thought of the Prince himself, but by all that being loved by him could mean.

Suffield had not really understood. He had thought she was shocked and timid, disturbed by the offer he had been sent to make. She had been shocked only for a second and then all she had been able to think was, why now? Why now

303

when it was too late, when she had promised herself to Arthur?

When she had first begun to meet the Prince in secret, she had been prepared for him to make love to her. It was a conscious decision, taken with the expectance of adventure and with pride at having the heir to the Throne and the Empire as her lover. She had adjusted, instead, to being his intimate companion, to flirt with him and keep him entertained and amused. While she gloried in the position and adulation it brought her, undoubtedly it added to her own frustration. Without that, when it seemed to have ended, would she have given herself to Arthur? But now she felt bound to him. And the Prince was coming to see her, to hear her decision.

It was arranged very deftly. A seemingly chance meeting between Edward and Sir Allen Young led to an invitation to a week's fishing holiday. Edward accepted eagerly, telling Lillie with amusement that, if she wished to be invited out from now on, she would have to learn how to fish. The evening of the day he left, Bertie visited Norfolk Street for the first time.

The meeting between Lillie and him was tense, restricted for a while only to small talk. Lillie wore a loose, muslin dress, virginally white, fairly high cut. He complimented her on it and on the decoration of the drawingroom. 'It is very charming,' he said. 'The perfect setting for you.'

'Most of the ideas came from James Whistler,' she smiled.

He was standing by the table. On it was a large blue glass bowl in which a single yellow waterlily floated. 'I thought I detected his touch.' He could not keep skirting the real purpose of his visit, which both knew must be reached. 'I have missed you,' he said quietly. 'I was looking forward, of course, to seeing you again – but I did not realise how much I would miss you.'

His voice was deep and sincere. Lillie did not know what to reply. She had to admit she was afraid of him. He was the only man who had ever made her feel afraid. She had seen how easily other people gave in to him. It had taken all her courage to make him wait, as she still did.

'Did you ever . . . think of me?' he asked.

'Many times, sir,' she said, truthfully.

He smiled briefly to her and moved round towards the fire. 'I cannot remember when I was last in London at this time of year. You have never been to Scotland, I believe.'

'Once sir, with John and Effie Millais. I was sorry to hear there was illness in your household.'

He nodded. 'It's a foul disease, typhoid. It seems to have a fondness for my family. It killed my father and two cousins. My elder son was struck down earlier this year and is still recovering. I, myself, nearly died of it a few years ago.'

'So did I, sir,' she told him, 'about the same time.'

'Indeed? Then we are both living on borrowed time.' He smiled again. 'I have been invited to the Sassoons' at Brighton for the weekend after next, a house party. I wonder if you and Mr Langtry would care to join us?'

Again Lillie made him wait. 'We would be honoured to, sir.'

Bertie breathed out slowly. 'I gather that Mr Langtry is on a fishing holiday,' he remarked casually.

She was equally casual. 'He left this morning, for the week.'

'Then you are left with only your maid and your gibbet-fancying butler at home.'

'He was given notice,' Lillie said, 'to preserve what is left of the vintage port.' Bertie chuckled. 'There is only my maid, who is devoted to me.'

Bertie knew she had given him her answer and felt a sudden, wild elation, which he could not hide. Lillie was still tense. Again, her decision had been taken quite deliberately, depending only on the way he approached her. If he had been domineering or presumptuous, she would have turned him away without caring about the consequences. She had to be certain that he wanted her, and more than wanted her. Suffield had reported that the Prince had been unable to settle in the two months they had been apart, that he had been able to think only of her. But she had to see it for herself. She would not give herself, if she was to be used for a few months and then discarded. The stakes were the highest she could play for and what she did now would fix the course of her entire life to come.

In the silence, they heard the jangle of the front door bell and a murmur of voices. 'No doubt, now people know you have returned, they will beat a path to your door,' Bertie said. He was taut.

Dominique knocked and came in. 'I beg your pardon, Signora.' She bobbed nervously, overawed. 'But Mr Frewen has called. He wishes to see you.'

Lillie knew Bertie was watching her. 'Would you tell Mr Frewen,' she said evenly, 'and anyone else who calls, that I am not at home.'

Dominique understood. 'Si, Signora.' She bobbed again and went out, closing the door.

Bertie felt the tension flood out of him, to be replaced by a new, triumphant excitement. He had known many women, but had not suspected he could want anyone half as much as he had come to want her. The weeks without her had been torment. He smiled, when she looked at him. At her faint, answering smile, he strode to her and took her in his arms.

Lillie hung back, half afraid at what she had done. Forcing him to wait these extra days had been calculated to make him more eager. His look, everything about him told her now that he loved her, but she was not even sure she could respond to him.

The directness of his lovemaking surprised her. 'We've been fools too wait so long,' he muttered. Her neck was bent back. He kissed the angle of her throat, then the white slope of her shoulder as he pulled the dress from it. His body was bulkier than Arthur's, his arms thicker and stronger round her. Her eyes were open and she was almost bemused. After the erotic tension between them, she found his direct, masculine approach instantly arousing. Part of her fought against it, but as he kissed her mouth at last, not gently or playfully as he had always done before, but fiercely, her eyes closed and her own arms went round him to hold him tightly.

The week that followed was like the honeymoon she had never had. Bertie completed her sensual awakening. As a lover, he was experienced and considerate, yet knew when to be dominant. His virility astonished her. He seemed inexhaustible, drawing her on and on to heights of response she had never thought possible. There were whole nights when they did not sleep, then rose before dawn to canter through the mists in the deserted Park, clearing their heads before returning to her room. Seeing him once, silhouetted against the window, she thought of her father, the same strong neck and shoulders, deep chest and masterful way of standing, legs braced and apart. The thought was perverse, but she could not get it out of her mind and it added to her excitement.

She was everything and more than he had dreamt. Her strength and needs matched his. Her skin breathed a musky perfume that intoxicated him. He had discovered to his surprise that she was inexperienced and her gratitude for his gentleness and the speed with which she learned bound him to her. She was not ashamed to show her delight nor talk about it and he found himself laughing with her. He wanted to know everything about her and for hours she would lie, curled in his arm, answering his questions, telling him her whole life. She told him everything. Except about Arthur. And he told her of his own childhood and his unhappiness at being given no chance to serve his country except by stealth, things he had never told anyone before.

She felt affection for him and sympathy. She knew she did not love him, but a sexual bond was forged between them that was very close to love.

He paid an official visit to Norfolk Street the day Edward came back from his trip and Lillie was amused to see how adroitly he behaved as if he never been there before, complimenting Edward on the taste of the drawingroom and catching sight of the painted ceiling, as though for the first time. Edward was overjoyed that they had not been dropped, after all. He was taken up again by Freake and Sir

Allen Young, Henry Chaplin, Christopher Sykes and others of Bertie's friends. More fishing trips were arranged.

The Langtrys were invited to a series of house parties in the new year. At all of them, the Prince was chief among the guests, accompanied by several friends. They loved to tell the story of a Countess who was condescending to Lillie, whom she considered a nobody. Lillie paid her back superbly. Overhearing the Countess arrange for her lover to come to her that night and promise to leave a plate of biscuits outside her door so that he could find her room, Lillie waited until everyone had gone to bed, then removed the plate. Bertie and she sat on her bed, eating the biscuits and laughing, listening to the lover's slippered feet pad up and down the corridor trying to find the Countess's room, until he gave up.

At house parties, husbands and wives rarely shared rooms. On most evenings, the servants were dismissed after dinner. It was a time for relaxed conversation and games. One sport developed by Lillie and Patsy, which immediately became popular, was for sliding downstairs seated on polished, metal trays. It was especially exhilarating in country houses with long, steep stairs. Bertie and others joined in with gusto and the speeds and spills were sometimes dangerous. The fainter hearts among the ladies declined, but the gentlemen thoroughly approved of it. There was always a chance of a skidding spill at the bottom and an intoxicating flurry of silken legs, white thighs and garters. Hide and seek was popular, too, and the seeker always took care to knock before opening any door. At bedtime, candlesticks were left in the hall and the gentlemen escorted the ladies to their rooms. It was the hour for tender goodnights and whispered arrangements for lovers to meet later, and sometimes for more boisterous games and pillow fights.

Hostesses very quickly learned to put Edward in a separate wing from Lillie and that she was to be in the same corridor as the Prince. All the proprieties were observed during the day. Night was the time for freedom, when no one remarked on floorboards creaking nor heard the soft closing of a door.

Few people were remotely aware that there had been any break in Lillie's relationship with the Prince. It was noted with amazement that she had survived into the new season and seemed to be more firmly the favourite than ever. She went everywhere with him, even to the royal box at Ascot. During the day, they rode together as always. Frequently, they lunched with friends and Lillie took him to Oscar's rooms and to Miles' and Whistler's studios. He commissioned Frederick Leighton, now president of the Royal Academy, to do a portrait bust of her. Her engagments were reported daily in the social columns and the newspapers reported in detail every new dress she wore. Her credit was infinitely extended and she began to indulge her long-stifled taste for extravagance. She had additional wardrobes fitted in her bedroom and the spare room for her day dresses, hats and accessories. Her parade of evening gowns created a sensation. Dominique was in constant raptures, but Edward grumbled at each new dress. Even at the reduced prices the courtiers charged her, it was costing a fortune, although he enjoyed the luxury of their life too much to protest too loudly. She took care not to quarrel with him. She still needed him to accompany her everywhere they went in the evenings, even though he scarcely saw her from the moment they arrived until it was time to leave.

She still had no jewellery, except small pieces she bought for herself. Bertie secretly bought some of her dresses for her, but could not give her jewels. Edward was stupid, yet not blind. He preferred not to think too precisely about Lillie's friendship with the Prince. A diamond necklace could not have been ignored.

He could even be unpredictably roused by smaller things. He came back from a second weekend visit to Lord Malmesbury at Heron Court in a drunken temper, unable to restrain himself even in front of their cab driver and Dominique. Bertie had given all the ladies at the party a present. Hers had been a small, exquisite gold and ruby pendant and Edward had been jealous but passed no comment. The next day, he had been in Lillie's room and seen her handwriting on the blotting paper, where she had blotted a letter. He had held the blotting pad up to the mirror and been able to make out most of what she had written. It was a thank you note to the Prince and its affectionate phrasing infuriated him. 'D'you know what I call that kind of behaviour? he raged. 'Am I supposed to accept it?! What right has he got to give your presents?'

'He gave all the ladies something,' Lillie soothed.

'But yours was special! And what do you think his wife would make of that? His precious Princess – or is she too damned used to it to worry?!'

That night, at an after theatre party at Christoper Sykes', he was still surly and did not respond to attempts by Allen Young and the bearded, humorous Sykes to cheer him out of it. He even refused a fishing trip to Dorset that Young had arranged. 'I don't think I'll be leaving town for a while,' he said, glancing over to where Lillie and the Prince were talking quietly.

She was wearing the pendant and Bertie frowned when she told him what had happened. 'He's not going to make you give it back?'

'I said you'd be angry.'

'And so I would be!' Bertie growled. 'It's only a – well, it's nothing to what I'd like to give you.'

'Lord Malmesbury saw I was upset,' she told him. 'I had to explain why – oh, only that my thank you note was a little indiscreet.'

'A little,' Bertie agreed, smiling. 'What did he say?'

'He was very annoyed with his servants. He's given orders that the blotting paper in the guestrooms is to be changed every day from now on.' Bertie chuckled, and she smiled. 'Yes, it's funny, but it's made Ned suspicious. I don't think he minds what happens – as long as he doesn't know about it.'

'Don't worry, my dear. I'll see to it,' Bertie assured her. 'And I've been thinking. It's time you met my wife.' Lillie was shocked for a moment. She had only ever seen the graciously beautiful Alexandra at a distance. 'I've seen how some of those old dowagers look at you,' he went on. 'How dare they? Anyway, once you're accepted by Alix, there's nothing they can do or say.'

Lillie was worried. 'Are you . . . sure it's wise?'

'Oh, yes. She's said she wants to meet you,' Bertie nodded. 'And don't worry about Ned. 'I'll take care of it.' He turned, rubbing his hands, calling to Sykes. 'Now then, Stopher! Where's the cards?' He had just discovered Baccarat and his infectious enthusiasm for the game was making it popular.

Sir Allen Young had been concerned over Edward Langtry's sullenness, which threatened trouble. He could only admire the deftness with which the Prince drew Langtry into the game to help him run the bank, confiding in him, asking his advice on the cards and thawing him with the warmth of his personality.

Throughout these months, Lillie had been writing more or less regularly to Arthur. She had not told him about the Prince, only that they met now and then socially. None of it affected how she felt about Arthur and she treasured his replies, upset when they did not come by return. She thought of Jersey and Portelet as a haven to which she could escape, if the world crumbled round her. She needed the certainty of his love for her to keep in touch with reality.

She was writing to him, half listening to Dominique and laughing. Her maid's pride at how her photographs had ousted those of all the other Beauties from the shops was unbounded. Many of her rivals, like Mrs Wheeler, simply refused to be photographed any more, rather than try to compete. Lord Suffield had tried to bring Mrs Wheeler and her together by taking them both for a drive in his superb four-in-hand carriage. The attempt had ended in disaster when *Town Talk* reported that he had drawn all eyes in the Park, driving with Mrs Langer and Mrs Wheeltry. Lillie had been annoyed, but laughed. Mrs Wheeler had been so offended she wished to sue the newspaper.

'And just think, Signora,' Dominique said. 'I saw a butcher's boy with a photograph of you pinned to the

311

basket of his bicycle.'

'To be admired by butcher's boys,' Lillie smiled. 'That is real fame, Dominique.'

She just had time to hide the letter she was writing under a magazine, when Edward came in. He was scowling, carrying a small presentation box. The Prince had sent him a pair of gold cufflinks, with his Prince of Wales monogram. 'Does he think he can buy me – with a little present?' he demanded.

'It's what he sends to his friends, as a sign of his special favour,' Lillie told him. 'Most men would feel honoured.' Edward was brought up short. He looked at the box with new respect. 'And have you read the card?' she asked him. 'I didn't want to tell you and spoil the surprise.'

A separate envelope had come with the gift. He opened it. Reading the embossed card inside, he gave a little sob of surprise. 'The – the Queen,' he faltered. 'I'm to be presented at Court.' It was true. He had been summoned to Windsor.

'*Che meraviglioso!*' Dominique exclaimed. 'Oh, Signore . . .'

'And afterwards, we have been invited to dinner at Marlborough House, with the Prince and Princess of Wales,' Lillie said.

Edward stared at her. Never in his whole life had he imagined – 'What do I have to do?'

'Write to thank him for his gift,' Lillie smiled. 'And to the Lord Chamberlain.'

He was nearly overwhelmed. 'Yes, yes. I must do it straight away.' He suddenly smiled to her and hurried out.

Dominique was alarmed. The Signora was to meet Princess Alexandra at her home? She watched as Lillie uncovered the letter, signed her name and sanded it. She no longer trusted blotting paper. How could she stay so cool?

'I want you to post this for me, Dominique,' Lillie said. 'It must catch the mailboat to Jersey.'

The conservatory at Marlborough House off Pall Mall was a long, mirrored, white and gold room, with tall French doors leading to the gardens. Filled with palms and potted plants, it was used as an extra drawingroom in the summer, for small dances and family parties.

Lillie had thought herself past being impressed, but Marlborough House impressed her. Originally built by Wren, it was Bertie's official London residence and displayed all his liking for opulence and comfort. There seemed to be hundreds of liveried servants. The blue drawingroom where the guests were received was faultlessly elegant. The State diningroom was enormous, yet dwarfed by the main ballroom of which she had only a glimpse. Throughout dinner, a footman stood behind each chair at the long table. The meal itself was beautifully prepared and presented, not the gargantuan feast most hosts thought it necessary to provide. Bertie enjoyed food, but not to the exclusion of everything else. He considered half the usual sixteen to eighteen courses as more than adequate and was trying to establish an average of eight as the rule for any normal dinner. He also enjoyed champagne and brandy, but drank sparingly. It made him animated and good humoured. He was never drunk.

Princess Alexandra had been looking forward keenly to meeting Lillie. At thirty-three, she was serenely beautiful, her hair with a touch more auburn in it than Lillie's swept up to a mass of curls on the crown of her head. Her eveningdress was lavender, revealing her perfect figure, still slim although she had borne six children. Round her neck, she wore a pearl choker, a fashion which nearly all ladies now followed. She had devised it to hide the tiny pucker of a scar on her throat, left by a childhood illness. Rheumatic fever during pregnancy some years before had left her slightly deaf and lame in one knee, which she disguised with a graceful, gliding walk that was also widely imitated. Brought up as a girl in fairly modest circumstances in Denmark, she still had a trace of a Danish accent. She was warmhearted, generous and wholly delightful.

She had married Bertie for love and it had been some years before she discovered that the intolerable pressures of his forced inactivity and his restless temperament had driven him to look for distraction with other women. She had been deeply hurt, yet understanding. The only time it

313

had been hard to forgive him was after the shame of his appearance in the witnessbox at the Mordaunt divorce trial. She had gone home to her parents, now King and Queen of Denmark, and had not known if she would return to him. War had broken out between France and Prussia and he came to fetch her home. Their third son, the child of their reconciliation, lived only for one day. Since then, there had been no more.

Inevitably, there were more women in Bertie's life. Eager friends had told her of Lillie when she returned from Greece the previous year and she expected his interest to be fleeting, as usual. When it persisted, becoming more like an obsession, she was forced to take notice. Her one fear had always been that Bertie might fall into the net of an unscrupulous woman. Rumour said that Mrs Langtry was amiable and sensible and she was relieved. Against the advice of her friends, she was also determined to meet her. At dinner, she had seen that Lillie was very, very pretty, although subdued, which was natural. In the conservatory, while they waited for the gentlemen to join them, she asked Lillie to sit with her and drew her out.

Lillie had carefully chosen a modest dress in very pale lemon. She was glad that Patsy and Lady Dudley were with them. Beyond Princess Alexandra sat Charlotte Knollys, her Woman-of-the-Bedchamber and confidante, uncompromisingly plain and undisguisedly disapproving. Of them all, Alix and Lillie were the only two who seemed completely calm and poised. All over the room, other ladies watched and listened, on tenterhooks.

'I believe your husband and mine have in interest in sailing in common,' Alix said.

'Mr Langtry is – or was – a noted yachtsman, ma'am,' Patsy put in, quickly.

Alix smiled. 'Yes, my brother-in-law Leopold told me he had won the Le Havre race.'

'In very bad conditions, Your Royal Highness,' Lillie said. 'I know. I was with him.'

'How exciting!' Alix exclaimed, enviously. 'Have you been in any other winning races with him?'

'Yes, ma'am,' Lillie told her. 'Though he has not had his own yacht for some time.'

'Yes, it's dreadfully expensive. 'I'm always telling Bertie,' Alix nodded and the others laughed. 'I'm sorry, Mrs Langtry. What was the race?'

'The Thames race, from the Nore to Erith, four years ago.'

Charlotte Knollys' mouth pursed. 'I don't remember that Mr Langtry won that,' she said accusingly.

Lillie inclined her head. 'Well, you see, Miss Knollys, there was hardly any wind and we drifted for hours. In the middle of the night, I had had quite enough and went to sleep in the cabin. Just before dawn we floated first past the winning post – but, not to wake me up, my husband didn't fire his signal cannon. Next day, because he hadn't fired it, he was disqualified.'

'What a shame,' Alix sympathised. 'And what did he say?'

Lillie smiled slightly. 'I don't think I dare repeat it, ma'am. But I slept very well.'

Alix laughed with the others. Leopold had assured her she would like her, and she was beginning to believe him. Of curse, poor Leopold was more than half in love with pretty Mrs Langtry, himself.

A footman opened the main doors and Bertie and Leopold came in, followed by Edward and the other gentlemen, bowing as they entered. Bertie and Leopold crossed immediately to Alix to find out how it was going. Edward came behind, with Suffield, Allen Young and Bertie's astute and discreet private secretary, Francis Knollys, Charlotte's brother. Edward was still partly dazed with the events of the afternoon. Actually to have been presented to the Queen, to have touched her hand . . . He could not remember what she had said to him, nor what he had replied. But the Prince had been most affable, and he felt ashamed at his crude suspicions and jealous behaviour.

'Here they are!' Alix smiled. 'I swear the gentleman these days spend less and less time before joining us after dinner.' She knew exactly why they had been so short a time.

315

Bertie bowed. 'No brandy and cigars could compensate for the pleasure of your company, my dear.'

'Don't mumble, Bertie,' she told him. I'm sorry, Mrs Langtry, I am a little deaf. But I can hear *you* perfectly.' Seeing her smile to Lillie, Bertie and his friends relaxed. Alix turned to Edward. 'Your wife has been telling us how you lost a race out of consideration to her. I call that truly noble.'

Edward was greatly gratified and bowed to give himself longer to think of something to say. 'Uh – it was the rules, ma'am.'

'Quite,' Bertie said.

There was a second or two of silence, which Alix ended with a sigh. 'I wish there was some music. I feel like dancing.' She looked at Lillie. 'Do you feel like dancing?'

'I'd love to,' Lillie smiled.

Alix smiled back, sensing they had a great deal in common. 'So what shall we do about it?'

An orchestra had played during dinner and the members were now having refreshments. 'Ask them to play outside, when they've fininshed,' Bertie told Francis Knollys. 'We'll leave the doors open.'

'Certainly, sir,' Knollys bowed, leaving at once.

'Now, Leopold,' Alix warned, 'you're not to dance more than twice. You promised Mama.'

Leopold seemed about to object, but then submitted. 'Very well. I shall dance first with you – then with Lillie.'

Alix noted that he used her Christian name.

'Each lady must choose what she would like to have played,' Bertie decided. 'Starting with you, Lillie.'

'Well, if everyone else is going to call you "Lillie", so must I, Alix said. They smiled to each other. It was going better than anyone had imagined. Alix saw Allen Young murmur to Suffield and could not resist teasing. 'I'm sorry, Alleno?'

Young was caught off guard. 'I was just saying – eh – how charming this conservatory is, ma'am.'

'Yes, it's almost my favourite room,' she laughed. 'I've been thinking, Bertie – would Lillie and Mr Langtry like to come with us to Cowes?'

There was a start of surprise as she intended. Even Lillie's poise was jolted briefly. It was Alexandra's method of saying she had accepted her.

'I'm sure they would,' Bertie smiled, and looked at Edward. 'Would you?'

It was almost too much for Edward. 'I – I'd – we'd be more that . . .' he began.

'That's settled, then.' Bertie knew Alix' sense of humour and did not wish to tempt her any more. 'If you'll excuse me, I think we should circulate a little.'

He looks worried, Alix thought. How unlike him. 'Do so, by all means,' she granted.

Bertie turned casually to Lillie. 'You're interested in plants and things. I don't suppose you've really seen this room yet.'

'Not yet, sir,' she told him. She rose and, with a slight curtsey to Alix, took Bertie's arm.

Alix watched him lead her away, expressionlessly. She saw how at ease they were with each other. The group around her was breaking up. She turned to Charlotte Knollys. 'Well?'

'I still don't think His Royal Highness should have brought her here,' Charlotte said intensely. 'I wonder you can be so pleasant to her.'

Alix smiled gently. 'Jealousy, Charlotte, is at the bottom of all the troubles and misfortunes in the world. Besides – I know Bertie.'

The orchestra had begun to play outside. Lillie and Bertie paused by a giant yucca plant, just coming into bloom. 'Well, what do you think of her?' Bertie asked.

Lillie glanced back at Alix. She had never met any other woman with whom she had had a more instant rapport, with less reason. 'I think your wife is the most wonderful woman I've ever met,' she said sincerely.

He nodded slowly. 'So do I.'

The following afternoon, Lillie was at her writing table in the drawingroom, finishing a letter to Arthur and rose, startled, when Edward showed in Arthur, himself, who had just arrived. He told them he had come to London for a few days on business for the farm.

'I hope we'll see something of you, while you're here,' Edward said, expansively.

'I hope so, too,' Arthur agreed, smiling to Lillie.

Dominique was out doing some shopping and Edward left with bad grace to answer another ring at the doorbell.

Arthur moved closer to Lillie as she gazed at him. 'I can't believe it?' she whispered. 'I'm just writing to you.'

'Let me see it,' he smiled, and reached for the letter.

She laughed and snatched up the letter, crumpling it in her hand. 'Certainly not!' She had been thinking of him as she wrote and to have him really here was disturbing. He was just as she remembered.

She wore a cream afternoon dress with a high, ruffled collar. No matter how often he saw her, each time she was more lovely. 'You look well,' he said.

'So do you.' They both smiled because it sounded so polite and impersonal. 'Are you really here on business?'

His eyes answered her. 'To see you.'

Edward came back to the door. 'It's Whistler and Wilde,' he said, disgruntled.

Why did they have to come now?, Lillie thought. She did not want to share Arthur's time here with anyone. But they were infinitely preferable to Ned. 'Bring them in,' she said. Edward grimaced and left.

'Whistler, the painter?' Arthur asked.

'Yes.'

'And Wilde?'

'A friend of ours, a poet,' she told him.

Arthur smiled. 'I've never met a poet.' He kissed his fingertips and touched Lillie's cheek. She pressed his hand for a second, disquieted not only by his touch but by the gesture, knowing that he thought of it a special sign between them. Both Oscar and Whistler would have recognised it.

She stepped away as they came in. Whistler was at his most dandified, Oscar his most flamboyant self. He had a cigarette in his right hand, his lavender gloves in his left.

Both carried canes. Arthur tried not to show his astonishment. If it were not for their style, both might have been caricatures.

'A good day to you all,' Whistler barked.

'This is an old acquaintance of ours from Jersey,' Edward told them. 'Arthur Jones. Mr Whistler and Mr Wilde.'

They bowed to Arthur.

'How do you do?' Arthur said.

'Remarkably well,' Oscar sighed, 'considering I have had such a tiring day.'

'Why, Oscar?' Lillie asked.

'This morning I took out a comma. This afternoon I put it back.'

Edward was the only one who did not laugh. 'If you'll excuse me,' he grunted.

Whistler stopped him, as he started to leave. 'No, no, you mustn't disappear, Mr Langtry. I have something here of tremendous import.' He had a folded newspaper under his arm and shook it out. 'Proof that our divine Lily's fame has spread not only throughout Europe, but to the other side of the world.'

Lillie was intrigued. 'What is it, Jimmy?'

'A friend has sent this newspaper from the States. I quote.' He screwed his eyeglass into his eye and read out, '"For followers of the social milieu. Among the phenomena of the London scene known as the Professional Beauties, a new star has arisen to dim all the others, Mrs Edward Langtry. A vision never to be forgotten; the colouring brilliant and at the same time delicate; the attitude all grace; harmony and contrast all in one, but the whole impression one of vital force. Public pets may be objectionable, but few could so well have survived the ordeal of public admiration and remained so natural as Mrs Langtry!"'

'That's marvellous,' Arthur exclaimed.

Edward took the paper from Whistler. 'Let me see it.'

Oscar saw that Lillie was thrilled. 'It is only a pale reflection of the original,' he murmured.

'Where is the paper printed?' she asked.

'Boston,' Whistler said. 'But the article is syndicated

throughout America.'

Edward was chuckling. 'You didn't get to the end of it,' he broke in. 'I quote. "Mrs Langtry and the other Professional Beauties have a rival in the shape of a beautiful youth named Oscar Wilde, a poet and aesthete. His picture adorns all the shop windows and is even taken in aesthetic style with a bunch of lillies in his hand. He must look as lovely as a yellow cat having a fit in a dish of stewed tomatoes."' He could hardly read for laughing by the end. Arthur began to laugh, too, but stopped when Lillie glanced at him. 'What do you think of that?' Edward spluttered.

'It is not very well written,' Oscar answered coolly.

'I think it's a masterpiece,' Edward chuckled. He handed the paper back to Whistler and went out. They could hear him laughing all down the hall.

'I'm sorry, Oscar,' Lillie said quietly.

He shrugged. 'Jimmy and I had already laughed at it. The joke was passé.'

Whistler presented her with the paper. 'Please have this – to start your transatlantic archives.'

She smiled, but she was watching Oscar who had turned away, concealing his hurt pride.

He stopped in front of a painting mounted on an easel and covered with a cloth. 'What's this?' he asked.

'Yes,' Whistler wanted to know. 'Have you been enriching the hyena art dealers?'

'It's my portrait by Edward Poynter,' Lillie told them. 'He presented it to me.'

'Then we must see it!' Oscar declared. He took the cloth and threw it up over the top of the easel. The painting showed Lillie seated, in a rich, golden dress, very low cut to show the swell of her bosom. Her right hand held a yellow rose to her breast and her left held a simple white rose. Her single strand of pearls was round her throat. Her eyes were downcast, pensive, the roses symbolising the choice between two lovers. Poynter was also perceptive.

'It is perfect,' Arthur breathed.

'He hasn't caught my colouring,' Lillie said flatly. 'Not

like Millais.'

There was a touch of arrogance and Arthur glanced at her, slightly perturbed.

'But then, who could?' Whistler commented. 'Perhaps, not even I.'

Oscar had not taken his eyes from it. 'I, too, find it perfect,' he murmured.

'Would you like it?' Lillie said. He looked at her in surprise. 'If you would like to borrow it,' she offered, 'take it with you.'

He was moved, realising she was partly apologising for Edward. 'Divinity,' he vowed, 'it will become my most treasured possession.'

That evening, Lillie heard from Bertie of something else that had happened during the afternoon. Prince Leopold had exhausted himself dancing and had to stay in bed. His mother, Queen Victoria, came to see him and was disturbed to find him pale and weak. She scolded him for following Bertie's example, then kissed him and bade him get well, as she depended on him.

Turning to leave his room, she had caught site of the framed sketch of Lillie above the desk. When he told her it was a sketch of Mrs Langtry, a lady in society, Victoria said, 'Indeed! She is much too pretty.'

To his disbelief and dismay, she climbed on to the chair by the desk and, in spite of his protests, unhooked the sketch and climbed down again. 'This has no place here,' she informed him primly. 'I shall see it is disposed of.'

Next day, at a small party in Whistler's Studio in Tite Street, Lillie told Frank Miles, who promised to make Leopold an exact replica.

Edward had not left the house for more than half an hour and it had proved impossible to meet Arthur alone. She knew she still had the same loving feeling for him, as he for her. To be near to each other, yet out of reach, unsettled them both  Her problem was by far the greater. She had grown used to deceiving Ned. Now she found herself also deceiving both Bertie and Arthur. Her fear was that someone would suspect her relationship with Arthur and that word of it might reach Bertie. Even more, that Artie might hear gossip about her affaire with the Prince. The only one who guessed her dilemma was Jimmy Whistler.

She had brought Arthur to his party and saw them standing together, discussing one of Jimmy's highly stylised paintings, which he called a Nocturne in Black and Gold. It was a night piece, showing a fireworks display across the river Thames at Cremorne Gardens, the smoky sky spangled with the impression of a falling rocket.

'I think I like it,' Arthur said slowly.

'You think so,' Whistler repeated ironically. 'Are you one of those people who know nothing about Art, but know what they like?'

Arthur smiled. 'I know what I don't like.'

'And what is that?'

'Paintings that pretend to be photographs.'

'Lillie, my dear,' Whistler declared, pleased, 'there is hope for your protegé.'

Arthur was not too happy at being called her protegé. He had seen the people who hung around her and did not wish to be classed merely as one of them. He refused another drink and excused himself to Lillie. 'I have an appointment. I'll see you tonight.'

She hesitated. 'I'm sorry, Artie. I have a sitting with Sir Frederick Leighton for my bust.' She was aware of Whistler listening with considerable interest.

Arthur was disappointed. He had hoped for at least one evening with her. So far, they had only kissed briefly in the hall at Norfolk Street. 'Tomorrow morning, then?' She smiled and nodded. She would send an excuse not to ride with Bertie. Arthur smiled back and she watched him leave, wanting nothing more than to go with him.

Whistler was beside her and murmured, 'I thought you were going to the Opera with the Prince tonight.'

'I am,' she said. 'But Arthur wouldn't understand.'

Whistler clicked his teeth. 'How long is he staying?'

'Another two days.'

'You're going to Cowes,' he reminded her.

'The day after he leaves.'

The day after he left, making her promise to spend longer with him next time, she followed him to Southampton with Edward. Then the fun and animation of the Yacht Week at Cowes lessened the pain of losing him. King Christian and Queen Louise of Denmark were on the *Osborne* with Bertie and Alix. Edward and she were on Allen Young's yacht, *Helen*, moored alongside. They had parties and dances on board and ashore. Ned came into his own and was quite a favourite with Alexandra's parents, rowing them round the bay every morning in a dinghy. Lillie and Alix discovered they had the same sense of humour and became almost inseparable, leading the games, arranging outings. Prince Leopold sneaked out of Osborne House and went sailing with them in the royal yacht, *Alberta*, all three of them hiding below the level of the rail until they were out of sight of the House, knowing that Queen Victoria would be watching with her telescope.

Bertie was not sure how he felt about the developing friendship between them. It was the most enjoyable week he had ever spent at Cowes, although with his wife and children, innumerable relatives and her husband there, it was never possible to get Lillie alone. He would soon be leaving with Alix again for Homburg. He had to do something.

He arranged for Edward to borrow one of his smaller yachts, the *Hildegarde*, with a crew from the Royal Navy, and to take it on trials on a day when Alix and her family were visiting the exiled Empress Eugénie of France at her rented summer home on the Isle of Wight. He, himself, sailed with Lillie and his two small sons, Eddy and George, for Poole Harbour, where the *Osborne* anchored and he took Lillie ashore. An open carriage was waiting for them and he drove her up to the outskirts of Bournemouth.

It was a clear day and the drive along the top of the sandstone cliffs was pleasant, with an unbroken view of the sea off to their right. Bertie wore a cap and reefer jacket and Lillie was also dressed for sailing, in a straw boater and a blue dress with a sailor's collar. She looked so fresh and tempting, he had to stop and kiss her, no matter who saw.

That was the wonder about her. He was never sated. The more he was with her, the more he wanted her, and could not bear the thought of losing her or of sharing her with others.

They drove on, reaching a secluded spot, a natural clearing of cropped, green grass among the trees. 'This is the view I promised you,' he said.

She looked round, smiling. 'It's lovely.'

'Jersey's somewhere to the South. The Isle of Wight and Cowes just over there.'

They sat for a moment, experiencing the peace and the strangeness of being alone. 'Shouldn't we get back to the yacht?' Lillie suggested. 'They'll be asking where we are.'

'I wanted to bring you here,' Bertie told her. 'I've bought this piece of land.' Lillie was more interested and looked round again. He had chosen a perfect spot. 'I'm tired of us meeting in other people's houses. I'm having a place built for us here,' he said. She swung round to him and smiled. 'It will be in your name. You can do it up in any way you choose. It will be our house – for us to meet and just be ourselves, whenever we can get away.'

He was studying her, waiting for her reaction. The reins were slack, but he was gripping the ends so tightly his knuckles shone like bone. She had never seen him nervous before and all at once her heart went out to him, as she realised how deeply he had come to love her. 'Bertie . . .' she whispered.

He kissed her. With one arm still round her, he turned the carriage and they trotted away, back towards the harbour.

# CHAPTER TWELVE

The plot of land on East Cliff and the contracts with the builders were in the name of 'Mrs Emily Langton.' The house was to be Lillie's and there had to be nothing to connect it in any respect with Bertie. Since the house was hers and secrecy essential, she easily persuaded him to leave everything to her. She designed it, inside and outside.

It was tremendously exciting. She managed to inspect the site again and to fix it in her mind. Alone in her cabin at night or when she seemed half asleep on a long cruise, she was planning, visualising, clarifying her ideas. No one had ever seen her so animated. Her enthusiasm spilled over into everything she did, playing tirelessly with fourteen year old Eddy and Georgie, thirteen, Bertie's and Alix's sons, who were naval cadets, dancing and flirting at the balls on shore, joining in games and pranks with Alix. The whole Marlborough House Set was there, in holiday mood, and before and after the races the party was unending, merely shifting from yacht to yacht.

With Bertie and Alix, she became particularly fond of the highspirited young son of former Empress Eugénie, Louis Napoleon, the Prince Imperial. One hilarious evening, they planned a seance at the Custs' summer cottage. The blinds were drawn, the lights put out and everyone sat round the table holding hands in a chain. For many minutes nothing happened, then there were gasps and shrieks as furniture in the room began to shake and bump. The young son of the house, Harry Cust, lit a match and revealed the Prince Imperial banging a wine-table with one hand and rattling a chair with the other. He had been sitting between Lillie and Alix, who had both laughed and kept the secret when they felt him break the chain.

He was put out of the house and the doors of the room locked. The table-turning began again, more seriously,

Again there was a long wait and then everyone felt the strangest sensation, a choking, coughing feeling, as though they were being smothered. The ladies became nervous and, this time, when matches were struck, there was real alarm. Many of the people round the table, particularly the Prince of Wales, had turned white, hair, face and clothes. The villain turned out to be the Prince Imperial again, who had found some bags of flour in the kitchen, climbed up a wisteria to the open sittingroom window, silently entered and thrown handfuls of flour into the air over the table. The experimenters all turned on him, pelting him with his own flour.

The next night, Lillie joined Bertie and Louis Napoleon in an exploit that was never to be forgotten at Cowes. Goodlooking Harry Cust with his fair hair and romantic profile already considered himself a Lothario and upset the Prince Imperial by continually stealing the prettiest girls from him. Having overheard him arrange to smuggle one up to his room in the cottage after a dance on board the *Osborne*, Lillie, Bertie and Louis Napoleon slipped ashore first. They found a small donkey and hoisted it up with ropes into Harry's bedroom, where they dressed it in his nightshirt and put it to bed. The intended seduction did not take place and the young lady suffered from nervous palpitations for days.

At the end of July, Bertie departed reluctantly with Alix for Baden and Copenhagen. He would not return until the family moved to Abergeldie in late September. Privately, he promised to see Lillie in London before then. Work had already started on the house and plans were made for Edward to be invited on a series of fishing and shooting trips, to give her a chance to inspect the stages of building.

The yacht *Hildegarde* with its naval crew was left at their disposal and they sailed for Jersey, where they were welcomed with some ceremony by the Lieutenant-Governor. They were only there for two weeks, but they stayed again at Portelet House and, much of the time, Edward was on the yacht. For days and nights, Lillie and Arthur could at last be alone, looked after only by Dominique. They walked and rode and made love and swam naked in the moonlight, with no need to hide their feelings. Any doubts which Arthur had had in London about her love for him were swept away.

Lillie surprised herself. It was not as if she had gone straight from Bertie's arms to Arthur's, but she had wondered how she would react. In fact, when they made love, it was just as perfect as the first time. He was trusting and uncomplicated and the relief of being able to be completely natural was immeasurable. Materially, he could give her nothing, but she felt more secure and protected with im than with anyone. He wanted to know every detail of her life in London, so that he could understand it, and she told him everything. Except that she barely mentioned Bertie, and said not a word about the house they were building. The two sides of her life were separate and she was a different person in each. She felt no sense of strain in passing from one to the other and had learnt to enjoy each to the full, while it existed. Both sides of her nature were fully satisfied and she saw no reason why she should be forced to choose between them.

Arthur had grown to dislike the fondness in her voice, when she spoke of Oscar. He did not doubt her, yet he could not help being jealous. She assured him he had no need to worry about Oscar and, the night before she left, her passion convinced him. He resigned himself to waiting until they could be together, knowing that the waiting was just as hard for her.

Edward and she had no sooner arrived back in London than he left again for a fishing party in Norfolk. Lillie took the next available train for Bournemouth.

The house was making astonishing progress. Already the foundations were laid and some walls beginning to take shape. Her enthusiasm had infected the builders, almost as much as the bonus she promised them. Mrs Langton, they assumed, was a wealthy young widow, very lovely and ladylike. They took great care not to damage the trees as she had asked, for she wanted the house to be well set back in its gardens and secluded. She had chosen a mellow red brick for the walls. It was not to be an enormous mansion, just a comfortable, large size, and the builders could appreciate the need for seclusion, since the plans called for so many windows. The house faced south and Lillie wanted it to be filled with light.

Back at Norfolk Street, she was kept fully occupied choosing materials and colours for the inside, from wall-papers and carpets to fireplaces, tiles and cornices. There were hundreds of things to remember. The Cornwallis Wests were going through a difficult financial period and had had to let Ruthin Castle, their place in Wales, so Patsy was in London. Lillie saw as much of her as usual, and of Oscar and Whistler, but she was becoming so adept at splitting her life into compartments that none of them suspected there was anything on her mind.

Edward noticed nothing. They did not spend much time together. When they did, he was quarrelsome and spiteful. He enjoyed the attention they received, but had never lost his resentment that it was due to Lillie. He had all the vanity of the shy and his pride was hurt by the constant exposure of his inadequacy. The rent of Norfolk Street used up most of his allowance and he had at last been forced to sell the *Gertrude*, which he could no longer afford to keep in dry dock. Unable to improve his finances, he simply gave up and lived on credit. Most days he was drunk. Since it was not the season, Lillie did not need him to visit those of her friends who were still in town. He seldom bothered to ask even where she had been. She could take the early morning train to Bournemouth and be back by the evening, without him ever realising she had gone. Sometimes she wished she was building the house for herself and Arthur, but just to be building it was enough.

It had not been possible for Bertie to return to London and, in early October, Lillie and Edward were invited to stay at Glen Tanar, the Marquis of Huntly's superb lodge in Aberdeenshire, not far from Abergeldie. During the day while the men fished or shot, the ladies sketched and had picnics and Lillie often joined Alexandra and her three little daughters, with whom she became a great favourite.

Frequent parties were arranged, attended by Bertie and Alix, and Lillie introduced her new sport of toboganning downstairs on a teatray. It was so popular that the host ordered all his best silver trays to be locked away.

She adored the Highlands, the lonely heather moors, the blue mountains hazy with mist or standing out sharp and clear against an eggshell sky, rank upon higher rank receding to the far horizon. She had been amused to see Bertie in a kilt, which he always wore in Scotland, but she came to like it. It suited his powerful body, showing his strong legs in tartan stockings, and the shorter, tweed jacket worn with it setting off his chest and shoulders. She only once went stalking with him, and was so sickened when the majestic stag they followed was shot that she refused to go any more. 'A woman's mission is to give life rather than take it,' she said.

One afternoon, she drove over to Balmoral Castle with Lord Strathnairn and Lady Erroll, one of the Queen's ladies-in-waiting. Lillie was disappointed in the royal castle, designed by the late Prince Consort in Scottish baronial style. Queen Victoria missed them, coming back twenty minutes after they had gone. She had heard much of Mrs Langtry, both from Leopold and Louise, and was sorry not to have seen her. An equerry was sent after the carriage to bring them back, but it was too late.

In November, Lillie and Edward stayed with the Romneys in Norfolk. Their estate was next to Sandringham and the visit was planned so that Lillie could attend Bertie's birthday ball. Some of the guests wondered at him allowing the relationship to come more out into the open and were sorry for Alix, but Alix, herself, felt no resentment. She had come to like Lillie more and more and was only pleased that he had made what seemed to be a lasting attachment to someone of whom she could approve.

Only to be able to see Lillie, to dance with her and talk politely in public was no longer enough for Bertie. Her independence and slight reserve challenged him as much as her beauty and personality drew him. She was the only one who did not automatically give in to him. She could be yielding, yet there was a strength of spirit in her that matched his own. With the return of spring weather, he suggested that Allen Young might care to take Edward for a cruise of several weeks on his yacht. He, himself, took Lillie to Paris.

He had a permanent suite of rooms at the Hotel Bristol, where he stayed as the Duke of Lancaster. Discreet and cosmopolitan Paris respected his incognito, although everyone knew exactly who he was. Paris was his second home, where he had first enjoyed freedom from the stuffy protocol surrounding him in England. He was as much the leader of society there as in London, and even more popular, Lillie saw. She was amazed by the smiling welcome given to him, even by people in the streets.

As for herself, she was treated like royalty. It was a heady experience. Bertie had always had his pick of French actresses and dancers before, of the great cocottes with their gilded salons and of the sophisticated wives of Parisian society, whose rules of romantic behaviour he had introduced to England. He had never before brought anyone with him, his chosen favourite, and Paris found Lillie not only intriguing, but even more *spirituelle* and alluring than reports had indicated. Her conquest was much more rapid than it had been in London. Within days, women were tinting their hair to match hers, wearing the Langtry knot and copying her flowing walk. It was whispered that he had actually been seen to kiss her while they danced at Maxim's. Friends of Bertie hurried in from their country estates to entertain them and join in the adulation of The Jersey Lily.

Lillie had never felt closer to him, had never known him so relaxed and loving. The only irritation was the squad of plainclothes detectives that followed them everywhere to guard them, staying almost, but not quite, out of sight. Lillie made him laugh by handing one of them her shopping to take home one afternoon. They delighted in giving them the slip, dodging out of the back door of shops and restaurants, to stroll arm in arm on the boulevards or climb to Montmartre and sit in an openair cafe, sipping wine and watching the life of the streets. Bertie never carried money, so Lillie had to pass banknotes to him under the table, which occasionally caused raised eyebrows. He took her to Worth's and insisted on buying her a whole range of exquisite dresses, to Cartier's for jewels which she could only wear in private at home, but which dazzled their fellow diners at Voison's or the Café Anglais. He chose all her accessories, wanting to know that everything she wore, from top to toe, came from him. How could he ever be certain?, she asked. The evening before they left, she asked him which were his favourites among the hats and shoes he had bought for her and startled him ten minutes later. Completely nude apart from white satin shoes and a small pink hat with a tilted brim, trimmed with osprey plumes, smiling and utterly unselfconscious, she walked into the drawingroom of their suite just as he was pouring a glass of champagne. The champagne went all over the table. They were two hours late for the Opéra Comique, arriving just in time for the finale.

She had another, even greater, surprise for him when they reached home. The house was finished.

She called it The Red House, from the colour of its lower walls. It was in Tudor style, the upper storeys white crossed by external beams. The huge windows were filled with many small square panes. With its steeply pitched, many-gabled roof in dark olive tiles, it was romantic and idyllic. Lillie's initials, E.L.L., were on the foundation stone. On the south wall was the inscription *Dulce Domum*. Bertie's suite on the west was spacious, with a palatial bedroom. Lillie's was smaller but faced south and there was a balcony outside on which she could take breakfast or sunbathe in privacy in the summer. Downstairs were reception rooms and a high-ceilinged dining hall with a minstrels' gallery, at the side of which was a squint, a small hatch, from which Bertie could check their guests. Along the front of the gallery the motto which she had chosen for herself and the house was inscribed, 'They say – What say they? Let them say.'

Bertie was captivated by it. Everywhere there was some-thing to interest the eye, carved wooden fireplaces, decorated tiles, coats of arms set into the windowpanes, some real, some fanciful, all selected with wit and style. Above all, the house was light and warm and comfortable, just as Lillie had promised it would be. He was more and more besotted with her.

When he walked into his private sittingroom on the first morning, in his pyjamas and dressing gown, he saw the table already laid for two. By one place was a pot of coffee for him, by the other a pot of tea for Lillie. On the sideboard was a row of silver salvers with silver covers. He lit a cigarette and sat in the high-backed chair by the fire, smiling when he noticed her initials concealed among the carving of the fireplace.

He looked round as she came through her own door. Her hair was loose and she wore a white lace wrap, trimmed with ermine. She was wearing nothing underneath and her body gleamed through the lace. 'Good morning, again,' he said.

She smiled. 'Good morning, again.' She came to him and sat on his lap and he kissed her gently, his hand sliding in through the opening of the wrap to caress the undersides of her breasts. She murmured as he kissed her. She had never been exactly in love with him, but she found him attractive and exciting and, through him, her sensuality had first been liberated. She sat back and made a face.

'What?' he asked.

'You've been smoking, Bertie. You promised you wouldn't smoke before breakfast.'

'Cigars – I promised I wouldn't smoke cigars.' He held up his other hand and showed her. 'Cigarette.'

She laughed. 'What am I going to do with you?'

'Now?' he chuckled.

'Not now,' she told him. 'I've just had my bath.' She kissed his cheek and rose and he had to let her go. She saw the untouched table. 'Oh, I thought you'd have started.'

'There was no one to serve it,' he explained.

She smiled. 'What did you expect? We're at home. Here we serve ourselves.'

He was amused as she headed for the sideboard. As he rose, he saw he had dropped ash on the new carpet. He glanced guiltily at her back, rubbed the ash into the carpet with his slipper and tossed his cigarette into the fire, before following her.

She was lifting the covers off the salvers. 'Chops – sausages – kidneys and bacon – haddock – eggs – woodcock. What would you like?'

'Oh, a little of each,' he said. 'I feel quite peckish. Here, let me.' He bowed. 'Let me serve you, Madame.'

'No, no, I'll just have some scrambled eggs. You help yourself.' She took a spoonful and went back to the table. She poured his coffee, then sat at her own place, watching him. He was helping himself from the salvers with an endearing greediness, like a child at a birthday tea. When he turned, his plate was piled high. 'Are your sure you've taken enough?' she asked.

'I've left the haddock and woodcock, in case I'm still hungry,' he answered seriously, then laughed with her, realising she was teasing. 'Well, I have a good appetite.' He came and sat opposite her.

'You'll put on weight,' she warned.

'I'm sure I'll find some way to take it off,' he murmured, and they smiled to each other. She had buttered some toast and put it on his side plate. 'I'm glad we left Paris,' he said, suddenly.

'Oh, I loved it,' she protested.

'Yes,' he nodded. 'But I couldn't wait to be alone with you – to be in our home. Dulce Domum – isn't that what it says on the wall outside? The sweet house, the gentle home. How right it is.'

She looked pleased. 'You really like it?'

'I adore it, Lillie. Almost as much as I adore you.' He looked at her fondly. 'I wish I had something to give you. something to remember my first visit here.'

She shook her head. 'You've given me too much already.'

'Nonsense! Anyway, half the things I offer you, you won't accept. That pink dress now – Worth was most upset.'

'It was lovely, but how could I explain where they all came from?'

'You're not living up to your motto,' he pointed out. 'What was it? "Let them say."'

'That's other people,' she said seriously. 'They can *say* what they like, as long as they can't prove anything.'

He considered her. 'You're thinking of Ned. Has he been complaining?'

'No. But I don't know what he's thinking.'

'He really knows nothing about this house?'

'Nothing. Here he doesn't exist. When I'm away from him, even for a few days, it's like being reborn.'

'My poor dear . . .' Bertie said softly. 'I didn't realise you disliked him so much.'

'So much that I don't even want his name mentioned here.'

'That's one promise I'll keep,' he told her. 'I'd still like to see you in pink.'

As they laughed, there was a knock at the door. It was Dominique to tell them his secretary, Francis Knollys, had arrived. Officially, Bertie was on trials with his yacht. Knollys came ashore every morning on the pinnace, to report and receive instructions.

Lillie finished her tea and rose. 'I think I'd better go and change.'

'Yes, you'd better,' he agreed. 'If he sees you like that, he'll have a heart attack.'

The wrap had opened slightly all down the front. Lillie drew it together demurely. 'I seem to remember my night-dress getting rather torn,' she said.

He chuckled. 'I seem to remember.' He patted her hip as she passed him and watched her go up the stairs to the door to her own rooms. She smiled to him over her shoulder as she went out. Last night he had been like a boy of twenty in love, impetuous, almost unable to keep control. Even now he wanted to follow her and send Francis to the devil.

His secretary's news cut short their first stay at The Red House. Crown Prince Rudolf of Austria was coming on a visit to London and Queen Victoria had returned from Balmoral to Windsor. The Austrian Embassy had taken rooms for the Crown Prince and his chaperon at Claridge's

Hotel. The visit was only semi-official, so the Queen did not have to plan entertainments for him, but she expected Bertie to do so. He had to go back to London before the end of the week.

Bertie felt sorry for young Rudolf, who led a very restricted life at home, at the court of his autocratic father, Kaiser Franz Joseph. He wanted him to enjoy himself for once and recruited all society to help him. Most of the arrangements were made at a party at Marlborough House.

Almost as soon as Lillie arrived with Edward, Ferdinand de Rothschild drew her aside. Originally Austrian, himself, he had married an English cousin, following the Rothschild tradition. She had died tragically soon after the marriage, but Ferdy stayed on in England, liking the culture and the way of life. Lillie knew the younger Rothschilds, charming, urbane and fabulously wealthy, through Bertie, who liked and admired them and had stifled social prejudice against their Jewish origin by making them his friends. Alfred had given a dinner for her, at which all the guests were gentlemen and she the only lady, an 'adoration dinner', he had called it, and afterwards had presented her with a diamond brooch. He had left it lying on one of the side tables among his treasured collection of antique objets de'art and asked her to take her pick, expecting her to go at once for the diamonds. When she pretended, instead, to choose a priceless little Tanagra statuette, he was stricken, until he realised she was teasing. Now Ferdy asked her to come by herself, without fail, to lunch at his mansion in Piccadilly. Seeing her with the tall, cultivated Ferdy, Bertie nodded distantly in passing. Lillie acknowledged the nod just as impersonally. It amused them to seem distant at times in public, to keep the gossips guessing.

Seated in a corner alcove watching, his left hand resting on his cane, was a man in his seventies, wearing evening-dress with the sash and star of the Garter. He seemed even older with his lined, basilisk face, his hair thin and dyed black with one defiant curl still trained to fall over his forehead, a short tuft of beard. The Prime Minister, Benjamin Disraeli, Earl of Beaconsfield, was shortsighted and held a monocle to his eye with his right hand. Francis Knollys and Lord Suffield stood on either side of him. 'Is he cooling off?' he asked quietly.

'Far from it, Lord Beaconsfield,' Knollys assured him.

'What is it now – nearly two years? None of the others has lasted that long.'

'Mrs Langtry is the first one whose energy matches his,' Suffield said. 'The first person, male or female, who's been able to keep up with him.'

'Her mind must be as lively as her . . . physique,' Disraeli murmured. 'I think it is high time I met her.'

Lillie had seen Disraeli, remote and inscrutable, at various official functions and was excited as Suffield led her over. 'Lord Beaconsfield,' Suffield said, 'may I present Mrs Edward Langtry?' Edward had followed them. 'Oh – and Mr Langtry.' Lillie gave a slight curtsey and Edward bowed.

'Forgive my not rising,' Disraeli said. 'It is an old man's privilege.'

'Then I shall sit beside you,' Lillie told him. 'That will be mine.' His face was an expressionless mask, but she had detected the humour lurking in his eyes and had no fear of offending him as she sat on the small couch beside him.

He was delighted. 'My dear Suffield,' he suggested, 'do entertain Mr Langtry.'

Suffield smiled. 'With pleasure. Ned –' He took Edward's arm and led him away.

Disraeli turned to Lillie. 'One of the joys of my position is that I no longer have to be unnecessarily polite to husbands.' She laughed. 'Your portraits do not do you justice.'

'Have you seen some of them?' she asked.

'The two by Millais. When I sat for him, he could talk of nothing else. Which is probably why his portrait of me is not a success.'

'He has also painted Mr Gladstone,' Lillie said. Disraeli's eyebrows lifted faintly and she smiled at his look of complete indifference. 'The Prince says we are fortunate to have two such statesmen as yourself and Mr Gladstone living today.'

'I would agree wholeheartedly,' Disraeli confided. 'With half of that remark.'

All over the drawingroom, people were conscious of them smiling and talking. No one could remember the last time Dizzy had seemed so animated.

They were discussing the amazing number of artists who had tried to capture her on canvas. Disraeli could understand why. 'Considering the social life you must lead, I wonder you have time to sleep,' he said.

'I don't need very much sleep,' she explained.

'How fortunate . . .' he murmured, envying the Prince even more. Meeting her in Paris, it was said, the eighty year old Victor Hugo had sighed and confessed that she made him wish he were three years younger. A sentiment Disraeli echoed. 'From now on, whatever I hear about you I shall believe.'

'I believe everything I hear about you,' she said innocently.

'Such as?'

She smiled. 'I hear that when Mr Gladstone thinks of you in 10 Downing Street, he has Dizzy spells.' His mouth twitched and he nearly laughed. 'What can cure them?'

'Nothing,' he told her. 'And long my he suffer from them.' His drooping eyes missed little that went on and he had seen Ferdy move from lady to lady. Now he was surrounded by a whole group and Disraeli was intrigued. 'What plot do you think Baron de Rothschild is hatching with the ladies?'

Next day, Lillie arrived for lunch at 143 Piccadilly to discover all the other leading Beauties already there. 'It is a little *déjeuner galant*,' he explained. 'The opposite of Cousin Alfred's dinner, for here all the guests are ladies and myself the only male.' He had invited the twelve most beautiful women in society, including Patsy, Georgiana Dudley and Mrs Wheeler and led them into the famous, spotlessly white, Louis Sixteenth ballroom of his mansion to reveal the mystery.

He had undertaken to give a grand ball in honour of Crown Prince Rudolf and, to ensure its success, he wanted

Lillie and all the Beauties to be present. As an inducement, he offered each of them a new gown specially created by Doucet who would come over from Paris for the fittings. They could choose their own style and colour.

It was a great talking point and, when she attended Whistler's next Sunday Breakfast with Patsy, they were immediately surrounded.

Lillie wanted to talk to Jimmy about his exhibition with Edward Burne Jones at the Grosvenor Gallery. He had shown 'The Falling Rocket' and others of his delicate impressions of night on the river, his Nocturnes, and some of his stylised portraits, Arrangements in Line and Colour. While Burne Jones had been praised, Whistler's work had been savaged by the critics, particularly John Ruskin. Oscar had brought the bearded, ailing Ruskin to meet her at 17 Norfolk Street and she had been surprised by the vehemence with which he denounced the Nocturnes and Arrangements. When she tried to defend them, Oscar thought Ruskin would have a brainstorm, he became so agitated. She simply could not understand how the man who championed the impressionism of Turner could dismiss Whistler as a daub. But people only wanted to talk about Ferdy's offer.

'Twelve Doucet gowns . . .' Oscar marvelled. 'The price of *one* would keep my creditors happy for a year.' Everyone laughed. 'What colours did you choose?'

'Green, of course,' Patsy said.

When he looked at Lillie, she hesitated. '. . . I haven't decided.'

'Of course, not,' he smiled. 'Not without consulting Frank and myself.'

'I with my pencil and Oscar with his pen were her creators,' Miles announced loudly.

Lillie felt a flash of annoyance, which she hoped no one noticed. She eased away from the group. Near her on a stand was a sketch of her by Whistler, her body in profile softly outlined in umber. It was worth ten by Edward Poynter and twenty by Miles, she thought. She was worried about Jimmy. Bailiffs had moved into his house, to ensure the payment of his debts. He accepted the embarrassment with style, making them serve as waiters at his little parties. After the critics' attack no one would buy any of his paintings and she had begun to sit for him, hoping that a portrait of her at least would sell.

Moreton Frewen had come to the breakfast, expressly to see her. She always rode with the Prince now, instead of him. He had made her a present of Redskin and she had been grateful, yet showed no sign of surrendering, although he had been so sure of her. He had tried to get her to come away with him for a weekend, when Ned was out of town, but she avoided him. As she was doing now.

Lillie sat in the throne-like posing chair, isolated from everyone. In spite of her enormous and continuing success, she felt unsettled, a combination of so many things. She looked up to find Whistler beside her.

'A penny for them,' he offered. She shook her head. 'A trouble shared is a trouble doubled – or something.' She smiled. 'That's better. Now, are you going to tell me, or shall I save my penny by guessing what's on your mind?'

'What is it?'

'Which first?' he asked. 'Oscar and Frank irritate you by being possessive. Your husband bores you by always being bored. The handsome Mr Frewen no longer appeals, but will not accept that for him the sun has ceased to shine.'

So far, he had been completely accurate. Lillie's surprise was tinged with anger. 'You read me too easily, Jimmy,' she said evenly.

He smiled. 'I have not got beyond Chapter One – and you know it. There's something else.'

Lillie regretted her anger. She had become too used to being flattered and admired and to never being questioned. With it all, it was difficult not to be conceited, and to live always behind her facade. But not with Jimmy. She shrugged. 'I keep thinking – how little meaning my life has, how repetitive it's become.'

'Success can feel repetitive,' he nodded, 'and as monotonous as failure. What you mean is, you have no one to share it with. Or not the right one. You were thinking of that young man on Jersey. What was his name – Arthur?'

She had gone tense and glanced round quickly, but no one else had heard. She looked back at Whistler and whispered, 'How did you – ?'

'Seeing you together,' he told her simply. 'It was obvious.'

She could not deny what he had said. She still wrote to Arthur and thought of him more and more. Already her affaire with Bertie had lasted longer than she had imagined possible. She could see how astonished his friends were. She had reached a pinnacle from which she could only come down. Her life as it was could not last forever and, when it ended, she would be left with Ned and a pyramid of debts they could not pay. She would be a fool to depend on Bertie remaining faithful. It was not in his nature and she could not blame him. The only certainty in her life was Arthur and, when uncertainties came, she calmed herself by dreaming of the peaceful, contented life they could have on the island, when it was time to go to him. 'What can I do, Jimmy?' she asked.

'Forget him,' Whistler said. 'All that is behind you. He is the might have been. That's why you keep thinking of him. You are unique, Lillie. You have achieved a great deal and could climb even higher – but not unless you put him out of your mind.'


The ball at Ferdy de Rothschild's was the most spectacular for many seasons. Ferdy and his sister were hosts to a distinguished gathering, including the Prince and Princess of Wales and other royalty, members of the Government and of the foreign Embassies and the elite of aristocratic society.

The gowns of the Beauties were all in pastel shades to complement the white marble ballroom and everyone agreed they had never looked lovelier, especially Lillie. Her gown was in pale pink crêpe-de-Chine, clinging and heavily fringed. It seemed to shimmer with her movements as she danced. Bertie was proud, as he knew she had chosen the colour for him. It made him all the more reluctant to leave.

Alix had been so unhappy since their sons had set off on a long training cruise for the Navy that he had promised to take her for a few weeks to Denmark. He was even more reluctant when he learnt that his friends, thinking she was going by herself, had arranged for Edward Langtry to spend two weeks fishing in Yorkshire and that Lillie would be alone.

The guest of honour, Crown Prince Rudolf, was a tall, slim, fairhaired young man of nineteen, wearing a white hussar's uniform. With deepset eyes, a long upper lip and projecting ears, he was not goodlooking. Watched by his strict chaperon, Colonel Hertzl, he danced dutifully with his hostess, then Alexandra. And all the time he was thinking of Lillie. He had looked forward keenly to meeting her. Gossip and stories circulated about her even in Vienna. He had read that when Cleopatra's Needle had been shipped from Egypt and erected recently on the Thames Embankment, among the artefacts placed in a sealed container beneath its base, as a memorial to future generations, was a photograph of Mrs Langtry, the most beautiful woman of her day. Now he believed it. He refused to accept any others of the partners selected for him. Instead, he danced with Lillie.

At first, she was flattered. Like Bertie, she was sorry for him. He was very inexperienced, a mixture of boyish impulsiveness, charm and arrogance, inclined to be abrupt because he was unsure of himself. But as he claimed dance after dance, ignoring the other Beauties, she was aware of them becoming offended and of everyone whispering. She tried to leave him between dances, but he always came to find her. Alix was amused, sitting next to Bertie and seeing the fingers of his right hand drum on his thigh, a sure sign of his irritation.

Patsy was sympathetic and managed to whisper to Lillie that Rudolf was spoiling her dress. All the other gentlemen wore gloves. Rudolf kept his tucked into his belt and his hand had left dark smudges on her waist. When he led her out possessively for the next waltz, she paused and said, 'Forgive me, sir. May I ask you to put your gloves on?

There are marks on my dress.'

He was embarrassed. 'That is not my concern, Madame,' he answered stiffly. 'It is you who are sweating.' He seized her and swirled her off with zest.

It was a relief when the principal guests went out in procession to supper, led by Crown Prince Rudolf and Alice de Rothschild. Lillie had been made to feel extremely uncomfortable and Edward accused her unjustly of deliberately drawing attention to herself. The Cornwallis Wests, Sir Allen Young and others sympathised with her, but she could see the disapproval and speculation of most of the other guests, who were all whispering about her. The comment increased when Ferdinand de Rothschild hurried back alone, clearly in some distress as he explained that the Crown Prince had turned his back on his sister and insisted on having Lillie as his partner. To avoid an unfortunate scene, the Prince and Princess of Wales agreed to an extra place being set and asked her to join them. When she went out on Ferdy's arm, she could hear the murmurs and suppressed laughter and knew that she was once again deeply involved in a scandal, for once not of her own making.

She hoped that night would be the end of it, but soon the town was convulsed by the news that Rudolf was paying visits to Norfolk Street. With Bertie out of the country and Edward away in Yorkshire, he could not resist calling on Lillie, even though he had to bring his chaperon. In the evenings, he knew he was bound to find her at home as, without her husband, she could not accept invitations.

Lillie was grateful for Colonel Hertzl's constant presence. She did not dislike Rudolf and even thought his attempts to behave like a man of the world endearing. He brought her trinkets and little gifts, which she could not refuse, calling every day, even if only for five minutes. Hertzl was always a stolid witness of their meetings and Lillie often wondered if he laughed, as she did afterwards, at the Crown Prince's selfconsciously debonair manner. It was all totally harmless, but when Patsy and Lady Lonsdale warned her that tongues were wagging, she sent a telegram to Edward, bringing him back to London.

One evening as she came downstairs, the front door bell jangled. It was Dominique's evening off and she waited for Edward to answer it. When the ring was repeated, she looked in the diningroom and saw Edward sprawled over the table in a drunken sleep. The doorbell jangled insistently and she hurried to open the door.

Crown Prince Rudolf came in quickly past her and she waited, but there was no sign of his chaperon. She closed the door and saw that Rudolf was hatless, his sandy hair dishevelled. His short, checked coat was muddied down one sleeve and he was in a state of excitement. She remembered and curtsied quickly as he stood, grinning to her. 'Where is Colonel Hertzl?' she asked.

Laughing, he told her that their fourwheeler had overturned in Oxford Street, throwing them. He was perfectly all right, but Hertzl was knocked unconscious. 'We were so near you, I could not resist the opportunity,' he laughed. 'Heaven sent!' He opened the door of the drawingroom and bowed as she went past him into the room.

It was decidedly awkward. Without Hertzl, with Edward incapable and Dominique out, she was virtually alone with him. Clearly, he saw it as a great adventure. She had to admit she had partly encouraged him at first, thinking it a harmless flirtation and pleased by the attentions of the heir to the Austrian Empire. But she did not intend to lose Bertie because of it, nor what was left of her reputation.

'You see?' he chuckled. 'I know how to open a door.' She did not understand. 'My father has a mistress, Katherine Schratt. He went to visit her one morning and stood for nearly two hours outside her garden, because there was no one to open the gate.'

She smiled slightly, when he laughed. 'Would you care to sit, sir?'

'Ah, no. Rudolf – when we are alone,' he told her. 'After all, I'm sure you don't call Cousin Bertie "Sir", when you are alone.' Quite unaware that he had insulted her, he stripped off his coat and dropped it on a chair. Without his chaperon, he seemed older and more self-assured. He sat on

343

the sofa, spreading out his arms along the back, and looked round the room appreciatively. 'It is so pleasant here – *gemütlich*. Adorable. Like you.' When she did not speak, he looked at her. 'Why did you open the door yourself?'

'It is my maid's evening off,' Lillie said, and immediately regretted it, seeing his smile.

'And where is your husband?'

'Just across the hall,' she said levelly.

She was wearing a tan housedress of soft muslin with silk panels. Her arms were covered, but the neck of the dress widened towards her bosom, a lacy frill just concealing its upper slopes. The material was so fine he could make out distinctly the shape of her unconfined breasts. His palms felt sweaty and he rubbed them on the back of the sofa. 'Why don't you sit down?'

She did not move. 'I was not expecting you, sir.'

'Rudolf.'

'. . . Rudolf. I am dining this evening with Colonel and Mrs Cornwallis West. I must go up shortly, to change – with your permission.'

'I do not give my permission,' he said haughtily, then he smiled to take away the sting. He was enjoying the situation enormously. As a Royal and Imperial Prince, his authority over every member of society from royalty down was absolute.

In spite of herself, Lillie smiled back, amused by him. She had no doubt that she could handle him, although his overwhelming social position despite his youth made it more difficult. 'Is there no way I could convince you that – ?' she began.

'You could come and sit beside me,' he broke in. He was quite definitely different on his own, more direct. For a moment, Lillie was intrigued. She suspected this was his first romantic adventure and, while she had no intention of giving herself to him to assist his education, she did not want to squash or humble him. She moved to the sofa, sat and turned to face him. He grinned. 'I thought you were going to be angry.' The warmth of her body seemed to reach out towards him. He was almost lightheaded.

'I'm not angry, sir – Rudolf,' she said, coolly.

'You must prove it,' he told her.

'How?'

'By letting me kiss you.'

Her face gave away nothing. 'Then may I go and change?' she asked. She could not prevent the hint of a smile.

He could not credit his luck that she was not angry. He smiled and shook his head, reaching into the pocket of his grey suit. 'Look what I have bought you.' He took out a small, leather ring box and handed it to her. She opened it, expecting another little pearl stickpin or silver trinket such as he had given her. She nearly gasped. Inside was a large and extremely valuable emerald ring. 'It's matchless,' he told her. It had cost him as much as the entire trip.

She gazed at it, seeing the green fire that flickered in its exquisitely cut facets when she moved it in the light. She was tempted, owning nothing so gorgeous, but it would be foolish. 'I couldn't possibly accept it,' she told him gently and handed it back.

He would not take it and looked hurt. 'Why not? I've given you things before.'

'Nothing like this.' She laid the box between them on the sofa.

'Cousin Bertie must give you beautiful things,' he muttered, disappointedly.

She had begun to warm to him, seeing that he really cared for her. But his words killed the sympathy which she had begun to feel. 'That is another matter.'

'Why?' Rudolf protested. 'He is your lover.' He was quite ingenuous, really not seeing the difference. She stared at him. 'It is no secret. I know about these matters. I told you, my father has a mistress. Like you, she is not presented at court.'

His gaucheness was almost incredible. 'I think you are mistaken in me, sir,' she said coldly.

She made to rise, but he caught one of her hands, stopping her. 'Don't pretend to be offended!'

She saw she would have to be more blunt. 'Have you thought what the Prince will say, when he returns?'

It was not going exactly how Rudolf had forseen it. He had heard of the *cocottes*, *les grandes horizontales*, that none of them could resist a priceless jewel. She was surely not going to claim fidelity to Bertie? These things were governed by a code. 'How could he object?' he shrugged. 'When he goes to Paris, other gentlemen lend him their mistresses. It is understood.' He released her hand and took the ring from the box, offering it to her.

'I am not for sale,' she said, deathly quiet.

'Of course, not. This is merely a token.' He smiled. 'You are not a professional.'

He could not resist any longer. The soft shapes of her body, so teasingly revealed by the thin dress, mesmerised him. He had dreamed of holding her, touching her, of actually possessing the Jersey Lily, since the moment she entered Rothschild's ballroom. The memory of her perfume and the supple sway of her waist under his palm had prevented him from sleeping. His hand was unsteady as he reached out to draw her to him. She rose abruptly moving away, and he swivelled, grabbing at her to stop her. His hand caught her dress and ripped the silken panel at her hip roughly. She cried out and stood for a second, looking down at it.

The reality was not turning out to be anything like his fantasy. He was distressed and slumped forward on to his knees in front of her. He was still holding her dress and, when she tried to pull away from him, it ripped even further. He clasped her round the legs. 'I'm sorry!' he sobbed. He held her more tightly, pressing his cheek against her thighs, feeling their yielding strength under her dress. 'I'm sorry. I didn't mean to! Forgive me . . .' She twisted to escape, but he still clutched her, his hands climbing her back as he rose from his knees, pressing her to him. 'Don't push me away! Don't turn away! I love you. I have dreamt of nothing but you. Please, Lillie . . .' He tried to kiss her, but she jerked her head round, struggling. He let her go and captured her left hand, forcing the ring into her palm. 'Here – take this! I'll give you more. One day you will have all Austria!'

She threw the ring away blindly and it landed in the fire. He gave a strangled cry, then ran forward, horrified, falling to one knee. He snatched up the poker and began to rake out the burning coals to get at the ring. He found it, but when he picked it up, it was already too hot and he dropped it with a yelp. As she watched him, Lillie's anxiety turned to contempt.

At that moment, the door opened and Edward came in. Lillie pulled her torn dress together with one hand and Rudolf stood up quickly, flustered and scared. 'What's – what's going on?' Edward demanded.

'The Crown Prince is just leaving,' Lillie said, very clearly.

Edward stood swaying, trying to focus. The words 'Crown Prince' reached him. Mustn't intrude on royalty. 'Oh, I – I 'pologise,' he mumbled, bowing.

Rudolf hesitated, gazing at Lillie who did not look at him. He crossed abruptly to the chair where he had left his coat, picked it up and went out. Edward followed him, still apologising.

Lillie was shaking after what had happened. She felt cheapened and degraded. How many other people thought of her in the same light as Rudolf? After a moment, she looked down at the hearth. Slowly, she knelt and picked up the ring. It was still warm and she blew the ash from it. She slipped it on to the third finger of her right hand and held it up to see its own fire flicker in it again. She knew she should return it to Crown Prince Rudolf with a curt note, but as she turned and the fire danced from facet to facet of the huge emerald, she knew she would not.

Bertie was the most affable of men, except for his rare rages which terrified everyone around him. He came back from Denmark as soon as he heard, scarcely able to contain his fury until he was inside Marlborough House. He threw his hat aside as he strode into the study. 'Puppy!' he roared. 'How dare he?!'

Francis Knollys had remained by the door. 'I'm sure there was some misunderstanding, sir.'

Bertie turned on him. 'No excuses for him, Francis! Get

in touch with the Austrian Embassy. He is to be recalled at once!'

'The Emperor Franz Joseph – ' Knollys began.

'Can be told what they like. But I want Rudolf out of this country!' Knollys bowed as Bertie glared at him. 'Not fit to be presented, is she?' Bertie muttered. 'We'll see about that . . . Puppy!'

That very evening at the fashionable hour, society became aware that Bertie had returned when they saw him ride into the Park, very erect and imperious. Lillie rode beside him proudly, just as regal. At first, he merely surveyed the crowd coldly, defying their disapproval, but as the gentlemen hastened to raise their hats, the ladies curtsied and those further back were helped up on to their chairs to see, he gradually relaxed. If any attempt had been made to snub Lillie, he would have turned his horse and ridden out of the Park for ever.

Going to Goodwood Races that year, Lillie had devised a toque out of a square of blue velvet to match her dress, pleating it and gathering it together in front where she fastened it with a dyed goose quill. Bertie had admired it and, noticing that many of the ladies now wore 'the Langtry Toque', she flicked her eyes towards them until he noticed them, too, and smiled to her as they rode on. His smile was proudly possessive. She had been placed in a difficult position, but had decided to use it, instead of trying to hide it. Everything had worked out exactly as she had planned.

Further along the path, Moreton Frewen had dismounted and stood with the dapper Lord Rosslyn and Sir Allen Young. He raised his hat with them as Bertie and Lillie passed. She did not smile, only giving a small, very regal inclination of the head.

'Now she can climb no higher,' Rosslyn commented drily.

'What do you mean?' Frewen asked.

'He's taken her under his protection,' Young told him.

Frewen did not believe it and looked from him to Rosslyn, who confirmed it. 'His first official mistress. Word's gone out.'

'He's acknowledged her?' Frewen gasped.

'Even havin' her presented to the Queen,' Rosslyn drawled.

'That's what she's been after!' Frewen said angrily. 'She's just used the rest of us. I – I gave her Redskin. That horse she's riding.'

'So you keep telling us,' Young smiled.

Frewen watched Lillie riding away. 'Well, she can keep him,' he said, with bad grace. 'And good luck to her. After all . . . lilies can be dreadfully boring, when they're not planted in a bed.'

Rosslyn and Young laughed quietly, amused by his sour grapes.

Arrangements were already in hand to have Lillie presented to the Queen at one of her Afternoon Courts at Buckingham Palace. Plump, friendly Lady Romney, with whom she had stayed in Norfolk, was to be her Presenter and both the Dean and Mrs Le Breton came from Jersey to lend their support. Mrs Le Breton's widowed sister was also brought in to help.

For once, Dominique was speechless. She was clumsy with excitement and Lillie's aunt had to fasten her into her gown. It was of ivory brocade, garlanded with pale yellow Maréchal Niel roses, as was the long court-train which hung from her shoulders, lined with the same pale yellow as the flowers. The neck of the gown was low, the arms bare.

Lillie was apparently the calmest of them all, although they kept warning her not to be nervous and arguing whether she should or should not eat something, in case she felt faint. They went over and over the ritual of the presentation with her, rehearsing her in catching her heavy train over one arm as it would be thrown to her by the pages in attendance, and in her specially deep, royal curtsey. They worried about the ostrich plumes she was to wear in her hair. They were obligatory and, as Bertie had warned her his mother was growing shortsighted and objected to ladies wearing tiny feathers she could hardly see, she had ordered the three longest available. She kept asking her mother if anyone in Jersey had sent messages and only stopped when Mrs Le Breton remembered that Arthur had said he would be thinking of her.

Most of all, they worried that she would be late, but Lillie would not hurry.

There was great speculation at what would actually happen when Lillie came face to face with the Queen. Supposing Her Majesty actually refused to receive her? Lillie did not believe it possible, yet Bertie's mother was so moral and such a law to herself that no one could be certain. Sensible Lady Romney suggested the solution. To avoid the long wait in the Mall, gaped at by the crowds in their open carriage, it would be best if they arrived as late as possible. The Queen became fatigued with standing and never stayed to the end of a Presentation, her place being taken by Alexandra, Princess of Wales. So Lillie would be received by Alix. She would have been presented officially at Court and have avoided any possible unpleasantness.

Lady Romney waited downstairs with Dean Le Breton and calmed him, as he kept checking his watch. He remembered his own presentation to the same Queen over thirty years before and the awesome moment during her visit to Jersey with the Prince Consort, when he had handed her a pen to sign a document at Victoria College. The pen did not write properly and she had simply dropped it on the ground and waited icily for another. He remembered the chill of her pale blue eyes. He went out into the hall, when Dominique answered the door and collected an enormous bouquet of real Maréchal Niel roses, which matched exactly the ones on Lillie's dress. He knew who had sent them before he even looked at the card.

He heard Lillie coming down at last in her ivory gown, her mother and aunt holding her train up carefully behind her. The three tall white plumes rising from the white veil attached to the back of her head were strikingly and unmistakably in the form of the Prince of Wales' emblem. Whether it was courage or bravado, he was proud of her daring. She seemed very composed. He advanced to meet her and took her hand as she reached the foot of the stairs. 'You look . . . very lovely, my dear,' he told her quietly, and handed her the bouquet. 'These have just arrived, from the Prince of Wales.' He glanced at his wife who was fussing with the train and either did not know or would not admit the realisation that their daughter was the Prince's mistress.

Mrs Le Breton had her suspicions but would not let them be confirmed. She was so proud of Lillie, she would not criticise her in anything. She had folded the train and laid it over Lillie's left arm. 'The pages will spread your train,' she fussed still. 'You mustn't look round. After the presentation, they'll throw it to you. You must catch it!'

'Yes, mother,' Lillie smiled. Lady Romney and Dominique were by the door. All at once, she could not hide her nervousness any longer and trembled. Her father touched her arm and she steadied. He kissed her cheek and she smiled to him, then to her mother and aunt and went out with Lady Romney to their carriage.

They had nearly left it too late altogether. When they reached the Palace, the Afternoon Court was nearly over. They were rushed to the anteroom where a few tense, white gowned debutantes, their heads crowned with three small white feathers still waited and advanced one by one with their older Presenters. The ushers in court uniform reacted in consternation when they saw Lillie's Prince of Wales' plumes. Among those in attendance was Suffield. He was the only one who smiled.

No one's shock was greater than Lillie's when she reached the door of the throne room and realised that the Queen was still in her place, with the Prince and Princess and other members of the royal family stretching beyond her. She felt the pages spreading her train and Lady Romney was urging her forward. As she advanced, perfectly poised, she heard the Lord Chamberlain say distinctly, 'Mrs Langtry comes next, Your Majesty.'

Queen Victoria was very short, not even five feet tall. At sixty her hair was grey and her figure stout, her face grown lined and pouchy. She wore a low necked, shortsleeved, black dress with a black velvet train. Across her bodice was the blue ribbon of the Garter, jewels and diamond orders on her corsage. Round her neck were strings of pearls and her headdress was of black feathers above a small diamond crown and a veil of white tulle. Bertie stood beyond her in a scarlet Field Marshal's uniform. He had not expected his mother to stay so long and looked at her anxiously. She was tired and serious, unsmiling. In spite of her short stature, the sense of majesty which radiated from her was immense.

Lillie had never needed her poise so much as now. And had never felt so nervous. As she neared her, Victoria straightened and looked directly ahead, regal and forbidding. Very stately, carrying the bouquet of roses, Lillie stopped in front of the Queen, turned and curtsied deeply.

Bertie was taut, watching from the corner of his eyes as his mother seemed to pause for an eternity before extending her hand abruptly for Lillie to kiss, with not the slightest trace of a welcome. Then Lillie was rising slowly and moved to curtsey to him. He had started to relax and, as she took his hand, he looked down with meaning at the bouquet which he had sent her for luck and smiled. Lillie was grateful. It was only the bouquet which prevented her hands from trembling and betraying her.

As she moved on to curtsey to Alexandra, Queen Victoria was still gazing grimly ahead. But her eyes turned to her left with the slightest turn of the head and she could see how Alix, then Louise, Leopold and Beatrice all smiled and greeted Mrs Langtry like an old friend. Very pretty, although a trifle pale, far too pretty for her own good, she thought. And those feathers . . . Probably no better than she should be, although Alix speaks highly of her, which at least shows that Bertie, in this instance, has shown some discrimination. She watched Lillie step back at the end of the line. The waiting page gathered up her train and threw it round. She caught it over her left arm and backed with dignity out of the far door. Very neatly done. Victoria glanced at Bertie who was beaming most unbecomingly. He should take a lesson from Mrs Langtry in how to control his expressions. She gazed ahead again. Her legs were aching. Thank heavens, there were only two more and she could go home.

That night, at a ball in her honour at Marlborough

House, Lillie was ravishing in a gown of yellow silk, draped with a wide-meshed, gold net, in which hundreds of preserved butterflies of every size and colour seemed to be trapped. Her gaiety at surviving the ordeal was captivating and Bertie laughed, telling her his mother had only waited till the end of the presentations in order to see her, and had been well satisfied. As she danced, the smallest of the butterflies slipped through the meshes of the net and fell to the floor and the other guests picked them up, laughing, to keep as favours.

Bertie found more on the ballroom floor in the early hours of the morning and brought them to her room at Norfolk Street, impulsively, before anyone else was awake. Except Lillie. She had known he would come and was waiting for him.

# CHAPTER THIRTEEN

Oscar's fast rising reputation as a poet and his mission as self-styled Apostle of the New Aestheticism had turned him into a well-known figure. That's one Apostleship too many, Whistler thought sourly. The two were still friendly, although Jimmy was gradually growing to resent the way Oscar absorbed his ideas and theories and presented them as his own, without acknowledgement now. Times were hard for Whistler, with bailiffs representing his creditors living permanently in the White House. He had only been saved from bankruptcy by the astuteness of his agent, who found a collection of his early etchings fogotten in a drawer and brought out a set of prints at bargain prices. In public, he was as jaunty and bitingly witty as ever.

One of the more practical lessons Oscar had learnt from him was that the cheapest white wine could be disguised more easily than red. Chilled and decanted, Whistler served it to his richest guests and was inscrutably amused as they tried to guess the vintage. Oscar went a step further, inventing vintages and vineyards to ennoble the even cheaper wine he served.

The centre piece of Oscar's room was the Poynter portrait of Lillie holding the two roses. Patsy admired it at one of his early evening drinks parties. 'If Poynter had done a portrait of me, I don't think I could bear to part with it,' she declared.

'She thinks, quite rightly, that it doesn't catch her colouring,' Whistler told her.

Lady Wharncliffe had been listening and protested. 'How can you say that, Mr Whistler? Edward Poynter has just been made a member of the Royal Academy.'

Whistler gave a short bark of derision. Since his portrait of his mother had only been admitted grudgingly, he had sent no more paintings to the Academy.

'I was at the Academy, last varnishing day,' Oscar remarked, apparently inconsequentially. 'I have never seen so many Academicians – all disguised as artists.'

As the laughter died, Whistler sparked it off again by agreeing. 'Varnishing is the only artistic process with which Royal Academicians are thoroughly familiar.'

Patsy smiled to him, while Miss Sally refilled their glasses. Frank and Oscar really ought to dress that child in something more appropriate, she thought. Sally was wearing a short, filmy dress of flowered material, showing most of her legs and held up by two narrow straps that left her arms and shoulders bare. In the past eighteen months, she had become an extremely pretty girl, with high, budding breasts and sweetly feminine hips and legs. Her relationship with her two protectors was more enigmatic than ever. She had even become something of a celebrity, since Leighton had used her as his model for his popular painting, *Daydreams*.

Oscar and Whistler were discussing Frederick Leighton, who had recently been knighted, unable to decide whether it was because of his success as President of the Royal Academy or due to the Prince's gratitude for his portrait and bust of Lillie. As usual their bantering conversation delighted and engrossed the party. 'When you two are together,' Lord Rosslyn asked, 'do you always talk about nothin' but art?'

'Of course, not,' Oscar denied. 'When Jimmy and I are together, we never talk about anything except ourselves.'

Judging his moment in the laughter, Whistler capped it. 'No, no, Oscar, you forget – when you and I are together, we never talk about anything except *me*.'

The laughter was louder, and became a shout, when Oscar nodded. 'That's true, Jimmy. We do talk about you – but I think about myself.' He looked round for Frank's appreciation.

Miles was seated in an armchair, apart from everyone, sunk in his own thoughts. Sally had finished serving and gone to sit crosslegged on the floor beside him. He had slipped one of the straps from her shoulder and ran his hand slowly up and down from the nape of her neck along her shoulder to her upper arm and back, intent, rather morose. Sally was looking at a picture book open on her knees and paid him no attention. Whistler had also noticed and looked a question to Oscar. Oscar shrugged.

'Where *is* Lillie, by the bye?' Rosslyn asked.

'She's been to Biarritz with the Prince,' Patsy told him. 'Should be back any day.'

'How does she explain it to her husband?' Lady Wharncliffe wondered.

'I think she's stopped bothering to explain. He's in Scotland for a month – salmon fishing.'

Whistler had missed her. 'When she's back, I must try to finish my portrait of her.' He had sketched her several times, but the portrait kept being delayed.

Oscar smiled. 'Poor Burne Jones is going frantic because she will not sit for him.'

'Burne Jones . . .' Whistler muttered. It was an unfortunate subject for Oscar to bring up.

'You've – uh – you've read John Ruskin's review of your joint exhibition?'

Whistler pursed his lips. Ruskin's review had been savage. Although Whistler affected to ignore criticism to follow his own artistic vision, it had wounded him sorely. Worse than that, it had frightened off the timid art buying public and badly affected the sale of his work. He had been reduced to the humiliation of pawning his paintings to survive.

Ruskin had condemned all his work, even his incomparable portrait of Thomas Carlyle. Most of all, he had taken exception to the *Nocturnes* and *The Falling Rocket*. 'What was it he said?' Oscar murmured. '"I have seen, and heard, much of Cockney impudence before now; but never expected to hear a coxcomb ask two hundred guineas for flinging a pot of paint in the public's face."'

'Sounds uncommonly like libel,' Rosslyn observed.

'Well – that I shall try to find out,' Whistler said blandly.

'How?' Oscar smiled.

'I intend to sue him.' The quiet remark had the effect of a

bombshell, exactly as Whistler intended.

The whole town knew about the forthcoming libel suit by the time Lillie returned. Nothing like it had ever taken place before.

Her holiday with Bertie had only been possible because he was in mourning. The young Prince Imperial of France, Louis Napoleon, had insisted on repaying his debt to the country which had given him refuge by service in the British Army. Strings had been pulled to allow him to join the campaign in the Transvaal, where the Zulus under their great King, Cetewayo, had risen against the Boer settlers. During a reconnaissance, Louis Napoleon and his escort were ambushed. His aide-de-camp and escort abandoned him and fled and he was put to death, although the Zulus, impressed by his boyish bravery, killed him mercifully quickly and afterwards sewed up the cuts their spears had made in his patrol jacket.

In his sadness, Bertie had been grateful for her understanding. They had both lost a dear companion and the French resort with its fashionable life and gaiety had jarred on them. They slipped back in secret to Bournemouth and the Red House, where the pleasure of just being with Lillie without ceremony or company restored Bertie's spirits. Their only visitors were his favourite young relative, Prince Louis of Battenberg, now serving as a lieutenant on the royal yacht, *Osborne*, and his commanding officer, Lord Charles Beresford.

Louis was oddly like the Prince Imperial in some ways, though more handsome. Tall and slim, with fair hair and blue eyes, he was the nephew of Bertie's dearest sister, Alice, who had married a Prince of Hesse in Germany and died there the previous year, nursing her children through an epidemic of diptheria. One of the four sons of Prince Alexander of Hesse from his morganatic marriage to Julia, Countess of Hauke, his one ambition since childhood had been to serve in the British Navy. At the age of fourteen, he had been naturalised and enrolled as a naval cadet. Conscientious, popular and extremely capable, success in his career was assured. He had accompanied the Prince of

Wales on his tour of India and Bertie and Alix were very fond of him, leaving a set of rooms permanently at his disposal at Marlborough House. In turn, he idolised his 'Uncle Bertie' and modelled himself on him, even wearing the same close-cropped beard which added to his dashing appearance in his naval lieutenants's uniform.

Beresford, commander of the *Osborne*, was another handsome charmer, Irish and daring. Like Louis, he was a determined career officer and, quite unashamedly, used his friendship with the Prince of Wales to advance himself. He was famous for his amours and his sense of humour, but Lillie thought his quips and pranks were often cruel, at the expense of others. She much preferred Louis, who was something of a romantic figure. After Disraeli's triumph at the Congress of Berlin, settling the terms of peace between Turkey and Russia, the vacant throne of Bulgaria had been offered to Prince Louis. Preferring to remain an officer in the British Navy, he had relinquished the throne to his younger brother, Alexander.

Bertie went back to Paris for a week and Lillie returned to London, two days before Edward arrived home from Scotland.

He was more maddening than ever. She had gone so far beyond him that even he had had to accept it, yet never willingly. He was either hangdog and sullen or sneered and complained, but, except when he was drunk, would not risk a quarrel. His comfortable life depended on Lillie and he would not risk offending her. Little articles criticising Lillie's friendship with the Prince and others and sniggering at Edward had begun to appear from time to time in a cheap scandalsheet, *Town Talk*. He refused even to discuss them with anyone, preferring to ignore them. To Lillie, it was one of the few sensible things he had ever done.

Shortly after his return, she was in the drawingroom at Norfolk Street, preparing to go out. He hurried in, fairly buoyant for once, and his face fell, seeing her put on her hat. 'I have a sitting for Jimmy Whistler,' she told him.

'But I haven't seen you for weeks!' he protested. 'And there's someone else you'll – '

She had scarcely paid him any attention and went out past him. A young man was standing in the hall and Lillie stopped short as he turned. It was Arthur.

'I tried to tell you,' Edward complained. 'It was to be a surprise.'

'I was up in town,' Arthur said. 'I thought I might find Ned at his Club. He insisted I came back.'

'Of course,' Lillie said. She was still not over the shock.

'It's good to see you,' he smiled.

'She's just going out,' Edward told him.

She was conscious of Arthur's disappointment and of Edward watching her. 'Yes, I'm afraid so, Artie. What a pity,' she said coolly. 'I have to go to James Whistler's for an hour or two.'

Whistler was amused when she told him. At least, he thought he was amused. His feelings for Lillie were ambivalent.

He stood painting at his easel, not wearing a smock but, as always, him most dandified clothes, his monocle fixed firmly in his eye. His table pallete which he sometimes took days to prepare before a major work was meticulously arranged and he handled his brush with a master's delicacy. On the canvas, the outline of a nearly naked figure, filmed by drapery, was beginning to emerge.

Lillie was standing in the light by the thronelike chair, one hand on its back, one leg thrust forward. All she wore was a partly transparent, yellow robe through which the shape of her body was provocatively suggested, in the flowing line of her outthrust leg, the shadow of her belly and curve of her hip, the domes of her breasts, their tips a darker smudge through the clinging material.

It was impossible to be with her, especially like this, and not desire her, Whistler thought. Occasionally, he had caressed her on impulse, a fleeting caress, which she had not rejected but accepted, smiling, as a tribute. It might have gone further, but Whistler for all his cynicism was constant and, for some years, had had a mistress, Maud Franklin, who frequently modelled for him. Only his mother's return from America had prevented Maud from coming to live with him, and even though Mrs Whistler had gone to live in Hastings for health reasons, he still kept Maud quietly in the background. But Lillie strained his fidelity. 'So you think he'll come here?' he commented.

Lillie smiled. 'I hope so.'

'If he understood,' Whistler pointed out. 'I should be steaming with jealousy! It's not that I mind my studio being used for secret rendezvous – just that it will take me even longer to finish this portrait.'

She laughed. 'It it really so important?'

'Oh, very really,' Whistler confirmed. He had to sell something soon, and a portrait of Lillie was a gift from the Gods. He was grateful to her.

'And you're really going to sue Ruskin?'

'I've no option,' he said. 'It is the most debased criticism I've ever had thrown at me. If I don't challenge him, it will make everything I have ever done worthless.'

'Yes,' she agreed. 'But he is bound to plead justification. And most of the other establishment critics will back him.'

'Let them. I sign my paintings with a butterfly. They will find it has a sting,' he said, with a gesture of his brush. 'And a portrait of you, like this. Sensational . . . sensational. You're sure you don't mind?'

'Why should I?' Lillie smiled. 'In any case, I have a fair idea who will buy it.'

'You are amazing,' he chuckled and began to paint again, murmuring, 'Amazing. Amazing . . .'

There was a knock at the door and one of the bailiffs showed in Arthur, who was hesitant as he came in.

'Well, bless my soul!' Whistler exclaimed. 'Look who's here.'

'I was in town,' Arthur said. 'I thought I'd pay my respects.' He was momentarily unsure, unable to look fully at Lillie.

'I am delighted, Mr Jones,' Whistler assured him. He dropped his brush into the pot on his palette table. 'I was just saying, I'd have to pop out for half an hour. And I wondered who I'd get to keep Mrs Langtry company.'

Arthur bowed. 'Good day, Mrs Langtry.' Lillie

smiled to him.

Whistler glanced from one to the other. 'If you'll forgive me,' he murmured. They were looking at each other and neither heard. Whistler moved quietly to the door and went out.

For a time, neither Lillie nor Arthur moved nor spoke, then he stepped towards her, and stopped. 'Was it all right to come here?' he asked.

'I meant you to,' she told him quietly.

He relaxed slightly. 'I couldn't stay away any longer.' Her letters in these last months had been so intimate and so longing that he had had to come to her.

'It was clever of you to look up Ned first,' she said.

He smiled. 'It seemed wiser. I don't want to make him suspicious of you.'

She was gazing at him. Obviously, he knew nothing about Bertie. Only yesterday she had had a letter from him, telling her he had planted some mignonette she had sent, her favourite flower, in the garden facing the west, as she had asked. She had grown so used to thinking and dreaming of him in Jersey, she could not get used to the thought of him being here.

His smile faded and he took another step towards her. 'Lillie?' he asked, made unsure again by her silence.

She came to him quickly and he took her in his arms.

With Bertie still in Paris and Edward used to her absences, it was easy to cancel all invitations and spend most of the next few days with Arthur. To be alone, they went out into the country on picnics, and Lillie wore a veil until she was unlikely to be recognised. In town, they lunched together and he accompanied her shopping, dutifully, like a brother. His father, Lord Ranelagh, had a small apartment in Berkeley Street, which Arthur used when he was in London. Although it was risky, sometimes she saw him there. One afternoon, as they passed through Burlington Arcade, he insisted on buying her something and disappeared into a glass and china shop. She had to wait till they reached home before she could open it and tore the paper from it in the hall. It was a little Staffordshire figure of two lovers kissing by a stile, simple and charming. 'Oh, you shouldn't have – but it's lovely,' she said.

'I wanted to buy you something,' he smiled.

She led him into the drawingroom so that she could kiss him, and they stopped in confusion. Oscar was seated in one of the chairs by the fire, smoking a cigarette, his hat and cane over his knees. He was disappointed she was not alone, but concealed it. He resented Arthur, for whom she palpably felt a more than sisterly affection, and attempted to conceal that, too. He had never stopped desiring Lillie. He had lost his opportunity, through fear of committing himself and, even more, through fear of his own individuality being endangered by hers. it was not merely her beauty which had drawn him to her, but her strength of will. Beauty, male or female, attracted him and, when it was yielding and complaisant, seduced him, by giving him the illusion of dominance. Lillie became unnattainable to him, as soon as he recognised it was he who would have to surrender. 'Dominique let me in,' he said brightly. 'I hope you don't mind.'

Lillie had recovered quickly and smiled. 'Of course, not. Artie – you remember Oscar.'

'How do you do, Mr Wilde,' Arthur said, crossing to shake hands, as Oscar rose.

'Ah, no, you must not call me "Mr Wilde", nor "Wilde". I shall certainly not call you "Jones". I am Oscar.' Lillie laughed, but Arthur did not really respond. There was something about Oscar which he did not like and he resented his possessiveness with Lillie, when he turned to her, ignoring him. 'Now, my Lily, you will ask why I am here? It is to bring tidings of the approach of Sarah.'

'Sarah?'

'The divine Sarah Bernhardt,' Oscar breathed. I saw her in Paris, at the Théâtre Français.'

'An actress?' Lillie asked, then remembered. 'Oh, yes, I've read about her.'

'*The* actress – as the world one day will recognise,' Oscar stressed. 'The Prince of Wales is bringing her and the whole Comédie Française over for a short season.'

'The Prince?' Lillie frowned, surprised, then realised that was Oscar's real purpose in coming. She glanced at Arthur, who had noticed nothing.

'Didn't you know? They are very old friends,' Oscar told her, apparently casual. It had amused him to see her for a moment startled. 'She has not yet been given the acclaim in Paris, which the Prince feels she deserves. He wants her genius to triumph and be recognised first in London.'

'I see,' Lillie said calmly.

'You and I must help her to conquer,' he insisted. '"Soul of the Age! The applause, delight, and beauty of our stage!"'

'"*Wonder* of our stage,"' Lillie said, correcting him automatically, although her mind was occupied.

Oscar's eyebrows lifted. 'I beg your pardon?'

'Ben Jonson,' Lillie murmured. '"The applause, delight and wonder of our stage."'

Oscar coughed. 'I hate to admit it – but I stand corrected.' He shrugged, and smiled philosophically when Arthur laughed.

Lillie smiled, too, but she knew a turning point had been reached. Bertie's name had been connected with this actress some years before. It must have been to see her that he had gone back to Paris. And yet he had said nothing, and was simply going to bring her to London. She must have a much stronger hold on him than anyone had thought. More than that – it was the first time in over two years that he had shown preference for another woman.

The Prince and Princess of Wales were in the royal box of the Gaiety Theatre on the first night of the French company's season. By policy, the Comédie Française had no stars, although its leading actor, Coquelin, had a massive following. The evening began with Molière's *Le Misanthrope*, in which he had a great success. Lillie and Edward were in the Dudleys' box and she waited impatiently for Bernhardt's first appearance after the interval, in one act of the tragedy, *Phèdre*, by Racine. She could see Oscar gesticulating and rhapsodising in the stalls. He had seen nothing strange in taking Lillie off the day before to the British Museum, to search among the collection of Roman medallions for a resemblance to 'the divine Sarah' which he remembered. Once he had spent days hunting for a remembered likeness of Lillie. Once she had been the only Divinity. At least, Oscar's engrossing enthusiasm for her rival prepared her for Bertie's friendly, but watchful manner when they had met, as if he were prepared for her to be angry and upset. Lillie had known better and been as charming and loving as ever, although in these few days she had developed an even deeper sympathy for Alexandra.

When the curtain rose again, she saw the reason for Bertie's and Oscar's fascination. The vibrant, silken voice, the passionate temperament, the unique fire of Sarah's natural acting roused the audience to a frenzy. She was not beautiful, but immensely striking, so slim she almost seemed emaciated, with huge, dark-ringed eyes, a semitic nose and frizzy, auburn hair. When she took her solo bow wrapped in a highnecked, crimson cloak, the audience was drawn to its feet, cheering, led by Bertie, with Alix applauding beside him. Lillie watched her smile and curtsey to the royal box and knew for the first time how it felt to be eclipsed.

Sarah's conquest of London was spectacular. Presented to the public by Bertie and proclaimed by Oscar, she was acknowledged immediately by critics and theatregoers as the greatest actress of her day. The Lord Mayor gave a luncheon in her honour at the Mansion House. She was feted everywhere and became almost the only subject of conversation, he love affairs, her pet cheetah, her illegitimate birth, the fatherless daughter of a Jewish harlot. There had never been anyone more talented, more exotic, more incomparable.

Throughout it all, Lillie kept her head. Even when Mrs Wheeler suddenly championed her, outraged that the Prince should be snared by a foreigner. The Wests, the Lonsdales and the Rosslyns accepted an invitation to one of Lillie's rare supper parties and, to their astonishment, found the Wheelers there as fellow guests. All at once, they had become Margaret and Luke.

Throughout supper, most of the talk was of the engagement of the Rosslyn's lovely daughter, Daisy, to young Lord Brooke, the heir to the very rich Earl of Warwick. Brookie's only interest in life was sport and he was reputed to be the best shot in England. The stuffed peacock which served as a firescreen in Lillie's drawingroom had been shot by him at Warwick Castle and given to her as a tribute. She was glad that Sarah was not mentioned, for Arthur was with them and already some of the remarks he had heard clearly puzzled him.

But after supper, Mrs Wheeler had been unable to restrain herself. 'I have to say it!' she complained indignantly. 'It is sickening the way the Prince fawns over that shameless woman! The divine Sarah, indeed . . . And the way he shows her off!'

'Yes,' Patsy agreed. 'He's taken her to meet Watts and Leighton and Whistler, all the artists. And half society.'

'I think she's superb,' Lillie said.

'She may be,' Mrs Wheeler snorted. 'But I can tell you that a lot of ladies are shocked at how he expects them to receive her – just as if she were you!'

Lillie could see Arthur and Rosslyn coming towards them and was anxious. 'They really have no need to be concerned, Margaret,' she said.

As she tried to turn away, Patsy protested, 'Maybe not. But are you just going to let her take him over?'

'He cannot stand possessiveness,' Lillie told her. 'You know that. It would drive him away.'

'You have to do something about it!' Patsy insisted.

Arthur and Rosslyn had been stopped by Edward. Lillie did not think they could hear. She had to finish the conversation. 'I already have, Patsy,' she said quietly. 'I saw her play again last night and called on her this morning. We had breakfast together.'

Mrs Wheeler's eyes opened wide. 'Breakfast?'

'I liked her,' Lillie went on. 'She knows very few people in London, all of them men. I think she'll be glad of a woman friend.'

'A friend? . . .' Patsy repeated, and smiled admiringly.

'How do you do it? That's brilliant, Lillie!'

Mrs Wheeler and she laughed, congratulating her. It was, indeed, a brilliant manoeuvre. The men turned, smiling, but Arthur was troubled as he looked at Lillie.

In fact, Lillie sincerely liked Sarah and had the most profound admiration for her as an artist. In turn, Sarah was entranced by Lillie's beauty and sense of humour. She was not popular with the other actresses in her company and the only woman in London who had taken the trouble to visit her was Ellen Terry, who knew no French. Sarah had, of course, heard of Lillie and was delighted that they could speak freely in her own language. She found Lillie sympathetic, amusing and unshockable. The actress's complete naturalness and lack of hypocrisy appealed to Lillie and, although Sarah was nearly ten years older, they were soon like sisters. When Sarah confessed a total envy of Lillie's looks and figure, Lillie told her she would gladly give up her so-called beauty for a tenth of Sarah's talent, then made up a little epitaph for her that was widely quoted.

An actress adored from pole to pole,
Here lies Sarah, beyond all praise,
Who filled each role,
But not her stays.

Bertie was far from sure what to make of the relationship developing between them, although at least it meant that there were no embarrassing scenes. He was still affectionately attached to Lillie, although, paradoxically, since he had acknowledged her officially, their affaire had begun to lose its special excitement. She had kept him captive longer than any woman before, but his restless nature fought against her hold over him. If she had been jealous, she would have lost him altogether. Instead, her friendly acceptance of Sarah made him value her even more highly. Yet he was irrationally uncomfortable at seeing the two of them laughing and gossiping together, while Lillie's friendship with Alix had only pleased him.

He called with Sarah one morning on Whistler, who was doing a sketch of her, and was disconcerted to find Lillie there with Oscar and Sally. He suspected, rightly, that it was by arrangement. Before returning to Paris, Sarah wanted to make sure there was no split between her friend and the Prince, certainly not on her account.

Lillie had been keen for Frank Miles to meet Sarah and could not understand why he had not come, too. 'He is hiding,' Oscar explained quietly.

She was puzzled. 'Who from?'

'The Police,' Oscar told her, reluctantly. 'Only for a day or two. It will blow over.' The night before detectives had come to Salisbury Street. Oscar had barred the door, pretending to think they were thieves masquerading as policemen, giving Frank time to escape through the sky-light and across the roof.

'But why?' Lillie asked, concerned. 'What's wrong?'

Oscar hesitated to tell her. It was a secret known to only a very few of Frank Miles' friends, a compulsion which overcame him from time to time, although he struggled against it. It had been better since he had lived on terms of non-sexual intimacy with Sally. Oscar shrugged. 'He has a love of exhibition natural enough in an artist – but repre-hensible, when only small girls in single spies are invited to contemplate.' Lillie was amused, yet partly shocked.

'What are you two whispering about?' Bertie demanded, curious.

'Is he making love to you, Lillie? Sarah smiled. She was teasing Oscar who had sworn himself her slave, and yet was evidently as much a slave to Lillie.

'He's telling me how much he adores you,' Lillie said.

Sarah laughed. 'I don't believe you. Not while he's sitting with you.'

Bertie puffed on his cigar. 'You seem to have formed a mutual admiration society.'

'How true . . .' Sarah affirmed. 'C'est bien vrai. I have admired Lillie, ever since I met her.'

'And I admired Sarah, even before I met her,' Lillie said.

'How is that?' Whistler asked.

'Oscar took me to the British Museum to hunt for coins and vases showing her profile.'

'Coins?' Bertie grunted.

'Of the Roman Empire, sir,' Oscar told him.

Lillie smiled. 'He has a theory that my profile is pure Greek and Sarah's pure Latin.'

'She looks more like a gypsy,' Sally put it, and they laughed.

'You've caught her, Miss Sally,' Bertie chuckled. 'In a nutshell.' He looked fondly at Sarah. In her trailing, white, beaded gown with the large bow of white tulle round her throat, a picture hat, she looked as slender as a serpent and ravishingly sensual. She even made Lillie look plumply rounded, and she was slimmer than most other fashionable women. They made an enchanting pair. Lillie in blue and Sarah in white.

'It's strange,' Sarah marvelled. 'I used to think the British were so cold and distant. Now I feel so at home here.'

'You can stay as long as you wish,' Bertie assured her.

'Would your ladies of society accept me – an actress?' Sarah teased. 'I think not. Not unless I was presented at Court, like Lillie.' It was daring. Oscar and Whistler began to smile, but stopped when Bertie glanced at them. 'She told me all about it,' Sarah said 'How wonderful!' She must have been magnificent. I wish I had been there.'

Aware of Bertie, none of the others could comment, then he chuckled, himself. 'She rather overdid it with the feathers.'

The others laughed with him, relaxing.

'I do wish I had seen her,' Sarah went on. 'That carriage, that voice – what an actress she would make!' Lillie smiled to her, although the others were surprised.

'You think so?' Bertie asked, intrigued.

'With that chin she would go far,' Sarah told him, and they laughed again, agreeing with her. Whistler brought the coffee pot to refill her cup, but she shook her hand. She rose and bowed to Bertie. 'I must ask your pardon, Mon Prince. But I am reminded I have a rehearsal with Coquelin.'

'Oh, yes,' Bertie agreed. 'He doesn't like to be kept waiting.'

'Exactly. Thank you, James.'

'I hope you will come again,' Whistler said.

'With great pleasure.'

Bertie had risen, keen to get Sarah off on her own. 'I'll take you to the theatre,' he offered.

'It will be an honour,' she replied. 'And you, Lillie?'

Bertie was surprised, and even more so when Lillie said, 'I'd love to come to your rehearsal.'

'Très bon,' Sarah smiled. She looked from Bertie to Lillie. 'Mon ami – et mon amie.'

Oscar bit his lip, seeing how thrown the Prince was for a second or two, then had to admire his aplomb, as he laughed and gave one arm to Sarah, and the other to Lillie. They turned to the door, which Whistler hurried to open.

'Much obliged, Mr Whistler,' Bertie chuckled. He nodded to Oscar and Sally and went out with Lillie and Sarah. Whistler followed them, winking to Oscar. Sally rolled over on the floor, giggling.

Later in the afternoon, Sarah lay on Lillie's bed, supported on one elbow, watching her pack a small travelling case. 'I am grateful to London,' she said. 'It has made me a star – thanks to the Prince and Oscar and you.'

'Your own talent did that,' Lillie told her.

'Oh, yes,' Sarah shrugged. 'But someone had to make people see it. I'm not beautiful like you.'

'But that's all I am,' Lillie said.

There was a note of disillusionment in her voice and Sarah sat up. 'What do you mean?'

'You've done something with your life,' Lillie smiled. 'There's a purpose to it.'

Sarah was not deceived by the smile. 'But not to yours? You have everything. What more do you want?' Lillie did not answer. 'Do you love the Prince?'

Lillie hesitated. She could be frank with Sarah, she decided. '. . . No, I admire him. And I need him, to be what I am.'

Sarah considered her. 'And that is why you are going off with this young man?'

'Yes,' Arthur had to go back to Jersey. His visits were always so short, Lillie could not bear him to leave and had thought of a way to keep him with her longer. She could tell that he was unsettled. She had to reassure him.

'So you are going to Bournemouth, to the house you told me about. Even for a few days, won't that be dangerous?'

'I have to do it,' Lillie said simply.

'Yes,' Sarah agreed. 'We have to do it.' She rose and moved to Lillie, putting her arm round her affectionately. 'We are very alike.' She saw their reflection in the cheval mirror and turned Lillie so that they could both look into it. 'I don't mean just our colouring. We've both had to come a long way, learn how to use other people – and yet stay true to ourselves. What a deadly combination we would make.' She saw Lillie smile to her in the mirror and hugged her gently, smiling back. 'And how fortunate that both of us prefer men . . .'

The tension that Lillie had sensed in Arthur was eased during their stay in the Red House. His passion for her was as overpowering as ever, and her response to his was total. Even when he collapsed in her arms, exhausted, he knew that her slightest touch would rouse him again, and he blamed himself for the uneasiness he had felt in London, for the pride that made him question and doubt.

It had taken all Lillie's courage to bring him to the house in Bournemouth. She had come on impulse, only telling Edward she would be gone for a few days. She did not care where he thought she was. But if Bertie suspected, and came or sent someone to find her, and Arthur was discovered, she did not like to imagine his fury. She had to risk it, aware of Arthur's perplexity growing, the longer he stayed on in town, seeing the deference paid to her, puzzled by oblique remarks and her unavoidable, only partly explained absences. Sarah, when she met Arthur, had made much of him, patting his cheek, cooing over him like a lapdog. At first, it had been amusing, then Lillie saw his embarrassment at being treated the way Parisiennes cossetted their young lovers. That was how Sarah had thought of him, as would others.

But he was not Lillie's plaything. He was much more. She had lived for so long on a tightrope, poised over a fearful abyss, and she thought of Arthur as her lifeline, like the almost invisible wire attached to the acrobats balancing and dancing high in the air in the dome of the Cirque Médrano. She knew the adulation and homage had gone to her head for a time. Her fame had come so quickly, it was only through Arthur that she kept in touch with reality. He loved and needed her, but she needed him even more and bound him to her. There was no risk of losing him, as long as he did not ask one question. Finally he asked it and she could not answer.

They had walked on the beach in the moonlight, when it was safe for her to go out, hand in hand along the edge of the water. There was almost no wind and the sea sparkled like beaten silver. For once they were silent, and the silence drew them even closer together in the still night. She kissed him, when they turned at last to follow the long, dark track of their footprints back to the path up the cliff. He had been so sure of their love for each other that he had asked her not to wait any longer, but to leave Edward now and come with him. She kissed him again, but he told her he was serious and that it was the only honest thing for them to do. If only they could, she answered. For years, she had done everything to avoid quarrelling with Ned. Now when she wanted him to, he refused to quarrel and give her an excuse to tell him to go. She could not leave him in cold blood or she would lose all her friends, and Arthur and she would need friends later.

Arthur argued, but accepted it. She was enchanting when they got back to the house, lighthearted and amusing, remembering incidents from their childhood. His first pony, which she had shared. And the old man who threatened to shoot her brothers and herself if they played at being ghosts in the churchyard again. They had already removed his doorknocker. As a further retaliation, they tied a long string to the handle of his bell and the other end to a rock which they dropped over the wall on the opposite side of the road, so that every horse and cart that passed rang the bell and, each time, old Mr Wilkins had popped out like a cuckoo from its clock. She was like a girl again, shy and girlishly provocative, and sleep had been a long while coming.

She woke in the morning, drowsy and contented, to find him packing his case. He had not slept, he told her, but lain and thought over all that she had said and had decided to go back now to Jersey.

She followed him into the private sittingroom from her bedroom, unable to accept that he really meant it. She was nearly in tears. He had never seen her cry and had to fight to stay calm and in control. 'Stay just another day,' she pleaded. 'Please, Artie.'

'I can't,' he told her. 'I sent a telegram to say I'd be back two days ago.' He put his suitcase by his coat and hat, which lay ready on a chair by the door.

'Is it so easy to leave?' she asked. 'I need you.'

'I wish I was sure of that,' he muttered. He heard her catch her breath and was sorry, knowing he had hurt her. She had risen to follow him, pulling on only her wrap. He was afraid to look at her, in case he weakened. 'I thought Ned was all that stood between us. You say you don't love him – why won't you tell him it's finished?'

'I've tried to,' she explained again. 'But now when I want him to, he won't quarrel with me.'

'So you keep – What does that matter? Why is it important? Leave him!' When she was silent, he turned to face her. 'It's not him, is it? It's your new life – that's what you won't give up.'

'I love you,' she whispered. 'I've never loved anyone else.'

She could not say those words like that, unless they were true. He wanted to believe her, desperately wanted. 'But I can't stand having to meet you in secret! Lying, pretending. Even here. Even –' He shook his head. 'There's so much I don't understand. That I try not to understand.'

She was over the first shock and was trying to think more calmly, but before she could find the words to reassure him, he went on.

'I know Ned has no money. Yet you have expensive clothes – jewellery. That horse you said he bought. Ned said it was given to you. And this house – you said you

372

borrowed it for a week.'

'Yes,' she smiled, taut.

'Lillie, I'm not blind!' he protested. 'It has your initials everywhere ELL. Emilie Le Breton Langtry.'

She could never tell him the truth, but she had to tell him some of it. It had been madness to think he would not notice. 'It was built by friends of mine,' she said slowly. 'For me to use whenever I wish. My new friends are so wealthy they don't think in terms of money. They give presents we would never have dreamt of.'

Again, he wanted desperately to believe her, that that was all. Even so, it was too much. 'And how long will you go on taking?'

The suggestion of scorn in his voice stung her. 'There was a time when we lived in three rooms,' she reminded him. 'I had one black dress and a wedding ring. I knew no one and no one had ever heard of me. Don't ask me to go back to that – not now.'

'I know you can't,' he said quietly. 'That's why I'm going home.'

It was unthinkable. She wanted to run to him, to hold him. But she would not beg. 'I love you,' she whispered again.

Once, he would have given his life to hear those words from her. Her eyes, the pain in her voice, the way she stood, one hand by her side, the other just holding the wrap together and her body softly shadowed beneath it, all urged him towards her, to hold her and swear he believed her and would never leave. Yet he clung to the decision he had reached during the night, when he lay awake beside her. He would not be another Edward, would not be kept by strangers as she was. 'And I love you, with all my heart,' he said. 'When you are ready to live my kind of life, I'll be waiting.'

She was silent and motionless, watching him pick up his case and his hat and coat. He hesitated, but did not come to kiss her, did not even look at her. He turned to the door and went out. Even then, she did not move.

Lillie was sombre, when she returned to London. She had spent a day completely alone in The Red House. For a time she had been crushed. She had not wept, because she had learnt that that was not the answer to anything.

She had been bitterly hurt by Arthur leaving, then angry. It was easy for him to reject what she had achieved. He had not lived through the excitement and been lifted as she had been by a swelling tide of admiration and popularity. Like Ned, he resented her winning more for herself than he could ever give her. Yet in her own unhappiness she thought of his, the strength of will it had taken to leave. Arthur still loved her, she was certain of that. He offered her all he could, himself and the tranquil, eneventful life at Portelet for which she had longed. Why couldn't she accept it? Would Ned give her a divorce? She had prayed to be free of him, but the thought of divorce and all that it implied was frightening.

She let none of her turmoil show, when she arrived back at Norfolk Street, prepared for angry scenes and accusations. Only to find that Ned had also left the house, without even asking after her. Bertie had been occupied with saying goodbye to Sarah and seeing her off to Paris, loaded with gifts, proud of her new acclaim. Oscar had won his share of publicity by seeing her off at the station and strewing lilies at her feet. Lilies . . . Then a note arrived from Bertie, telling Lillie he regretted that he had been so busy of late and hoping he might call. It was a formality. He would call, anyway.

The more Lillie thought about it, the less she was able to accept it. Arthur had reproached her for not behaving like a prudish, provincial housewife. If she had done, he would never even have kissed her. Edward sneered at and resented her social prominence, while living on the credit and hospitality it brought. And Bertie – he had been infatuated with her, until his appetite demanded a change. Now it was satisfied and he had returned, expecting her to take her place again automatically at his side – the other side from Alix. Until the next time, and there would inevitably be a next time. And yet in all this, if it became known, as a woman she would be the only one the public would condemn. Her spirit rebelled against it. Especially in the knowledge that, to exist as she did, she would have to submit.

When Bertie arrived, charming and affectionate, she was as loving as ever. Society breathed more freely. The intrusion of the French actress had come and gone and life would continue as unruffled and pleasurable as before. It was tacitly agreed, since Mr Langtry was away so frequently on his fishing trips, that it would be unfair not to allow Mrs Langtry to attend social functions in his absence. She could come in the party of the Cornwallis Wests, the Dudleys or Suffields, or with a suitable escort, Lord Lonsdale, say, or Prince Louis of Battenberg or Lord Londesborough. In any case, she would partner the Prince. Her grace and infectious gaiety became even more admired.

As she was thinking of going up to change one evening, Dominique showed in James Whistler. He was at his most elegant, jaunty and blithe as he swept off his widebrimmed hat with a flourish and told her he had won his libel case against Ruskin, vindicating himself against malicious criticism.

Lillie hugged him, laughing with relief. 'You've won! You've won your case?'

He bowed. 'The jury found in my favour – with damages.'

She knew the strain it had all put on him. Ruskin had had a nervous breakdown and been unable to appear. Instead, a series of leading artists had been summoned to evaluate Whistler's work, some hostile, some reluctant, while he spoke superbly for himself. 'How much did they award you?' she asked, excitedly.

'A farthing,' he told her, smiling. She did not understand. 'One quarter of a penny.'

'You can't mean it . . .' she breathed.

He had gone straight to a jeweller's and showed her the tiny copper coin mounted on his watchchain. 'I shall keep it as a reminder of my victory.'

She still could not take it in. 'What about the costs of the trial?'

'I have had to pay them, of course,' he shrugged. Unfortunately, it has made me bankrupt.'

Apparently he did not have a care in the world and Lillie saw that his pride was protecting him, helping him not to show any pain at the shattering insult the art establishment had given him. 'What will it mean?' she asked.

He shrugged again. 'That I will lose my studio, my house, my works, everything I own.' He smiled. 'But I won.'

'Oh, Jimmy . . .' she faltered, distressed for him.

'Now, I mustn't stay,' he said quickly. Sympathy was dangerous. 'Dominique said you are going out.'

'It doesn't matter.'

'No, no, I mustn't keep you. Where are you off to?'

'A fancydress party at Lady Dudley's,' she told him.

'A masquerade,' he murmured. 'Mine is over.'

She followed him out into the hall. 'Shall I see you?'

'Sadly – not for some time,' he said. He took her hand and kissed it gently. 'So I shall never finish the portrait.' Dominique held the front door open and he kept Lillie's hand a moment longer, before turning towards it.

'Where are you going?' Lillie asked.

'Paris . . . Venice,' he said. 'Venice, I think. Today I resigned with several others from the Society of British Artists.' He turned in the doorway, putting on his hat and tilting it over his right temple. 'The artists have left. Only the British remain.'

He left her laughing, as he smiled impishly, touched the brim of his hat and went buoyantly down the stairs.

The party at Georgiana's was fairly informal, with the masks and dominoes adding to the gaiety. Rosslyn caused much amusement by turning up dressed as, and being mistaken for, a footman. Some of the guests were so disguised, it was impossible to recognise them. Others had only added a rosette or sash to their normal eveningdress and wore halfmasks. Georgiana was imposing in a sumptuous Pompadour constume, while Margaret Wheeler attracted much attention in a shako and long, fitted hussar's tunic, which flattered her slim figure. Patsy had come as a Grecian shepherdess and her husband as a cosssack. Lillie wore the chequered costume of a Pierrette with a loose, white, ruffled collar and a black satin cap. Like Patsy and the others, she carried a velvet mask on a short handle.

She was depressed and, for once, could not hide her feelings. Even the champagne, of which she drank more than usual, did not lift her spirits. 'You might at least pretend to be enjoying it,' Patsy whispered. 'Georgiana looks upset. Cheer up!'

'I just don't feel like it,' Lillie said. The laughter and flirtation, the chatter all round her, seemed empty.

'Don't worry about Jimmy Whistler,' Patsy maintained. 'He'll survive. Won't he, Poppets?'

'Bound to,' her large, amiable husband agreed.

'It's not only that,' Lillie told them. Jimmy had been driven away by people who could not remotely appreciate his genius. Like all artists, he depended on favour. It had reminded her how much so did she.

'Tell you what,' Patsy offered. 'You can dance with Poppets. That'll make you laugh.' Lillie glanced down at Colonel West's huge Russian boots and smiled. 'That's better.'

Lillie toasted them both and drank off her glass in one.

'Here – steady on,' Colonel West laughed.

Georgiana Dudley was watching Lillie, concerned. She had been perturbed as soon as she saw her and hoped she knew what she was doing. Many people admired Lillie's costume. It was dashing and eyecatching. But not very wise, Georgiana thought.

Her majordomo came to the entrance of the ballroom and bowed to her. She signed to the orchestra, collected her husband and they hurried out. There was a stir of anticipation when the music was cut off and lines quickly formed in an avenue leading from the entrance.

There came a ripple of applause, when Princess Alexandra appeared with Lord Dudley, wearing a nautical dress and jacket and a sailor's ribboned hat. Bertie followed them in, smiling, with Georgiana on his arm. Francis Knollys and an equerry walked behind. There was astonishment at Bertie's costume as he progressed down the avenue with Alix, acknowledging the bows and curtsies on either side. He was dressed as a Pierrot, with the same checks, loose, ruffled collar and black satin cap as Lillie.

Lillie stood poised, almost with a hint of bravado, knowing that everyone was looking at her. Beside her, Patsy hid her face with her mask and whispered, 'Did you know what he'd be wearing?'

'Yes,' Lillie said, calmly.

Patsy gasped and lowered her mask as the Prince and Princess came nearer. Across from her, she could see that Suffield and Allen Young were worried. Margaret Wheeler was rigid with anticipation. She had come to like Lillie, but this was too thrilling a moment. Everyone waited for the confrontation and the royal snub.

When Bertie and Alix reached Lillie and she curtsied, there was utter silence. Bertie's expression was stern. He was seriously displeased. He saw that Lillie was flushed, as if she had drunk more than she was used to – that did not excuse her choice of costume.

When he did not speak, Alix said clearly, 'How nice to see you, Lillie. And how charming you look.' She smiled and moved on with Bertie and the Dudleys. The tension relaxed and the threat to the evening was over.

Lillie had chosen the same costume as Bertie as a gesture against hypocrisy, to assert her own status and individuality. As soon as they had stopped in front of her, she realised she had made a miscalculation. She had thought Bertie would laugh and had forgotten it might offend Alix. Alix's graciousness did not make her feel any better.

She was not at all drunk, but the champagne made her recklessly gay and partners crowded round her. She had never looked more lovely. She only danced once with Bertie and he held her stiffly, at a distance, aware of the picture they made as Pierrot and Pierrette.

He invited her to join him, however, at the buffet supper table. All down the long table, footmen served the gentlemen who, in turn, served their partners. He made the gesture for her sake as much as his own, to prevent unfortunate gossip. He was ready to forgive her, but was still annoyed because she had not apologised. 'How could you?' he muttered. 'I should never have told Georgiana and you what I was going to wear.'

'I think it suits me,' she smiled.

'Dammit, that's not the point!' he snapped. Then forced himself to appear calm. They were towards one end of a large group, with Alix and the Dudleys at the other. A slight space had been left round them and everyone else chattered animatedly, carefully not overhearing them. 'You've drawn attention to us.'

'It's only an informal party.'

'You've embarrassed Alix,' he growled. 'And you've not even said you're sorry.'

Lillie would have apologised earlier, but his scolding had grated on her. Alix was different. 'Very well, I'm sorry.'

The footman had refilled their plates with breast of pheasant and truffles. Lillie smiled to him, declining it. Bertie seized his. A cross temper made him hungry. 'I don't know what's got into you,' he complained.

'I feel aimless.'

'Aimless?' He was puzzled. 'In what way?'

'I don't know,' she told him. 'Nothing I do has any meaning. Don't you ever feel useless?' She finished her champagne.

'No, I'm always too busy.' The pheasant was delicious. He did not want to fall out with her. 'Have something to eat. You'll feel better.'

'I don't want to eat, Bertie.'

'Not here!' he hissed, glancing round. 'Don't call me that here. For Heavens sake!' The others had pretended not to notice. He made himself smile. 'Oh, come on, Lillie – come on. It's a party.'

She knew he would never understand what troubled her. 'That's what's wrong,' she said flatly. 'It's always a party.' Her glass was empty and her throat felt parched. She turned to the buffet, where a bottle of champagne stood beside her in a silver bucket filled with crushed ice.

The equerry was hovering near them and took the bottle to serve her. 'A little more champagne, Mrs Langtry?'

As she held out her glass, Bertie shook his head sharply. The equerry hesitated and lowered the bottle. Lillie had also noticed Bertie shake his head and turn away. She was incensed for a moment and, almost without thinking, snatched a handful of crushed ice from the bucket and thrust it down the back of Bertie's wide collar. He gasped and hunched his shoulders. Since everyone else had been secretly watching them, while pretending not to, the reaction was instant and Bertie's gasp was re-echoed round the room.

He could not credit what happened. In the silence, he heard Lillie laugh behind him. A defiant, challenging laugh. He looked round slowly, expressionless, feeling the ice trickle down his back, and saw her smile to him, her chin held high. He turned abruptly to Georgiana Dudley, bowed to her and held out his hand to Alix. Alix was watching Lillie compassionately, sorry for her. She moved to Bertie. Without another glance, he stalked out of the ballroom with her, followed by the equerry and Francis Knollys. Georgiana and Lord Dudley hurried after them.

The silence in the great ballroom continued. Mrs Wheeler could not resist smiling. Suffield made to speak to Lillie, very upset, but turned and left with his wife, saying nothing. The Londesboroughs and De Greys went with them.

The people nearest Lillie moved further away, turning their backs. She remained frozen, seeing how backs were turned to her and she was shunned, after what she had done. In the whole room, only Patsy was looking at her.

# CHAPTER FOURTEEN

Next day, her invitations began to be cancelled, one by one, some curtly, some apologetically. Guests she had been expecting sent their regrets. When she went out with Dominique to do some shopping in Bond Street, people she smiled to walked past as if she did not exist. In the draper's shop where she bought her material, two ladies seeing her walked out at once. Society was sending her to Coventry.

She had left Dudley House alone and come home by cab. No one had spoken to her, not even Patsy. It was not until she awoke that morning that the full consequences of her mockery and defiance of Bertie begun to occur to her. Even her own home felt unnaturally silent, as though it too had been isolated. Dominique was distressed and afraid to speak to her.

Then the doorbell rang. It was Patsy Cornwallis West.

'You didn't have to come,' Lillie said.

'Don't be silly,' Patsy smiled. 'You need a friend.'

Lillie was touched and grateful. Her sudden loneliness had shaken her. Even Edward seemed to have disappeared and she had no idea where he was. She told Patsy about the cancelled invitations and the snubs in the street.

'It will get worse,' Patsy said. 'I suppose like most of us you live on credit. Today, the tradesmen will hear the Prince has dropped you and, by tomorrow, their bills will start to come in.'

'I can't pay them.'

'Take a tip from Jimmy Whistler,' Patsy advised her. 'Move the most valuable stuff out at once, before they send in the debt-collectors and bailifs. They'll grab whatever you have that's worth selling to settle their accounts.'

Everything began to turn out exactly as Patsy foretold. Not only a few, but all her invitations were cancelled. When she called on Georgiana Dudley to apologise, she was told she was 'not at home.' Neither was Lady Wharncliffe, nor Mrs Wheeler. After that, Lillie did not pay any more calls on anyone. Her only visitors, besides Patsy, were Lady Lonsdale and Oscar with Frank Miles, who had been staying quietly in France until the police lost interest in him. She was grateful to all four, particularly to Patsy and Lady Lonsdale, who had put their own social positions in jeopardy by standing by her.

And the first probing bills began to come in, with a request for 'the favour of an early settlement.' Lillie was staggered by the amount they owed.

Then Edward arrived home. He had not paid his wine bills for over a year and, with pressure from other personal debts, he had gone to Southampton to arrange the sale of Cliffe Lodge at last. It was a poor time to sell and he had not received as much as he had hoped. It barely covered what he owed. When Lillie showed him the other bills, he panicked, drinking himself into a stupor. In the morning, Lillie roused him and sent him to Lamb, the moneylender, to borrow what he could. A percentage of the first bills had to be paid to prevent an avalanche, if their creditors feared no money was available.

Our of the blue, she had a visit from Lord Suffield and the manufacturer, C. J. Freake. Freake, who cultivated the Prince so shamelessly, was the last person she had expected to see. The reason for their visit, Suffield explained, was that the Prince had been so unsettled and irritable since the night of the fancydress party that all his friends and all social life had suffered. They wanted to bring about a reconciliation. Freake was giving a party for charity at his townhouse in Cromwell Road and its centrepiece was to be a series of *tableaux vivants* of famous modern paintings, staged by the artists who had created them. Millais had agreed to present *Effie Deans*, provided Lillie agreed to pose.

It was all carried out in great secrecy. The band platform in Freake's ballroom was curtained off and, when Bertie and the other guests assembled on the night of the party, there was much speculation as to which paintings had been chosen. Lord Carrington, one of Bertie's oldest friends, whispered that he hoped they would include some of Alma-Tadema's classical nudes. Bertie chuckled as expected, but the fingers of his right hand were already drumming on his thigh in anticipation of more boredom, which was confirmed by the first tableaux, Holman Hunt's *The Awakening Conscience* and Leighton's *The Music Lesson*. Then Millais appeared and bowed, introducing *Effie Deans*.

There was astonishment as the curtains parted to reveal Godfrey Pearse who had posed for the outlaw seducer, the original dog and a stone dyke and backcloth painted by Millais, and Lillie in her simple skirt and blouse, her hair unbound, her lips parted and her violet eyes raised in penitence. The symbolism was striking and appropriate. Suffield had crossed his fingers, but smiled happily to Freake when Bertie began the applause, although the loudest clapping came from William Gladstone who was moved to tears by Lillie's repentant beauty. Freake came bustling round to find Lillie while the platform was being cleared. Bertie wished her to sit with him at dinner and to remain in her simple, Scottish costume.

The next morning in the Park, those who had not been at Freake's party, were startled to see the Prince and Mrs Langtry riding and laughing together, as if there had never been any disagreement between them.

Dominique marvelled at the flood of invitations which poured into Norfolk Street. In the next few days, she was forever answering the door to callers and messengers. Lillie received everyone with a graciousness which only Alexandra could match. No one, not even Oscar, could guess her thoughts. Suddenly, she was everyone's favourite again. People who, only hours before, had been ready to write her off as a provincial upstart, her beauty vastly exaggerated and her intelligence overrated, showered her with praise and admiration. But now she knew how insincere it was and just what it was worth.

Alexandra was genuinely glad to be able to invite her to Marlborough House again and young Louis of Battenberg, who was off active service and had taken up his rooms there to become an aide to Bertie, was increasingly attracted to her. He partnered her and danced with her in the evenings and took the equerry's place on their morning and evening rides. When Lillie came to tea, he amused Alix by unfailingly thinking of an excuse to come into her private sittingroom on the second floor so that he would be invited to join them. She met Gladstone again there. The old man was a favourite of Alexandra's and surprised them by telling them how he counted the hairstyles of women he passed in his carriage, finding that half wore Alexandra's, swept up into a mass of tiny curls on top, and half wore Lillie's smooth on top with a fringe and the loose, figure-of-eight knot in the nape of the neck. Gladstone had a liking for the ladies, Lillie saw, and was not surprised when he started to call on her, dropping in with books he thought she might like to read, for tea and a chat. The political parties were preparing for a general election, but he still found time to read parts of his translation of Homer to her or discuss the poetry of Shakespeare. At over seventy, his attachment to her was mental, rather than physical, yet none the less romantic.

Lillie was grateful to Bertie. He had no inkling of the pressures that had driven her to flout him in public, believing she had merely had too much champagne, and his forgiveness was due to the dullness of his life without her and a trace of guilt over Sarah, yet he had saved her from her own rashness. He could not ignore the insult to his dignity and had been extremely angry, but he was immensely kind, where he was fond, and he had given her another chance, hoping she had learnt her lesson.

She had learnt it well. The suddeness of her fall and her immediate rejection by so many people she had thought were friends had shaken her. Even more, she despised the way they came running back, fawning over her, trying to pretend that nothing had happened. Some, who were close to the Prince, she could excuse, and only them. One thing she swore, that none of them would ever have the opportunity to snub her again. Bertie was the key. As long as she kept at least his friendship, and Alexandra's, her position might be lessened but she would never lose it. Even the pressure for the payment of bills eased, as few tradesmen dared to offend the favourite of the Prince of Wales.

Life had retuned to normal. Ned returned to his drinking companions and his fishing trips, unquestioning, only thankful that he had been saved from bankruptcy. He did not even comment on the magnificent diamond pendant and bracelet which Bertie gave her to seal their reconciliation, nor the matching tiara which appeared when they were invited to official banquets. Although they continued to live together as man and wife, their marriage was virtually over.

Then, one day when Gladstone sat in the drawingroom at Norfolk Street reading a selection of Shakespeare's sonnets aloud to her, Patsy arrived in a flurry. She was evidently agitated and Gladstone tactfully ended his visit, leaving the edition of the sonnets as a present for Lillie. When he had gone, Patsy threw down on top of it the latest copy of the scandal sheet, *Town Talk*. There were a number of small satirical news sheets and comic magazines, filled with titillating gossip, like *Tomahawk* and *The Pink 'Un*. *Town Talk* was one of the most acid. The Beauties were all prime targets for jokes and hints of scandal and, in her position, Lillie was inevitably singled out. *Town Talk* had often published snippets about her, at first admiring, then more and more vitriolic, hinting at her involvement with many different men. This latest issue was already sold out and was being passed eagerly from hand to hand. Lillie was incredulous a she read, 'A petition has been filed in the Divorce Court by Mr Langtry. H.R.H. The Prince of Wales, and two other gentlemen whose names up to the time of going to the press we have not been able to learn, are mentioned as co-respondents.'

'Is it true?' Patsy demanded.

'Of course, not!' Ned would never throw away his comfortable life by divorcing her, even if he could overcome his Quaker upbringing. Besides, with divorce, his allowance from his family would stop at once.

'Then you must do something about it,' Patsy insisted.

'Get hold of Ned. This rag must be forced to print a retraction!'

'Edward was somewhere in Dorset. Instead of contacting him, Lillie went straight to Bertie, who had already been informed by Francis Knollys. Bertie was flatly against any public denial. 'Just ignore it, my dear,' he told her. 'And you're not to worry. I'll take care of it.' To Knollys he said, 'First, we must find out if there *is* any truth in it.'

He sent for the solicitor, George Lewis. Lewis, Jewish and very capable, had built up a large practice through wide knowledge of the law, commonsense and total discretion. All Society went to him and many marital problems and scandals were settled in his office, without ever coming to court. He knew and liked Lillie and was happy to be able to report to the Prince that there was no sign that a petition had ever been filed. The story had been invented to sell more copies of *Town Talk*. But also a little more than that.

The weekly news sheet was edited and almost entirely run by a young man named Adolphus Rosenberg. Rosenberg lived in poor circumstances in Brixton with his wife and two children. Over the past two years, he had developed what amounted to a fixation on Lillie, buying every photograph of her that was ever printed and avidly following her career, as a symbol of democratic, feminine triumph. When she laid aside her black dress and began to appear in gorgeous plumage on the arm of the Prince, outdoing her rivals in extravagance, his admiration had changed to criticism, mixed with jealousy. Lewis's advice was the same as Bertie's, no public denial. The whole matter would blow over sooner for being ignored.

Rosenberg had waited in considerable excitement and some fear for either the Langtry's or Marlborough House to contact him, prepared to admit that his sources of information might be mistaken but that he had published in good faith. When no reaction came, he decided they were afraid to take any action and seized his chance. *Town Talk* placards appeared in the streets, 'The Langtry Divorce Case: Further particulars', and he reported that the divorce was to be heard *in camera*. In following weeks, he disclosed that Lillie had decided to contest the case, which was to be tried privately, since the details would rock the nation. He declined, magnanimously, to be more explicit. In his next issue he told his readers that the Home Secretary had ordered that no joking references to Mrs Langtry and the Prince of Wales were to be allowed in the musichalls.

As interest in the supposed Divorce Case mounted, he was forced to invent further details, when other newspapers ridiculed his reports. In spite of her anger, Lillie laughed when he named the other two co-respondents as Lord Londesborough and Lord Lonsdale. Londesborough . . .

Handsome Hugh Lonsdale was only a close friend. If she had given him any encouragement, of course . . . But she never did. He was a madcap. One night, she had climbed into a single-horse cab waiting outside her house, giving the driver Reuben Sassoon's address. They had started off almost at a gallop, jolting her, and she had called to the cabby to drive more carefully. His only response was to crack his whip, and the cab sped on even faster, lurching round corners, forcing other traffic out of the road. Hanging on in the unlit interior, thrown from side to side, Lillie had seen streetlights and buildings whizzing past and heard shouts and police whistles. When all her commands and appeals only made them go faster, she realised she was in the hands of a madman. She had no idea where he would take her nor what would happen, as the breathstopping journey went on and on. When they halted at last, miraculously without an accident, she leapt out, ready to fight for her life. And discovered to her surprise that she was outside the Sassoons' and that short, swarthy Reuben was waiting at the open door, anxious because she was late. The driver was climbing down and she cried to Reuben to stop him getting away. Reuben started forward and the driver grinned, taking off his hat and muffler. It was Hugh dressed as a cabby. It had not occurred to Lillie that only a master horseman could have handled the cab like that. He had driven her often enough in his four-in-hand. She thumped him hard on the chest in laughing protest and Reuben invited him in to join the dinner party.

Lillie had to persuade Lonsdale against seeking ou Rosenberg and whipping him. Edward had returned and was distraught, sure that people were pointing and sniggering at him in the street. His brother and sister wrote, horrified at the scandal which had even reached Belfast, begging him to deny the rumours. Bertie had to stop his friend Londesborough from suing Rosenberg. George Lewis agreed when Lillie said that something now had to be done. He went to the office of *Town Talk* in dingy premises off Fleet Street.

Rosenberg was thin, intense and also Jewish and Lewis spoke bluntly to him, warning him that he was putting himself increasingly in danger of the law. Rosenburg, however, was flushed with success and notoriety. Intoxicated by the thought that he had the Jersy Lily on the run and with visions of fame as a scourge of public morals, he refused to retract. Yet Lewis had worried him and he decided that, in any case, he had milked the story long enough. He had to find a way out of it, while still retaining his credibility, and his next issue created a sensation. 'I am now informed on authority, which I have no reason to doubt, that Mr Langtry has withdrawn the petition which he had filed in the Divorce Court,' he wrote in part. 'The case of Langtry v. Langtry and others is therefore finally disposed of, and we have probably heard the last of it . . . I am told also that it is not unlikely that Mr Langtry will shortly be appointed to some diplomatic post abroad. It is not stated whether his beautiful consort will accompany him.'

Bertie read the issue and exploded with fury at the suggestion that he had bought off Langtry and was abusing his position to have him shipped out of the country on a government salary. It did not matter that it was not remotely possible. A sufficient number of radicals and fools would be willing to believe it. He sent again for George Lewis, who hurried from him to Lillie. He found her equally determined. Rosenberg had gone too far to be ignored any longer. They had given him enough rope and he had tied his own noose.

Having finished for the moment, as he thought, with Lillie, Rosenberg turned on her friends, starting with Patsy. He reported that, behind her house, she had built four photographic studios where she spent the entire day, posing for a series of photographers, only stopping to change her clothes, that each of them paid her a fee and that she went round all the shops in person to collect commissions due to her on the sale of her photographs.

Colonel Cornwallis West was not a man to sit quietly under insult and had Rosenberg arrested on a charge of uttering a 'filthy and foul libel.' Rosenberg expected to be admonished or made to pay a small fine, after sticking to the timeworn excuse that he had published in good faith. Brought before the magistrates, however, he found himself facing a second charge of maliciously publishing a defamatory libel on Mr and Mrs Langtry, knowing it to be false. He was remanded in custody until his trial at the Central Criminal Court in the Old Bailey. By the time he appeared there, to make certain he did not get off, a third charge was made against him of publishing a malicious libel on Lord Londesborough.

The most serious of the charges was the one of libelling Mr and Mrs Langtry and that was the one with which the court proceeded. Edward, Colonel West and Lord Londesborough were all present, but neither Lillie nor Patsy. The prosecuting counsel easily established that the libels had been published for profit and deliberately to defame Lillie. Edward in the witness box, stuffy and gentlemanly, indignantly denied that there was a single word of truth in the libels or that he had ever filed or contemplated filing any action for divorce. 'I have always lived on terms of affection with my wife,' he insisted, 'and am living with her still at Norfolk Street.'

'Is there any truth about you having been offered a diplomatic appointment?' his counsel asked.

'Not a word!' Edward declared, to applause.

The court was completely packed with reporters hoping for sensational revelations. They were disappointed. Rosenburg was beaten and knew it. He had no further titbits to give them and could only keep claiming that he had not known his information was false. The jury did not even leave the box. They found him guilty and the judge, Mr Justice Hawkins, sent him to prison for eighteen months, with the regret 'that I cannot add hard labour.'

The final irony which Rosenberg never knew was that, throughout the trial, Lillie had not been present because she was in Paris with Bertie.

With Prince Louis of Battenberg, Carrington and various other friends in attendance, they had a most enjoyable week. Sarah entertained them royally and the Princesse Jeanne de Sagan, who had a son by Bertie, gave a dinner in Lillie's honour. Maxim's, the Café Anglais and the crowds in the gaslit boulevards greeted her raptuously as the *maitresse en titre*. Bertie bought her a wonderful rope of amethysts.

They returned in time for the races at Newmarket, where they stayed at Leopold de Rothschild's racing box. Afterwards, Bertie slipped back to Paris.

Lillie had not known he was going and only learnt by accident, when Prince Louis called to take her riding. He was covered in embarrassment that he was the one who had let out where Uncle Bertie was. 'I am not at all upset, Your Royal Highness,' she assured him. 'Why should I be?'

'No, no,' he said. 'I am not a "Royal". I am a "Serene".'

She laughed. 'Very well – Your Serene Highness.'

'Ah, but to – to friends,' he hesitated, 'I only answer to the name Louis.'

She had always liked him and found him even more charming and amusing on his own than when he had been conscious of Bertie and Alix with them. There was only a few months difference in their ages and, like her, he was interested in art and music and literature. Like her, too, he had very little money, existing on his half-pay as a naval lieutenant. He had supplemented his pay on Bertie's state visit to india by sending back illustrations for the *Illustrated London News* and been elected as Honorary Member of the Institute of Painters in Water Colours. He also played the piano very well. She had seen him as a dashing, carefree young naval officer, completely dedicated to his career. The unexpected sensitivity added to his attraction and she was happy to welcome him as a friend.

On their ride in the Park, she smiled and laughed listening to his stories of his life in the Navy. As an aide to his other uncle, Prince Alfred, he had visited Monaco, where they had been joined by Bertie. They had taken him to the casino at Monte Carlo and he had been partly fascinated and partly horrified at the bets placed on the roulette tables, each more than he earned in a year. When Uncle Bertie had twitted him on his lack of courage, he had put his only two gold louis coins on the red. It had won and he left it there. Red came up nine times and he had had to use a hotel towel as a sack to carry his winnings to the bank.

Lillie laughed, but she was thinking of Bertie. Obviously, he had gone back to Paris to see Sarah or Jeanne de Sagan or even some unknown who had caught his fancy. She was not distressed. She had seen the signs and been expecting it. Funny, she thought, I know exactly how Alix feels. It did not make her any less fond of Bertie. Although she had never fully loved him and always been slightly afraid of him, she was very fond of him. He had helped her through the Rosenberg scandal, but now was slipping away. 'Chère amie,' he had begun to call her in Paris, no longer 'my dearest.' She forced her attention back to Louis. He was telling her how he had been with the British fleet sent by Disraeli to stop the Russians from taking Constantinople, the excitement of the day their ironclads had steamed up the Bosphorus and anchored between the Turkish and Russian armies. His brother Sandro, now Alexander I of Rumania, had been with the Russians. Strange. He, Lieutenant Prince Louis of Battenberg, had gone ashore and paid his respects to his brother and to the Russian commander, Grand Duke Nicholas, in his tent.

That evening, Louis partnered Lillie at a ball, at Alfred de Rothschild's and next day he took her in to dinner at the Hamilton's. He called for her to ride in the morning and escorted her to lunch with Alexandra in Marlborough House. Gladstone was there, with his wife, Catherine. The old Liberal was once again prime minister after the surprising defeat of Disraeli's Conservatives in the General Election. The Queen had been violently opposed to appointing him and angered that Hartington would not accept the post. Hartington had had no choice but to stand aside and let Gladstone resume the leadership of the Liberals. If he had not, he knew that Gladstone would deliberately split the party, as Bertie had explained to his mother. There was no sign of the ruthless politician in the gentle old man who sat at the table, still touchingly grateful for the letter of congratulations she had sent him.

After lunch, she had walked in the gardens of Marlborough House with Louis and he confessed that he had been deputised to squire her by Uncle Bertie, to make sure she was not lonely. 'I had guessed that,' she told him.

It had cost him a great deal to make the confession, but he had felt dishonest. 'I look on it not as a duty, but as a privilege,' he said. 'And as a pleasure.'

'I am glad,' she smiled.

They were in a long arbour of Russian vine, screened for the moment from the others. Louis seemed unable to look at her. 'I had to tell you,' he said. 'I should have told Uncle Bertie that I was the wrong person to trust – since I would wish to see you on my own behalf, not on his.' Lillie was not certain what he meant, until he looked at her. 'At the risk of you forbidding me to see you again, I – I cannot see you under false pretences.'

Although they were so close in age, Lillie felt much older. She was used to men swearing devotion to her and smiled and teased them. She did not smile at Louis. 'You must not say anything you would regret,' she warned him gently.

She made to walk on, but he stopped her. 'No, please. Even if I never have another chance, I must tell you that I love you. That I have never loved anyone else, and never shall.'

Alexandra came into sight with Charlotte Knollys and the three little princesses who ran laughing to Lillie. As usual, Alix was surrounded by at least half a dozen dogs and they ran, too, barking and frisking, until it seemed there was a small menagerie round Lillie and Louis and she laughed, beginning to play tag with the dogs and children.

In the late afternoon, Lillie was sitting quietly at home, when Dominique showed in William Gladstone. Lillie had not been expecting him. She had been thinking about Louis, aware of a mixture of feelings and trying to decide what to do. For his sake.

'I can see you are occupied,' Gladstone said. 'I apologise for intruding.'

'Oh, no, it was only a foolish thought,' Lillie smiled. 'It is I who should apologise. Let me ring for some tea.'

'Thank you, but I cannot stay.' Gladstone declined. 'Much as I would like to, dear Mrs Langtry. No, I only came to give you this.' He handed her a slip of paper. Drawn on it were the Greek alpha and omega signs, interlocked. 'I would ask you to memorise it and not reveal it to anyone else.' Lillie did not understand. 'It is a private cipher I have devised,' Gladstone explained. 'If you are ever in need, if you ever require my assistance in any matter, you may write to me in complete confidence by drawing that cipher on the envelope. Enclose the envelope inside another and, when any of my secretaries perceive it, the envelope inside will be passed immediately to me, unopened.'

Lillie thanked him sincerely. She could not imagine what she had done to be given the honour of direct access to the Prime Minister, yet here he was, offering to be her adviser and protector. He would not accept thanks. As he went on, she realised that he thought it was through her persuasion that Bertie had spoken in his favour to the Queen. Certainly, she had discussed the inevitability of Harty Tarty's resignation with him, but that was all. She was about to tell Gladstone that, when she changed her mind. The devious old man was not making a simple, generous gesture. Because of Queen Victoria's antagonism to him, he urgently needed friends at Court and was ensuring that Lillie would continue to use whatever influence she had on his behalf. It was part of the pattern. He liked and admired her, but was ready to use her. Then he must be prepared to be used in his turn, Lillie thought. She smiled. 'I am sure you overestimate the little I have done, sir, but I am deeply sensible of the honour you have done me. I shall try to use it sparingly.'

'Oh, not too sapringly, I hope, dear Mrs Langtry,' Gladstone smiled. 'I trust, indeed, that you will find time to write me a line or two, now and then, just to say you are well. That would cheer me. And any little piece of news that might help me in my task would be welcome.'

Lillie smiled after he left, folded the paper with the cipher and put it in the secret drawer of her writing table. It would not often be useful to her, but it might be extremely useful to Bertie to have a safe channel of communication with the Prime Minister. Holding the key to it made her feel much more secure.

Gladstone had offered to act as her adviser. The one question on which she needed advice at this moment was one he was least qualified to judge.

In spite of being, perhaps, the most famous woman in the country next to Alexandra and the Queen, she was very alone. She knew her few real friends. The rest who fluttered round her, thinking themselves all the time vastly superior, were nonentities with money and titles. The men who professed to adore her kept at a distance, afraid of Bertie. Edward was usually absent on his interminable fishing trips. Moreton Frewen had finally given up and gone to America, to raise cattle in Wyoming. She was not certain if Bertie would return to her in any positive sense. Arthur . . . She had not heard from him. She had enjoyed these few days with Prince Louis in attendance, courteous and amusing. In a world of handsome men, he was outstandingly goodlooking, with his blue eyes and slim figure and surprisingly shy smile. She suddenly thought of Michel, the half-brother she had fallen in love with all those years ago. How many years, since she last thought of him?

Just as suddenly, she realised she would have to be very careful with Louis. The lesson she had learnt was that survival was the greatest talent. And that most people were willing to let themselves be used, even enjoyed it. Louis was one of the few she would not wish to use.

That night, she went to the Lyceum with the Dudleys and he came to their box. She smiled and he asked Georgiana's permission to stay. Afterwards, they joined a select group with Henry Irving and Ellen Terry. Nelly had proved almost as much of a draw as Irving, himself, and they had become inseparable in the public's mind, as in their own. It was fascinating to see how courteously Irving treated her and how charmingly Nelly responded, both respecting each other's position, and quite unmistakably falling in love. At least, my private life is not such a muddle as Nelly's, Lillie thought. At least, I can control my emotions. Louis saw her home and kissed her hand at the door. She was touched.

Next day, Bertie returned from Paris and Alix told him she was worried that Louis might be developing an infatuation for Lillie. He chuckled. 'Why not? Why not?' It was the first hint Alix had that his heart was free again, and roving. At almost the same moment, Lillie was in Patsy's boudoir in Eaton Place, impatient and waiting to speak to her privately.

Patsy had put on a little weight and was trying on a new corset, a new one-piece garment in rose satin stiffened with strips of steel alternating with whalebone, encasing her from her plump breasts to the tops of her thighs. Under it she wore a filmy chemise and silk drawers. 'Oh, it's all right for you, Lillie,' she gasped, as her maid hauled on the tapes to compress her waist still further. 'That'll do! You'll cut me in half,' Patsy said, and the maid looped the tapes round the metal tags at the back, crisscrossed them deftly and tied them. Patsy passed her hands down her ribs and waist to her hips, grimacing when she felt the bulge of her thighs under the corset's lower edge. The maid brought her negligee. 'For pity's sake, fetch me a glass of water,' Patsy said.

The maid hurried out and Lillie seized the chance to tell Patsy what was troubling her, that she found herself attracted to Louis.

'Why not?' Patsy laughed, almost exactly like Bertie. 'Has he made advances?'

'No, nothing like that,' Lillie explained. 'It's serious. I'm trying not to see too much of him.'

Patsy was tying the sash of her negligee. She sat and rose again almost at once, as the rigid corset dug into her thighs. 'Well, you can hardly avoid it during Cowes Week,' she observed. 'With both of you on the Osborne.'

'I'm on the Suffields' yacht this year,' Lillie said.

'Too bad,' Patsy sympathised, and smiled. 'I hope he can swim.'

Before she left for Cowes, Lillie had a surprise visit from her parents. Her father was tired after the journey and went to lie down. Lillie was too keen to hear news of the island to notice the strain her mother was under, at first. Yes, Mrs Le Breton told her, Arthur was well. He had got in with some rowdy company at the Victoria Sporting Club, but had settled down again. There had been some talk of him with one of the Price or Courtney girls, but it had come to nothing. All at once, she sobbed and covered her mouth.

'What is it? What's wrong?' Lillie asked, concerned.

'It's your father,' Mrs Le Breton whispered. 'He's been dismissed . . . told to leave the island.' The scandal over the Dean's womanising had come to a head and the Parish Council had demanded his removal. To preserve the good name of Jersey, William Corbet Le Breton could retain the title of Dean to his death, on condition he did not return. His salary would be paid to the vice-Dean, who would take over his duties. Mrs Le Breton had only come to help him to find suitable accommodation, then she was going to leave him and go back to the island.

Lillie had more understanding of her father now, and more sympathy with his weakness. But his lack of discretion angered her. He was a fool to make everything so obvious. She was relieved, at least, that his dismissal was to be kept a secret.

Lord Charles Beresford was Commander now of the ironclad H.M.S. *Thunderer*, which was stationed off Cowes during the week of the regatta. She was one of the newest warships and he was proud of her, when he showed round his friends the Prince and Princess of Wales and party. Prince Louis was with the group and joined Bertie in congratulating his former commander on her immaculate condition. They inspected everything, from her enginerooms to her hydraulically-operated guns.

While tea was being served on the upper deck, Alexandra mentioned how much space there was compared to most of the yachts, which were often too cramped for dancing. Beresford took up her suggestion and proposed an impromptu dance on *Thunderer*. He could telegraph the yachts for their friends to come on board. The Marine Band could play and the ship's cooks provide refreshments. While the preparations were made, Beresford suggested, the ladies might care to rest in the quarters of the ship's officers, who could entertain the gentlemen in the wardroom. Alexandra and the other ladies were conducted down to the cabins below the waterline, small but comfortable, with fresh air pumped down to them through ventilation shafts.

Lillie was escorted by Prince Louis. She had been subdued when she arrived at Cowes, after hearing of her father's disgrace. He was a changed man and seemed to have lost all his fire and authority. The final destruction of her childhood idol.

In the exhilarating atmosphere of the regatta, her spirits had revived. Louis had been waiting ardently for her and made no secret of it. She felt herself responding to him and stayed at a slight distance, anxious for him. She did not want to come between him and Bertie. Slowly, however, she began to realise that Bertie himself was pushing them together, delighted to see their growing affection. Bertie did not wish to lose Lillie's companionship, although he no longer felt exclusively bound to her. At the same time, he wanted her to be happy. An affaire between Louis and her, mutually desired, keeping them both in the immediate circle, was the ideal solution. Lillie's misgivings vanished and Louis became her constant companion at all the parties and dances, sailing with her, talking and laughing with her, not hiding his feelings. And Lillie knew she was falling in love. She fought against it. It was too pat. An attractive, romantic figure, he had appeared from nowhere when she was alone and needed someone. She knew that was why she had responded to him, but she could not help it. And what she felt for him she had never felt before, a tenderness, not the passionate reassurance she had needed from Arthur, nor the pride she had known in capturing Bertie, but a true, gentle joy at being with him, to be able to hear his voice and see him smile. Over the days, it was exciting to find out each other's likes and dislikes, the many points of agreement, to become absorbed in each other's lives. They had not made love, but that did not matter. Just to touch hands, to kiss in the shadow of the deck when goodnights were said was enough.

Lillie entered the cabin on *Thunderer*. She took off her hat and turned. Louis had followed her in and closed the door. The cabin was warm and silent, except for the soft pulse of the air pump. The silence stretched on for a long moment and Lillie, seeing how he looked at her, knew the time had come. 'Hadn't you better lock the door?' she said.

Louis snapped the bronze catch shut. When he looked round she was already undoing her dress and he hurried to help her. He was excited and nervous suddenly and his hands were clumsy. Lillie smiled and stopped him. 'I – I wanted – ' he began.

'I know,' she said. 'Will they come to look for you?'

His throat was dry. 'I don't think so.'

She smiled again and slowly undid the buttons of his uniform jacket. She was like a handmaiden. When he was undressed, he was not embarrassed, as he thought he would be. All she wore was a light summer dress over a linen petticoat and gauzy underthings, because of the heat. She stepped out of them. Her silk stockings were the palest ivory, gartered high on her thighs, almost matching her skin. Without her shoes, she was shorter, only reaching his chin, when he took her in his arms.

The single bed was bolted to the metal floor. They sank on to it and he held her tightly, suddenly eager and demanding, but she made him restrain himself, and hold back, and hold back, until both their minds were swirling and the universe contracted and expanded around them. When it ended, they were limp, their lips numbed with the length of their last, desperate kiss to prevent each other from crying out. Smiling, marvelling at each other, in the warm drowsiness they fell asleep.

Bertie had left the wardroom after a token brandy with the junior officers and walked round the deck with Beresford and Charles Carrington. They had enjoyed many exploits together. He did not miss Louis for some time and, when he did, paused with one hand on the taffrail, realising where he must be. He frowned and drew on his cigar. Well, he thought, bound to happen sometime.

'Has Your Royal Highness observed that Lieutenant Prince Louis is not with us?' Bereford said. Bertie nodded. 'No doubt you are aware, sir, where he might be.'

'Good luck to them,' Carrington said.

'Exactly, Charlie,' Bertie agreed.

'Nevertheless, not the best of form,' Beresford drawled.

Bertie chuckled. 'He could hardly ask the Captain's permission.'

'Hardly, sir,' Beresford conceded. 'Nonetheless, I have ventured to make a slight gesture of reprimand.'

'How so?' Bertie asked.

'The cabins below the waterline are ventilated by a hydraulic system. I have made things . . . a trifle hot for Lieutenant Prince Louis, by switching off the ventilation to Mrs Langtry's cabin.'

Bertie and Carrington stared at him, then started to laugh. Beresford joined in and their laughter sent the gulls perching round the stern squawking and fluttering in alarm.

It was fortunate that Lillie woke. The cabin had been warm before and now it was like an oven. Her head was swimming and she found it difficult to breathe. Louis lay beside her, inert, as if he had been drugged, his arm heavy across her body. They felt fused together by a film of sweat. She was drifting off to sleep again and fought against it. Something was wrong. She suddenly knew what it was. She could not hear the sound of the air pump and the oxygen in the little, metal room was nearly used up. She could not rouse Louis. Pushing his arm off her, she managed to get out of bed, stumbled to the door, unbolted it and wrenched it open.

Colder air flooded into the room and she leant on the handle gasping. She was wearing only her stockings, rumpled to her knees, and at any moment someone might pass. She heard Louis mutter as the fresh air revived him. She closed the door and hurried to pull him to his feet, so that he could dress and see to the pump.

The story of Beresford's joke went round all the yachts and everyone laughed, not knowing the names of the couple involved, nor how nearly it had become a tragedy.

What had happened was only the beginning for Lillie and Louis. It was impossible for them to be together, yet they could not exist apart. They had to spend some time alone with each other, to be sure of what they really felt. There was one obvious place they could go, but Lillie was reluctant to take Louis there. He did not care. His love for her dwarfed every other thought and, after Cowes, with only Dominique to look after them, they went to The Red House.

They had nearly two weeks that were so perfect neither could ever forget a moment of them. Lillie need not have been anxious. After the first hour in the house, she thought of no one else. No ghosts came to spoil their idyll. On the last evening, she sat with Louis on her balcony, watching the high, drifting clouds above the trees turn from white to salmon to fire and fade slowly, as the sunset faded, to a dark mauve tinged with smoky grey. Even the birds had fallen silent after their sunset song. This time, when Louis said he loved her, she confessed her own love, half afraid to speak the words, but smiling, too, when he laughed with happiness and drew her to him.

It was August, when they returned to London, Lillie to Norfolk Street and Louis to Marlborough House. Bertie was glad to have them back. It had been a most enjoyable season, capped by his yacht *Formosa* winning the Queen's Cup at the Cowes Regatta. He had his sons with him, too, back from their training voyage. Both boys adored Lillie, especially the elder, handsome, sleepy-eyed Eddy, who was now sixteen. She had bought each a little silver trinket at a jeweller's shop in Cowes. Eddy had taken off his grandmother's picture locket to make room for it on his watchchain. Like father, like son, Bertie thought, smiling, but he hoped the Queen would not notice her locket had gone. The boys were due to go off on another training voyage, this time lasting two years, and Alexandra was upset at the thought of losing them for so long. Lillie and Louis always cheered her up and he was determined to have them both with them, when they went north to Abergeldie, even if it meant taking the unprepossessing Edward Langtry as well.

However, there was something on Louis' mind. He was often silent and preoccupied, only coming alive in Lillie's company, detached and thoughtful again when she had gone. As bad a case as ever I've seen, Bertie thought. Others were beginning to notice. Bertie's youngest sister, Beatrice, had her eye on Louis, herself, and was becoming quite jealous. After a ball at Marlborough House for Alexandra's brother, Willy, the King of Greece, he decided to give Louis some advice. Lillie had looked particularly enchanting that night, but her husband had been with her for once and Louis had had no chance to see her home. He had let his disappointment show far too obviously. When everyone had gone, Bertie took him into his study, where they would be quite private, for a last brandy. He made the invitation quite casually. He had never spoken to his nephew about Lillie and did not want to give the wrong impression. He did not disapprove of their liaison, but if a whisper of it reached the Queen, she would be stricken, and furious.

In fact, it was Louis who broached the subject, apologising for his distraction of late. 'I can't help it, Uncle Bertie,' he said. 'I've never been so in love.' Bertie handed him his glass and smiled, understandingly. 'You don't mind?'

'In the circumstances, I'd be the last person to,' Bertie assured him. 'However . . . for both your sakes, you must be more discreet.'

'That's the problem,' Louis said. 'I can't hide how I feel any longer.' He was silent for a time. 'You see, we're going to be married.'

Bertie was pouring his own brandy and his hand jerked, nearly spilling it. Gently, he told himself, gently . . . 'How can you?' he pointed out. 'She's already married.'

'She's going to ask her husband for a divorce.'

Bertie replaced the stopper in the decanter, surprised that his fingers were so steady. 'So you've discussed this with Lillie?'

'Over and over,' Louis said. 'I made her see it's the only answer.'

'Then, she wasn't entirely in favour?'

'Not at first,' Louis admitted. He felt encouraged. This was a moment he had dreaded, but Uncle Bertie was taking it much more mildly than he had feared. 'She thinks her husband might not agree to a divorce.'

'She's right,' Bertie murmured. 'I'd imagine it extremely unlikely. And what about your parents?'

'I wrote to them at the beginning of the week. We decided to do nothing, until I'd heard from them.'

Thank heavens for that, Bertie thought. He saw Louis smile to him briefly, shyly. Poor boy . . . So much in love. He sat in the leather chair by the fire and waved to Louis to take the one opposite. 'No one could understand more easily how you could feel about – about Mrs Langtry as you do,' he said. 'No one could be more pleased than myself that you are happy together.'

'Thank you,' Louis smiled. 'Naturally, I wondered – ' Bertie shook his head. 'She is the most perfect woman in the world, Uncle Bertie.'

'Close to it. Very close.'

'I never knew – never dreamt of anyone so perfect.'

Bertie nodded. 'Well, I'm not going to talk about public reaction, scandal, or even what the Queen will say. I suppose you've thought of that? But what are you going to live on? If you marry a divorced woman, you'll have to resign your commission.'

Louis was very serious. 'I realise that.'

Bertie grunted, covering his surprise. 'Well, I'm glad you've told me, and that you've done nothing hasty.' His brandy glass had warmed in his hand and he sniffed the aroma. 'I don't see your parents accepting it, Louis.'

'Because I'm . . . marrying beneath me? My father was accused of that, himself.'

'Yes, but your mother was a countess, and unattached. However, that's all academic.' Bertie said. 'I don't think there's a ghost of a chance of Langtry giving her a divorce.'

'He would have to,' Louis told him, quite simply. 'If Lillie and I lived together openly.' He was prepared to give up everything for her, his social position, career, friends and family, everything. 'If he still will not agree, then I would resign from the Navy and we would go to live in France or Italy. Anywhere, as long as we can be together.'

Great God Almighty, Bertie thought, it's even worse than I suspected.

Lillie had spent the week, since Louis had told her his decision, in a state of mingled joy and anxiety. Whatever happened, she was finished with ned, she knew that. Louis and she were so suited in spirit and temperament. His royalty sat lightly on him. She had no fear of him as she had of Bertie, even now. The tenderness of their love for each other grew with each meeting. Each day she felt a quiet happiness just to think of him. Yet she knew that what they were going to do would create a storm, and that they would be condemned. She, most of all. She was prepared to accept it for his sake. But then, she had little to lose. And would be giving up her present, uncertain life for one filled with love, a horde of friends in name for a man who would cherish her for ever.

She expected Louis to call, the morning after the ball. Instead, Dominique announced the Prince of Wales. She saw at once that something was wrong.

'You know why I'm here? he asked. She was taut, standing as he often remembered her, with the light from the window burnishing her hair.

'I think so, sir,' she said.

'Oh, come now, my dear, no need to be formal.' He wished there were some other way to break it. 'This business with Louis. It's not possible, you realise.' He saw her sudden pallor and was afraid she was going to faint. 'Here, come. Come and sit here.' He took her arm and sat her beside him on the sofa. 'I take it you're genuinely attached to him?'

It was unfair, Lillie thought. Louis said they would face him together, face everyone together. 'Very,' she said quietly.

Bertie took her hand and pressed it. 'And he to you, I know. We spoke for hours last night.' He sighed. 'I tried to make him understand. If you left your husband to live with him, you'd be shunned by everyone. I couldn't even receive you, myself. He would have to give up his career. He has no money. You'd have nothing to live on. His parents won't give him an allowance.'

'He's heard from them?' Lillie whispered.

'This morning. They say they'd have nothing more to do with him.' He felt the slight tremor in her body through her hand. 'Apart from that, there's the Queen. She would be deeply distressed. These are all other people, I know. And love is selfish, when it comes to the feelings of other people. But I want you to think of the effect on Louis. H'm?'

She had looked away, and turned back, forcing herself to concentrate. Her head felt light, her mind empty.

'It's not because it's you,' Bertie went on. 'Not only that. Louis' life is mapped out – a career in the Service, rising inevitably to the highest rank, a royal marriage, a respected and honoured future. He's known that all his life. The Navy has *been* his life. If he threw his future away to live with you, scraping a living somewhere abroad, you'd have a few months of happiness, no doubt, then the cancer of disappointment and regret would eat it away. And he could never return, neither could you. You'd end up bitter at the world, or hating each other. And that is as inevitable, and as certain as that he loves you now.'

He had thought she might cry, but Lillie's voice was completely unemotional. 'What does he want me to do?' she asked.

'He doesn't know I'm here.'

Her eyes searched his face.

'He wouldn't listen to me,' Bertie told her. 'Wouldn't see reason. You're the only one who can make him do that. You're sensible and practical. A romance like yours is for storybooks. It has no place in real life. You must make him see that.' He paused. 'I can depend on you?'

'Yes,' Lillie said.

'Good . . . Good!' Bertie kissed her hand and smiled. 'It needn't be so bad. You can still be friends. No one can object to that. It can go on as long as you wish, and end when you wish, without upsetting anyone. Perfectly civilised. I'll never understand why those young men won't be content with that.'

No, Lillie thought, you'll never understand.

She did not know how she lived through the hours till she met Louis. Nor how she lived through that meeting.

Louis applied for an immediate return to active service and was posted to a frigate in the squadron escorting the two young Princes, Eddy and George. Before the end of the month, he set off with them on their training cruise that was to circle the world. They would be gone for two years.

# CHAPTER FIFTEEN

Lillie did not go with Bertie and Alexandra when they spent September in Scotland. It was noticed. It had also been noticed that she had been less in the Prince of Wales's company in recent months and bills began to be presented again. Since Edward could not pay them, she ignored them, until Mrs Stratton and others among the dressmakers informed her politely that they could supply no further orders, unless something was paid on account, at least. She talked Ned into going to Belfast to appeal to his brother, but it was a wasted journey. The Langtry shipping line was not doing well and a disastrous harvest meant that rents from their Irish properties could not be collected. There was nothing to spare. Edward went on a shooting holiday, leaving Lillie to handle their creditors, alone.

The season was extended that year. So many royal visitors were passing through town that Bertie and Alexandra returned to Marlborough House at the end of September. By that time, the trickle of bills arriving at Norfolk Street had become a deluge. The cook and extra maid had been dismissed. The brougham and coachhorse which Edward had bought in a grandiose mood after his presentation to the Queen had been seized. During the day, Dominique had to scout the street for debtcollectors before Lillie went out.

Only Dominique and Patsy had seen her sadness after Louis left. She had never been nearer despair. For long hours she sat alone, remembering his stricken face when she told him she could not run away with him. At least, he had realised why. He had not thought it was cowardice, nor because she did not love him. He had held her and kissed her and she had nearly weakened, but she could not accept the sacrifice of his career and his future. And he had honoured her for it, although it broke his heart.

In the weeks that had followed, she went over that day again and again. Had she really given up for his sake, or did Bertie know her even better than she did herself? She loved Louis. He was the only man who had ever been prepared to sacrifice himself for her, who did not demand more of her than he would give, himself. But could she have lived in poverty and disgrace with him? She despised herself for not being able to answer. Although she knew the answer. The threat of poverty terrified her.

On an evening in early October, she was at a ball at Grosvenor House, held by the Duchess of Wesminster. She wore a gown of white satin, with white satin dance slippers, and the diamond necklace and bracelets the Prince had given her. Both Bertie and Alexandra were there and agreed with the old Duchess that she had seldom looked lovelier, her beauty paler and more refined. The men who clustered round her were drawn by the mysterious, detached quality she had that was not quite coldness, an aloof, challenging watchfulness that would suddenly be transformed by a smile which dazzled everyone who saw it. That night, she danced and flirted and responded to compliments but there were few smiles. Surrounded by power and talent, by wealth and nobility, she was more conscious than ever of how vulnerable she was. Not only vulnerable, but useless, fit only to dress up and be admired. At home she had a drawer full of bills, yet had agonised before coming out because she had already worn this dress twice. It was ridiculous.

She became more and more withdrawn. All at once, she felt she was here under false pretences. She had sworn never again to be dependent on anyone. Yet she was only here because of the patience of the tradesmen to whom she owed money. Her extravagance had become colossal and she had taken no thought of how it was to be paid for, and by whom. Certainly, not by Edward. Many others she knew worked hard to make their name and their living, Oscar, Jimmy, Millais, Swinburne, all worked constantly. And some of her women friends, Ouida, the novelist, and Ellen Terry. While she did and was nothing, a parasite.

On the wall near her was Reynolds's great painting of the actress, Sarah Siddons, as *The Tragic Muse*. She had been looking at it for some time. She excused herself to the group she was with and left the ballroom, without even saying goodnight to the Prince and Princess or to her hostess. She pushed through the knot of footmen, all eager to be the one to call her carriage or a cab, and walked out into the night. Oblivious of the rain and the mud that spattered her dress and ruined her stain slippers, she hurried up Park Lane and home to Norfolk Street.

She could not have stood another minute of the ball. She was unsettled, almost feverish, and Dominique was sure she had caught a chill walking home. In bed, Lillie could not sleep. Thoughts of Louis, of her husband, of the disastrous financial position she was in tortured her. She was totally defenceless and alone. She would not degrade herself by appealing to Bertie. Nor blame anyone but herself. Her mother was living with friends in Jersey, her father in charge of a poor parish in Marylebone. They could not help her either. There was a simple way out, she knew, but she would not take it. There were man, many men, each of them willing to become her protector, on any terms she wished to set. But she would not sell herself, to become a kept woman. She had sworn never to be dependent on anyone again. It was easy to swear, but what could she do? Her friend Edmund Yates, the editor and novelist, had mentioned her difficulties to Henry Irving. Irving was about to revive the old melodrama, *The Lyons Mail*, and Nelly had refused the female lead, who was required to do little except look poised and beautiful. Lillie had often told him how she admired and envied Nelly and Sarah and wished she could have been an actress. To her astonishment, he had offered her the part. It was not sheer generosity. He was certain that curiosity would draw audiences to see her. It was flattering and tempting, yet just as drastic a step as the other. No lady from society had ever appeared professionally in the theatre.

The next day was a Sunday and at dinner in Marlborough House, she apologised to Bertie and Alexandra for leaving the ball. She had to explain a little of what had been troubling her and told them of Irving's offer.

They and the other guests were shocked, although Bertie laughed and Alexandra was excited. 'But how thrilling, Lillie!' she said. 'Will you accept?'

Lillie smiled. 'I really don't think I can, Ma'am. Apart from anything else, I would be far too nervous. Although I was tempted.'

'I'm not surprised,' Alexandra answered. 'So would I be.'

Everyone laughed and the conversation moved on. Lillie was relieved. She was feeling feverish again, and light-headed, and it was an effort to appear bright and relaxed.

Bertie was talking to Charles Dilke, the Radical and former, convinced Republican, now a member of Gladstone's government. The two had begun to forge a friendship of considerable mutual value. Acceptance by the Prince was helping Dilke to overcome some of the prejudice against him caused by his republicanism, which he had now abandoned. In return, as Under-Secretary for Foreign Affairs, he was able to give Bertie information privately, so that his secret diplomatic work had a more positive result. Bertie had already decided to use his influence on Gladstone to make sure that Dilke was promoted to the cabinet as soon as possible.

They were discussing the new border of Greece and Turkey, a continual problem for his brother in law, the King of Greece, when Charlotte Knollys noticed that Lillie was swaying in her seat and attracted Alexandra's attention.

'My dear Lillie, are you quite well?' Alexandra asked.

Lillie had had a sudden wave of nausea and felt herself go faint. 'I'm – I'm sorry, Ma'am,' she panted. 'It's only a dizzy spell.'

'You don't look at all well. Does she, Bertie?'

Lillie was on Bertie's left and he took her arm, concerned, as she leant on the table for support. 'Perhaps you'd better lie down, my dear,' he suggested.

She managed to smile. 'I'm sorry, sir. I think, if you'll excuse me, I should go home.'

'We can't let you go alone,' Bertie said. Everyone was

watching them.

There was a moment's awkwardness and Alexandra ended it. 'Lillie shall have my carriage. Now, no arguments. You go straight home to bed.'

Dominique had scarecely helped Lillie to undress, when the doorbell rang. It was Francis Laking, the Household Physician, sent by Alexandra to make certain that she was all right. The nausea had gone and Lillie told him she felt much better. Dr Laking, a capable, courtly man, smiled. 'Nevertheless, I think I'd better examine you, Mrs Langtry,' he said. 'Otherwise, Her Royal Highness would never forgive me.' His examination was short, but thorough.

The following afternoon, Lillie lay on the sofa in the drawingroom, when Dominique came to her with un-disguised excitement and showed in Princess Alexandra. Lillie began to rise, but Alexandra stopped her. 'No, no, no, Lillie. Don't disturb yourself. I've only come to see how you're getting on.'

It was not strictly true. Alix had never visited Norfolk Street before and had to admit an overpowering curiosity to see where Lillie lived. She exclaimed over the gilded fans and the Whistler ceiling, the blue and white china bowls that were presents from Oscar. It was so petite and charm-ing, she could appreciate why Bertie with his sense of style had loved it.

It was nearly teatime and Dominique brought in tea-things and a teapot, then the kettle. Again Lillie was going to rise, but Alexandra insisted on making tea for them, herself. As she added the boiling water, she said, 'I was quite worried about you last night. So was Bertie.'

'You are very kind, Ma'am,' Lillie said quietly. She was touched by Alexandra coming to see her.

'Not a bit,' Alix smiled. 'My little boys would be incon-solable, if I had to write and tell them that Mrs Langtry was unwell.'

Lillie was grateful. Alix and Bertie's letters to the young Princes were a means of keeping in indirect touch with Louis. At least, they had news of each other. Alexandra

410

poured her a cup of tea. As she put it on the little table beside her, Lillie smelt the violet perfume which Alix had made specially for herself. 'The scent of violets always makes me think of you, Ma'am,' she said.

'Perhaps I shouldn't have worn it today,' Alix said. 'It's too strong for you, is it?'

'Not at all,' Lillie assured her. 'I'm very fond of it.'

'So am I,' Alix nodded. 'Only, I remember from my own experience, that little things like that can be upsetting for someone in your condition.'

And Lillie knew that Laking had reported to the Prince and Princess the news that had shocked her last night, although it was only confirmation of what she had feared and been refusing to believe. He had confirmed that she was over three months pregnant.

There was no doubt who was the father. She had not slept with Edward for over two years. Louis was the only man who had made love to her in these months. She had always taken precautions, particularly in the dangerous period of the month. The only time she had not was that afternoon on the *Thunderer*, when it had been forgotten in the heat and excitement.

It was a few days before her twenty-seventh birthday. She was pregnant, nearly bankrupt, and alone.

Bertie came to see her that evening. Alexandra and he were moving shortly to Sandringham and he wanted to reassure himself about her. Privately, he gave thanks that Louis had not heard she was to have a baby, or he would never have gone. They decided it would be unfair to tell him. At any rate, not just now. His squadron was en route for South America and there was no point in distressing him, since there was nothing he could do.

After Louis, the thing that made her most anxious was that Edward should not know. She was determined to have the baby. However, the law allowed Edward to claim it as his own and take it away from her. He was quite capable of it, especially as it would ingratiate him with his family. Her pregnancy would soon begin to show. She could not have a legal separation from him at this moment, in case news of her condition leaked out. Somehow, she had to get away from him, or he had to be removed, for at least four to five months, which seemed impossible.

Bertie arranged to speak to George Lewis, the solicitor, before he left. He was troubled about her. In her need, all his affection for her revived, but she would accept no further help. She told him she was perfectly well and could manage. In one way, he agreed that she was right. The less they were seen together now, the less chance of damaging scandal. He set off for Sandringham, telling her to send word at once, if she needed him.

George Lewis became Lillie's guardian angel. He arrived at Norfolk Street a few days later, hearing that Edward had at last come home.

Edward was nearly in a state of shock. The bills had continued to be presented in his absence and he had not a penny with which to pay them. Even those friends of Bertie's and Lillie's who had quite liked him or taken pity on him would do nothing for him any more. His self pity and drinking had alienated them all. But Lewis asked to see him on a business matter. He was trying to trace the descendants of members of a Devon family, he said, who had emigrated to America. And he needed someone with some legal training to go to the United States at once to carry out discreet enquiries. He had thought of Edward, as someone he could trust. There would be expenses, a reasonable fee and the probability of a bonus.

Edward could not believe his luck. It would be the first work he had ever done, but it was respectable, interesting and well within his capabilities. He jumped at it, explaining to Lillie rather grandly that he knew she would be disappointed, but he would be unable to take her with him. Lewis had stressed that it was not a pleasure trip and must not be looked on as a holiday for himself and Mrs Langtry. Lillie would have to stay behind, even though he would probably be gone for several months.

Dominique and she helped him to pack and she said goodbye to him, with the greatest sense of gratitude to George Lewis. Lewis would not say where the money for the trip had come from, but she knew it was from Bertie.

As soon as he left for New York, the sheriff's officers moved in. The patience of the shopkeepers, couturiers and tradesmen had run out and nothing could not stop Edward being declared bankrupt. Lillie had to face the shame of having bailiffs living in the house. She had followed Patsy's advice and copied Jimmy Whistler. Most of her best jewellery was already at Patsy's. Not all of it, or that would look suspicious. And friends who called often left with 'presents' to keep for her. Oscar walked blandly out past the bailiffs in the hall one day with a silver tray stuffed up under his waistcoat.

The house was to be repossessed and the contents auctioned. She had nowhere to go and George Lewis came again to her rescue. He and his wife had a villa near the river at Walton-on-Thames and they gave her refuge there. Very few people knew where she had gone and there was much speculation in the newspapers, in England and abroad. Oscar was one who knew and invited himself to stay for the weekend, bringing a copy of *The New York Times*, which carried an article under the headline, RETIREMENT OF MRS LANGTRY FROM SOCIETY. No one but the Lewises and Dr Laking new the reason for her 'retirement' and Oscar was concerned to find her in bed when he arrived, confined there by Laking's orders because of the strain.

The newspaper stories brought another unexpected visitor to London. A letter from him was forwarded to her, saying he had come officially to see his father, but really to see her. Arthur Jones.

It was the strangest sensation to hear from him. So much had happened since Lillie had last seen him, he seemed part of another world. She still felt very close to him, yet it was difficult to arrange a meeting. She had quickly realised that the Lewises thought the Prince of Wales was the father of her child. It was one of the reasons for their respectful care of her. But it also made Lewis extremely protective and, after Oscar's visit, he insisted that no one else should be told she was at the villa or soon half the fashionable set would start turning up. Lillie was grateful to him and had to agree.

She wrote to Arthur and arranged to meet him by the bridge over the Thames in the early afternoon, when Lewis was at his office in town.

Artie had not changed. He was as frank and open as ever, deeply worried about her financial troubles and her problems in the reported collapse of her marriage. He did not suspect, nor did she tell him, that she was pregnant. Portelet House was his now. If he could sell it to help her, he would, he told her, but there were no buyers at this time of the year. It was already let for the autumn and that was all the money he had. Lillie was moved to discover that he still cared so much for her. The slight awkwardness there had been between them at first vanished, and they talked of the island and friends and her garden at the House.

He came to see her every day, still in secret, and she looked forward to their meetings more and more. With Louis half the world away and out of reach for ever, George Lewis and his wife treating her kindly, yet also as an embarrassment to be kept hidden, her attachment to Arthur was renewed, not romantically, nor passionately, but out of a genuine affection. Finally, she had to tell him the true reason why she was living here in seclusion, that she was to have a baby that was not Edward's.

They had stopped by a group of trees bent over the river, their branches almost bare. There was no sign of the drenching rain that had ruined the harvests and the late Autumn weather was warm and perfect. 'You are one of the few people I really love,' she said. 'Yet I am ashamed to look at you.' He was silent for so long that she turned to him, hurt.

'It's my fault', he told her.

'No, Artie.'

'I should never have left you. Or I should have made you come home with me. it's my fault.' He had been angry and disbelieving only for a few seconds, when she confessed. Then his own reaction sickened him, when he thought what she must have been going through. He had heard rumours in Jersey about her and the Prince of Wales. Because he was afraid they were true, he had got into fights defending her.

'What – what is your father going to do?' he asked.

Lillie was very quiet. 'He doesn't know about it. I'm not sure I'll ever tell him.'

'Then we must start making preparations.'

'We?' Lillie asked.

He smiled faintly. 'I can't let you go through it all on your own.'

She could not speak, but kissed his cheek and he held her gently.

Having Arthur to help her, she began to make plans. However kind the Lewises were, she could not stay at the villa indefinitely. To have her baby so near London increased the threat of discovery immensely. She could not go to the Red House, as she had become too well known in Bournemouth. She would need a doctor and midwife and could not swear them to secrecy.

As the end of the month approached, she had to send Dominique to buy a corset for her, the first she had ever worn. She had to get away soon, or even that would not be enough. She had not seen Arthur for several days and was anxious. She felt guilty about him, sometimes. He almost seemed happy she was having someone else's child, to show her how much he loved her by helping her. To him it was destiny, proving that they had been meant for each other from the beginning. She was no longer naive enough to believe there was only one man in the world for each woman. Affaires, love, she had learnt they were a matter of liking and desire, circumstances, adjustments and opportunity. Yet she did not doubt that Arthur and she could be happy together. She knew how well they were suited, and she could make any man happy.

Next time she heard from him, Dominique was surprised when she opened the letter, laughed and caught her arms, spinning her round the room. The Signora nearly made herself sick. But it was wonderful news. The autumn booking at Portelet had ended sooner than expected and they could have the House till January.

Lewis agreed that the move was wise. There would be much less risk of detection on the island. The islanders were

415

reticent with outsiders and any who suspected would be unlikely to give her away. Besides, Portelet House was so remote and her mother could move there from St Helier to help Dominique to look after her.

Arthur did not travel with Lillie and Dominique. He went on to Jersey ahead of them to prepare the House. Patsy Cornwallis West saw them off at Waterloo Station, then hurried back to Norfolk Street where a carpet hung from the drawingroom window to announce that an auction of the contents of the house was taking place. Many people turned up, curious to see where the Jersey Lily had lived. Among them were some of her friends, determined to buy some of her special treasures and keep them for when she returned – *if* she returned. Everything was sold, even the gilded fans from the walls, and quite high prices were paid, so the Langtry creditors were all satisfied.

Arthur was happy to have Lillie back at Portelet. The house came alive again with her there. It had so many memories for her and she felt so much at home that she was able to relax at last. The auction had barely covered her debts and there was very little money, but enough for their needs at the moment. Dominique's salary had been paid in advance for the year. What would happen after Christmas, she was not certain. Dominique solved it one day by bursting into tears. Somehow, she had got the idea that Lillie meant to send her away. She begged to be allowed to stay. She did not need money, only to share what food there was – if she could still serve the Signora.

The only problem was Mrs Le Breton. She could not understand why Lillie was making a secret of having a baby and refused to tell Edward. She was shocked when Lillie explained to her that he was not the father. For a time, she thought the child must be Arthur's, but Lillie swore to her it was not and she assumed, like everyone else, that the father was the Prince of Wales. After she had cried for a while in private, she accepted it and became quite practical. There were many arrangements to be made. Clothes to be got ready, a layette, a midwife and doctor to be on call. By December, Lillie was entering the seventh month and would have to take care.

Lillie stopped her contacting a doctor. Unknown to any of them, she had swallowed her pride and written to George Lewis. It had become obvious to her that she could not have her baby in Jersey. Even here, there was too much curiosity. And some enterprising islander was making money by sending reports of her new, simple life to the mainland newspapers. Her letter to Lewis had been in reply to a newspaper cutting he had sent her, again from *The New York Times*, dated November 6, 1880. As soon as she read its opening words, 'Mr and Mrs Langtry have given up their London residence, and for the presence Mrs Langtry remains in Jersey. Is beauty deposed, or has beauty abdicated?', she knew that Portelet was not safe any more.

Her letter to Lewis was answered by a cheque from Sir Allen Young. It was a gift of two thousand pounds, to cover any expenses she incurred. Alleno did not have that kind of money and she knew it had come through him from Bertie. Shortly after, she received a highly confidential reply from George Lewis. The Prince had not known until the auction how precarious her finances had been. He was determined that she should want for nothing and be taken care of properly. On his instructions, Lewis had arranged for Lillie to travel at once to France from Jersey with her mother and maid, where they would be met by a doctor and a special agent of Bertie's. They were to stay outside Paris, with the doctor in constant attendance, until the agent, Dighton, found a suitably discreet apartment for them. Secrecy was essential, since even in Paris Lillie was liable to be recognised. She was to live in the apartment, seeing no one, until the child was born. She would receive occasional discreet visits from the Princesse Jeanne de Sagan, who would keep Bertie informed.

Arthur was disturbed, both by the money and the announcement that Lillie was leaving for Paris. He had thought they would make all the arrangements together. He was not rich, but everything he had was hers, enough for them to survive. He was happy she was at Portelet because, if news of the baby did leak out, he could stand by her and

L.—O

acknowledge it as his own.

They were in her room and Lillie was troubled by the way he looked at her, doubtful and questioning. She made him sit, then sat on his knee and kissed him. She had nearly forgotten how much she loved him, she told him. She had become more and more dependent on him, jealous when he was away from her, afraid that he would desert her. She would not let him speak. The money was from a group of her friends, she said, who had joined together to assist her. She could not refuse. And the arrangements Lewis had made were for the best. If Arthur claimed the child was his, Edward could sue him for crippling damages and the scandal would destroy them both. If its birth was secret, it need never be mentioned until after she had divorced Edward, and no damage would be done. And her baby protected. But she needed Arthur's love and support or she could not go on.

He asked her forgiveness and she told him she would only go to France, if he promised to come, too, if she needed him. He promised.

It was settled in a few days and she sailed, heavily veiled, with her mother and Dominique to St Malo, where they were met by the courier, Dighton, and the doctor, Pratt. They led her at once to a carriage and drove her along the coast to a smaller port where she was less likely to be known.

Arthur could not understand his feelings when she had gone. He missed her constantly, yet he was relieved at no longer having the responsibility. And that made him feel guilty. She wrote to him every day and he was impatient for her letters, while he found difficulty in answering them. She told him how the two men guarded her almost like a prisoner, hardly permitting her to go out for fresh air in case she was recognised. Just before Christmas, Dighton found a suitable, obscure but comfortable apartment in Paris and they moved to it. Arthur was glad she was settled. He had been uneasy about her, but now he could relax and take up his normal life again. He could attend to what business there was on the property and have a drink with his friends

418

at the Victoria Sporting Club. He even went to a party at the Courtneys, where he was popular with the daughters and was attracted himself to one of them. He had to admit, it was partly because she was so different from Lillie.

Then he had a letter from her, telling him she had insisted on being allowed out, even though the weather in Paris was appalling, with freezing winds and flurries of snow. Walking with her mother, she had slipped and fallen in the icy street. She was badly shaken and the doctor had put her to bed. In spite of her assurances that she was not really hurt, Arthur could tell that she wanted him. He hurried over to Paris and found the second floor apartment at 37 rue de Naples. He was greatly relieved to see her sitting up and the colour coming back to her cheeks at the sight of him.

Watching them together, Mrs Le Breton was concerned. She was aware of how much Lillie needed him and saw how much Arthur loved her. She did not want either of them to be hurt.

Lillie had insisted on an apartment with a spare room, so that he could stay when he came to see her. For the next two months, he scarcely had a quiet minute. He travelled backwards and forwards between Jersey and Paris. He brought her mail and took back letters and cards to post to Oscar, Patsy and Lady Lonsdale. He had his own business to attend to, but his visits cheered Lillie. She made good progress, but the waiting was tedious. He was afraid to be away, in case he missed the birth and she needed him. They talked of how life would be afterwards. He had plans to sell Portelet House, if the price paid was right. Not to live on that he got, but to invest it or to buy a farm. Ranelagh was bound to leave him something, but until then he wanted to be able to support them.

Apart from Arthur, Lillie's only visitor was the chic, charming, Princesse Jeanne de Sagan. She was married to one of the richest and most elegant men in France and their marriage was the most perfect marriage of convenience. They led totally separate lives. Both were close friends of Bertie and Jeanne had even been his accepted mistress for a while. The only occasion she and her husband had shared a bedroom after the birth of their heir, was when she had discovered she was going to have a child by Bertie. The dates would not quite match, but the Prince de Sagan moved into his wife's mansion and slept in her bed for a week to allay future rumours. She had a definite fellow feeling for Lillie, whom she adored. And Lillie in turn was grateful for her attention and learnt a considerable amount from the Frenchwoman's balanced and rational attitude to life. After one of her visits at the end of February, Lillie wrote to Arthur.

He had been anxious to return to Paris, as her baby was due any time now. She told him that Pratt had assured her it would not be for at least another ten days, not until the weekend after next. At the same time, she was troubled by a rumour that Edward had returned unexpectedly for a few days from the United States and was looking for her. In case he happened to turn up in Paris, she advised Arthur not to come until the end of the following week, when it would be safe. Her letter puzzled him, but it meant there was no urgency.

Bertie had been in Berlin for the wedding of his nephew Prince Wilhelm to the dumpy Princess Augusta Victoria. He returned to London via Paris where he stayed, incognito, with the Princesse de Sagan. Together, they visited the Rue de Naples. Bertie was disappointed that Lillie had not yet had the baby, in which he took the keenest interest, but he was delighted to see that she was in excellent health and to learn that all would be over in two to three days at the most. He regretted that he could not wait until then. Hearing that, Lillie breathed more freely. She could not hide Arthur's visits, but he passed almost as a member of the family. On the other hand, she did not wish them to meet, nor Arthur to know the Prince had been with her, if possible. He could be jealous and she did not want the two sides of her life to clash. Her luck held.

Bertie sat with her for an hour or two that day and the next, charming and affectionate, completely winning over Mrs Le Breton before he said goodbye. Arthur arrived the day after, the 7th, and on the 8th her baby was born. It was a girl and she called her Jeanne, after the Princesse de Sagan. Little Jeanne Marie.

Arthur was as thrilled with her as if she had really been his own. 'All that fuss over something as tiny as this,' he said, cradling her.

'She's beautiful!' Lillie laughed. Her mother and Dominique agreed and were quite cross with Arthur, until they realised he was joking. He had brought champagne and Dr Pratt let Lillie have half a glass with them as a restorative and to welcome her daughter.

Pratt insisted on her staying in bed for a week to ten days after the birth, but she chafed under it and got up every day, despite Dominique's protests, as soon as he had checked her. She had been inactive long enough. She only fed Jeanne Marie herself for the first week, after which a wetnurse was hired. Her figure was one of her most precious assets and she could not afford to lose it. Both Dominique and her mother were staggered to catch her doing exercises and she laughed at their disapproval.

Bertie returned to Paris before the end of March, accompanied by Alexandra. They had come for a more important reason than the birth of Lillie's baby, but they took time to visit the apartment. Alix brought presents for both Lillie and Jeanne Marie. Like Bertie, she was glad it was a girl, as there would be far fewer problems. They had broken their journey to St Petersburg where they were to attend the funeral of Czar Alexander the Second, who had just been assassinated. Alix's younger sister, Minny, was the wife of the new Czar, Alexander the Third. She was very worried about her in that country of repression and terrorists, and thanked Lillie for giving her a touch of joy at this moment.

Arthur had had to go back to Jersey. Now that Jeanne Marie was born, he expected Lillie to join him. However, there were problems. She could not suddenly arrive on the island with a new born baby. She decided against haste. In any case, she did not intend to leave Paris until there was no sign that she had just given birth. Lewis still kept Edward travelling round America. There was nothing to be gained by hurrying.

Fate had helped her so often and it did so again. They received news from India, from her brother, William, that saddened her. Her other, older brother, Maurice, who had done extremely well in the Indian Civil Service, was dead. A noted shot, he had been asked by villagers to rid them of a maneating tiger. He had stalked it with his bearer and his first shot wounded it. When he turned for his second rifle to finish it off, he discovered that his bearer had fled in fear. Unarmed, Maurice ran to a tree, but before he could climb out of reach the maddened tiger clawed one of his legs. He had died later of blood poisoning.

Mrs Le Breton returned to Jersey, in mourning, bringing her son's baby daughter, Jeanne Marie. Two days after her, also in mourning, Lillie arrived with Dominique to help her look after her little neice. They spent the summer at Portelet and all three were devoted to the orphaned baby, especially Lillie, who seemed to spend every possible minute with her neice.

It was a season of happiness, as ideal as Arthur had imagined, so he was all the more shaken when she told him one afternoon, as they walked up from the beach, that she would have to go to London. 'Edward's back from America,' she explained, 'wondering what I'm doing here. I have to show myself to stop any rumours.'

'How long will you stay there?' he asked.

She shrugged. 'That all depends. On how long it takes to talk him into giving me a divorce.'

Arthur had been tense. There were other people on the beach and normally they were very controlled in public, but he smiled and pulled her to him, kissing her, careless of who saw.

Edward was continually complaining to George Lewis. The trip to the United States had been more like a wild goose chase than anything else. He had been kept travelling from New York to Chicago, to Memphis and up to Portland, Maine, down to New Orleans and on to San Francisco by the sea route, and back to New Orleans again. Exhaustive enquries had produced not a single member of the branch of the family he was trying to trace. No one had ever heard of them. Not Licensing Offices, church records, hospitals, schools, police courts, no one. When he got back, Lewis had said, 'What a pity. Never mind,' handed him a cheque for fifty pounds and that was that. So much for the substantial bonus! And to cap it all, Lillie had virtually disappeared. Rumour had it she was on Jersey, but he had no money to spare to go hunting for her.

In early August, he heard a whisper that she was in town and went again to Lewis's office. Lewis confirmed that Lillie had taken a set of inexpensive rooms in Ely Place, but that she did not want to see him. What she wanted, in fact, was a legal separation. Edward refused to believe it. He went straight to Ely Place, where Lillie had taken a small apartment with Dominique.

Edward had lived well in America and put on a considerable amount of weight. His face had grown puffy, his moustache ragged. Living alone in a furnished room in Kensington, with no one to look after him, he had begun to look shabby. Seeing him, Lillie could not credit that she had once thought him handsome and dashing. When he announced his intention of moving in with her, the mere idea sickened her. 'It's out of the question, Ned,' she told him. 'Our marriage is over.'

'Don't be ridiculous!' he laughed. 'We're still man and wife.'

'In name only,' she said. 'Our marriage ended years ago. We only kept on with it because it was convenient to both of us. It's not convenient any more.'

Edward tried to bluster with her, but she was so quiet and determined that he could make no impression. Finally, she told him there was nothing more to say and asked him to leave. He gaped at her. 'You – you're throwing me out? . . . How dare you! You'd better come to your senses, my girl.' She meant it. She would not say another word and he marched to the door. 'Just as soon as I'm back on my feet again,' he sneered, 'you'll come running. Well, don't be so certain I'll take you back! You think about it. I'm prepared to provide a decent home for you – better than this hovel. You'll get nowhere without me.'

A little later, she asked her father to go and reason with him. The Dean was serious, when he returned. 'I spent an uncomfortable hour with him,' he reported. 'He was drunk, of course, and insulting. He blames you entirely for the failure of your marriage.' He sighed. 'You best forget any thought of him giving you a divorce, at any rate, for the moment. He won't contemplate it!'

Lillie had deliberately chosen the time when most of the people she knew were at Cowes. She could seldom remember the town looking so empty. The first person she contacted was Patsy, who hurried to Ely Place. 'It's been so dull without you!' she exclaimed. It was incredible. Lillie was wearing black again, in mourning for her brother, as if the clock had been put back three years. She was enviably slimmer and her complexion more perfect than ever. Obviously there was no truth in these whispers about a baby.

The next to arrive was Lady Lonsdale. In a rush, smiling and crying to see her. Patsy had brought Lillie's jewellery and some blue bowls she had bought at the auction. Lady Lonsdale went one better. Her coachman staggered up the stairs carrying the stuffed peacock with its tail outstretched and jewelled eyes that used to stand as a firescreen in Norfolk Street. She had bought it at the auction. Lillie was touched and did not tell her she meant to get rid of it at the earliest opportunity. Her brother Maurice had shot a sacred peacock by mistake, shortly before he was mauled by the tiger. The Indians said the peacock caused his bad fortune, and she meant to take no risks.

She called, herself, on Oscar. Shortage of money had driven Frank Miles and him to leave the rambling house in Salisbury Street. They were now in Keats House, Tite Street, Chelsea, a stone's throw from Whistler's former studio. They still had Sally with them, although they now had to protect her from young men who pretended to visit them, but really had come to see her. One young gentleman just down from Eton had wanted to marry her and his titled father shipped him off at once to Canada. He had sent Sally some money, which she indignantly wanted to send back.

Instead, Oscar and Miles had invested it for her, so that she would be provided for, if anything ever happened to them.

She was as pretty and unaffected as ever, wearing a long, loose dress. When she opened the door and saw Lillie, she threw herself into her arms.

'Divinity! Divinity!' Oscar cried. 'The sun breaks forth after nearly a year in eclipse! How have we survived?' He had become quite outrageous, Lillie thought, as he kissed her hand, her wrist and her forehead. He was wearing a black velvet jacket and ruffled shirt, velvet kneebreeches and silk stockings. It was his own 'aesthetic' dress, worn to startle and be noticed. His articles in newspapers and magazines on the appreciation of Art, on clothes, interior design and architecture had won him a large following, if little income. A volume of poetry that summer had increased his reputation. Most of all, Gilbert and Sullivan had modelled one of the two chief characters in their latest, successful Comic Opera *Patience* on him, with the other based, appropriately, on Whistler. He was now recognised everywhere and audiences rocked, when the poetic Bunthorne sang

'Though the Philistines may jostle, you will rank
    as an apostle in the high aesthetic band,
If you walk down Piccadilly with a poppy or a lily
    in your mediaeval hand.'

He was delighted to have his tribute to Lillie immortalised, he swore.

Frank Miles was also pleased to see her. He had an uncompleted pen and colourwash portrait of her from three separate angles, which he acknowledged as the best thing he had ever done. He had been afraid to touch it in her absence. Now he could finish it.

Arthur was bitterly disappointed that Edward had not let her divorce him. He accepted reluctantly that she had to stay on in London to try to make him change his mind.

Separated from Edward and not certain how that affected her position, Lillie had hesitated to go out in society. Oscar and Frank gave a party for her and invited all her real friends still in town. It was a hilarious evening, but during it Oscar called for silence. The whole purpose of the gathering, he stated solemnly, was not to indulge in a bacchanalian rout, but to consider the Lily and advise her on how she was to spend the rest of her life. In short, how was she best to support herself?

It was a question all her friends had considered. Miles thought that, with her talent and knowledge of plants, she should run a market garden.

'No, no, Frank,' Oscar protested. 'It would compel the Lily to tramp the fields in muddy boots. Inconceivable.'

Sally thought she should open a teashop. More practically, Millais agreed with what Whistler had once said, that she should concentrate more on her drawing. Her caricatures of the people she saw and met were very effective. Unfortunately she would need to study, so that was ruled out.

Patsy thought she should open a dress shop, with her sense of fashion. Lady Londsdale suggested she might set up as a milliner. Everyone would buy hats designed by Mrs Langtry.

Oscar objected to every suggestion, until Patsy swore she would not make any more unless he told them his. 'You have all missed the obvious,' he said. 'There is only one possible career for the Lily. She must tread the boards.'

'The Theatre?' Lady Lonsdale gasped.

'She would shine like Venus in the night. As Desdemona, Juliet or Cleopatra, she would be the star of the age.'

The others laughed, yet Lillie knew he was serious. She had considered becoming an actress, too, had even discussed it with Ellen Terry. Nelly had been sympathetic but not encouraging. 'It is not a life for someone used to ease and luxury,' she said. 'The Theatre needs dedication and years of effort. I started, myself, when I was a child. It is hard work, long hours, most of them boring repetition and study, and the odds against success for anyone are enormous.' All Nelly had told her was undoubtedly true. Many doors would shut against her and there was no guarantee of success. Yet she was wrong about Lillie's determination and ability to work hard. She certainly had to do something fairly soon. There was Gladstone's offer, but the assistance she needed was not legal, nor political, and he would disapprove of the only alternatives open to her.

Bertie had been given her address by George Lewis and came to Ely Place. He half expected to see the baby. Lillie had thought of renting a room somewhere for Jeanne Marie and her mother or a nurse, but it was still too risky. She was as wise as ever, Bertie told her, and even more lovely. He was prepared to help her, but she would not accept any more financial help from him. To his surprise, she regarded the two thousand pounds she had been sent as a loan, which she would repay. It was not necessary, he assured her, but she insisted and gradually he was forced to accept her determination to be independent. She meant to be her own mistress. She would never be submissive again. It was she who would choose. If she gave herself to any man, it would be because she cared for him, not because she was paid for. The challenge made her even more irresistible and Bertie began to call quite frequently, flattered that she let their relationship resume its old intimacy.

She had been with him one day at Sandown Races and found someone waiting for her at home, a short, plump, energetic woman in her forties. 'I'm Mrs Labouchere,' she introduced herself. 'Or as some still remember, Henrietta Hodson.'

Henrietta had been an actress of some distinction before she married the rich Liberal M.P. and magazine editor, Henry Labouchere. After her marriage she had specialised in producing society's amateur theatricals and had succeeded in turning several ladies into reasonably accomplished performers. She had heard from Oscar of Lillie's interest in the theatre. It so happened that she was about to produce an amateur performance of one-act plays in aid of a local hospital at Twickenham, where she lived, and it occurred to her that if Mrs Langtry agreed to appear, it would create much local interest.

Lillie was much more than interested, although she concealed it, telling Henrietta that she had absolutely no experience. Henrietta knew that. She was proposing a short one-act play with only two characters, one to be played by herself, the other by Lillie. They would rehearse together and she would coach Lillie, if necessary, in every move and every inflection. Lillie asked for time to make up her mind, although she already knew her answer. It was a heavensent opportunity, to be rehearsed by a professional actress and appear before a small, local audience at Twickenham Town Hall. They would be indulgent and no harm would come if she failed. In any event, she would learn for herself whether she had any aptitude for the theatre.

In early November, she arrived at the Labouchere's home in Twickenham, Pope Villa, to study for the next two weeks. Henrietta was an extraordinary housewife. The cooking was the worst she had ever known. Labouchere, a droll, highly intelligent man, simply sent out a servant every day to fetch him a hot saltbeef sandwich. His relations with Henrietta were like cat and dog. While Lillie and she rehearsed endlessly in the garden, he would stroll up, listen and make dry, critical comments, provoking his wife into a rage. Lillie thought him amusing, if disconcerting.

To Henrietta's relief, she turned out to have a beautiful, clear speaking voice and a very retentive memory. She taught her where to place the stress in a line, how to pause for comic or dramatic effect and to react to the person to whom she was speaking. Forced to think about them, her gestures were stiff and Henrietta showed her how to use her natural grace. Over and over again.

The play was a popular comic duologue, *A Fair Encounter*, lasting for thirty minutes, in which two contrasting women scored off each other, sparring verbally. Lillie, as Lady Clara, was on stage first. On the Saturday in the Town Hall, the audience applauded as the opening curtains revealed her in one of her prettiest dresses, holding a bouquet of roses. At the sound of the applause, her mind emptied. She could remember not a move, not a word she had learnt and stood frozen with stagefright, smiling fixedly at the bouquet. The applause faded and Henrietta's voice could be heard, whispering Lillie's opening line, softly at first, then more loudly. 'Oh dear, oh dear. Four o'clock – and the new maid . . .' At last, just as the audience was beginning to become restive, the words penetrated and Lillie's head jerked as if she were coming awake. 'Oh dear, oh dear,' she exclaimed. 'Four o'clock, – and the new maid Mrs Murray promised to send me has not yet made her appearance.'

Behind the painted door in the scenery, Henrietta fanned her face with her hand. She heard Lillie's footsteps on the stage and knew she was crossing down to begin arranging the roses in a vase. Keep on going!, Henrietta prayed.

Lillie sailed through the rest of the play without being aware of any of it. She smiled, spoke, paused, moved and responded to her cues, exactly as she had been drilled. At the end, the applause was loud and enthusiastic and Henrietta congratulated her. 'Excellent,' she said. 'Very smooth.' Lillie disagreed. It had been a terrifying experience and one she never intended to repeat. 'Nonsense!' Henrietta declared. 'I'm going to make you a star.'

Unknown to Lillie, some of her friends were in the audience, among them Oscar, Patsy, Frank Miles and her father. They were agreeably surprised at her naturalness and charm on stage and praised her extravagantly afterwards. She was sure they were being kind, but several newspapers had sent their critic or gossip columnist and the reviews they gave her were glowing. 'She has talent to back her beauty.' 'She achieved a remarkable triumph and it was hard lines upon her that she had not an audience more critical and consequently better able to appreciate the singular delicacies of what we must now perforce term Mrs Langtry's style.' She cut some of them out and sent them to her mother and Arthur.

Aware now that she had returned and was more than restored to the Prince's favour, society flocked round her. Henrietta, however, gave her an ultimatum. She could either continue to study or attend balls and parties, not both. Lillie decided to study and Henrietta chose the part for her of Kate Hardcastle, the heroine of Goldsmith's *She Stoops to Conquer*. It was a long and difficult role, but Lillie learnt it very quickly, guessing why Henrietta had chosen it for her. It had been announced that a special, single performance of *She Stoops to Conquer* was to be presented by Squire Bancroft and his wife at the Theatre Royal in the Haymarket, for the benefit of the Royal General Theatrical Fund. Henrietta was a shrewd business woman and promoter. She had guessed that the Bancrofts would be unable to resist the lure of presenting Lillie in her debut in the West End, especially since her appearance would most certainly guarantee the attendance of the Prince of Wales and half of society.

First, Lillie had to be ready. If the Bancrofts accepted her, she would be the only amateur in a cast of leading professionals. In such an important part, if she could not hold her own, it would be disastrous. Once again, there were days of endless, gruelling rehearsal in the turreted, Gothic villa, with Henrietta drilling and correcting her, playing all the other parts, and Labby making wry, critical comments that distracted Lillie, until she learnt they could be useful.

Bancroft was in a quandary. He remembered Lillie from her first evening at Lady Sebright's and had met her often since. He knew what Henrietta was proposing. Also, after a performance one night, the Prince of Wales sent for him to his box, and, after congratulating him on his performance, asked casually if he could think of any way Mrs Langtry might be assisted to begin a theatrical career. It was Lillie, herself, asking him through the Prince. Bancroft had to be honest. With such pressure on him, he could not refuse Lillie an opportunity. She could read the part with the company at the first rehearsal. If after that they decided she was not fit to appear with them, that would be the end of it.

He had to admire Lillie on the day of the reading. Although she must be desperately nervous, she showed it far less than some of the experienced actors. The slightest tremor in her voice, when she was introduced, was all that betrayed her. Henrietta considered it an almost shameful ordeal and would scarcely speak to any of them. She could understand resentment in the profession at being forced to perform with a royal protégée, but at least they could remember their manners.

Lillie had not slept the night before. So much was staked on this and she knew she was facing the most critical test of her life. She sat with the actors and actresses in a semi-circle. She was too aware of them at the beginning and spoke too quietly. She made herself speak up and concentrate only on the words. Strangely, she felt an excitement at hearing other voices than Henrietta's and responded. She absorbed herself in what she was saying, remembering all she had been taught and thought for herself, every note of Henrietta's, every one of Labby's asides. She began to enjoy it and was surprised when it finished.

There was a pause for a minute, then the actors of the company rose and applauded her. She could only nod her thanks.

The work that had gone before was nothing. From now on, she saw no one except the other members of the cast and Henrietta. She rehearsed eight hours a day at the Theatre Royal, and nearly another ten at the villa. At times, the words seemed to lose all meaning through constant repetition.

She had heard from Arthur, asking her when she was coming back to Jersey. She replied, asking why he had not commented on her reviews. To her surprise and pleasure he turned up one evening at Twickenham, three days before the performance. Henrietta was upstairs resting. She was listening to Labby reminisce about his political battles. He broke off and, tactfully, left her alone with Arthur.

She kissed him, delighted he had come for the performance. He told her that was not the reason. He had come to take her back to Jersey. She was excited to see him, but his brusqueness disturbed her.

'Now?' she wondered. 'I can't leave now.'

'There's nothing stopping you.'

She laughed. 'But I'm working! The performance is only three days away. I still have a lot to learn.'

He was very tense. 'Once before, I made the mistake of not insisting. I want you to come with me.'

'I can't, Artie,' she explained. 'It's too important. I have

431

to prove that what happened at Twickenham wasn't an accident.'

'If you love me – if you meant anything you said, you'll come,' he told her.

She could see he was deadly serious. He was not like himself. 'Artie, please, that's not fair. I'll come to you one day, but not till I've proved myself.'

'So you didn't mean any of it,' he said harshly. 'You only pretended to be staying here because of Edward.'

'I came because of him!' she protested. 'But I'm staying on until I see if I have a chance of success.'

'As an actress?'

'Yes, it's the only way I can make some money – for both of us.'

'No.' He shook his head. 'It's not money. It's the flattery and admiration. That's more important to you than anything I can give you.'

She could not understand him. 'Why does it have to change anything? I thought we'd go on just as we are.'

'With nothing ever decided, and me waiting another ten years,' he said. 'You never meant to come back. You only used me. And now I'm not useful any more.' It was all the more hurtful because he did not raise his voice.

'That's not true.'

'Whether you admit it or not,' he said. 'Whether it was deliberate or unconscious, you used me just as you use everyone. Any thought of our being together permanently was a fantasy.'

There was enough truth in what he said to drive it home. She had drawn herself up. 'So I'm to do precisely what you want or we can't go on, is that it?' Her tone was biting. 'I don't accept those conditions. Not even from you.'

Arthur was flushed. 'I'm glad I've seen you,' he muttered. 'So I can remember what you've become.' He turned away from her. 'I wish you happiness, though I doubt if you'd recognise it if you found it.'

She watched him leave. The last time, she had been distressed. She was sad, but for Arthur, not for herself. She was now free. And responsible to no one. Except perhaps little Jeanne Marie.

The charity matinee at the Theatre Royal was completely sold out. All the columnists and critics for British and foreign newpapers had clamoured for tickets and marvelled at the audience, as well as the performance. Following the lead of the Prince and Princess of Wales who were in the royal box, the stalls and circles were crammed with every rank of society, politicians, literary and artistic celebrities and leading members of the Theatre. And from Pit to Gods, the audience roared out its appreciation of Lillie, again following the Prince as he rose to applaud. No one had really known what to expect, which added to Lillie's triumph. Henrietta's forceful gestures and mannerisms were softened by her own grace and gave her performance a rare and individual quality. The laughter of the audience stimulated her own provocative sense of humour and each fed on the other, until by the end nearly everyone was in love with her as young Marlowe in the play.

Before the end of the performance, she had signed a contract with the Bancrofts for fifty pounds a week for the rest of the season, a more than promising start. Irving was one of the first to reach her dressingroom, to ask to play Hero in *Much Ado About Nothing* to his Benedick and Ellen Terry's Beatrice. He was too late.

Her dressingroom became so crowded that no one could leave. Oscar kept trying to propose a toast. Bertie was almost speechless with pride. Alexandra kissed her. They were giving a dinner that evening in her honour and Bertie promised her he would write straightaway to his sons to tell them of her triumph.

When they finally left, it took Henrietta another quarter of an hour to clear the dressingroom. But there was one man who had been overlooked. Edward Langtry. He refused to leave without speaking to his wife, alone.

Yes, Lillie thought, I'd forgotten Edward.

He had been drinking and was dishevelled, unkempt. He was ruined, he told her, and all through her. Because of her notoriety and now going on the stage, his family had stopped his allowance. He had begged them, but they refused to listen. He had nothing, no money to pay for a room or food.

'Or drink,' she said.

'What's a fellow to do?' he demanded. 'I'm a gentleman. I'm not trained for anything. I can't run around making an exhibition of myself, like you do. And you're paid for it, paid well. There are things I could tell, if I wanted to.' She looked at him. Was he threatening her? 'Not that I'd stoop to it,' he said, but could not meet her eyes. 'I have my pride.'

'I'll help you as much as I can.'

'Only till I get myself set up,' he said quickly. 'I have irons in the fire. Expectations.'

'I'll pay you thirty-five pounds a month,' Lillie told him. 'On condition that you leave me alone. If you ever come to see me again, it will stop at that moment.'

The coldness of her voice almost frightened him and he licked his lips. 'You used to love me once.'

'Do you accept?' she asked.

He hesitated, and nodded.

'Go and see George Lewis tomorrow,' Lillie said. 'He will arrange it.' She turned to her mirror and began to remove her stage makeup, smoothing cream on her cheeks. She paused only briefly, when he went out. She wiped the smeared rouge from her cheekbones and thought of Henrietta who would be back any minute.

Henrietta had become her manager. She knew why. After the season with the Bancrofts, when Lillie was more experienced, she would suggest setting up their own company. Why not? That was exactly what Lillie wanted. She still had a great deal to learn from Henrietta, but, when the time came, she must be left in no doubt whose company it was and whose name was the attraction.

There was a great deal of money to made on tour, as manager of her own company. She could hire a nurse to help her mother take care of Jeanne Marie in The Red House.

Oscar had been excited, not only by her performance. He had just had a cable inviting him to give a series of readings and lectures in the New Year in America, where Gilbert and Sullivan's *Patience* was a great hit. He would make a fortune, he told her. Her name was even better known in America than his. It is not entirely unlikely that Oscar will turn out to be my Ambassador to the United States, she thought. He would like that. She smiled.

And the rest of the world? . . . It was waiting now for Lillie Langtry.

# UNQUIET SOUL

## Margot Peters

'A totally fascinating book about the Brontës – perhaps the best ever published' *Irving Stone*

'The story itself is so gripping and the telling is so good that one ceases to question and reads on to weep . . . a most readable book that cannot fail to move' *Margaret Drabble*

'This fine biography is both moving and revealing . . . a compelling narrative, never marred with indiscriminate sympathising' *Spectator*

# ROSE: MY LIFE IN SERVICE

Rosina Harrison

## A REAL LIFE UPSTAIRS DOWNSTAIRS

'The record of an extraordinary relationship . . .
fascinating and deliciously readable'
*New York Times Book Review*

'Fascinating, outspoken . . . a social document of
mistress and maid' *Daily Telegraph*

On 6 August 1918, Rosina Harrison left her Yorkshire
home for London to take her first job as a lady's maid;
eleven years later she was offered the post of personal
maid to Nancy, Lady Astor. This is the story of the
tempestuous 35-year-long relationship between Rose
and her brilliant, unpredictable employer, first woman
Member of Parliament and celebrated hostess: an
enthralling picture of life between the wars in one of the
great houses of England.

'Unique insight into the splendours and miseries of
Cliveden . . . stuffed with interesting and amusing
anecdotes' *Times Literary Supplement*

'Best-selling, eminently readable' *Financial Times*

# MACARTHUR

## Clay Blair Jr

At the end of World War I and the age of thirty-nine he
was a brigadier-general. As Superintendent of the
Military Academy at West Point his liberal reforms
played a crucial part in the development of the modern
army.

Alternately loved and hated, Douglas MacArthur was
sixty-one when the Japanese bombed Pearl Harbour,
yet he went to on become one of the heroes of World
War II, the man who by his tenacity and his genius
liberated the Philippines and drove the Japanese from
the Pacific.

A brilliant biography of the legendary American
general. Clay Blair Jr's book is a new appraisal of his
extraordinary genius and ties in with the Universal film
starring Gregory Peck as MacArthur.

# THE LIVES OF THE KINGS AND QUEENS OF ENGLAND

**Edited by Antonia Fraser**

## ONE THOUSAND YEARS OF ENGLISH HISTORY.

From William the Conqueror to Elizabeth II stretches the pageant of England's kings and queens and a story of wars and glory, conquest and exploration, usurpation and murder. Eight of our best-known modern historians tell the sage of England's realm.

'Lively . . . bursting with colour . . . demonstrates not only the way to enjoy history but also the way to marshall a mass of facts' *Economist*

'Well-written, terse and readable' *Times Literary Supplement*

'Lively writing . . . a comprehensive history of England in biographical form' *Sunday Telegraph*

# HUMPHREY BOGART

## Nathaniel Benchley

Humphrey DeForest Bogart believed that a man was
either a professional or a bum. He was pugnacious and
cold and yet he was a gentleman; a puritan who married
four times; mean but generous; a thug and a romantic.
All these contradictions converged in the person of a
complicated man, a dedicated professional and a
fabulous legend.

Written by Nathaniel Benchley, a close friend and
frequent guest, and with the complete co-operation of
Lauren Bacall, here is the real story of how Bogart got
his famous scar – and his equally famous lisp; how he
bungled his way into acting; how the big films were
made; and how he died of cancer at the age of 57. Here
is the story of the man who made the legend we all know
as BOGART.

'A fine, serious life, perceptive, humourous,
understanding.' *Financial Times*

'Affectionate . . . well-written . . . perceptive.'
*Sunday Express*

'A host of fascinating inside anecdotes' *Evening News*